A
PAINTED
WINTER

A
PAINTED
WINTER

H. BARNARD

SHADOWFAX
PUBLISHING

First published 2021 by Shadowfax Publishing Pty Ltd
Melbourne, Australia.

First edition

Text copyright © H.Barnard 2021
Maps and internal illustrations copyright © Shadowfax Publishing Pty Ltd 2021

Cover design by Sarah Whittaker Book Design
Book design and typesetting in Adobe Caslon Pro by Irissa Book Design

A catalogue record for this book is available from
the National Library of Australia

ISBN 978-0-6450429-1-7 (hardback)
ISBN 978-0-6450429-0-0 (paperback)
ISBN 978-0-6450429-2-4 (ebook)

Fiction – historical
Fiction – fantasy - general

www.shadowfaxpublishing.com

PLACE NAMES WITH MODERN LOCATION
(in order of appearance)

North

Caercaled	King's Seat hillfort, above Dunkeld, Scotland (Canmore ID 27172). The standing stone circle is at the base of a steep slope of Newtyle hill to the south of Dunkeld overlooking the Tay river (Canmore ID 27206). The row alignment of standing stones are the East Cult stones to the east of Dunkeld (Canmore ID 27127). The burial chamber/cairn is the Ninewells Cairn to the east of Dunkeld in line with the Loch of Lowes (Canmore ID 27115).
Caerdwabonna	Clatchard Craig Fort, Cupar, Scotland (Canmore ID 30074).
Caermhèad	Myot Hill Fort, Falkirk, Scotland (Canmore ID 45957).
The Ruined Wall	The Antonine Wall, Scotland.
Gowan	Govan, Glasgow, Scotland. Evidence of occupation since bronze age (Canmore ID 44189 also see work of Dr Claire Ellis).
Farming settlement near ruined Roman fort	Inverquarity Roman Fort, Kirriemuir, Scotland (Canmore ID 33713).

Caertarwos	Burghead promontory fort, Scotland (Canmore ID 16146). Burghead well (Canmore ID 16157).
Rīgonīn	Enclosure near village of Rhynie, Scotland (Canmore ID 87197, also see work of Dr Gordon Noble). The two stones described are the Craw Stane (Canmore ID 17199) and the Rhynie Man (Canmore ID 17128).
Caeredyn	Edinburgh, Scotland.
Banntuce	Hill fort at Mither Tap, Bennachie, Scotland (Canmore ID 85507, also see work of Dr Gordon Noble).

South

Saxon Shore	Series of Roman sea forts on the eastern English coastline – running from Norfolk to Hampshire, England and corresponding western side of France.
Londinium	London, England.
Corinium Dobunnorum	Cirencester, England.
Aquae Sulis	Bath, England.
Coria	Corbridge (near Hadrian's Wall), England.
Vindolanda	Vindolanda (near Hadrian's Wall), England.
Vercovicium	Housesteads fort – Hadrian's Wall, England.
The Great Wall	Hadrian's Wall, England.

PROLOGUE

In year 43 of the Common Era (c.e.) Emperor Claudius led an army to the island of Britannia with the purpose of conquest and occupation. By the end of the 1st century the Romans occupied all of southern Britannia. As the decades went on, the Romans controlled a vast and seemingly ever expanding empire. But despite attempts to conquer the north of the island, the mountains and Iron Age people of the Scottish highlands had remained beyond their control. The Great Wall was built to protect the Roman army and to keep away the 'barbarians' of the north from the civilised south. The Romans called these native north-erners the Picti or 'Painted People'. In reality the people living beyond the Great Wall in the glens, mountains, on the edges of lochs and rug-ged coastlines were not a single group of 'Picts', but rather were made up of many different kingdoms.

Away from Britannia, the Romans controlled an immense Empire, and were constantly at war. Under the strain of defending their borders, the Empire also fell victim to plague and famine. By the 4th century, many public buildings were no longer maintained in Britannia and the Roman legions were progressively withdrawn to mainland Europe to fight against the Germanic threat. The tribes of the north had long suffered at the hands of the Romans, but had remained unconquered and ruled the mountains and jagged coasts. As Roman law and order dissipated, the door was opened to Rome's enemies to descend on Britannia.

ONE

Winter, 366 C.E., Britannia

Thundering hooves echoed across the field, shattering the dawn silence. A young woman pressed her back against a towering grey rock on the edge of the stone circle. Perspiration trickled through her hair and down her neck, turning cold and clammy in the icy air. She peeked around the standing stone. Pale winter light pierced through the low, hanging mist and crept across gloomy fields as the silhouette of three mounted soldiers galloped towards her.

She jerked her head back and spread her hands across the rock, pushing the jagged edges into her palms until her skin throbbed. *I'll never escape.*

Once more, she craned her neck around the stone. The soldiers wore the gold-plated helmets and red cloaks of the Roman army. Outside the circle, they stopped their horses. Leather creaked as a soldier gripped the reins. One soldier reached behind his head, pulled an arrow from his quiver and drew the bowstring back.

Shaking, she stepped out from behind the stone to face the Roman soldiers. *I've avoided this for far too long.*

A soldier raised his hand and nodded to the archer, who stretched the bowstring back to his lips. Metal crunched against bone as a horse chewed its bit.

Her heart pounded in slow rhythmic beats, as though a blacksmith was striking an anvil. *Sulis, I am ready. Take me to Tirscath.*

The soldier lowered his hand. A crack echoed around the circle as the bowstring hit against the leather bracer on the archer's arm. The arrow spun towards her.

She shut her eyes and opened them again. *Light. Dark. Light.* The arrow struck her chest, ripping through skin, fat, and muscle, wedging deep within her heart. Her eyes watered. The wound seared. Stumbling backwards, her feet left the grass and her back slammed into the frosted ground. She coughed and her mouth filled with blood.

"Should we bury her?"

"No, the woman told me to leave the body here."

Blood dribbled from her lips and crept across her cheek, into her ear. *Light. Dark. Light.* She squinted at the sky. White flickering arms of winter sun flexed and punctuated the silvery veil of mist. *Dark.*

TWO

Seven years earlier, Summer 359 C.E., Caledon

A raindrop spattered on Brei's bowed head. He wiped it away with his wrist and looked at the black smear of watery ash that clung to his forearm. Acrid smoke stung his nostrils.

Brei knelt next to the surging River Tae and slipped his hands into the cool water to scrub another man's dried blood from his skin. *They've taken Anwen.* Tears gathered, threatening to spill over his inflamed eyelids. *We should have run away together. How can I forgive my mother for keeping me away from Anwen?*

He sniffed and spread his hands across his face. The stubble that had sprouted along his jaw prickled against his palms. *Will they be furious that I left the battle? Are they looking for me?* Two raindrops landed on the silty riverbank, forming a circular depression on impact. *No, everything was in hand. They didn't need me.*

A haunting wail of women keening echoed out from within the city walls. Brei sighed and pushed his hand against the gritty sand and stood up. Dawn glowed crimson onto the grey clouds clustered above the hill fort. Brei adjusted the fit of his linen tunic that fell above the knees and walked towards the city walls.

Savage fire had roared through the forest and, by morning, Caercaled, capital of the Kingdom of Caledon, cowered beneath a thick smog. The city sat on the west-facing side of the Hill of Caledon, on

5

the northern bank of the River Tae. Three stone tiers were cut into the slope, culminating in a stone tower that rose eight hundred feet above the river. The flat land around the hill's base was enclosed by an outer wall that held two garrisoned gates, Northern and Western. Inside, on the lowest level of the city, were hundreds of roundhouses that surrounded a great centre circle. As the hill sloped upwards, two further walls enclosed more roundhouses interspersed with small pens and stables. The hill steepened and gave way to a forest. At the summit was a ten-foot-wide wall and, inside, loomed the enormous stone tower.

Smog clogged Brei's lungs as he wandered from the river along a wooded path to the city. Many of the pine trees outside the walls smouldered. Ashes swirled through the air, and he spat out the chars coating his tongue. Giant oaks survived with blackened trunks and curling, crisped leaves. The roundhouses that cascaded down through the wood to the river had been torched by the Roman soldiers. Villagers huddled by the smouldering remains of their homes, their faces red and swollen as they clutched each other.

Bodies littered the path as he approached the thick outer stone wall of the city. Warriors and farmers, women and children lay where they had been slain. Despite the blood and ash that coated their bodies, he recognised them all. An elderly man, who once worked the bellows in the blacksmith's furnace, lay contorted on his back. Clotted blood smeared across thinning white hair where his skull had been struck with the lead sling-shot ball that lay at his feet. The wail of women intensified as Brei continued past the Western Gate. The warriors guarding it were crumpled on top of one another, slaughtered at their posts. A Roman soldier's body sprawled across a warrior of Caledon. Brei kicked the dead Roman off, and the limp body rolled onto its back with a sickening thump. Dead eyes stared back at him. The gold-plated helmet and red cloak were all that Brei needed to see to justify his hatred.

"Brei!"

He looked to where the wooden gate to the city should have stood.

The stones on either side of the gap in the wall were scorched black. Through the gap, the path opened into the large centre circle, covered in the battle's dead. Romans, warriors, and villagers, equalised by the disarray. Through the smoke he saw his younger brother, Taran, limping towards him, the tattoos covering his chest and biceps glistening black against his pale skin.

"Brei," Taran croaked as he collapsed into Brei's arms. "I thought you were dead. I thought I was all alone."

Brei pushed Taran back and examined the blood caked into his blond hair. A blade had slashed his head and lines of crusted blood streaked down his neck and chest. "What do you mean? Where's Father?"

Taran clasped his hands around Brei's neck and sobbed. "Everyone is dead. Father. King Uradech."

Brei's heart quickened. "And Mother?"

"I...I've looked for hours. I searched everywhere, but I can't find her. A villager said they saw her being taken by the Romans."

"Then Aife, Naoise and Dylan, are they gone too?"

"No, they're all safe. They were in the tower. The villager said he saw Mother here in the centre circle. She must have left the tower and... and been captured."

Brei held his brother and wept. "I thought everything was under control. What happened?"

Taran pushed away sharply and glared at Brei. "What happened? Did you leave the battle?" Taran scowled at Brei's silence. "Where the fuck were you?"

Brei studied his brother's face. They were the same height, even though Taran had seen two fewer summers than Brei. "They took Anwen." Brei's voice cracked as he spoke.

Taran's eyes narrowed. "I saw the farmstead burning. You saw it too, didn't you? Did you leave us, in the middle of battle, to chase after the farmer's whore daughter?"

Brei threw Taran's hands off him. "Anwen isn't a whore, Taran."

7

Taran smirked. "Not yet, at least. But she deserves what's coming, for your betrayal."

Brei pushed Taran in the chest. Taran was solid, despite his youth, and did not flinch.

Taran shook his head. "The warriors will kill you for this, Brei."

Brei scanned the circle. Blackened piles of ash were the only remains of the roundhouses. Women stood over corpses, wailing. His uncle, Gartnait, hovered over a body, and Brei wondered if it was the beloved King Uradech. He clenched his jaw, his chest tightening over his hammering heart.

Taran stepped closer, his eyes slits beneath the blood and ash. "But I didn't save you last night to watch your execution today." His hoarse voice slipped to a whisper. "I should kill you. You deserve to die for betraying Caledon." He lunged forwards and hurled a fist into Brei's eye.

Brei staggered backwards, his eye throbbing. Taran struck him again, knuckles smashing against Brei's cheekbone. Brei's brain jolted in his skull, the ground swayed beneath him, and he collapsed to his knees. Taran's fists found Brei's stomach and struck him repeatedly.

"Did you care if I died?" Taran shouted, between blows.

Brei choked and squeezed his chest against his knees.

"What about Father?" Taran yelled, punching Brei's ribs. "We fought back to back, and he died next to me. Where the fuck were you, Brei? When they took Mother, where the fuck were you?"

Taran's knee smashed into Brei's nose and he blacked out.

Brei cracked open an eye. The wooden roof of his chamber churned, and his head pounded. He screwed his eyes shut and realised something soft covered his face. With shaking fingers, he reached up and brushed at a cloth that sprawled across his cheeks. His nose seared at the movement, and he recoiled.

"I wouldn't touch it if I were you."

Brei opened his eyes and focused on a silver-haired man in white robes perching on the edge of his bed. He groaned as he recognised the man. *The Eldar Druwydd.* "Am I dying?"

The Eldar Druwydd smiled. "No, but your brother made a good go of it. Your uncle, Gartnait, pulled him off you just in time. Serenn has seen to you, she thinks you will live, but your nose is broken and will hurt for some time. When you can sit, she has made a potion for the pain."

Brei lifted his body with his elbows and leant against the stone wall.

"Have this," the Eldar Druwydd said and smiled as he thrust a silver goblet into Brei's hands. Brei sipped with his eyes closed. Serenn had attempted to mask the bitter herbs with honey, but the concoction was still revolting to swallow. He opened his eyes and studied the deep wrinkles that cut across the man's forehead. Most men Brei had known died before the decrepit hand of age marked them. Grey spots covered the Eldar Druwydd's retreating hairline, but he grew his silvery locks long, and they curled down onto his shoulders and into his lengthy white beard. The corners of his pale green eyes were unlined, and Brei wondered if this was the first time the Eldar Druwydd had ever smiled at him.

Brei drained the goblet and handed it back.

"You're probably wondering why I am visiting you," the Eldar Druwydd said, adjusting his long white robes, so the folds fell straight to the ground.

Brei cleared his throat. "I didn't even know you were in Caercaled."

The Eldar Druwydd nodded. "I was in Rīgonīn when I heard the news that King Uradech had fallen. We rode four days, with little rest, to get here. Serenn says you've barely woken. Such is the strength of your brother's rage. I wondered if he was trying to kill you so he could have the throne to himself. But Serenn pointed out that Taran had his sword but did not use it."

Beads of sweat ran from Brei's underarms and dampened his linen tunic. *That's why he's here. He's come to execute me for abandoning the battle.* "Did you ask him?"

The Eldar Druwydd inspected the folds of his robes and tugged. "Yes, I did."

Brei's pulse thumped. *Will it be the triple death? Is it so bad what I have done that they will prevent my soul from ever reaching Tirscath?*

"Taran said he was beside himself with grief and took it out on you. I am surprised. He seemed such a stable child. King Uradech often told me he favoured Taran over you for the throne of Caledon. But," he pressed his lips together and released them with a soft "pop", "it is good that we have seen his instability before it was too late. Caledon needs a stable leader to help heal the wounds of this attack."

Brei's head felt it might explode from the pain of the blood rushing around his body. *Why would Taran protect me?*

"I am sure you realise by now that it is you, Prince Bridei, whom I would ask to make a claim for the throne."

Brei frowned. The contracting of his facial muscles pulled at his nose, and he winced. "Me? Surely you would prefer my uncle Gartnait. Or my cousin Talorc?"

The Eldar Druwydd shook his head. "I would not ask either. I have plans for Talorc in Vortriu, and Gartnait is not a warrior. He knows how to plan harvests and organise trade, but he does not have the heart of a king. He would be better as your advisor. You are a warrior, Brei. Perhaps less passionate than Taran, but youth will give you the stamina to lead Caledon through this adversity."

Brei glanced down at the linen sheets on his bed. "I'm not a warrior."

The Eldar Druwydd arched his white eyebrows. "You were seen at the battle defending Caercaled. You have been trained by King Uradech and seasoned warriors," his face relaxed into a smile. "But you are young and injured, so I will forgive this momentary lapse of confidence."

A servant girl tapped on the entrance to Brei's chamber.

The Eldar Druwydd frowned. "What do you want?"

The girl bowed and addressed the stone floor. "Forgive me, but there is a girl from the farmsteads, Anwen. She wants to see Prince Bridei, but no one will let her in."

Brei swung his legs over the bed, but the floor swam before him and he threw up.

The Eldar Druwydd jumped off the bed. "Leave us!"

"No!" Brei coughed as he steadied himself on all fours on the stone floor. "Bring Anwen to me."

The Eldar Druwydd scowled. "This is not the time to be having a dalliance with a farm girl. We have work to do."

Brei lifted his head towards the entrance as Anwen hobbled into the room. Even without a fire, he could see blackish-blue bruises stamped onto her pale skin. Anwen glanced at the Eldar Druwydd and her bottom lip trembled.

"We'll have to resume this conversation later." Brei coughed again as his eyes swelled with tears.

"As you wish, Bridei, I will return in an hour," the Eldar Druwydd said and brushed past Anwen into the stone stairwell.

"Anwen," Brei whispered and raised a shaking hand.

She dropped to the floor and embraced him.

"I thought they'd taken you. I didn't think I'd ever see you again." He stroked her auburn hair and pressed into her mud-encrusted tunic. Heat rose in his cheeks as his eyes travelled to her split and swollen lips. Her beige tunic was ripped, but she had tied it together at her shoulders. Yellowing bruises peeked out from beneath the rags. "What happened?" he said, his voice deeper and louder than he had intended.

Tears began to fall from her blue eyes. "I'm so sorry, Brei."

"What did they do to you?"

She shook her head and her small body shuddered in his grasp. "I wanted to die. I wanted to kill myself, but I kept thinking of you."

Hot tears surged down his cheeks and soaked the bandage across his nose. "I will never let anything happen to you. Ever. I will not spend another minute without you being mine. You will never leave my side again."

"But your mother and father, what will they say?"

Brei stared past her shoulder into the stone stairwell. "It doesn't matter. They are dead."

Bristles scratched against Brei's dagger as he shaved a week's worth of brown growth from his jaw. Holding a polished bronze mirror with one hand, he scraped the blade downwards through the glistening soap of animal fat and herbs, taking pains to avoid the bandages that still covered his broken nose. Carved into the antler bone handle of the blade was a snake that slithered across an arrow bent in the shape of a "Z". It was the symbol of the bloodline of Caledon. He tilted the mirror and glanced at the bluish bruises that ran like war paint across his collarbone and ribs. Inked into his chest was the warrior symbol of a crescent atop a bent arrow, and curling around his biceps was the Snake of Caledon. Over his wrists he pushed two massive bronze armbands up his arm, to sit snugly below the serpent.

Footsteps shuffled outside his chamber and Brei's eyes flicked in the mirror to Anwen, standing in the corridor behind him. He smiled at her reflection as he finished shaving. Servants had cleaned and dressed Anwen in an ankle-length blue tunic that belonged to Brei's cousin Aife. A band of crimson adorned the cuffs at her wrists and the hem. Around her small shoulders was a short red cape, fastened in the centre of her chest by a silver, U-shaped brooch with the Snake of Caledon curved across it. Anwen's freckled face was framed by flowing, shoulder-length, russet hair.

"Are you sure?" she asked, as Brei pulled a matching blue tunic over his head.

Brei smiled and sheathed his iron sword into a leather scabbard belted around his waist. He squeezed Anwen's hand and led her from his chamber and along the corridor to the stone stairwell. They descended the stairs in darkness until, at the bottom, the summer sun poured into the damp shadows. A woman waited for them outside the tower entrance.

"Prince Bridei." Serenn bowed her head. She was almost as ancient as the Eldar Druwydd, but unlike him, the physical manifestations of time were almost inscrutable. Her eyelids and eyebrows were blackened with charcoal and her hair stained midnight blue with woad. Half her hair was piled up on top of her head, pulled back from her face with pins made of bone. The other half hung over her shoulders, braided into multiple plaits, each secured with an amber bead. The fine lines of her heart-shaped face were the only betrayal of age beneath the otherwise smooth skin. She had once been a princess, the daughter of the long-dead King Cailtram. However, for most of Serenn's life, she had lived with the Kings of Caledon, as a Bandruwydd, the female order of the Druwydds.

"Is everything prepared?" Brei asked.

"Yes. But there is one problem." Her voice had a slight husky edge. "I have not had time to acquire rope threaded with gold for the ceremony." She glanced at Anwen and tilted her head. "You are from the farmstead, my dear? Perhaps you will not mind that the rope is not gilded?"

Anwen nodded, her cheeks reddening.

"Any rope is fine," Brei murmured.

Serenn smiled as she extracted a length of intricately twisted black wool from a pocket in her black flowing tunic. "Shall we?"

Brei squeezed Anwen's delicate hand. "Are you ready?"

Anwen winced as she smiled with swollen split lips.

Encircling the tower were the roundhouses where nobles not of the Blood lived. Brei, Anwen, and Serenn walked between the roundhouses and descended into the Sacred Forest. Broad, knobbed, green leaves of the ancient oaks and narrow, toothy, dark leaves of rowans spanned overhead. They passed the grey, fissured trunks of ash trees and the light brown, scaly trunks of gigantic yew, as a sweet breeze curled Anwen's cape behind her. Underneath the tallest oak tree in the Sacred Forest, they stopped. Gnarled, moss-covered limbs twisted at odd angles like an arthritic hand, culminating in the hollowed-out base of the trunk that blinked under the dappled glow of its leaves.

Serenn's black-blue robes billowed behind her as she approached the Great Oak and stood amongst its knotted roots, which seemed to wrap around her in a contorted embrace. She studied Anwen's face. "I can help with the bruises and I can give you potions for the pain inside. The memories will haunt you forever, but I can give you dreamless nights."

A summer warbler watched them from a shady bough, and he chirped sweetly as Serenn wrapped the woven rope around Brei and Anwen's wrists.

"Prince Bridei, do you promise to the Gods to protect and provide for Anwen and any children she births while you are bound?"

"I promise."

"Before the Goddess Brig," Serenn said, holding her hands over theirs, "before all the Gods, I bind you, Bridei, Prince of the Blood of Caledon and Vortriu, to Anwen. I bind you in protection and provision in this life and pray that you will find each other again in Tirscath."

Serenn left them in the forest, tied at the wrists, as the afternoon sun glistened through the leaves and mottled their faces in shadow.

"There," Brei said and smiled. "Now I will never leave you again."

Anwen's cut lip trembled. "It wasn't your fault, Brei."

"I should have run away with you a year ago when my mother said we could not be bound."

"No, Brei. You're a Prince of the Blood of Caledon. You can't turn your back on your responsibility to the people for me. It wouldn't matter if I was a princess from Vortriu or Hibernia, no single person is worth more than an entire kingdom."

He held her hand to his lips and kissed it. "I wish I could kiss your mouth."

"If you are gentle."

Brei bent slightly. Anwen's blue eyes shimmered as his lips pressed, gentle and hesitant against hers. "You taste like honey," he murmured.

"Serenn's apprentice dressed the cuts with honey."

Brei licked his lips. *I have to tell her.* "The Eldar Druwydd has made a request of me." He cleared his throat. "He, ah, he has asked me to make a claim, to be King of Caledon."

Tears swelled in her eyes.

"I will not make a claim," he whispered.

She frowned. "Brei, this is your destiny."

He drew her into his arms and kissed the top of her head. "If I become king, I must bind myself to Caledon, instead of you. I must devote every waking minute to rebuilding. I must go to war against the Romans, if necessary." He gazed into her eyes. "I must abandon you again. And I will not do that. The crown is not my destiny. You are. Do you remember when we first met? When we were children?"

"I was chasing a rabbit and got lost. I was so afraid, but you found me."

"What did I say to you?"

"You held me while I cried. You said that I was yours. That you would always protect me."

A tear slipped from his eye. "I failed, but I will never fail again. *You* are my destiny, Anwen, I will not leave your side and one day, together, we'll be more wrinkled than the Eldar Druwydd."

Tears escaped from her blackened eyes and she shuddered against him. His chest felt hollow, and he wondered if he really would give up his claim to the throne. *It is my destiny.* He swallowed. *It* was *my destiny.*

Silver moonlight shone upon the wounded warriors gathered underneath the sprawling branches of the Great Oak to listen to the Eldar Druwydd. Bandages covered limbs, faces, and chests. Some men were injured to the point of requiring support from other warriors to stand. Robed in white, the Eldar Druwydd stood surrounded by eight of his Druwydds. Serenn and her apprentice, Eluned, wore black. Affixed to their heads were antlered deer skulls.

Brei leant against a yew behind the crowd, with his young cousins Naoise and Dylan. The armbands around his biceps were cold in the evening breeze. In the branches above them, a long-eared owl hooted.

Taran and Gartnait waited in the middle, facing the warriors. Gartnait was tall and slight, and drunkards in Elwyn's tavern often chided his physique as being more suited to Druwyddry than leadership. His hair was light brown like Brei's, but flecked with grey, and his gentle face more resembled his sister, Derelei, than his brother, the dead King Uradech. Gartnait twisted his head over his shoulder towards the Druwydds. The Eldar Druwydd nodded.

Brei clasped his hands in front of his stomach. It had enraged the Eldar Druwydd to learn Brei was declining the invitation to make a claim for the throne. He had raised his voice and told Brei he was throwing his life away for a shit-covered peasant.

Gartnait turned back to the warriors and cleared his throat. "I, ah, I don't know what to say really." He turned his palms upwards and smiled.

"Allow me," the Eldar Druwydd said. Moonlight glinted against the wide curve of his stag headdress as he strode forwards to address the warriors. "Gartnait is deeply mourning the loss of his brother, the great King Uradech, and of his sister, Princess Derelei. Whilst you may not know him as a warrior, Gartnait was the great king's advisor, and he is the man to help Caledon rebuild. He is the man to increase trade, and he will ensure the harvests are brought in. He may not be the man to lead you to battle, but he will ensure your swords are sharp. Most importantly, he is a man. Not a boy. And he is the choice of the Druwydds. We ask that you support our choice."

The warriors murmured. Brei held his breath as his eyes lingered on the Eldar Druwydd's wrinkled face and then flicked to Taran. His brother was watching him. Brei dropped his gaze to the forest floor, where a rock the size of his fist lay amongst twigs and dried leaves. He kicked it and watched it roll down the slope towards the city.

"I also wish to make a claim," Taran said, stepping forwards. He was already taller than Gartnait, but his chest was yet to fill out, and this was even more noticeable as he addressed them without his tunic. The same black ink that marked Brei as a warrior of Caledon also curved across Taran's chest. From his belt hung a long iron sword encased in a leather scabbard.

Taran's gaze was furious as he stalked around the circle of men. "Gruffydd." He nodded to their cousin once removed. "Owain." He nodded to another warrior. "Cináed." He paused and held his arms out wide. "Warriors of Caledon, I am young, but you know me. You have trained me. You have fought with me. You fought with my father and with my uncle, King Uradech. You know what to expect, and what you can expect is a warrior king! The Druwydds do not support me, but I don't need their support." Taran glanced at the Eldar Druwydd and clenched his fists. The massive armbands around his biceps seemed to swell as he flexed. "I have the support of the Gods! Taranis, Lord of Thunder, blessed my birth and gave me his name!"

A crease formed between the Eldar Druwydd's eyebrows, and he muttered to the other Druwydds and shook his head. The hint of a smirk played on Serenn's lips.

"Your support is all I need to lead you. I pledge my protection of Caledon, of you, of your mothers, sisters, and children, in return for your support of me. Caledon needs a king with stamina to rebuild. I promise I will never sleep, never rest, until I have restored Caercaled to its former glory, until I have revenge against the Romans for what they did to us. Follow me. Choose me, and there will be no looking back. Only forwards, to a new dawn for Caledon!"

Taran scanned the crowd and his eyes found Brei's. Brei held his gaze before dizziness enveloped him and he stared at the ground.

"You only need to look at Bridei to know why Taran cannot be king," the Eldar Druwydd said. "Look what Taran did to him."

Fabric rustled as the warriors shifted their injured bodies, and their eyes found Brei's face. His heart hammered. He knew the men better than Taran, and he knew they would throw caution to the wind and follow Taran if he told them to. *Taran protected you, surely you owe it to him.* Sweat moistened his upper lip as he observed Gartnait. *Does Gartnait even want this? Maybe he would be a good king.* Brei chewed his tongue. *I wish I had made a claim, what was I thinking? The Eldar Druwydd asked me, he believed in me.* His pulse was manic. *What should I say?* He opened his mouth, but his throat was dry. Taran's eyes shimmered in the moonlight, unblinking as he glowered at Brei and shook his head. A few men glared at Brei and wrinkled their noses, as though he were covered in an unpleasant odour.

Naoise, who had only seen ten summers, kicked Brei in the shin. "Dog."

Brei frowned and gazed down at the boy's scowling face beneath a mess of unruly black hair.

"I will presume all you warriors will vote with the Druwydds in favour of Gartnait? So all those who vote for Taran speak out now," the Eldar Druwydd said.

"I do!" Naoise yelled, his voice squeaking.

The Eldar Druwydd raised his eyebrows. "And do any *men* speak for Taran?"

The silence that followed was thick, and Brei wished he could leave rather than see Taran's face.

"Then, I proclaim in the sight of Cernunnos and all the Gods, the new King of Caledon…"

The Eldar Druwydd raised a plain silver circlet in the air and held it above Gartnait's head. His hands seemed to shake as he began to lower the crown. A wave of nausea rose from Brei's stomach. *What have I done?* Gartnait beamed as the crown touched his greying hair.

"… King Gartnait!"

Fuck.

THREE

Winter, 366 C.E., Caledon

*L**ight*. She squinted at the sky. White flickering arms of winter sun flexed and punctuated the silvery veil of mist. Her eyes closed, and her mind tumbled into unconsciousness. *Dark*. With both hands outstretched, she groped to either side. A familiar scent of crisp humidity and damp leaves permeated the air. A frozen, wet tickle landed on her cheek. And another. *Snowflakes*. Allowing the snow to settle on her, she listened for a moment to the desolate absence of noise and opened her eyes. *Light*.

Skeletal branches of an ancient oak tree hung above, silhouetted by blinding white. A dull buzz in her ear grew into the gushing roar of a river.

She turned her head and observed that she lay at the centre of an unfamiliar stone circle. Her body was naked but for a cloak of snow. She frowned and wondered at the length of her limbs. *My new body is taller*. The snow slipped away as she sat up and inspected her chest. Over her heart was a silvery, knotted scar. It looked as though it was long since healed, and she wondered how long she had dwelt in Tirscath, the shadowland of the Ancient Gods.

Mist and snow swirled beyond the grey shadows of the stones as she pulled her legs into her stomach and wrapped her arms around them. *I can't believe Mother went through with it.* Throughout the long lives her mother had lived, and the many firstborn daughters she had raised, she had never had a daughter who had refused the Gift.

A snowflake landed on her hand. She raised her eyes as others floated to the ground. If she stayed in the stone circle, it protected her. But if she moved, she would need clothes, shelter, and food. She dropped her head to her knees and scrunched up her eyes. If she remained, even if it were only when she dreamed, it would be as if the Roman soldiers had never chased her across the fields.

The biting wind swirled around her with a melancholy whistle. It whisked the mist far above the standing stone circle to reveal a labyrinth of deciduous oaks interspersed with conifers that seemed to glow like onyx against the white. She scowled at the trees. *Perhaps I will just sit here forever.* In her mind, her mother's voice returned, chiding her petulance. Strands of jet-black blew across her face, and she twisted her neck to survey her new hair.

She was not afraid to be alone, to stay there for eternity. *But I'm here for a reason.* The wind gusted and dislodged snow from an oak branch. She watched it cascade, like a foamy waterfall, to the icy ground below.

She sighed, scrambled to her feet, and trudged through the snow. Crossing the threshold of the standing stone circle, the frigid air stung as it glanced off her cheekbones and thrust into her eyes until they watered, forming frozen tears on the ends of her lashes. Her bare feet ached and burned as the snow squeaked beneath them.

A cluster of conifers on the edge of the clearing held the snow at bay on their branches. She broke off the lower branches from one tree, to allow herself to sit against the trunk and shelter. From under nearby dry conifers, she collected kindling. Her hands stung as she dug through the snow and into the dirt to retrieve a piece of chert, which she struck with a rock to light a fire. When the kindling was hot enough to place twigs on, she sat against the trunk and edged her swollen feet towards the flames. The heat was excruciating, but she persisted, breathing in the rich scent of wood and pine needles that whirled in the smoke.

She leant back against the trunk and placed a large branch on the fire. The flames crackled and steamed. Rough bark pressed into her skin, and she shifted her back. Her eyes grew heavy as she listened to the crackling fire. *I wonder if Mother misses me... Does she regret sending those soldiers to kill me?*

A raven cried and beat its wings. The hair on her naked arms prickled as her eyelids shivered into consciousness. Thick grey vapour had descended through the trees, propelled by an icy wind. As her eyes adjusted to the startling white, the mist swirled around two hooded figures standing knee-deep in the snow.

They had dismounted, and each held the reins of their horses. The figures wore long capes made of greying wolf pelts. Their faces were indistinguishable under the hoods, but from their height and the broadness of their shoulders, she guessed they were men. The harsh winter light glinted against iron hilts at their waists. One man clutched a bow, and a white feather-tipped arrow was drawn and pointed at her face.

"*Borego dag.*"

She did not realise at first that the men addressed her. It sounded like the Ancient Tongue her mother had taught her as a child.

"*Borego dag? Pui hui?*"

Good morning? Who are you? She understood him but could not place his strange accent. The man without the bow lowered his hood and waves of light brown hair tumbled out, resting at his neck. His forehead was high and broad, and his cheekbones were pronounced, rising almost to the corners of his eyes. She assumed he was a few years older than her and perhaps had seen twenty winters.

"Where are you from?" the brown-haired man asked in the Ancient Tongue.

She frowned. *What should I say?*

Her mind raced as she tried to deduce where she was. She remembered as a child her father pointing to an old peeling map painted on the wall of his private chamber. In her mind, she traced along the spidery rivers and woods of her home in Britannia to the Great Wall that cut the island in half and marked the edge of the civilised world. But beyond the Great Wall was another wall, fallen into ruin, above which the worst kind of barbarian dwelled. The Picti. *The Painted People.* They were so fearsome that the Romans had long since abandoned their aspirations to conquer the desolate northern lands.

Have I been sent north of the Ruined Wall? A dull ring filled her ears.

"I..." she began in the Ancient Tongue. Her throat tightened, and the snow-covered ground seemed to sway beneath her. "I am lost." She shivered to mask her accent. "Please help me."

The brown-haired man unfastened a large U-shaped brooch with a snake slithering across it and removed his fur cape. Under the cape, he wore a brown, thick-weaved, hooded shawl with tassels falling at his waist. A woollen tunic poked out from underneath and covered down to his knees, underneath which he wore fitted skin pants. He stepped over the dead fire and wrapped his cape around her shoulders. It was still warm, and her skin tingled against the fur. His nose was kinked, as though it had once been broken.

He cleared his throat. "What are you doing here? What happened to you?"

"I... I was attacked...and I woke up in the stone circle." Her brother had often told her that the most convincing lies are those closest to the truth.

The other man lowered his bow and then his hood. Taller than the first man, his honey-blond hair was pulled into a ponytail. They shared the same high foreheads and blue eyes. "Romans?" he asked.

If they know I'm from Britannia, they will kill me. "Yes."

The men shared a dark look she could not interpret. The brown-haired man reached out, and she slipped her hand into his. It was calloused, but his nails were clean and clipped. She watched his serious face as he lifted her up, but he was staring at her feet.

"You have no shoes either?"

She shook her head.

"My name is Brei," he said and pointed to his companion. "This is my brother, Taran. We'll take you somewhere safe."

Brei carried her to his chestnut horse and placed her onto the saddle, both legs dangling over the same side. The roar of the river grew louder as Brei led the horse through the icy forest, crunching through the snow on foot with his long sword unsheathed before him. Leather creaked as she twisted in the saddle and looked behind her. Taran followed from a distance, riding a white horse with his hunting bow drawn. His eyes darted across the misty forest, scowling at the ghostly trees, as if expecting something to emerge.

After less than a mile, the path dipped to the forest edge. Nestled against the northern riverbank, a small settlement sat in the clearing. *It's so close. No wonder they discovered me.* Smoke billowed from the roofs of ten snow-covered roundhouses. Empty stock pens were scattered between the roundhouses, and a broad rectangular building stood on the northern side of the settlement. Only the river, a bright midnight blue, altered the white and grey landscape.

Brei stopped outside the nearest roundhouse. A high roof, which sloped to a point, sat above a circular dirt wall. In places the dirt had crumbled away, revealing sticks of weaved hazel. Taran clicked with his mouth, and his white stallion leapt into a gallop, flicking lumps of snow into the air as they disappeared into the mist.

Brei reached up to lower her from his horse. For a fleeting moment, his eyes flicked across her face. Clenching his jaw, he looked away. He bent under the porch and carried her into the roundhouse.

Inside, the roundhouse seemed to have no order to it. It appeared to be both a room for sleeping, with cot beds fashioned out of animal skins arranged around the fire, and a meals area. A shoulder-height wall made of weaved hazel divided the back quarter of the room, and tanned skins and furs hung over it. Little light seemed to reach past the divider, but through a half-yard-wide gap a fire's light shone across a wooden barrel, linen sacks held closed with heavy lumps of wood, a weaving loom, undyed wool, and finished lengths of woollen sheets stacked on top of one another. Skinned rabbits hung from a roof beam above the fire, and a pair of pheasants were being plucked by two young girls sitting on the dirt floor near the door. An unpleasant odour of raw meat, dried dung, and wet feathers hung in the air. The room was unlike any she had ever seen, and she felt a terrible distance from the shimmering marble pillars and bright, coloured mosaics of her home.

A woman with ginger hair, streaked with white, dozed by the fire. Next to her, a younger woman with fox-red hair and shimmering blue eyes sat cross-legged, crushing grains with a smooth rock on a grinding stone. Brei placed her by the fire near the younger woman.

"This is Anwen." He gestured to the young woman, and then to the older woman. "And this is her mother, Morfydd. You may stay in Morfydd's house until we can take you back to your home."

"You're back late from patrol... Who is she?" Anwen asked.

"We found her in the forest. The, ah..." He crouched in front of Anwen and placed a hand on her shoulder. "She says Romans attacked her."

Anwen's eyes widened. "Where?"

"In the forest," Brei said as he pressed his head against Anwen's auburn hair. "They won't get the chance to even look at you. We're going to take a scouting party out to find the Roman scum, and if there are any, we will slaughter them all."

Anwen was breathing fast, and her wild eyes flicked to the children. "Who will protect us?" She reached her pale, slender hands up and clutched around his neck. "You can't leave me, Brei."

"I have no choice, I have to go with the others, darling. Please return to Caercaled, to the tower." He turned to Morfydd. "Taran has ridden to Caercaled to ask that they send men to guard the farmsteads."

"I won't leave Mother," Anwen said with a tremor.

"Fine, Morfydd can shelter in the tower as well."

Morfydd shook her head. "I'm not leaving the other farmers to perish while I cower with the gilded Snakes of Caledon."

"Please go to the tower, darling." Brei stroked Anwen's cheek with his thumb.

Tears slid from her blue eyes. "I can't leave her, Brei."

"I wish you would." Brei stood up. "But if you insist, I won't leave until men have arrived to guard the farmstead. Look after the girls. I love you." He stooped under the door, and the wood snapped against the weaved hazel and daub wall as it closed.

Anwen and Morfydd seemed to contemplate the door. *Have they forgotten I'm here?* The whistle and creak of the wind soon replaced Brei's crunching steps, and the women turned on her in unison with narrowed eyes.

FOUR

Winter, 366 C.E., Caledon

B rei held Anwen's cheek and wondered if he was right to leave her. *This is why you can never be king.* His gaze fell upon the strange woman sitting by Morfydd's fire. Long jet-black hair fell across her pale face. As she glanced up at him, the firelight reflected in her eyes, and the green irises disappeared, replaced by luminous yellow. Brei had seen this before in forest creatures at night, in wolves drawn to the smells of the campfire, the light reflecting in the animals' eyes like yellow moons glinting between the trees. But never had he seen it happen in the eyes of a human. The glow vanished in an instant as she tilted her chin upwards and her eyes returned to emerald green.

A frown creased his brow, and he wondered if his mind was playing tricks. He tore himself away and pushed the door open with his palm, stepping into the snow again. Tied to a wooden post was his chestnut stallion, named Rhuad, "Red", waiting patiently for him. A grey woollen blanket beneath the saddle ran from Rhuad's neck to his tail, and his legs were wrapped to the knee. Brei tried to slide his fingers under the girth, ensuring it was secure. As he checked the wrappings on each leg, Brei wondered about the woman. About her eyes. *Did I imagine they glowed? Why was she alone and naked in the forest? And now there are Roman soldiers raiding again?*

The rumbling thud of displaced snow echoed through the stillness

26

of the morning air. Brei turned as eleven warriors, led by Taran, galloped across the snowy pasture. They wore grey, red and brown capes of wolf and fox pelts over leather pants and thick woollen tunics. From leather belts around their waists hung long swords in elaborate scabbards. They reined up their horses to stop in front of Brei, just as he put his foot into the stirrup and swung his leg over Rhuad's back.

Taran leaned forwards on the neck of his white horse. "And?"

Brei raised his eyebrows. "'And?'"

Taran rolled his eyes and sat upright in the saddle. "I sent a messenger to King Gartnait and told him about the woman and the Roman soldiers. I asked a few warriors to come down to protect the farmsteads, I wasn't sure if you'd want Anwen and the twins moved."

"Thanks, brother." Brei scanned the warriors Taran had chosen. Owain, Cináed, and Gruffydd were experienced men, and he mentally checked them off as good picks. Next, his eyes fell on Dylan, who had seen but thirteen winters and resembled his brother, Naoise, also in the party of warriors. Dylan's black hair was cropped short at his ears, while Naoise grew his long and it sprawled in a black mess over his shoulders.

"Dylan, why are you here?" Brei asked.

"I thought he might like to come, he needs to be blooded," Taran said, grinning at Dylan.

"He's just a boy, Taran, and we don't know how many Roman soldiers are out there."

"I was about his age when the Romans last raided Caercaled," Taran said, frowning. "Or have you forgotten?"

Brei grimaced. "Of course I haven't."

"I can't wait to shank a Roman in the kidney!" Dylan beamed.

Taran and Naoise snorted, sharing looks of mischief as they took it in turns to push Dylan, in an attempt to unseat him.

"An initial scouting party will ride out first," Brei yelled over Dylan's shrieks.

As if spurred by an invisible force, Taran abandoned his game with Naoise and moved his horse forwards in front of Brei. He swung around in the seat to face the ten men. "The rest of the warriors at Caercaled are on alert to follow if we do not return by the quarter moon."

"Do you really think Roman soldiers are raiding?" Dylan asked.

Brei scowled at Taran. "It is too soon to tell, but we will find them if they are."

"We will head south and make camp at the ruins at Caerdwabonna tonight." Taran reined his horse's head around towards the south. "Move out, lads!" He pushed up into a gallop to lead the scouting party. Brei rode at the rear, glaring at Taran's broad back.

Following the River Tae east for an hour before it turned, they continued south. Then the party fanned out a quarter-mile apart through the forests, to cover as much of the land as possible. But their searching proved futile, and by midday they found a clearing and ate lunch on a fallen tree trunk.

"But how did she get there?" Naoise asked for the fifth time. "How is it she survived even five minutes in the snowstorm with no clothes?" he continued through a mouthful of bread.

Brei sighed. "I just want to know whether there are soldiers. We can deal with the woman later."

Dylan leant forwards. "What if the Romans have hidden in the mountains of northern Caledon and we missed them?"

Taran snatched the last bite of bread from Naoise's hand. "Then the garrison at Caercaled will deal with them."

Naoise punched Taran hard in the shoulder.

"What if the Romans attack the farmsteads?" Dylan continued, while Taran and Naoise wrestled on the log.

Brei watched as they tumbled onto the snow-covered ground. He stood up and stretched his arms above his head. "Guards were sent to the farmsteads." Brei cracked his neck and felt that if he heard "What if the Romans…?" one more time he would have to give Dylan an early taste of the violence he seemed so keen for.

By nightfall, they reached the bridge near Caerdwabonna, "the fortress at the two rivers". The bridge crossed where the River Tae met the Eryn. Brei gazed across the water at an ancient abandoned fortress. He used to play there as a boy. On a cloudless day, he could see from the river mouth to the River Tae that curved up to the north and the smaller River Eryn that flowed in a straight line to the west. Green hills and grey water for miles.

"No fire tonight, lads," Brei grunted as he led them into the round stone fortress. The roof had caved in long before he was born, and its only occupants were tufts of grass creeping between the mortar of the stone floor. He walked across to the southern-facing side and watched as shadows raced from behind the forest across the field towards the hill. Gruffydd joined him, leaning against the remains of the tower's stone wall, and handed Brei a pigskin drinking pouch.

"Mead?"

Brei grunted and took the leather bag and raised it above his lips. The mead tasted of honey with a hint of heather. He licked his lips, and Gruffydd grasped the bag from Brei and had a swig. Gruffydd was the eldest of the scouting party. A cousin of Taran and Brei's mother, Derelei, on the male line. Gruffydd's hair was dark auburn brown, with the first hints of grey about the temples. A soft-spoken man, he had known Brei his entire life and often provided quiet counsel when they rode together, patrolling the kingdom's borders.

"There are no signs so far of any soldiers," Gruffydd murmured.

"I know. It's strange. Perhaps they retreated north?"

"Unlikely, in this weather. The Romans never attack in winter, not for hundreds of winters, anyway."

Brei nodded and fingered the brown tassels of his weaved woollen hood.

"Where's your cape, lad?" Gruffydd asked.

"The woman has it."

"I'll let you have a corner of my pelts tonight. But no cuddling, mind." Gruffydd smirked.

Brei laughed and tugged the mead pouch from Gruffydd's hand.

As the light faded from the distant hill, the sound of metal grating on metal interrupted them. Brei and Gruffydd turned. In the centre of a circle of warriors, Naoise and Dylan were sparring with their long swords. Owain, a red-haired warrior who had served with King Uradech, grinned. "A silver coin on Dylan," he said to Taran.

Naoise glanced at him and smirked. "May as well give Taran that coin now, Owain."

Brei and Gruffydd joined the circle around the brothers. Taran stood opposite Brei and nodded his chin upwards at his older brother. "Chuck us that mead, Brei." Brei raised his arm high and lobbed the leather mead sack over Dylan and Naoise's heads. Taran caught it and smiled.

Dylan grasped his sword with both hands and glared at Naoise. "What I lack in size, I make up for in focus, Neesh. You'll get bored in a second."

Naoise snorted. "Convenient timing, little brother, it will only take me a second to whip you."

Dylan stepped forwards and lunged at Naoise, who caught Dylan's blade against his, the metal swords scraping against one another.

Cináed, a warrior of the same age as Brei, looked over at Taran. "A silver coin on the boy as well."

"I'll whip you next, Cináed," Naoise grunted as he leapt back.

Brei laughed. "Ten coins on Cináed."

Dylan leapt forwards and struck Naoise's arm. Naoise hissed and clutched his wrist.

Dylan raised his eyebrows. "Do you concede, Neesh?"

"Come on, Naoise!" Taran roared.

Naoise grinned at Taran and twirled his sword in his right hand, blood streaking from his scratched wrist.

"Dylan, you've got this," Brei yelled. "Neesh is a little pig, look how tired he's getting."

Gruffydd and Cináed snorted.

Naoise whipped around and aimed his sword at Brei's stomach. "That's big talk coming from you, Brei."

Brei glanced at Taran, whose eyes glinted in the fading light.

Dylan danced behind Naoise and pressed the blade against his brother's pale neck. "I knew you'd lose focus."

"Taran, that's two coins for Cináed and I!" Owain yelled.

Taran shook his head and reached into the small leather pouch that hung on his belt.

"Might spend them up at Elwyn's tavern when we get back, eh?" Cináed said as he took the coin from Taran's hand.

"Naoise's already fathered a litter at Elwyn's, haven't you?" Owain laughed as he slapped Naoise on the back. Naoise smirked and strode to Taran's side.

"I'd put ten coins on Brei against Taran," Dylan said as he sheathed his long sword.

"Brei's nose is crooked enough," Naoise murmured.

Brei smiled. "Perhaps we should just discuss our plan for tomorrow?"

Naoise nodded and leaned against the stone wall, dragging his fingers through his sweaty black hair.

"We'll split in half tomorrow," Brei said. "Owain, you'll lead a party south-east to the coast to watch for ships. I'll lead the other party south-west through the Kingdoms of the Maetae and Damnnones."

Naoise cracked his fingers. "Which party will I go with?"

"You and Dylan will stay with Taran and me. Wouldn't you like to visit Queen Cantigerna?"

Naoise shrugged. "I guess."

Brei looked up at the sky. Thick clouds concealed the moon.

"Are we sure soldiers even attacked that woman?" Naoise asked through the shadows.

"She said yes when we asked her if it was the Romans."

"She had a strange accent," Taran said.

Brei's mind wandered again to her eyes, glowing yellow in the fire, and he shivered.

Mist rose in silver clouds above them as their breath met the wintry morning. They had slept upright, their backs against the fortress wall. Naoise was still asleep, his tousled hair sprawled across Taran's shoulder. Brei strained his ears for a sound. Birds signalled the new day, but there were no signs of soldiers. He stood and stretched his back.

Taran opened his eyes as Brei motioned with his head to Naoise. Taran smiled and ducked down, removing his shoulder and body from Naoise's weight in one swift movement. Naoise fell in a heap to the right, and his head landed in Cináed's lap, jolting him awake with a yelp. Taran and Brei sniggered as Cináed shoved Naoise off and cuffed him around the ears.

"Stop it!" Naoise yelled.

Brei smirked and wandered behind the stone fortress to relieve himself.

After breakfast, Owain split off with five men, leaving Brei behind with Taran, Naoise, Dylan, Cináed, and Gruffydd. Their search through the forests was slow. The land was flat in the valleys where rivers flowed, but rough hills threatened to slow their journey. But they knew how to navigate through their lands. They knew where the marshes rose and where to cross them. On the third day, their search led them into the hilly territory of the Kingdom of the Maetae.

"Why can't we ride further west and avoid them?" Naoise moaned as Brei pulled his horse to a stop.

Brei closed his eyes. "Because I want to ask them whether they have seen anything." He paused, trying to control the annoyance in his voice. "Not to mention the fact we would incite a war if we passed through their lands unannounced and without seeing the king and our cousin, Queen Cantigerna."

He turned to Taran for support, but he was watching a falcon circling overhead. Brei clicked his horse on and continued through the valley in silence. They rode to the furthest end of the valley where, perched on a snowy hill on the southernmost end of the mountain range, stood Caermhèad, "Fortress of the Maetae".

"I'll ride up and announce us," Taran called to Brei as he pushed his hips forwards and his horse obeyed by breaking into a canter. Brei watched as he grew smaller, riding up the slope. Before Taran reached the summit, a group of warriors had gathered to greet him. Brei held his breath as they spoke to Taran. Then a horn bellowed from the hill, echoing through the crisp air. Brei exhaled and led the rest of the party up the hill to join Taran. When they reached the summit, Brei noticed the fortress commanded sprawling views across the surrounding land. To the south lay the snaking outline of the river called the Neidrabona, "Snake River".

King Nechtan welcomed the party into his circular stone hall, his brothers, cousins, and Queen Cantigerna joined them.

Brunette ringlets framed the queen's round face. She wore a green tunic trimmed with red, with a matching burgundy sash tied around her waist. "Hello, cousins," she beamed. "And little Naoise and Dylan, how you have grown!"

Naoise grimaced but allowed himself to be kissed on the cheek.

"It's been so long since I last saw you." Brei took her hand. "Not since your binding… I almost don't recognise you."

Cantigerna smiled. "I had seen but fourteen winters then Brei. We're all grown up now, aren't we?" Her hands moved to her stomach. "But I still have a little growing to do."

Taran pushed past Brei and hugged her. "Congratulations, Canti."

"This is Cináed and Gruffydd, warriors of Caledon," Brei said, catching Nechtan's eye.

King Nechtan smiled. "You are all welcome here," and he gestured for them to sit down at the long wooden table. "Come, let's eat."

King Nechtan's blue tunic pulled tight against his biceps and broad shoulders. Although he was much older than Cantigerna, his face was unlined, perhaps because his auburn hair was stretched tight into a bun. "How is King Gartnait?" he asked as he took a sip of ale from a silver goblet.

"The king is very well," Brei said.

Nechtan raised his eyebrows. "Is he? I have heard rumours of ill health."

"Where did you hear that from?" Brei asked.

The king smiled into his goblet before taking a swig. "Why does he send you on this errand in his stead?"

Taran cleared his throat. "Brei and I have always handled these operations for the king."

"Of course. He is more of a strategist than a warrior." Nechtan raised his goblet. "To Gartnait's health."

"To King Gartnait," Taran and Brei murmured.

Taran raised his drink towards Cantigerna. "And you have been well, Canti? How is your new life in the south?"

"It's been two winters, Taran, hardly new anymore. But I like it here. Although sometimes I miss the ocean, the way the waves used to crash into the fortress at Caertarwos."

"I bet you don't miss Talorc," Naoise smirked.

Cantigerna smiled. "I miss all my cousins in Vortriu."

"You will return soon, to raise the child?" Brei asked.

"Of course. My little Prince or Princess of the Blood will be raised in Vortriu," she said, patting her stomach.

Taran leaned towards King Nechtan. "But it may not be safe to travel at the moment. Have you seen any Roman soldiers in your lands recently?"

Nechtan frowned and turned to his men, who mirrored his expression. "No, we have not seen soldiers up here for many winters, not since…" He paused and looked around the table. "Not since King Uradech was slain."

One of Nechtan's men, an advisor called Domgal, leant forwards. "Why do you ask?"

"We had reports of Romans near Caercaled."

Domgal frowned. "Are these reports reliable?"

Brei coughed. "We are, ah, beginning to think they are not."

Taran sipped from his goblet. "But we are treating them as serious. The consequences of not taking any threat seriously are, as we all remember, dire. So we will continue onto the Damnnones' kingdom soon, to the city of Gowan. But if we may stay the night, we would be much obliged."

Nechtan cleared his throat and leant towards his advisor. "Domgal, have men sent to the west, we need to make sure Romans are not hiding on our lands." He turned back to Taran. "Will you go to Altclud?"

Taran shook his head. "We will speak with the garrison at Gowan only, but if the reports warrant it, then we will go to Altclud and visit our uncle Alwyn, the king."

Nechtan glanced again at Domgal. "And of course you may stay, it is an honour to welcome four Princes of the Blood of the Kingdoms of Caledon and Vortriu."

"And who else do you welcome in your halls? Are you still accepting Roman silver for peace?" Taran asked.

King Nechtan spat his ale back into the cup. "Steady on, lad."

"It's just a question," Taran said, smiling.

"No. We are not. It's not been offered for twelve winters, when the peace was first broken. Has Caledon been accepting Roman silver?"

"Caledon has never accepted Roman bribes," Taran said. "And never will."

FIVE

*A*n amber light flickered within a stone chamber at the end of a black passageway. She crept towards it, stooping under the low ceiling as gravel scratched beneath her feet. Entering the chamber, she straightened to her full height and looked around. Three walls opposite the passageway were inset with smaller chambers, and inside each were stone basins. Placed on the basins were immaculately cleaned skulls, which seemed to glare at her. She peered back towards the impenetrably dark passageway. The only noise, save for the crackle of a torch that rested on the ground, was her own breath. Crouching, she reached for the torch, but as her hands grasped the wooden handle, the flame extinguished, and the chamber plunged into darkness. Blood pulsed like drums in her ears as she strained to see anything other than black. An abrasive scrape of gravel reverberated along the length of the passageway. Followed by a crunch. Footsteps in the dark. One foot after another, until the drumming sound engulfed her.

Her eyes snapped open, and the thatched roof of the roundhouse whirled into focus. Sweat drenched the fur cape tangled around her body. Anwen's face hovered above her, a flaming torch clutched in her shaking hand.

"Who are you?" Morfydd asked, brandishing a knife.

She frowned as she tried to recall what had happened. Morfydd and Anwen had attempted to question her after Brei's departure, but she had been in no mood to talk. Lying amongst the barrels of stored wheat where they had made her a bed, her head had pounded and she had drifted into an uneasy sleep. Her dreams of home, of the vineyards that grew on her parents' estate, strayed into dark passageways leading her mind far from civilised Britannia.

Morfydd thrust the knife forwards. "Are you a Roman spy?"

"A spy? Why do you think I'm a spy?"

"You were screaming...and you were speaking like..." Anwen closed her eyes. "Like them."

Morfydd lunged down and pressed the knife against her throat. "Tell me your name or I will kill you."

She hesitated. Her name was Lucia. *I'd bet all the denarii in the world that Lucia is not a name of the Ancient Peoples. It's a Roman name.* "Sorsha," she croaked against the force of the blade, recalling the name of her mother's cousin.

Morfydd frowned and leaned her head to one side. "Sorsha?"

Sorsha pursed her lips and hoped the furious pulse in her neck was not visible.

"Where are you from?" Morfydd asked as she removed the blade from Sorsha's throat.

"I come from south of here from...from near the wall." She tried to recall anything of what her father had said about northern trade routes. "My father was a merchant and he...he traded with the Romans. That's why I can speak Latin."

Morfydd frowned. "Latin?"

Sorsha flushed. "Yes, that's what the Romans call their language. Where am I? What is this place?" She pushed herself up and pulled Brei's cape around her.

"This is the farmstead on the edge of Caercaled, in the Kingdom of Caledon."

Caledon had a strange familiarity to its sound. One of the tribal labels on her father's map had read "Caledonii". *Just one of the many barbarian tribes beyond the Great Wall. They are all the same.*

37

Morfydd exhaled through her nose. "Anwen, keep the girls busy somewhere else. I'll help..." her eyes narrowed, "her."

Anwen nodded and disappeared through the gap in the screen that divided the main room from the storage area. "Ceridwen, Nia, come away from the screen and help me repair my comb."

Twin girls shuffled forwards, and Sorsha caught sight of them briefly through the gap in the divider. One had brown hair and seemed to tremble. The other was blonde, and her eyes glistened as she peered at Sorsha before moving out of sight.

"The Romans are our enemies. Are they also your enemy?" Morfydd asked.

Sorsha swallowed. "Yes."

"How did you get here?"

"Brei and Taran found me."

Morfydd stepped towards her. "But how did you get to Caledon?"

"I, ah, I don't remember. I just woke up here, in the stone circle."

Morfydd's eyes darted across Sorsha's face. "I see. And you're wearing Brei's cape because you have no clothes? No shoes?" She pursed her lips. "I guess we'll have to stitch you a tunic..." Morfydd ran her fingers along a neat pile of beige linen sheets. "The flax was a gift from Anwen. I spun these myself and weaved them into sheets to make clothes... They took me weeks to make." Morfydd's voice was so low, Sorsha wondered if she was talking to herself. From a wicker basket next to the sheets, Morfydd grabbed a handful of what appeared to be rags. "You can have these." Morfydd thrust a fistful of scratchy wool into Sorsha's hands.

"I am so grateful you are helping me. It was so fortuitous that Brei and...and..."

"His brother, Prince Taran?"

"Yes... So lucky they found me."

Morfydd motioned upwards with her fingers. "Come, take that off. I need to look at you so we know how much fabric we need."

Sorsha stood but did not remove the fur cape until Morfydd stepped forwards and tore it off. Her skin prickled as Morfydd fitted pieces of rough-spun wool. When Morfydd had collected enough scraps to fit Sorsha's frame, they sat on the floor in silence, fastening the pieces together with a needle made from deer bone. Morfydd's method of instruction involved pointing, grunts, and curt slaps if Sorsha made a mistake.

As dusk frosted over the farmstead, Sorsha pulled the finished tunic over her head and tied a strip of leather around her waist. The beige fabric dropped to her ankles and rested in a modest position on her chest. The gusseted arms were loose and came to her wrists.

Morfydd fingered the hemming on one sleeve. "Tomorrow we'll make an apron and socks."

"Thank you," Sorsha mumbled.

That evening, Anwen and Morfydd hung an iron cauldron from metal rods across the fire. The liquid inside gurgled ominously, and Sorsha noted the distinct absence of a delicious scent. Ceridwen, who did not seem to share the same fear of Sorsha as her twin sister Nia did, held up small, carved wooden bowls as Anwen ladled out a beige, puffy slop. The fire fluttered across Ceridwen's heart-shaped face, which she had inherited from Anwen, but her braids were blonde, like her uncle Taran's hair. Nia sat hunched over on her cot bed, murmuring to herself as she played with a polished wooden horse. She shared her father's stern expression and light brown hair.

Ceridwen shuffled to Sorsha and held up a bowl of what looked like soupy grains.

Sorsha smiled down at the child as she accepted the warm bowl and a ruggedly carved spoon. "What is it?"

Ceridwen frowned, and Sorsha wondered if she had given herself away.

"It's porridge. Oats and water," Ceridwen said.

Morfydd glared at Sorsha over the cauldron. "Eat back there and go to sleep!"

Sorsha slid behind the screen and sat on the bed of skins, squashed between a loom, spinning wheel, and stacks of woollen sheets. Her stomach rumbled, but the lumpy beige muck looked unappetising. She swallowed a mouthful of creamy grains and watched Anwen and the twins join Morfydd by the fire.

"What do you think?" Anwen whispered to Morfydd.

Morfydd glanced towards the storage area. "I don't trust her."

Sorsha slid back into the shadows.

"What can we do?"

"Nothing until Brei gets back," Morfydd whispered and then, raising her voice, said "there are warriors guarding the farmstead and the forest if anyone were to try anything!"

SIX

Winter, 366 C.E., Maetae

Brei and his scouting party departed Caermhèad at dawn and crossed the Neidrabona. Riding their horses at a gallop, they curved around the mountain range before the land flattened into grassy lowlands. The change in geography marked the border between the Kingdoms of Maetae and Damnnonia.

As the sun reached its highest position, Brei raised his hand to slow the rest of the group as he surveyed the ruins of an abandoned Roman wall. A ditch lay in front of a grass mound, carpeted in snow, about three yards high. It stretched to the horizon on either side. On top of the grass wall were the remains of a wooden fence. In many places, it had rotted away, enabling them to see through it from horseback.

Brei looked to the west, waiting for Owain and the others to join them. Gruffydd and Taran watched southwards through a gap in the fence. The city of Gowan lay near the wall, but there was no evidence of a disturbance.

Riders galloped from the west along the wall. Owain and his group of scouts reined up in front of them. Owain leant against his horse's neck to speak to Brei, red hair plastered to his sweaty face. "Nothing. A few trade ships heading south from Caertarwos, but other than that, nothing. We passed a good many farmsteads on our way. None had seen any sign of Romans, not for many winters."

"We saw no traces of soldiers in the forest either."

Owain dismounted. "So, what now?"

Brei had been trying to process the same question in his mind. "I think we should still enquire with the Damnnones."

Taran leaned against the wooden fence. "If the Damnnones saw nothing coming through here, then we should revisit King Nechtan on our way back to Caercaled to see if his scouts found anything."

Brei nodded, his thoughts returning to the strange woman, who he was now certain was lying. *Why?*

Brei, Taran, Naoise, Gruffydd, and Cináed stood on the southern side of the wall and watched as Dylan slid gingerly down through the snow on his bottom. Brei helped him stand as the others sniggered, having managed the distance at a jump themselves. Dylan's cheeks reddened as Taran ruffled his black hair.

They walked towards Gowan, a town within the Kingdom of the Damnnones on the banks of the River Clud. The stench of animals and inhabitants was overpowering. Along the city's narrow lanes, snow was piled up against stone roundhouses with brownish-grey roofs, thatched and slanting. The murmur of a hundred conversations rose and carried in the icy air.

Brei stopped and turned to the others. "Spread out and find Damnnones' warriors and traders. Ask whether they've seen any Roman soldiers. We'll meet back at the wall before nightfall."

Jostling through groups of market buyers and sellers, Brei pushed past two large men carrying swords outside a stall selling ale. "Are you in the service of King Alwyn?"

The taller of the pair spoke. "Depends who's asking."

"I'm Prince Bridei of Caledon and Vortriu. King Alwyn is my uncle."

The shorter man raised his eyebrows. "What brings you so far south?"

"Answer my question first."

The tall man smiled. "I am Rhodri, a warrior in the service of King Alwyn's son, Prince Coel, and this is Aaron."

Brei nodded. "We fear there may be Romans ranging in Caledon, perhaps planning an attack. Have you seen any soldiers?"

Rhodri glanced at Aaron. "None crossing over the Clud. But we have seen them ranging further south. Their scouts travel freely in Gwoddodin."

"We see them quite a bit, actually," Aaron added.

Brei frowned. "In Gwoddodin?"

Rhodri shook his head. "No, Aaron means something else."

Brei turned to the stall owner, an elderly man wearing a grubby beige apron. "A round of ale for us, please," he said, pressing a clipped piece of Roman coin into the stall owner's hand. The old man dipped three wooden tankards into a foaming barrel of ale and handed them to Brei, Rhodri, and Aaron.

Brei grasped the wet wooden cup and took a sip of the bitter ale, surveying the Damnnone warriors as he drank. "So, tell me, why have you been seeing soldiers?"

Aaron smiled. "We've been paying visits to our friends over the Great Wall."

Brei spat out a mouthful of ale. "You what?"

Rhodri and Aaron grinned. "There's not many soldiers left on the wall anymore," Aaron said. "Hardly any of the towers are occupied like they were in our grandfathers' time. The ones that are left, they've been recruiting them locally and, ah, they're a lot friendlier than those foreign soldiers."

"And what have you been doing?"

Rhodri drained his cup. "Raiding beyond the wall. They just let us. We let them have some of our spoils on the way back through. You have to avoid the big forts but the smaller towers, they just let you right through the gate, no problems."

"I don't believe you."

Aaron pulled back the cloak he wore and displayed a golden brooch. It dazzled even in the fading winter light. "I took this from a big white farmhouse. Their farmers are filthy rich, a single man ruling over an

43

estate with slaves growing food for him. Not like our farms. But they are just as unprotected."

"Do you worry they will launch a revenge campaign?"

Rhodri shook his head. "They don't have the men to range very far beyond the wall. The news we have from traders is something's distracting them, some war with the tribes beyond Gaul."

As the sun dipped behind the forest, Brei climbed over the wall to join the rest of the scouting party.

Naoise's cheeks were tinged with pink. "Did you hear about the raids?"

Brei nodded. "But more importantly, none of the Damnnone warriors had seen soldiers on their land."

"And most of the army has left the Great Wall," Naoise continued, as though he had not heard Brei. "And the Roman garrison are less hostile than normal they have been allowing the Damnnones through the wall with only a small bribe of silver."

Brei grunted and continued walking to the woods just north of the Ruined Wall to make camp.

"What are you going to do about it?"

Brei frowned as he undid Rhuad's girth strap. "What am I going to do?"

Naoise nodded. "Isn't this the perfect time to strike? Get revenge for what they did?"

Brei hauled the leather saddle off Rhuad's back. "Maybe," he said as he led Rhuad away from Naoise. *If I can get revenge against the Romans, maybe Taran will forgive me.* Sticky needles grazed his hands as he tied Rhuad to a fir tree, giving him enough rope to lie down. Brei stroked Rhuad's forehead. "We'll be home in a few days."

A twig snapped, and Brei turned to see Taran leading his white horse through the snow towards him. "Did you hear–" Brei began.

"Even if I didn't, Naoise has made sure we are all informed."

"He is nothing but enthusiastic," Brei said and smiled.

Taran twisted another rope around the tree. "What do you think?"

He cleared his throat. "I want revenge, Taran. More than I want to sleep or to eat. I want to kill the men who murdered our father, our uncle, and who took our mother."

Taran raised an eyebrow. "And the men who hurt Anwen?"

Brei clenched his jaw. "Obviously."

"This woman is a sign from the Gods. She led us here, soldiers or no soldiers. Now we know they are weak and we can strike. It's destiny."

Brei studied Taran's face. He had the colouring of their mother, but the looks of their father. "We should speak to King Gartnait."

Taran grinned. His milky white smile was seldom bestowed on Brei alone, and Brei felt the colour rise in his cheeks as he grinned back.

When they had built a fire, Brei sat on the icy ground. His bones creaked as though they had aged beyond his years in the space of a few days. He moved his feet closer to the fire, relishing the luxury of heat.

"Why would someone lie about being attacked by Romans?" Cináed shook his head.

"Perhaps she's a spy?" Owain said.

Gruffydd raised his eyebrows. "A spy without clothes?"

"Maybe to lure us into taking her in?" Owain shrugged.

Brei closed his eyes and wished he had trusted his first instinct not to leave Anwen alone with the woman.

Taran reclined and rested his head on his saddlebag. "Do you remember the stories of the Gallar? They disappeared and reappeared wherever the Gods sent them, always where there was evil or sickness. Didn't they always have green eyes?"

Brei recalled the haunting glow of the woman's eyes, and he began to second-guess himself. Perhaps he had not imagined it, after all. *Maybe the light of the fire really had reflected yellow in her eyes. Like a wolf.*

Naoise threw a twig at Taran. "No, it's faeries that have green eyes."

45

"No, they don't!" Dylan yelled. "Faeries have purple eyes. Like summer heather!"

Brei grew deaf as his thoughts turned inwards. Beads of cold sweat dripped down his sides and he closed his eyes. He imagined returning to the farmstead, hearing Nia and Ceridwen scream "Papa!" as they raced towards him with smiles. But there was no sound except the faint creaking of tall pines swaying in the wind. In his vision, he walked to Morfydd's roundhouse, but when he reached the door, blood seeped out, turning the snow red.

SEVEN

Winter, 366 C.E., Caledon

The days blurred into one as Sorsha helped Morfydd and Anwen around the farmstead, making woollen sheets on the loom and grinding husks to make flour. By the third day, Sorsha's palms were forming calluses. Dark circles spread beneath Anwen's eyes and her movements became erratic. Sorsha seldom left the smoky confines of the roundhouse, but when she did her eyes trailed across the hardened faces of the guards Taran had sent to watch over them. When the chores were completed each night, Sorsha was banished to languish in her place behind the weaved hazel-branch screen and furs. While it was warm in the roundhouse, the pungent stuffiness of smoke, dried herbs, and raw sheep's wool had Sorsha longing to be outdoors, even if it meant freezing. She was relieved when, on a bleak morning, Morfydd told Sorsha to search for hazelnuts in the forest.

It had snowed hard the night before, and her boots sunk knee-deep into the crunching snow. As she walked up the rise, at the eastern edge of the clearing, she came upon two warriors cloaked in greying furs. Their cheeks were icy pale beneath shaggy red hair. One had freckles leaping across a pronounced nose, while the other had skin so smooth it looked as though it were frosted over. They glanced at each other as she approached.

"Hello," Sorsha said as she stopped where the shadows of the forest met the brightness of the snow.

"Are you the woman Brei found?" one man asked.

Sorsha tilted her chin upwards. "Yes. And who are you?"

"The warriors sent to guard you," the man with freckles said. "I am Brin, and this is Deryn."

"Guard me?"

"Well," Brin cleared his throat, "not just you. Everyone in the farmstead, in case those barbarian Romans come back."

Sorsha raised her eyebrows and wondered how they could hope to defend the farmstead against professional soldiers.

"But it's not just us," Deryn said. "This is just our post."

"Well, I won't keep you any longer. If you'll excuse me," she said, stepping towards the forest.

Brin stepped in front of her. "Where are you going?"

"In there." She pointed to tall pine trees shrouded in the snow that lined the edge of the forest. "I'm looking for hazelnuts for Morfydd," she said, holding up a leather pouch Morfydd had given her.

"Well, don't stray too far," Deryn said. "There are more warriors in the forest, and they are shaky enough to shoot anything that moves."

Brin touched the hilt of his sword. "You're lucky you stumbled on us first, not everyone is as steady as us."

"Right. I'll keep an eye out," she said and continued into the forest.

Breathing in the fresh winter air, her shoulders relaxed for the first time since she arrived in Caledon. She trudged through the white forest without a clear sense of direction, hoping to find a coppice of hazelnut trees, but with no urgent desire to return to the farmstead. At times she tripped and fell in the snow. Her skin tingled beneath a film of soot as the crisp air swirled around her, and she longed to bathe in the hot spring baths that were so common in her homeland. At last she spotted a solitary hazelnut tree standing desolate among the pines and oaks. She crouched down and dug in the snow underneath the tree to find any hazelnuts that had fallen during autumn, and that squirrels had not taken. By the time she had collected over twenty nuts in the leather pouch, her stomach was growling.

Despite her hunger, she did not want to return. Instead, she lay in the snow in an oak grove and watched the clouds. They had turned from fluffy white to ominous grey. She flirted with the idea of leaving, of returning to Britannia. *I wish I knew what to do, wish there was a Druwydd I could speak to. They would know what I am here for.* Her stomach knotted and ached as she thought of home, of her mother. *I wish our last words hadn't been in anger.* Tears rolled across her cheeks and into her hair. *I wish I could tell her I was sorry. If only I had listened to her lessons. If I had accepted the inevitable, I would know what to do right now.* She imagined stealing a horse from the stables and riding south for as long as it took. *Maybe I can leave. Maybe I can return to her and go back to my old life.* Her throat constricted, as though invisible hands choked her. She spluttered and coughed until the tightness subsided. Through a watery veneer, she watched a snowflake twirl in the breeze until it landed on her forehead.

"Sorsha?"

She sat up and dragged the back of her hand across her cheeks.

Ceridwen crunched across the clearing. "Are you okay?"

With a drawn bow and arrow, Taran followed her.

Sorsha scrambled to dust off the caked snow. "I'm fine." She looked at Taran. "Is something wrong?"

Taran put his hand on the child's shoulder. "Ceridwen was worried because you were gone for so long when it looked like another snowstorm was coming in."

Sorsha looked down. "Sorry, you startled me."

Ceridwen stepped closer to Sorsha. Her cheeks were flushed and her blue eyes sparkled against the snow. "Why were you sleeping?"

Sorsha frowned. "I wasn't sleeping."

"Then what were you doing…?" Taran asked, the right side of his mouth curling up.

"Are you crying, Sorsha?" Ceridwen asked.

"No."

"But I could see tears."

"I… yes, well, I guess I was. I'm just tired." Sorsha surveyed her knees, surrounded by hardening snow. "When did you get back?"

Taran fingered the feather tip at the end of his arrow. "Just recently. Why have you been gone for so long?"

Sorsha took out the leather pouch and gave it to Ceridwen. "I was collecting hazelnuts."

Ceridwen investigated the contents of the pouch. "You didn't find many!"

"Oh, I thought I had quite a few."

Taran smirked. "Perhaps you should spend less time lying on the ground."

Sorsha glanced at the bare oak branches, covered in snow, and said nothing.

Taran tugged at one of Ceridwen's blonde braids. "Come, Ceridwen, let's head back. Dinner will be ready."

Sorsha followed them out of the grove. "Dinner? I didn't realise it was so late."

Ceridwen extended her hand towards her. "That's why we came looking for you."

She accepted Ceridwen's small hand. "How did you find me, anyway?"

Taran frowned. "There's an entire garrison of warriors guarding the farmstead. Surely you didn't think we'd let you roam around unfollowed? Plus…" He smirked. "We could see how many times you'd fallen over."

Her walk into the forest seemed like days ago, and tripping over was already a distant memory. "Oh."

Beneath dark clouds Brei stood outside the roundhouse with an older man. Brei still wore the same tasselled shawl. She pulled his fur cape tighter around her shoulders. *He must have been freezing without this.*

"Hello," Brei said, almost inaudibly. A shadow hovered beneath his blue eyes, and thin lines she had not noticed before were etched across his high forehead.

"Hello. I didn't get to say it before, but thank you for rescuing me."

He nodded and picked up Ceridwen, who showed her father the pouch of hazelnuts. "She didn't find very many, Papa."

Brei glanced at the other man. "Goodnight, Gruffydd." He nodded at Taran and bent to enter the roundhouse.

Gruffydd patted Taran on the shoulder. "I'll see you in the morning."

Sorsha and Taran watched in silence as Gruffydd mounted a grey stallion and cantered through the snow to the north.

"Do you live here too?" Sorsha asked.

"No." Taran gestured in the direction Gruffydd had ridden. "I live in the fortress at Caercaled. We all do, except for Morfydd. Surely, Morfydd and Anwen told you that by now?"

"They have barely spoken a word to me."

Taran's eyes narrowed. "And why do you think that is?"

She shrugged. "The first day, they accused me of being a Roman spy."

"Why?"

"I don't know. I talk in my sleep. I always have. So, I probably said some things in Latin... In the language the Romans speak. But how do Anwen and Morfydd know what the Romans sound like?"

"That's not your concern. We should go inside, dinner will be ready."

Sorsha frowned, not moving.

Taran exhaled. "Go inside, please."

Sorsha looked him in the eye. "Why is everyone here so hostile?"

Taran stepped closer, his voice dropping to a whisper. "Why are you so strange?"

"I'm not the one who is strange, it's all of you who are..." *Barbarians.*

Taran smirked. "Forgive me, of course, it's all of us, it's the entire

Kingdom of Caledon who are strange, not you, the woman who spontaneously appeared naked in our forest."

She opened her mouth, but Taran's smile vanished. "Go inside."

The blood rose to her face, but she forced a smile. "After you."

He shook his head and opened the door of the roundhouse.

Sorsha dragged her wooden spoon through yet another meal of porridge as she listened, unfocused, to Brei as he told Anwen and Morfydd of how a king, named Nechtan, had known that another king, called Gartnait, was sick. She was dazed to be inside after the stark freshness of the outdoors, and the room seemed even more claustrophobic with the addition of two grown men.

Brei's eyes narrowed. "Sorsha?"

She tried to frown the fog away. "Sorry, I wasn't listening."

"I asked how you got so far north."

The fire was scorching against her legs, the relentless glare of Anwen and Morfydd suffocating. "I…" She closed her eyes. She could not imagine an adequate explanation. "Um…" She leaned forwards and opened her eyes as the light of the fire fell across her face. Anwen gasped and clutched Brei's hand. Sorsha frowned and wondered if a stray spark from the fire had burnt Anwen. Taran tilted his head, a frown creasing his brow.

"Did the soldiers bring you here?" Brei asked, unblinking, as tiny pinpricks of fire glistened in his pupils.

"I don't remember."

EIGHT

Winter, 366 C.E., Caledon

"I asked how you got so far north," Brei said.

"I..." Sorsha closed her eyes. "Um..."

What's wrong with her? Brei glanced at Taran, whose face seemed to mirror Brei's own thoughts. *She's hiding something. Maybe she is a spy.*

Sorsha opened her eyes and leant forwards. The light from the fire flashed across her face and her green eyes glowed yellow. *Like a wolf.* Anwen inhaled and grasped Brei's hand.

Brei swallowed. "Did the soldiers bring you here?" *What is she?*

"I don't remember," she mumbled and looked at the ground.

"You must be tired," Taran said. "You should sleep."

Sorsha nodded without looking at Taran and rose. She was tall for a woman, broad-shouldered but slender, and gave the impression she could run fast if she so chose. Brei studied Taran's face as his eyes trailed Sorsha's exit.

When Brei was certain Sorsha and his twin girls had fallen asleep, he motioned for the adults to join him outside. They trudged in silence up the rise and into the forest.

"Tell Taran what you told me earlier," Brei said as they huddled together under the shimmering, silver clouds.

53

"She talks in her sleep." Anwen stroked the brooch that clasped her cloak, over and over. "She…she talks in *their* tongue."

Brei reached for her hand and squeezed it.

"I think she's a Roman spy," Anwen whispered.

The muscles in Taran's cheeks strained. "But, Anwen, we saw no evidence of any soldiers. Even the Damnnones and Maetae have not seen the scouts for a long time. If she is a spy, she's come a long way on her own."

Anwen's hand shook. "She will…she will bring the soldiers back."

Brei's throat constricted as Anwen's voice cracked. "Anwen, my love, the soldiers are not coming, I promise. Their power is weakening even in the south. You have nothing to fear." He squeezed her hand tighter.

"Why is she here, then? And did you see her eyes change? She is a witch, an evil spirit sent from Tirscath," Morfydd hissed and put her arm around Anwen. "She should be executed."

Taran raised his eyebrows. "Which is it? Roman spy or spirit from Tirscath?"

Brei glared at Taran. "Morfydd, please, I will take this to the king, and he will deal with it. It's out of our hands now." He took Anwen into his arms and kissed the top of her head. "Return to the girls, darling, I need to speak with Taran alone."

Taran waited until Anwen and Morfydd were out of earshot. "If she is a spy, then why did they just leave the twins alone with her?"

"Don't start." Brei scowled.

Taran shook his head and began to pace. "If she is a spy, she has to be the worst spy I've ever seen. She doesn't want to talk to anyone. Ceridwen said she hasn't even been to Caercaled. And today I found her lying alone in the forest."

"Then who is she and what is she doing here?"

Taran stopped pacing. "She's not telling the truth, I'll give you that, but she's not a spy."

"Why do you even care?"

Taran's face relaxed. "Don't you want to know the truth, Brei? I keep wondering about the stories, and her eyes are... Did you see the way the fire—"

"Yes, I saw it!" Brei sighed and lowered his voice. "I don't think there is any good that can come from keeping her alive, Taran. How can it be otherwise when we were attacked not six summers ago? Did you learn nothing from it? The effort to kill her is small, and yet the potential consequences of keeping her alive are catastrophic."

Taran grabbed Brei's shoulder. "Oh yes, I learnt from it! When I watched Father die in my arms, where were you? When they took Mother, where were you? Chasing after the farmer's daughter!" Taran's hand fell to his side. "Do you want to know what I learnt, Brei? I learnt that you will never be king. When you told me you'd abandoned Caer-caled, I knew you weren't the one to lead us. I'd believed it up to then. I'd have followed you to certain death if you'd asked me to. But a king would never abandon his people. Your own mother and father. You are so selfish. But I never told anyone what you did. The warriors would have begged for your death, but I protected you. I could have let them and then I would be innocent of your death, and you wouldn't have stood in my way. But I protected you. So why didn't you speak up for me when I made my claim to be king? I saved your life twice and you still don't believe in me. And now you don't trust in my judgement about Sorsha. Why is that?"

"You were just a boy. And I was barely a man. What weight did my opinion have against the Druwydds?"

"They cared what you thought, and you know it! They asked you to make a claim, and you denied them." He lowered his voice. "I heard it. I heard the Eldar Druwydd ask you... You know, I thought the Eldar Druwydd would ask me next. I ran back to my chamber after you'd denied him and I waited. I heard his footsteps leave your room, and then he paused. I imagined him looking into my chamber. He was going to ask me to make a claim, and though I had always thought it would be you, I was ready." Taran kicked at the snow. "And then it was as though an icy bucket of water had been thrown on me. The Eldar Druwydd turned and went down the steps to visit Gartnait. Even though I knew he wasn't coming for me anymore, I waited for hours for him to return. But the steps were silent."

"Taran, I don't know what I could have done."

"You could have done anything. Even if it didn't work, the fact you did nothing, it was like you were betraying me all over again."

Brei raised his hands and dragged his fingers across his face. "This is all such an unnecessary distraction."

Taran turned his head and spat. "From what?" Brei remained silent and watched Taran's shoulders drop. The intensity in his eyes vanished. "You mean the Damnnones bribing the Romans to let them through the Great Wall?"

"Yes," Brei said.

"We should speak to the king tomorrow."

"Once this is settled, yes. But I will go to Caercaled to speak to the king now about this woman. Do you want to join me?"

Taran scowled. "And leave your family unprotected with a spy in our midst?"

"Fine. I'll go alone."

Under cover of darkness, Brei dismounted before the circular stone tower. A red haze shone from the entrance, emanating from the great hall. *Servants have left the door open again.* As Brei walked into the tower, he paused under the arched stone entrance to scratch Beli, the tower guard dog, behind the ears.

"Brei, is that you?" A raspy voice called from inside the hall.

The circular hall took up the entire ground floor of the tower. Recessed into the stone wall was an enormous fire, and in front of it sat a long rectangular table with benches on either side. The king sat alone, hunched over the table close to the fire. He wore a simple tunic, dyed green, and his greying brown hair hung limp over his ears. Before him were two glossy red jugs and more silver goblets than the king needed.

"Yes, Uncle, it's me. Why are you sitting here alone?"

Gartnait's eyes crinkled as he smiled. "You're good to care, lad. Elfinn will be back in a moment, he's just speaking to Serenn for me. She's making me a potion." His voice was soft but crackled, and the shadow of a smile forever lingered on his thin lips.

"Can't sleep?"

"No, just feeling a bit off. When did you get back from the south?"

Brei moved to the fireplace and sat on the bench next to the king. "I got back today. I would have come sooner, but…" His eyes lingered on the king's pale, strained face.

Garnait reached across the table and patted Brei's hand. "I'm fine, lad. Go on."

"We found no evidence of soldiers."

"That is excellent news." Gartnait gestured to the jugs and goblets. "Will you have some ale? Wine?"

"Wine, yes, thank you, Uncle. But this woman we found, Anwen, suspects her of being a spy for the Romans."

Gartnait used both hands to lift the jug, and they shook as he poured wine into the goblets. "And do you think the woman is a spy, Brei?" His voice wheezed, as though out of breath.

Brei frowned. "Are you sure you're well?"

The king waved his hand. "Serenn will sort me out."

"Right. Well, I have no proof, other than Anwen's word that she speaks in the Roman tongue while sleeping. Maybe she is a spy, or perhaps there is an innocent explanation. But as she has avoided our questions, and given the risk is so great, I think it would be best for us to act now."

"Are there others who have a view?"

"Yes, Uncle." Brei clenched his jaw. "Taran does not think she has been truthful with us…but he does not believe she is a spy."

"Then I think the correct course of action would be for the Gods to decide this woman's guilt. I will speak with the Bandruwydd tomorrow."

"When will you hold the trial? Are you...well enough?"

"Yes, dear boy, I'm fine." He smiled. "Serenn and Elfinn are taking good care of me. We'll hold the trial as early as I can fix it. Tomorrow, before dusk."

Brei nodded. "Well, I can't stay long, we are staying at the farmstead."

"When are you returning to Caercaled?"

"Soon, a few days perhaps. And I will need to speak to you about the Damnnones."

Gartnait raised his eyebrows. "The Damnnones?"

"Yes, they have been raiding south of the Great Wall, apparently with the help of Roman soldiers."

Gartnait's arm paused mid-lift to his mouth, and he lowered his hand without taking a sip. "That's very interesting, Brei. I would like to hear more, though I expect you are waiting for Taran to be part of such a conversation?"

Brei tightened his hand around the stem of his silver goblet and wondered if he could break it. "Yes, Uncle."

NINE

Winter, 366 C. E., Caledon

"Wake up." A strained whisper in the dark pulled Sorsha from another nightmare of skulls in the spectral chamber. Pinpricks of silvery light filtered through cracks in the thatched roof, but the rooster had yet to grace them with its guttural cries. Taran knelt over her, nudging her arm. "Get up now."

Groggily, she dragged on skin boots and wrapped her legs with strips of wool. Taran crept between the weaved room divider and she tiptoed behind him. After pulling Brei's fur cape over her tunic, she stepped into the pale dawn. The startling freshness, after the stale aroma of tanned skins and human breath, was a relief.

Taran trudged across the trampled lane separating the line of ten roundhouses and led her to the river that flowed in front of the farmstead. Dark clouds gathered overhead, and a biting wind blew from the northern mountains. Sorsha scanned the patchwork water. *Why has he taken me here?*

Taran avoided her gaze and looked at the gaunt forest on the southern bank. "Do you know what lies beyond the forest across the river?"

"No."

"The lowland Kingdoms of Maetae, Damnnonia, and Gwoddodin. Do you know what is south of those lands?"

She shrugged. "The Great Wall?"

59

He turned to her. "Are you a spy?"

"Why do you all think that? Just because I don't remember how I got here doesn't mean I'm a spy." Her lips shivered as she spoke.

"Where are you from, then?"

Gwoddodin was the only tribe she knew about with any certainty because her father had often sailed north to trade with them. Their city, Caeredyn, was a misty harbour, with a great tower on a hill overlooking the sea. Her chest tightened as she remembered her father's words, how his black eyes sparkled when he told her of his adventures. It was Gwoddodin he had sailed to the last time they said goodbye. "Gwoddodin, near Caeredyn," she stammered, blinking away the sound of her father's soft voice. "I can try to return to my family if you will lend me a horse."

"No. We can't let you go, in case you are a spy. It's just a question of whether we execute you."

Sorsha's eyes widened. "But I haven't done anything wrong. Isn't that a bit extreme?"

His blue eyes glinted in the dawn light. "Is it? If you'd seen what I've seen…what we've all seen, you wouldn't take any chances on some stranger who appears from thin air."

She dropped her gaze to the silty riverbank, her heart hammering.

"It doesn't mean it will happen," he said, lowering his voice. "It just means you will be subjected to a public trial."

She lifted her eyes to meet his. "Can I speak to a Druwydd before I…before a decision is made?"

Taran frowned. "No, there aren't any Druwydds visiting in Caercaled right now."

"Oh." Her eyes prickled.

"But Serenn, the Eldar Bandruwydd, will be involved in deciding your fate. You will meet her soon."

Sorsha's chest rose and fell faster than she wanted it to, and the itching in her eyes threatened to spill. *Why was I sent to this place, if they are going to execute me? Is this the Gods' sick punishment for refusing their gift?* "Can I speak to her now?"

"If it is the will of the Gods that your life is spared, then you may speak with Serenn." Taran turned back to the river. "Brei says King Gartnait will come down before dusk."

The crashing of the river buzzed in her ears.

"You can remain out here, or in the stables, if you get cold, but I think you should avoid Anwen and Morfydd. I'll bring you something to eat," Taran said and walked up the bank towards the farmstead.

"Thank you," she murmured to his broad back when it was already a few yards away. She watched as he grew smaller, a grey shadow disappearing into the roundhouses. *Perhaps I should make a run for it?* She walked towards the stables at the end of the settlement. *But where would I go? I must have been sent here for a reason. Even if I don't know what it is.* Two large wooden doors barred her way into the stables. She heaved a rough metal handle and pulled one door open. The building was split into two large pens, one for cattle and one for sheep. At the entrance, smaller pens held horses, which stared at her as though she might carry some delicious treat. She wandered towards a chestnut mare and clicked her tongue. The mare whinnied and Sorsha raised her hand for the horse to sniff.

"Such a pretty girl, aren't you," Sorsha murmured, stroking the mare's forehead, breathing in the familiar scent of dry grass and earth. *Surely, they wouldn't execute me?* She patted the mare's nose. *But what if they do? Will I return to Tirscath? Or will the black abyss be forever this time?* She rested her forehead against the horse's neck and tried to calm her racing heartbeat.

A tabby cat slunk across the hay-covered floor, avoiding Sorsha, who sat with her back against the cold stable wall. Over and over, she turned in her mind whether things could have been different. *If I had been a*

dutiful student and had willingly accepted the gift of the Gods, would I have been sent here? Would I still be facing a permanent death? She ran her hands through her hair and pressed her forehead against her arms. *I pushed so hard to avoid my fate, but now here I am.* She screamed into her arms, the muffled anguish strangling out into sobs as she released hot tears down her cheeks.

The door of the stable creaked open, and leather boots scraped on the dirt floor towards her. She lifted her head and wiped the back of her wrist across her eyes and nose. Taran knelt in front of her and held out a chunk of grainy bread.

She scrambled upright. "I can't eat, I feel sick."

Taran exhaled, stood up, and wandered along the pens to stroke a white, muscled stallion.

"Is he yours?"

Taran smiled up into the horse's face. "Yes, his name is Ri."

"Ri," she repeated. *King*, she thought. Sorsha joined Taran next to the white stallion and patted his glistening neck.

"I don't want to alarm you, but King Gartnait is coming down now, with Serenn the Eldar Bandruwydd," Taran said.

Sorsha concentrated on stroking Ri's forehead and tried to count the strands in his fringe. She felt Taran watching, but when her eyes flicked to his face, he looked away.

"I spoke to Serenn and…" The sound of boots crunching in the snow made them both start.

"Taran!"

He glanced at Sorsha before responding. "Uncle Gartnait! How are you?" he called back and disappeared through the opened door.

Sorsha's palms grew sweaty as she continued to stroke Ri's forehead. Ri seemed to sense her anxiety and tossed his elegant head in the air, stamping his front hoof on his bed of straw. Sorsha wondered whether it was still possible to escape. *Perhaps if I run to the river and jump into the fast-flowing water, I could see how far it would carry me before I died of the cold.* She gazed up into Ri's face. *I survived in the snow without clothes, so perhaps I could survive in the icy river too?*

Taran reappeared and hurried towards her. "My uncle, Gartnait… the king that is, he came early," he whispered.

A few men wearing the wolf pelt capes she had come to associate with the warriors stood just outside the stable door, gawking in. She recognised the guards from the forest, Deryn and Brin, but the other men she did not know.

Taran motioned for her to follow him. Nausea pulsed from her stomach into her head. *There is no point even trying to calm my heart.* It hammered with such intensity she thought it would burst through her chest.

The entire farmstead had come to hear the matter of the Roman spy adjudicated. Many more had arrived from Caercaled. They gathered in a semicircle near Morfydd's roundhouse, standing ankle-deep in brown snow.

The king and three strange women stood in the middle of the semi-circle. The women's faces were painted in dark blue woad. White paint encircled their eyes, accentuating their features so that they resembled enormous birds. *They must be of the female Druwydd order, the Bandruwydds.* One woman pulled her shoulders back and surveyed the gathered crowd by looking down her nose. A section of her hair was secured under a leather cap, atop which a deer's skull and antlers had been affixed. The rest of her hair was stained dark blue and hung in long plaits over her shoulders. *She must be Serenn.* Serenn's two companions seemed much younger and wore their hair loose about their shoulders. All three women were cloaked in thick black robes.

As Sorsha was led through the crowd, she glanced at Brei, but his deep-set eyes stared through her. King Gartnait stepped forwards and raised his hand to silence the whispers. Despite the cold, the king's cape was draped low around his shoulders, exposing his upper chest. A large, twisted gold necklace hung around his neck.

"We have heard from the accusers, Anwen and Morfydd, that this woman, Sorsha, is a spy from south of the Great Wall," the king began, in a soft but commanding voice. He was not so tall that he had a natural advantage for leadership, but his tone was reassuring. "The decision to allow Sorsha to live is not mine, but the Gods'. If Sorsha is allowed to live, I will decide what happens next." He nodded to Serenn.

The Bandruwydd women chanted in low voices. The blonde Bandruwydd had a noticeable limp as she shuffled towards Sorsha. When she reached her, she clasped Sorsha's hands and applied a dark blue paste from a wooden bowl. The nerves in Sorsha's hands tingled from the brush strokes. She looked into the painted face of the young woman. "Help me. I am a descendant of the Gallar from Tirscath."

The whites of the young Bandruwydd's eyes expanded against the white of the paint that encircled them, but she continued chanting. The Bandruwydd finished painting Sorsha's hands and limped to Serenn's side. They spoke in whispers not even the king was privy to. Serenn's eyes glistened as she strode towards Sorsha. When Serenn stopped in front of her, a potent scent of cinnamon and smouldering wood clung to her robes. A long-nailed hand grasped Sorsha's cheeks and raised her head up. "Look at me," Serenn said.

Sorsha raised her chin, staring back into Serenn's eyes. Her grasp tightened, her stare manic. The icy ground seemed to bend beneath Sorsha, and she tried to remain composed and focus on the massive antlers and deer skull affixed to Serenn's head.

Finally, Serenn released Sorsha and raised her hands to the sky, chanting to Nodens, the Ancient People's God of Healing. The wind howled through the creaking trees as Serenn lowered her arms and walked towards King Gartnait, who hovered a few paces behind her. They spoke in whispers for a moment and then, with glistening eyes, he followed Serenn back to Sorsha.

The king stood inches from her, and she could feel the vapour as his breath turned to condensation in the frigid air.

"How were you killed?" Serenn whispered.

Sorsha frowned. "I'm sorry, what?"

Serenn turned to the auburn-haired Bandruwydd standing next to her. "Check her heart."

The two younger Bandruwydds removed Brei's fur cape from around Sorsha's shoulders and let it fall to the ground. The auburn-haired Bandruwydd grasped the front of Sorsha's tunic and wrenched it down.

Sorsha struggled against them, her skin tingling in the frosty air. "What are you doing?"

The king motioned to a man in the crowd. "Restrain her."

A tall, red-haired warrior stepped from the semicircle and held Sorsha's arms behind her back. The Bandruwydd ripped Sorsha's dress down to her chest and exposed the deeply knotted scar above her heart. Serenn ran her fingers over the mangled scar and smiled at King Gartnait. He reached a trembling hand out, but Sorsha threw herself back into the man restraining her so that the king's fingertips fell just short of their target. The muscles around her mouth quivered and her eyes stung.

King Gartnait stared at Sorsha, his eyes drifting between the scars and her face. She looked at the ground and let her body go limp against her captor. *There is no point fighting the inevitable.*

Nodding to Serenn, the king walked back to the centre of the semicircle. The warrior released Sorsha, and the blonde Bandruwydd handed her Brei's cape. Sorsha pulled it on before her captor restrained her again.

Once more Serenn and the king conferred. Sorsha could not see Serenn's face, but the king was frowning. He stepped away from Serenn and addressed the crowd. "Where is Naoise?"

"He must still be at Caercaled. Shall we send for him?" Brei asked.

The king nodded, and Gruffydd stepped forwards to perform the task. He ran for the stables and disappeared inside. The wind picked up, and intermittent snowflakes fell across Sorsha's face. *What on earth is going on?* Moments later Gruffydd emerged from the stables, already mounted, and urged his horse into a gallop.

Sorsha turned back to the semicircle. She recognised half the crowd as the farmers and their families. Her eyes moved to Anwen and Morfydd, talking with their heads close together. Her feet ached, and she shifted from foot to foot. *Perhaps Naoise is the executioner?*

"Keep still," her captor whispered, tightening his grip on her.

By the time Gruffydd returned, the snow fell thick and the wind wailed. He was followed by a dark-haired man, just into adulthood, whom Sorsha guessed was Naoise. Naoise leapt from his saddle and strolled over to the king. Sorsha could see no weapon. *Perhaps they will drown me in the river?* She swallowed and wondered how she would prefer to die. *Burning to death would be the worst.*

The king spoke to Naoise, who twisted to look at Sorsha and glared. The onlookers were silent as they watched a furious argument, in which Naoise was the only one to speak. The king shook his head and turned to Serenn. "Bind them."

Serenn beamed as she looked at Sorsha. Her teeth flashing white against the dark blue paint. Sorsha dug her nails into her palms and prayed to the Goddess Sulis-Minerva.

"The Gods grant life!" Serenn yelled.

Sorsha opened her eyes. She felt as though all her body weight had left her, and she was nothing but air and water.

King Gartnait raised his hand to suppress the protests from Anwen and Morfydd.

"The Gods granted life, but our laws dictate that the accused must still be vouched for." The king paused, and Sorsha saw Anwen and Morfydd smirk. "Is there anyone here who is willing to bind themselves in obligation to this woman and swear to me they will be responsible for her crimes?"

Sorsha's cheeks flushed. She had hoped for banishment if they did not kill her.

Naoise scowled. "I am willing."

Sorsha wondered whether she could still escape. Her mind raced as she tried to work out a plan, and she barely noticed a new voice speaking. The crowd gasped.

"No," the king said, his voice shaking.

Taran was at her side. "Let her go, Owain."

Her captor released her and stepped aside as the king hurried across. "Taran." He stopped in front of them. "Naoise has agreed, there is no need for this."

Taran lowered his voice. "Uncle, is it worth it to have me challenge you openly?"

The two men stared at each other, unblinking.

"If Taran is stepping in, then I don't think you need me anymore," Naoise called out. "If you do, I'll be back at Elwyn's tavern!"

The king shook his head. "Fine," he muttered and walked back to the centre of the semicircle.

Serenn and the younger Bandruwydds approached, chanting, and bound Taran and Sorsha's hands together with a thick rope made of dried grass. Serenn called for Cernunnos, the Horned God, and Belenus, the Lord of Light, to bind them in obligation, and asked that Sorsha's crimes become Taran's crimes, and his crimes become hers. When Serenn was finished, she shuffled aside.

"I give you my protection," the king murmured and departed through the gathered crowd towards a horse held for him by Gruffydd. When it was clear there would be no further spectacle, those who did not live in the farmstead followed him.

Serenn approached Sorsha. "There are people who need healing. Visit me soon," she said huskily, before she too disappeared with the crowd, trudging north against the gale.

Sorsha caught Taran's eye and pulled against the itchy restraint that bound them.

Once most of the farmers had returned to their homes, Brei approached the pair. "We will wait till the full moon to return to Caercaled."

"A blizzard is coming," Taran said. "Are you sure you want to stay out here?"

Brei did not respond, and they stared at each other with such tension that Sorsha flushed. Realising she was still wearing his cape, she unclasped it from around her shoulders and tossed it to Brei, whilst trying to hold up the front of her ripped tunic. Brei accepted the cape in silence, nodding to Taran before he returned to Morfydd's roundhouse.

The door slammed, and Sorsha and Taran stood alone. The blue paint covering her hands was tight and itching in the wind, and she imagined how satisfying it would be to wash it off.

"Why didn't you tell me you were going to do that?" Sorsha asked as she flexed her hands against the paint, curling and uncurling her fists until it cracked.

Taran shrugged. "I didn't know I was."

He pulled a small blade from his belt and hacked off the rope that bound them. "This was all just a formality to keep you safe. We're only bound in obligation, so don't worry." He threw the rope on the ground.

"What now?"

Taran glanced at the dense falling snow and removed his fur cape, handing it to Sorsha. "I guess I'll have to take you home. To Caercaled."

TEN

Winter, 366 C.E., Caledon

The cold wood had grazed Brei's palm as he nudged open Morfydd's roundhouse door. A lump rose in his throat as he thought of the pain Sorsha's arrival had caused Anwen, and he wondered how he could begin to convince her that justice had been served.

Inside, Anwen was rebuilding the fire, her back towards him, while Nia and Ceridwen played with straw dolls beside the growing flames. Brei closed the door and knelt down beside Anwen. Tears cascaded from her blue eyes down her freckled cheeks.

"I know you're scared, darling, but remember I will not let anything happen to you." Brei hugged her against his chest. "I hate what they did to you. Every day my blood boils thinking of it. But it will never happen again, do you understand?"

Anwen sobbed, and he felt her nodding. "I just wish I could forget," she choked.

"Nothing is more unfair." He clenched his fists. "Those evil men walk in the light of ignorance while you are shadowed by the memories of their violence." He kissed her on the top of her head.

"I can't believe Taran betrayed you like that," Morfydd said, slinking from behind the wicker screen dividing the roundhouse.

"He didn't betray me," Brei snapped.

Morfydd raised her eyebrows and Anwen pushed away, staring at him through swollen eyes.

"What I mean is," Brei sighed. "It was Serenn who convinced Gartnait to have Sorsha stay. Like it or not, this is the justice the Gods willed." Brei glanced at the fire. He thought he understood Taran's motivations. *But why did Serenn persuade Gartnait that Sorsha was so important they should tie her in obligation to Naoise, a Prince of the Blood? Why Naoise? When any of the warrior class or higher could have vouched for her?* "In any event, it is done now." Brei turned to Anwen. "It is all done with, and there is nothing to fear. You don't even have to speak to her."

"But where is she going to live? The tower? If Serenn and the king think she is important, they will surely keep her in the tower with them. You can't expect Anwen to return there now," Morfydd said.

Brei frowned. "Why? Is there still a problem with Sorsha?"

Anwen exchanged a look with her mother, but neither spoke.

"I'm going hunting," Brei said, picking up his bow and quiver of arrows. He turned to Anwen and lowered his voice to a whisper. "Which is something I wouldn't have to do if we returned to the tower, Anwen."

Anwen busied herself with the fire, refusing to meet his eyes.

"Nia, Ceridwen, let's go for a walk in the woods and see if we can't get a nice hare for dinner." He opened the door, and his daughters followed him into the frosty air.

Relief swept along his shoulders, even as the icy gale burned his cheeks. As he watched Ceridwen and Nia race into the frosted wood, his mind wandered back to Sorsha's trial. *Serenn ordered Sorsha's dress be pulled down so they could inspect something. What did they see? Perhaps she is not a spy, but something more terrible.*

ELEVEN

Ice tore through the air at Sorsha and Taran as they followed a track along the river. The farmstead disappeared, and the forest swelled until the river veered sharp to the north. A dense fog descended over the hills on the northern bank, and if not for the stench of smoke and human lives lived close together, Sorsha would not have believed there was a city. Plump snowdrifts perched atop a bleak wall that snaked around the base of a hill and melted into the misty sleet. They entered the stone walls of Caercaled through the Western Gate, guarded by warriors draped in fur capes. After a short lane of roundhouses they came to a large round space cleared of snow.

"What is this?" Sorsha yelled over the gale.

"The centre circle," Taran said, without stopping.

"The what?"

"It's where markets are held, and festivities," he called over his shoulder.

They kept to a straight path running between rows of roundhouses and followed it through two further stone walls. The trail steepened, and the roundhouses disappeared, replaced by a forest of ghostly trees wrapped in winter's cloak. They continued up the hill, pushing against the gale through the barren forest. At the top, they reached a final thick wall, guarded once more by faceless grey hoods. Taran approached,

71

never altering his pace, and the warriors parted for him, bowing their heads. Inside the last wall, the trees were cleared and Sorsha could just make out a short path lined with snow-covered roundhouses. As they trudged along it, she could see flames flickering beneath a soaring shadow and, gazing up, she realised it was an enormous stone tower fading into the grey clouds.

In an alcove recessed into the curved stone entrance of the tower were flaming torches, and beneath sat a thick-set mastiff. As Taran approached, the black dog sat straight and whined. The mastiff's head came to Taran's waist, and he scratched the dog's ears as he ducked below the stone arch. The dog's eyes flicked from Taran to Sorsha and growled.

"Beli," Taran said in a low voice.

Beli licked his lips and dropped his stomach to the ground.

"Did you name your dog after the Shining God?" Sorsha asked.

"Yes. He was born on the festival of Beltane. We found him in the stables after we'd released all the cattle for the fire run. He was the only pup from the litter who wasn't trampled to death."

The massive dog looked up at Sorsha and she imagined him a blind, terrified newborn. She crouched in front of Beli and stroked his sleek black head. His tail whacked repeatedly against the stone wall of the tower.

Taran snorted. "He must be getting soft in his old age, he never usually likes strangers."

Sorsha smiled at Beli and stood up.

"Let's go inside," Taran said, rubbing his arms. Without his fur cape, he wore only a blue linen tunic, caked in ice.

The tower was made of two thick dry walls of interlocking stones, and in-between a stone staircase curved upwards. Taran's foot hovered on the first step. "This is the King's Hall," he said, gesturing to the doorway in the inner wall.

"Beli, go inside," Taran said, and the dog trotted inside the hall.

"Loyr!" Taran yelled. "Loyr, close the door now. Brei's not coming, we're the last ones."

A young girl sprinted across the gloomy hall, as if from nowhere, bowed to Taran and closed the heavy wooden door.

"This way," Taran said, stepping into the shadowy staircase between the walls. The gale whistled and echoed against the stone as they climbed the stairs in darkness. After ten steps they reached a landing with a flaming torch hanging on the wall next to a wooden door. The flames illuminated stone etchings of snakes and strange beasts, and as Sorsha moved along the walls into the light, she saw bulls and wolves dancing in the flickering glow. Taran pointed to the closed wooden door. "This is the king's floor, and it has the warmest rooms in the tower. Gartnait occupies them with his son, Elfinn, but when King Talorc, the Over-King of the North, or the Eldar Druwydd visit, they also stay here."

"Where does the Bandruwydd, Serenn, live?"

"You were serious about wanting to speak to her? I'll take you there now. They live on the highest floor of the tower." They climbed more stairs and soon reached a second landing. "This is my floor, along with my cousins," Taran said. "I'll show you when we come back down." They continued up the dark staircase, the howling wind growing louder with each step until they reached a third landing. "Brei and his family live here," Taran said, without stopping.

On the fourth and final landing, Taran knocked on a wooden door. The sound of a steady clunk and scrape drew closer until the door was opened by the young blonde Bandruwydd. The girl nodded as she admitted them into the room, her face still painted blue and white from the ceremony.

An intense concoction of herbs, smoke, and cinnamon filled Sorsha's nostrils. The room was much smaller than the great hall below, and she wondered how that was possible. A fire glowed, flickering with violence as wind gusted down the chimney. Over the fire, on a long metal rod that seemed to float in the middle of the hearth, a giant bubbling cauldron emitted a greyish cloud of steam. Ornate, inter-lacing pictures and symbols decorated the cauldron, and Sorsha rec-ognised Cernunnos, the Horned God, Lord of Nature, sitting on the forest floor surrounded by woodland creatures while he held in one hand a snake, and in the other a Torc necklace.

Serenn sat on a chair nearest the fire and motioned for them to join her. She had removed her deer skull and antler headdress, and her blue hair slithered across her shoulders in tentacle braids. Save for the black charcoal outlining her eyes, her face was cleansed of paint.

Sorsha dipped her head and stepped into the room through the curved opening. The roof was low, and she had to bend her knees to prevent her head from banging against the rafters. She glanced at Taran, but he did not follow her. The glow from the fire caught on a golden object lying on the bench. Its metal had been twisted countless times and formed a U-shape.

"Are you admiring my Torc?" Serenn asked as she sipped from a silver goblet. She smiled and gestured for Sorsha to approach. "I was not expecting you to visit so soon. This is Arian," Serenn nodded to the blonde girl with the limp. "And this is Eluned."

Sorsha glanced at Eluned, who had auburn hair and a strange, haughty way of holding her mouth. The fire plunged her painted face into shadow one moment and then flickered across the whites of her eyes.

"They are my apprentices," Serenn continued. "Have something to drink."

Arian pulled a wooden ladle from the cauldron, poured a steaming liquid into a goblet, and handed it to Sorsha.

Taran cleared his throat. "Sorsha, I should show you your chamber now."

Sorsha raised the drink to her lips, inhaling the acrid herbs. The boiling liquid burnt her tongue and her throat. Her eyes watered, and the pungent, steamy room seemed to sway beneath her. Serenn's lips curled upwards as Sorsha handed Arian the empty cup.

"See me again soon," Serenn said. Her voice rasped, as though she had dwelt for too long by the pungent fumes.

Taran guided Sorsha back down the stairs, past Brei's closed door once more, and on to the second landing, where he pushed open the wooden door. He ducked his head under the stone arch and beckoned Sorsha to follow him. The roof was much higher than it had been in Serenn's chamber, and Sorsha could stand at full height. Unlike Serenn's chamber, walls of wood divided Taran's floor into four separate rooms.

Taran pushed open one of the doors. "This is my chamber, but it will be yours now. Sorry if it's a mess." He ran his hand over his forehead and ruffled his blond ponytail. "This has all been a bit unexpected. My things are everywhere," he said as he picked up a bow and quiver strewn on the cot bed. "I'll send servants to fix the room for now, and later I'll see if we can set you up in a roundhouse below the tower."

Sorsha peered inside. As well as the cot bed, the chamber contained two wood chairs, a low table, and a small hearth with a fire burning. Along the wooden wall was a long bench with a bronze mirror and basin, a dagger, and a carved wooden snake that looked as if it were a children's toy. Taran piled all the items into his arms, including the mirror. Sorsha smiled as she watched him struggle to hold on to everything.

"Where will you stay?" she asked.

He pointed with his chin to the wooden wall. "With my cousin Naoise in the room next door. Can you hold the door open for me?"

She followed him and opened the door to the next room along. Clothes and weapons littered the room, and a stale sweat stung her nostrils. Taran emptied his arms on the cot bed and shook his head as he avoided stepping on the legs of a pair of deerskin pants. "I'm almost regretting saving you now."

Sorsha tilted her head. "And why did you?"

Taran leant against the doorframe and ran his hand across the stubble on his jaw. "A conversation for another time, perhaps. Servants will be up shortly to assist you, Eiry and Loyr are their names. They'll fix my room for you and help you out of those rags. I will be in the hall if you need me… but you won't… can I have my cloak back?"

Sorsha blinked. "Um, yes."

"Thanks," he said, holding his hand out.

Sorsha unfastened the silver brooch, and Taran pulled the heavy cape off her shoulders, so she could hold up the front of her ripped tunic. As soon as the cool air washed over her, his leather boots clicked along the wooden floor, echoing across the landing and down the stone steps.

As she closed the door to her new room, Sorsha realised how heavy her head had become, and wondered how her neck bore it. She shuffled to a chair by the fire and stared into the flames. Her mind wandered through the vineyards on her parents' estate, her hands trailing across red autumnal leaves. She saw her mother's face, her shoulders draped in a silk wrap that rustled when she moved her arms. A tear crept over the edge of Sorsha's eyelid as she drifted to sleep.

A subtle aroma of cooked meat and fresh bread floated through the warm air. Sorsha rolled over in the tiny cot bed and opened her eyes. Orange light shimmered across the grey stone wall.

Taran sat by the fire, eating a rib of venison with his hands. He caught her eye and nodded towards a glossy red clay dish of meat, kale, turnips, and buttered bread. "Forgive the intrusion. I thought you'd be awake by the time the servants had laid this all out, and…" he shrugged. "I was hungry."

Two silver goblets sat on the table with a clay wine jug. Sorsha recognised the red clay serving ware, she had eaten from similar dishes in her home in Britannia. She wondered if a merchant such as her father had sold it to the barbarians, or if it was the reward of plunder.

The door to the chamber creaked open and the serving girl, Loyr, mousy-haired and timid, shuffled into the room. Loyr glanced at Taran and her eyes widened. "I'm so sorry, my lady, I only stepped out for a moment. I was hoping to dress you properly before…" she glanced at Taran. "Before you had any visitors." He rolled his eyes.

Sorsha's parents had kept slaves in Britannia, and it was almost a relief to be dressed by someone else again. Loyr pulled a blue tunic over her head, trimmed with yellow, and tied a matching yellow belt around her waist. Sorsha admired the concentric knots weaved into the belt.

Loyr bowed herself out of the room, as Sorsha lowered herself into a chair by the fire. Taran turned around and plucked another rib from the plate and smiled. "Sleep well?"

She rocked her cup in her hand and nodded. *What time is it? Perhaps I can talk to Serenn and find a way out of here.*

"Do you have everything you need?"

"Oh…um, yes, thank you," Sorsha glanced around the room. There was no natural light. "What time is it?"

Taran shrugged. "The blizzard is still raging, but I'd say afternoon."

"I was asleep this whole time?"

"Well, you drank Serenn's wine, didn't you? I did try to make you come with me before you had any."

Sorsha frowned.

"Don't fret." He smiled. "She makes it for Brei, Anwen, and I."

Sorsha studied the weave of the woollen tunic stretched across her knees. "Do you have trouble sleeping?"

"Yes. You have trouble sleeping also?"

"Why do you say that?"

"You said you talk in your sleep, remember? A fact most upsetting for Anwen." His lips curled into a smirk.

Sorsha's cheeks flushed.

"What do you dream about?"

Sorsha shifted her legs away from the fire. Sweat beaded on her top lip. "I don't know."

Taran leant forwards, his features plunged into the glowing light. "Tell me something."

77

"Something?" Sorsha sat upright in her chair.

"Tell me something…" He paused, a smile lingering at the corners of his mouth. "About where you grew up. Did you grow up in a city or in the country?"

"The country," she murmured.

Taran raised his eyebrows. "Don't tell me you're a farmer's daughter?"

"No," she grimaced. "My father was a merchant."

"Strange for a merchant to live in the country, isn't it?"

She raised her goblet to her lips, careful not to drink anything from it. "He wasn't home often."

"He may not know you are gone, then?"

Sorsha leaned in towards the fire. A hot sickness rose in her abdomen.

"Not that he wouldn't miss you," Taran continued.

"He died two years ago, so no, he won't be missing me."

His face, darkened by shadow, was incomprehensible. "I'm sorry… and your mother?"

"She's alive."

"Do you miss her?"

"No."

"Why not?"

"I feel an ache, a sickness, whenever I think of her."

He reached to recover the glossy red jug and splashed more wine into his goblet. "When was the last time you saw her?"

"I…" She traced the intricate bumps and notches of leaves etched into the silver cup. "We'd had a fight…and I was very far away from home when the soldiers attacked me." Sorsha tilted her head. "And where are your parents?"

Taran stared into his goblet and swirled the contents around. "Dead." The chair creaked as he leant back. "I think."

TWELVE

Winter, 367 C.E., Caledon

"Why can't we stay here?" Anwen looked up at Brei pleadingly as he brushed a strand of coppery hair from her face.

The blizzard had broken, and white sunlight glared through the clouds. Brei and Anwen stood beside the half-frozen river on the edge of the farmstead.

"Darling, I am bound to you, but I am also a Prince of the Blood and my place...*our* place is in Caercaled."

"But I want to stay at the farmstead to look after Mother."

"Anwen." Brei drew her in and held her. "I know you're afraid, my darling, but Sorsha will not hurt you."

Anwen's eyes widened. "But she will tell the soldiers where I am!"

"If she wanted to kill you, she would have done so when she stayed at the farmstead. And if she wanted the soldiers to kill you, it would be a lot easier for them to do it here."

"They took your mother from the tower," Anwen whispered.

"Maybe. We don't know where she was. Perhaps she had left the tower and was caught later." He shook his head. "But it doesn't matter, I won't let anything happen to you. Don't you trust me?"

"Of course I trust you." She kissed his cheek. "But how can you trust her?"

"I've never said I trust her, ever. I'm just saying I don't think you have anything to fear."

"I'd feel better if I knew I didn't have to see her again. Can you find out if she's staying in the tower? And ask that she be moved out if she is?"

"That would be so awkward for me, Anwen. Taran is bound to her in obligation and is responsible for her crimes, isn't that enough?"

"I don't trust Taran. I don't trust anyone but you. There's something not right about her and I…" Her breathing became erratic. "I'm sorry, Brei. Whenever I see her, it reminds me of…" She screwed up her face and shuddered against his chest.

"Shh. Breathe, darling, I'm here." He stroked her hair. "And I will ask her to avoid you, if you promise to move back to the tower with me today. But if the king or Serenn want her with them, there's nothing I can do. She won't harm you. No one will."

She nodded against his chest but did not move out of his arms. He glanced at the frozen edges of the river and in his mind followed the forested bank to the stone walls of Caercaled. His stomach tightened as he imagined how the conversation with Sorsha would play out. *Taran will not be pleased about this.*

Caercaled bustled with activity as Brei rode to the tower alone. Anwen had insisted he go on ahead and ask Sorsha to stay away from them. He had promised her. But as he gazed at the grey tower, he wondered whether he should honour it. The last thing he wanted was more conflict with Taran.

Cináed guarded the gate in the final rampart before the tower, and he took the reins from Brei. "I'll have one of the boys take Rhuad to the stables."

"Thanks, Cin." Brei pulled a bundle of furs off the saddle and trudged between the row of roundhouses towards the tower. Beli whined and reared onto his hind legs as Brei approached. "Good boy," Brei murmured, ducking his head under the entrance arch of the tower. On the third landing, he pushed open the wooden door to his floor and threw the pack of furs on the ground with a thud. A wooden table and chairs stood in a large living area next to the fire. In the back, a wooden wall divided the floor in half, and two doors led into bedrooms, one for the twins and one for Brei and Anwen.

Brei shrugged his cape off, letting it fall to the ground. The floorboards creaked beneath his boots as he crossed to the table. *What is Sorsha going to say? Will Taran be furious?* He traced a circular pattern in the tabletop with his finger. *This is so awkward.* The pad of his index finger numbed as he traced around it over and over. Finally, he clenched his fists, strode across the floor to the door and grasped the handle. The iron was cold beneath his palm. *Anwen's wellbeing is more important than offending Taran.* Wrenching the door open, he stepped into the glow of the landing and down the staircase. As he pushed open the door to the second floor, his palms were covered in a film of sweat.

Muffled voices escaped from Taran's room.

"What was it like growing up here?"

Brei hesitated. Sorsha's voice was soft, but with a crisp, pragmatic edge, as though she wanted the answer for her own sake, rather than for the meandering pleasure of conversation.

"I don't know, different to now, I suppose. Uncle Uradech was king then, he was different to Gartnait, and he was…"

Brei thought Taran was whispering and could not hear the response.

"What were your parents like? Is Brei your only sibling?"

Brei listened intently, and he wrestled with his promise to Anwen and an acute desire to leave.

"Just Brei… Ah, I guess I was very close to my father. He was a younger son of the King of the Damnnones. He taught me everything. How to fight, how to shoot a stag. In summer he'd show me the safe paths through the bogs and marshes, and we'd ride to the coast, to Caertarwos, to see my cousins of the Blood."

"Tell me again how it works. To be a Prince of the Blood."

"The claim to kingship passes through the female line. My mother was a Princess of the Blood in the Kingdoms of Caledon and Vortriu. Her brothers, Uradech and Gartnait, both became Kings of Caledon, and her nephew, Talorc, is King of Vortriu. It means Brei and I both have a claim to the thrones of Caledon and Vortriu, but our children will not, because the right to make a claim does not pass from father to son. Although, if I had a son with a Princess of the Blood, he would have a claim. If I were to bind myself in protection and provision to one of our cousins like Aífe, for example."

"Why don't you do that, then?"

Taran laughed. "She is my second cousin, so I would be allowed to bind myself in protection to her. But she grew up here with me, like a sister. I kissed her once, but it felt wrong."

Sorsha laughed.

"I have a cousin in Caertarwos," Taran continued. "Princess Eithne, and she is exquisite. Her hair is like a veil of gold. Sadly, she is my first cousin, and the Druwydds would never consider it. But I don't want to be bound in protection and provision. Not right now, anyway. It's bad enough being bound to you in obligation and having to worry about all the crimes you're committing when my back is turned."

Brei heard muffled laughter from the pair.

"And what about you? Aren't I bound to your crimes as well? How do I know you're not up to mischief?" Sorsha asked, and Brei could hear the smile in her voice.

"Caledon is my mother and my father. It is my child. I would never do anything to betray my country."

"You want to be king, don't you?" Sorsha asked.

Brei took a step closer.

"More than anything. But not for me. Not for the sake of power. But because I know…I truly believe I'd lead Caledon to glory. I'd restore her to her rightful place in the Northern Alliance. King Uradech was Over-King of the Northern Alliance, and I will be too."

Brei rubbed his hand over his face, his palm grazing the bristles of his beard. "Taran, are you there?" he shouted.

There was a pause, before Taran called, "Come in."

Brei walked into Taran's room. It was devoid of all his possessions, even his mirror had been removed. Taran faced the door, sitting by the fire, while Sorsha sat opposite, a goblet resting on the wooden arm of the chair. She twisted in her seat to look at him, and Brei met her green eyes.

Taran smiled. "You've returned?" He stood up and walked to Brei. They embraced, and Brei's cheeks reddened.

"Anwen and the girls will be back soon, I arrived early." Brei cleared his throat, wishing the blush would dissipate. "Are you living in the tower, Sorsha?"

"She's staying here, in my old room." Taran smiled. "I'm bunking with Naoise."

Brei grimaced. "Ugh."

"I had Loyr and Eyrie clean it up. Poor girls." Taran laughed.

Brei looked at the ground, and the crackle of the fire seemed to roar as the room fell silent.

"So, were you after something?" Taran asked.

"I just, um…I just wanted to speak to Sorsha, actually."

Taran eyed him questioningly, and Brei wondered how Taran had grown so much taller and broader than him.

Sorsha had remained impassive throughout their discussion, studying Brei as she took a long sip of wine. As she lowered her arm, her movements seemed deliberately slow. "What can I do for you?"

"Well, you see, Anwen is awfully cut up about… I'd just like to ask if it's possible for you to give Anwen and the girls space. That is to say, ah, could you please stay away from them?"

Sorsha's stony face barely moved. "Of course." She shrugged.

Taran considered her, and his face relaxed. "Is that all?"

"Ah, yes… Thank you for understanding," and he frowned as he realised she did not care.

Brei backed out of the room and stepped into the flickering glow of the landing. Footsteps echoed below, and he turned to see King Gartnait emerging from the darkness of the stairwell.

"Hello, lad!" Gartnait smiled, wrinkles creasing around his eyes. "Is Taran in? I thought I would catch you both now that you are back, so we could continue that conversation, Brei."

A chair scraped in Sorsha's room and, just as Taran stepped onto the landing, Brei touched his arm and whispered, "I'm sorry about that Anwen–"

"You did what you had to." Taran shrugged Brei off and stepped towards Gartnait, grasping his hand. "Uncle, are you well?"

Brei frowned. *Garnait does seem thin.* The skin was stretched so tight over his cheekbones that Brei thought he could tell what his skull would look like when he died.

Gartnait noticed his nephew's concerned expression. "Don't trouble yourself with me, dear boy. I'll be visiting Serenn after we chat. She has a fresh batch of potion for my aches. Anyway." Gartnait paused and smiled. "I wanted to continue that conversation we were having Brei, before all that nasty business with the trial."

Taran looked at Brei, his eyebrows raised slightly.

Brei nodded. "About the Damnnones raiding south of the Great Wall."

"Yes. Taran, my boy, what do you think of it all?"

Taran answered without hesitation. "I think it is an opportunity, Uncle, one we must act on quickly."

"An opportunity… Perhaps, but at what cost? We must do it properly, Taran. These things cannot be done as swiftly as you would like." Gartnait's calm voice crackled with age, and yet his understated wisdom never failed to command Brei's attention.

"We must call a meeting of all the warriors of Caledon, and then take it to Talorc," Taran continued.

"Yes, of course, Taran." Gartnait sighed. "We must raise this with the warriors. I'm not sure if it is what I would do, but Talorc will know best."

"I understand, Uncle, and you are right. Talorc will know best." Taran draped his arm around his uncle's shoulders, and the king smiled up at him.

THIRTEEN

Winter, 367 C.E., Caledon

Sorsha squinted against the harsh natural light as she passed through the guarded wall separating the Sacred Forest and the city. The blizzard had finally broken, and she wondered if she would ever be able to step inside the oppressive tower again. Imprisoned for a week by snow, the damp walls of the shadowy stairwell had seemed to constrict and clutch around her neck. Often she wondered if the chamber from her nightmares lurked somewhere in the tower. As she ambled down the winding lane that divided Caercaled, the crisp scent of snow was cut with the earthy odours of horses, sewage, and smoke billowing from the roundhouses. Men and women cloaked in furs and tasselled shawls passed her, travelling in all directions, avoiding the piles of snow heaped on either side of the paths.

A sharp, rhythmic hammering of metal against metal echoed across the central lane. A blacksmith was working in a three-walled wooden building, and he knelt on the ground, hammering a long blade against an anvil. The metal clanged, and sparks flew as the hammer hit the searing red blade. The blacksmith was young, with black hair tied loose at his neck. A greasy film of sweat and soot covered his face and muscled arms.

"Do you like it?" he panted, as he put the blade into a bucket of water. The water sizzled and spat.

Sorsha stepped closer to get a better look at the iron blade. "It's beautiful, but how does it work when it's so thin?"

"It's easier to protect yourself when you are further away from your opponent. The Romans like to use spears and hide behind their big shields, so we need a long reach."

"How do you make the blade?"

He put the blade on the dirt floor and stood. "You have to make the iron first, that's turning rock to metal, and then you melt the iron into a mould of a blade, or what have you. When it's red hot and no longer a liquid, you hammer it into shape. And then you refine it even further against a wet stone."

"Could you show me?"

He grinned. "I'd like to, lady, but my apprentice is not with me today and I need someone to work the bellows," he said, pointing to what looked like a leather sack with a wooden handle that was attached to the furnace. "But come back another day, and perhaps I'll show you."

Sorsha turned at the sound of female voices floating down the lane behind her. Serenn's apprentices, Eluned and Arian, wore thick black robes, and a wide leather band was strapped across their torsos, attaching brown leather satchels.

Sorsha stepped in front of them. "Where is Serenn?"

Arian smiled, her blonde hair flowing loose in the breeze. "We are going to see her now, she is at the Shining Lakes."

Eluned's auburn hair was braided, pulled tight on either side of her long face. She grimaced as she watched the blacksmith wipe sweat from his brow. Then she looked at Sorsha. "You may follow," Eluned said in a dour voice, brushing past Sorsha as though she had smelt a nasty scent.

Sorsha spun back to the blacksmith. "I will visit again soon. I would like you to show me. What is your name?"

He smiled. "Gwyddion."

Sorsha waved and walked with Arian as she limped behind Eluned. As they crossed into the centre circle, cleared of snow, market stalls had been set up for sellers of cloth, bread, vegetables, and meat.

Eluned paused in front of the Western Gate, turning to watch Sorsha and Arian catch up. "Can you two hurry? I hate keeping the Eldar Bandruwydd waiting." She spun around and marched past the warriors on guard, her black robes unfurling behind her in the wind. Sorsha glanced at Arian, and they turned their faces away in silent laughter.

Outside the city walls, Sorsha and Arian had to wade knee-deep through the compacted snow, following Eluned's brisk tracks. They trudged until they approached a shimmering lake bordered by distant, snow-covered mountains. Mist hovered above the lake like ice-cold breath. On the lake's edge Sorsha could see a fire, the snaking flames outlining a figure swaddled in a cloak. Alerted by the collective crunching of their steps, the figure turned. It was Serenn, draped in a long, fiery-red cloak made from the russet pelts of foxes and squirrels.

"I am glad you have sought me," Serenn said in a husky voice.

Sorsha stepped closer. "I've been wanting to ask you," she paused, "some questions."

"I know." Serenn studied Sorsha through charcoaled eyes, and the sides of her mouth wrinkled into a smile. Time had been kinder to Serenn than to other inhabitants in Caercaled. The greying of the roots of her blue hair betrayed an advanced age, but the fine lines on her heart-shaped face were a mere shadow of what an ordinary person would carry after years of hard labour.

Serenn motioned for Sorsha, Arian, and Eluned to sit on furs laid out by the lake's edge. The fire crackled in front of them, and Arian poured wine into wooden cups. An icy wind swept across the glittering surface of the lake, blowing Serenn's scent of cinnamon, herbs, and wooded smoke.

The undiluted wine was bitter, but the Bandruwydds seemed content to finish it before the conversation could begin. The wine warmed her fingers, and her limbs became heavy.

Serenn reached forwards and took the goblet from Sorsha, the amber beads tied to the ends of her blue braids chinking together as she moved. "Now, tell me what you want to know."

"I suppose you know how I came to be here?"

Serenn nodded. "You are a Healer? Descended from the Gallar, who dwell in Tirscath."

"Well, my mother was."

"And you are the firstborn daughter of one of her lives?" Serenn asked.

"Yes."

"Then you know that the firstborn daughter of a life of a Healer is the only offspring from that life to become a Healer, if they accept the Gift."

Sorsha nodded.

"And you have passed through Tirscath?"

"Yes."

"How many times?"

Sorsha shifted into a cross-legged position. "Just once."

"Once?" Serenn looked at Eluned and smirked. "Then I see why you have questions."

"Yes, well, I didn't really want to. My death was…not altogether consensual."

Serenn raised her eyebrows. "Go on."

"I didn't want to accept the Gift. I refused. But my mother couldn't accept that." Sorsha swallowed. "This is her… I'm not sure, her ninth life, perhaps? She was born before the Romans first sailed to Britannia. All her other firstborn daughters had been ready to receive the Gift. But I was different. We fought so much about it, for years. And so, a week before I turned twenty-one, after which the Gift can no longer be accepted, my mother had Roman soldiers assassinate me in the standing stones near where I grew up."

"Why didn't you want to accept the Gift?"

"Is it a gift, though? To be forced to serve the Gods for all eternity sounds more like a burden. And I felt like I didn't even know who I was or what I wanted to do with my life, let alone for one hundred lives or more. When I was a child, I wanted to experience adventure with my father, on one of his voyages. But accepting the Gift is permanent, and I still don't know… I still don't know who I am. I guess it doesn't matter anymore, does it, who I am?"

"Who you are?" Serenn leaned forwards and clasped her hands around Sorsha's. "My dear, we do not care who you are, only *what* you are. Individuals perish, but the Ancient People survive."

Arian and Eluned nodded and repeated, under their breath, "individuals perish, but the Ancient People survive."

"We cannot help you if you seek meaning beyond the purpose that has been given you by the Gods. You must realise this?" Serenn pulled a sprig of mistletoe from her leather satchel, withered and crisping, as though it had been hiding in the bag for weeks. "You should know how thankful we are that you have come to us at last, we have been asking for some time," Serenn said as she twirled the mistletoe in her fingers. "The Eldar Druwydd picked this on the sixth night of the last waning moon. He promised us we would have our wish before the life left the stem." The crinkled leaves scratched between Serenn's fingers, but it was not quite dead. A pale greenness clung to the stem. "You came too early…" Serenn whispered, as if to herself. "And we were not prepared. But no matter," Serenn looked up and smiled. "I always make things go to plan in the end."

"And the plan is what? My mother helped people in the city where we lived. Is that what I must do, too?" Sorsha asked. "Is that what you want me to do?"

Serenn tilted her head, the amber beads clinking. "Do you know how to do it?"

Sorsha frowned. "I've seen it done. But my mother said it wasn't something that could be taught. She said I'd just know how when the time came."

"Let me help you," Serenn said and nodded to Arian.

Arian rummaged through the leather satchel and extracted a small blade with a white bone handle.

"Give me your arm, Arian," Serenn said. Arian nodded and placed her arm on Serenn's palm.

Sorsha's heart pounded. *Surely not.* Serenn rolled up the sleeve of Arian's tunic, exposing the pale flesh of her forearm. The shining lake reflected in Arian's eyes, and she stared out as though there was nothing more fascinating in that moment than counting the distant mountains.

Sorsha's gaze darted from Arian's pale, ethereal face as Serenn lifted the dagger and sliced through Arian's upturned skin from wrist to elbow. Arian inhaled, but her head did not turn away from the lake. Blood oozed from the wound, lingering in a pool on her arm, as if considering which way to go, and then dribbled over the edges, trickling along the skin, through the tiny hairs, until droplet after droplet fell onto the furs on which they sat.

"Heal her," Serenn whispered.

Sorsha's eyelids felt heavy, as though a cold fog had descended upon them. Serenn pushed Arian's bloodied arm towards Sorsha. Blood dripped from the wound, relentlessly. Sorsha recoiled.

"She will die soon," Serenn said.

But Serenn's husky voice seemed far away, lost in the thick clouds swelling in Sorsha's mind. She sensed Serenn grab her hand and place it on Arian's wound. The warm blood was wet under her palm, and she stared, transfixed, into Arian's silvery-blue eyes, their light fading. *Please don't die.* Sorsha's heart raced and a strange, intense heat pulsed from her chest. It spread down Sorsha's arm and into her hand. The heat concentrated in her palm as Serenn guided her hand along Arian's arm. Sorsha's eyes never left the steely grey of Arian's, and she was determined not to look down.

As sudden as it had come on, the fog lifted from Sorsha's mind, and she was left, heart hammering, hand clasped around Arian's arm. Arian had never wavered from her casual calmness, as though this had happened before. Serenn pried Sorsha's hand off and Eluned poured water from a decorated jug over the girl's bloodied arm. There was no wound. Nothing more than a thin white scar.

"What happened?" Sorsha asked, unable to keep the shake from her voice.

Serenn shrugged. "You healed her."

Eluned took Sorsha's hand and poured water over it. The liquid trickled red onto the furs beneath them.

Arian glanced at Sorsha over the lip of her goblet as she drank, her eyes sparkling in the waning white light.

"Do you have more questions?" Serenn asked.

"Would it be possible to see my mother?"

Arian fetched a wooden bowl from her satchel and mixed a dark powder with water.

"Where is she?" Serenn asked.

Sorsha watched as Arian took her arm and painted it blue in long, soothing strokes with her icy hands. "Ah…" Sorsha paused, disturbed by how relaxed Arian continued to appear. "Corinium Dobunnorum, south of the Great Wall. She knew the land before the Romans came… But I cannot explain this to the people here. They already think I am a spy."

"Yes, I think it would be unwise."

Flames whirred and fizzed as the wind picked up. Sorsha flexed her hands to crack the dried paint and peeled a long strip off, from her fingernail to her knuckle. "But I think it would be better if I went back south," she whispered. "I want to see my mother… I need to go home."

Without warning, Sorsha's throat restricted painfully, as though someone had hit her, and she coughed. She searched for a culprit, but the Bandruwydds watched her without a sign that they had noticed anything amiss. Sorsha cleared her throat.

"You are not a captive here, but you understand that you are under the control of the king and his nephew, Taran," Serenn said, and Sorsha felt her body sink into the furs.

"But Taran told me the ceremony was a mere formality, to save me."

"He means, you are not bound like Brei and Anwen. Brei is bound to Anwen in protection and provision, he has promised the Gods he will protect her and provide for her along with any children he fathers. But you are bound in obligation."

Sorsha frowned. "Then why am I under his control?"

"It depends on the intention. You were bound because someone needed to vouch for you. You were bound by the Gods in obligation, and Taran is responsible for your actions, your crimes. I, myself, am bound in obligation to Eluned and Arian. For as long as they are my apprentices we are bound, I am responsible for their actions, their crimes are my crimes."

"So I must get Taran's permission to leave? Or the king's?"

"If either were to allow it, then yes, you could see your mother. I think it unlikely, though. The king knows your value, and if Taran does not, he will figure it out soon enough."

Wind whistled and howled, filling her mind like slow drums in the depths of a cave. Sorsha walked along a dark stone passageway, her bent back occasionally scraping against the low roof. The air was thick with the smell of damp grass and the saltiness of the ocean. She followed a flickering light along the low passage to a square chamber where a lit torch lay on the ground. The wood crackled and spat. She bent to pick up the torch to get a better look at the chamber, but as her hands touched the wood, a gust of wind blew up the passageway, and the torch went out. Then the wind dropped, and she could hear footsteps. Someone was running along the passageway towards her. Her heart beat frantically as the footsteps drew closer.

Sorsha choked and opened her eyes. Sweat beaded across her forehead as she panted. The dying fire in the hearth cast long shadows across her room, and a strange howl, like wind, echoed in the stairwell. The muscles in her legs tensed and she lay still, listening to the dull crackle of the fire. Another low howl, like a wounded stag, reverberated against the stone once more. Edging herself off the bed, she crept to the door and peered into the empty corridor. The noise groaned again from behind the entrance to the staircase, and she tiptoed towards the landing door. Her hand hovered on the iron door handle. *Maybe I should wake Taran and Naoise?*

She grasped the handle and pulled it open. The torch on the landing had blown out, but she could still make out a strange, lumpy shadow lying across the entrance. The lump moaned. *It must be an animal… or a demon.* The lump raised its head, and she inhaled. It was a man, crunched over on his knees. He wheezed. A strange empathy, a tremor in her stomach, lured her forwards, and she bent down and put her hand on his shoulder. Tears smudged his cheeks as he looked up at her. A hideous odour wafted, and she wondered if he had shat himself.

She recoiled as recognition dawned on her. "King Gartnait… What is wrong?"

"My stomach," he moaned. "I was trying to reach Serenn…but it is so far." He doubled over his knees once more.

Perhaps I should find Serenn. She looked across the dim landing to the spiralling staircase that faded into black. The king's breathing was rapid and his shoulder wet with sweat. An intense urge to help him rippled through her, like an itch, a blind compulsion. Reaching forwards, she pushed her hand into the space between his knees and his stomach. Agonised cries echoed around the stairwell as she pressed her hand against his wet robes, up into his abdomen.

"Shh," Sorsha whispered.

Heat travelled from her heart, down her arm, and into her palm, and she pressed until his breathing returned to normal. He lifted himself onto his knees and gazed up at her, wide-eyed. She stroked the sweaty grey hair out of his eyes and pressed her palms across his forehead until his face relaxed. "Do you feel better?"

He nodded, looking up at her like a puppy rescued from a stream. "It is true, then, what Serenn said about you."

The compulsion to heal faded from her body like waves pulling back from the shore.

King Gartnait clutched her hand, a sweet smile crinkling his eyes. "Thank the Gods you came to us."

FOURTEEN

Brei followed Taran and King Gartnait under the ancient boughs of oak and yew, into the Sacred Forest. The warriors of Caledon waited for them beneath dark jagged clouds outlined by the creeping pale dawn. Brei's stomach tensed as he practised the speech he had spent the night memorising, instead of sleeping. *We have gathered to decide whether to avenge the deaths of our fathers and defend our lands, as our ancestors did from a greedy and persistent foe.* Brei and Taran had spoken to every warrior in Caercaled of their plan to attack the Romans south of the Great Wall. Brei felt confident that no matter what he said, they had mustered enough support before the vote.

King Gartnait stopped at the top of a slope and gazed at the warriors gathered in the trees below. Dylan and Naoise were leaning against the trunk of a yew. Naoise yawned, his black hair sprawling across his shoulders. Brei scanned the crowd and saw Owain and Gruffydd. When Gruffydd nodded, warmth spread across Brei's chest. *I'm ready.*

King Gartnait raised his hand to silence the murmurs that rippled through the crowd. He turned to Brei and Taran. "You have a proposal for consideration?"

Brei cleared his throat. The faces of the warriors stared at him in anticipation. *This is it.* He fixed his eyes on Gruffydd and opened his mouth to deliver his speech.

Taran stepped forwards and, in a loud voice, addressed the crowd of warriors. "Many of you have heard that, on a recent scout, we spoke with the Damnnones about the Roman movements beyond the Great Wall."

Brei's stomach dropped. The blood rushed to his cheeks, and he looked at the ground, hoping that Gruffydd was not looking at him.

"Before the Romans came, with their hearts full of greed, this island was united by the Gods of the Ancient Peoples. Before the Great Wall cut this island in two, we all spoke the Ancient Tongue. There are Ancient Peoples still living in the south. The Romans use these southern Ancient Peoples as soldiers and turn them into the oppressors of their own people. But we have discovered that the loyalty of these native soldiers is now being tested. The Damnnones have told us that these native soldiers are easily paid off and that they are letting the Damnnones pass through the Great Wall." Taran paused. Feverish muttering had broken out, and he grinned.

"Brei and I have also spoken to merchants who told us that many Roman soldiers have been withdrawn from the southern lands beyond the Wall. The merchants complain that trade across the empire is disrupted and that they are attacked by Saxon pirates because the remaining Roman soldiers can no longer protect them."

Taran nodded as muttering broke out once more. He walked down the slope, along the rows of men, looking into their faces as he spoke. "And while the merchants complain, I say we rejoice! I say we thank the Gods for this opportunity! This opportunity for vengeance!"

Taran put his hand on the shoulder of a young, red-headed warrior, Deryn. "Revenge for what they have done to us! Revenge for the towns they have destroyed! Revenge for the lives they have taken! Our fathers, who were cut down! Our mothers and sisters, who we will never see again! And if we die, the Gods will welcome us in Tirscath! Join me, brothers! Revenge or Tirscath!"

The warriors roared and thrust their fists in the air. "Revenge or Tirscath! Revenge or Tirscath!"

"Do we have the backing of the warriors of Caledon?" he yelled over the chanting. The warriors roared for Taran.

Taran rejoined Brei and King Gartnait at the top of the slope. "I ask our king, will you send us to Caertarwos, to seek the unity of the Northern Alliance?"

Brei studied Gartnait, thin in the dim light but stronger than he had seemed for months. The warriors were shouting with such vigour that Brei knew it would be impossible to deny them blood.

The king lifted his hand. "I agree to your request. You may speak with King Talorc and see if he will summon the rest of the Northern Alliance." He paused and waited for the cheering to subside. "If vengeance can be ours, for my brother, King Uradech, for the life of my sister, Princess Derelei, then I say we must embrace it!"

Taran grinned and grasped the king's arm. The warriors cheered and banged their swords on their wooden shields. Brei gazed at the crowd. Many of the villagers of Caercaled had joined, creeping up the hill into the Sacred Forest and flowing into the streets below. It seemed as if the whole of Caledon was celebrating. Brei closed his eyes and willed himself to join in. *Revenge or Tirscath.*

Before dawn, Brei walked to the stables, listening to his feet crunch in the snow. His fingers were raw in the frigid air, and he pushed them under the lip of Rhuad's saddle as they rode out. The shadows of naked branches passed over him as he rode through the Sacred Forest and into the city. Beneath frost, the sloping roofs of roundhouses and workshops still slept, and cats skulked out of the way of Rhuad's hooves. Puffs of mist escaped his mouth as he hailed the guards at the ramparts to each tier of the city. "Morning," they called back, tugging at their fur capes, and following up with variations on the theme of "it's cold out."

He rode through the Western Gate and lifted his face to the dawn. Thin clouds betrayed no sign of rain or snow. Brei urged Rhuad into a gallop to the east, towards the Shining Lakes, hoping Taran would not chastise him for sleeping in.

As Brei approached the lake, he pushed deep into his seat, slowing Rhuad to a canter, then a trot, and reined up close to the lake's edge. Taran waited on Ri's muscled white back, watching as three white swans, with vivid red beaks, waddled across the frozen edge of the lake.

Brei cleared his throat. "Shall we get on, then?"

Taran shifted in the saddle to face Brei. "Just waiting for Naoise," and he nodded in the forest's direction. The swans flapped their wings, and the rising sun outlined the feathers as they took off into the air.

"I thought it was just us?" Brei murmured as he watched the swans circle once and then fly to the east.

Taran shrugged. "He asked to come."

They waited and, before long, Naoise came trotting out of the forest towards them. "Sorry about that," he yelled. "Drank too much at Elwyn's last night."

The three of them urged their horses into a gallop, and they arched around the first Shining Lake and rode along the valley, between its smaller sister lakes. A corridor of broken water, bounded on either side by forest. In the middle of the lakes, large roundhouses called crannogs sat on stilts above the icy water, connected to the shore by a jetty. The farmsteads soon vanished, and the pasture merged into the forest. They kept to a narrow track alongside a frozen creek and continued through the valley until they reached a river that ran north to south and blocked their eastwards journey.

"We've come a bit too far north," Taran called out, twisting to look at Brei.

Brei surveyed the river. The edges were frosted, but the water still surged through. It was about fifty yards wide and looked too high to cross. They followed south along the bank until they found the sandbar they were searching for. The water was high, but it was not as turbulent as the waters that raged past Caercaled.

"Time for a swim, boys," Taran called as he jumped off Ri and led the white stallion down the riverbank into the water. The sandbar, which acted as a stepping-stone across the river in summer, was submerged. Brei suspected the water would be waist-deep, at most.

Naoise cursed as he stepped into the river. "I can take it anywhere but my balls!"

Brei snorted and jumped into the icy water, leading Rhuad in after him, being careful to hold his cape above his head. The water came to his waist, but after a few steps, he could walk at knee-height across the sandbar, before plunging again to cross to the other side.

As Brei splashed up the snowy bank, Taran and Naoise were already re-mounted and keen to continue. They followed the river southeast, sitting sodden and freezing in the saddle, and passed through ancient lands of a long-forgotten kingdom. Brei knew there was a minor fortress atop a hill in the lands to his left. He looked up at the hills for the ruins, but the snow-dusted trees obscured them. Brei closed his eyes and listened to the rhythmic sound of the horses' hooves on the dirt road, imagining past battles between the kings of his ancestors.

They continued until they reached a snake bend, where they had to cross two rivers. There was an island where the rivers met, and they used the shelter this provided to cross behind it. The water was much deeper there, and they could only just touch the bottom. Their horses managed better than they did, arching their heads up out of the water and pushing forwards off the bottom with their long legs. It took them a good ten minutes to cross. On the other side, Brei flopped on the snowy bank next to Taran and Naoise, shivering as he gasped for air. Rhuad shook himself and droplets of water sprayed on Brei's face.

"Need to keep moving, or the horses will freeze," Brei said, standing up to stretch. The pants and bottom of his tunic clung damp and heavy to his limbs. They re-mounted in silence and rode northeast along the river to join a wide dirt road, where they were able to travel at a faster pace. It had once been a road the Romans used. Brei clenched his jaw. *The Romans made footholds into our ancestors' land by using our own network of tracks and settlements.*

The further east they rode, the lighter the snow covering on the road, and by afternoon the road was mud. Forest thinned into pasture and, in the distance, Brei saw a small farmstead near the ruins of an abandoned Roman fort.

"Shall we carry on?" Naoise asked.

"I think we should spend the night here. It is safer than being on the road come nightfall," Taran replied.

Brei nodded. "We should visit the farmstead, save us having to hunt for dinner."

They rode up to the little settlement of roundhouses. "Hello!" someone called from inside the rubble, and Brei reached for the sword hanging from his waist.

A white-haired man emerged from the ruins. "We've been wondering when we would see the young princes again." He grinned. "Not so young, all of you, of course." He nodded to Brei and Taran.

Taran smiled. "How are you, Sam?"

Brei glanced at his brother. *How on earth did he remember his name?*

Sam flushed. "Well, my lord, I thank you for remembering. Are you visiting King Talorc?"

Taran nodded. "Are you using the ruins now?"

"Only to keep the sheep. We still live in the roundhouses, of course, but we've started taking back some stone to build more houses. We are growing," he said, pulling his shoulders back.

"And will you be coming to market in Caercaled soon?"

"Yes, after Imbolc I will."

"I'll look out for your stall."

Sam bowed. "You are generous, my lord." He paused and gestured to the roundhouses behind him. "We have a loom here now, we're going to sell cloth and raw wool."

"Do you have any cloth ready now? I will buy some on our way back in a week or so if you do."

"Yes, yes, of course we do. It would be my pleasure. Will you be staying for the night? It would be an honour to host you for dinner, my lords."

"Thank you, yes, we would welcome dinner."

"Excellent, come to me at dusk. My family's roundhouse is the first there by the river."

Taran bowed his head. "We'll see you then, Sam."

They watched as Sam hurried towards the closest roundhouse, where a woman stood waiting for him by the wooden door.

"I need to get out of these clothes." Naoise thrust his hand into his leather pants. "I'm chafing so bad." He winced.

Brei chuckled. "Let's go further along the river where it's more private."

After they unsaddled their horses, they let them roam along the bank to eat the lush grass, while they removed their clothes and lay them out on the grass to dry. They were closer to the coast, and even though a chill clung to the crisp air, there was no snow.

Brei lay on the ground. Cold grass pressed against his back, and he closed his eyes.

"I'm going for a swim," Naoise announced.

Brei opened his eyes and squinted at Naoise. He stood naked with his hands on his hips.

Taran plucked a tuft of grass with a lump of soil attached and flung it at Naoise. The dirt hit him in the stomach. "Go on then."

Brei snorted. Naoise turned his back on them and bent over, displaying his pale cheeks.

"Did you get any dirt up there?" Naoise called, peeking at them with his head between his legs.

Brei threw a lump of dirt at Naoise, striking him on his back. Naoise squealed and, tripping over himself, ran into the river and dived under the water.

Brei caught Taran's eye and smirked while they watched Naoise float on his back like an otter. Taran stood up, sauntered to the riverbank and plunged under the water as well. Brei watched the white ripples spread across the surface, and when Taran re-emerged, he was far from the point of impact.

FIFTEEN

A rian pointed to a tall, thorny weed. "Thistles grow by the road-sides, and on pastoral land."

Sorsha groaned inwardly as the lesson continued. They stood on the edge of the farmstead by the River Tae. The smell of manure and the earthy hides of animals in the stables wafted towards them in the biting wind.

"We extract the oils from the roots and use them to heal those who cannot breathe," Arian continued. Her voice was gentle, and the corners of her delicate lips curved upwards as she spoke. "The thistle flowers in summer, a big purple floret, and we use it to brew a tea as a curative for the weak heart."

Sorsha squinted across the river to the impenetrable forest on the southern side. Mist rose from the bank and clung to the snow-cloaked pines and gaunt oaks. *What is the point of these lessons, when I can cure anyone with just my hands?*

"Sorsha?"

She turned back to Arian. "Mm?"

"Look at that hawthorn tree, do you see the messy balls up there?"

Sorsha gazed at a cluster of tall trees on the edge of the icy field. They were bereft of leaves and covered in clumps of scraggly green balls. "It's mistletoe," Sorsha said.

Arian smiled. In the presence of Serenn, she was aloof, suppressing a raw charm that she did not fear revealing when alone with Sorsha. "Yes, and it is easiest to find in winter when the hosts have lost their leaves. The Druwydds harvest it for us."

"What do you use it for?"

"Mostly it is used with other plants, valerian, for example. We use it to help those at the tower who have trouble sleeping, but on its own it is useful for those with a nervous disposition, for anxiety. It is rare, used by the nobles only, and it is punishable by death for anyone other than a Druwydd to harvest it."

"Has anyone actually been killed for taking mistletoe?"

"Oh yes." Arian paused and shook her head. "Every year someone is caught."

Sorsha looked up at the messy balls. *Such a strange thing to die for.*

Arian screwed her eyebrows together and seemed to lose her balance.

"What's wrong?" Sorsha asked, reaching out to take hold of Arian's arm.

Arian shook her head and closed her eyes. The clouds cracked apart, and Arian's golden hair glowed in the sun as she stooped and sat on the snow.

Sorsha crouched on the ice next to her. "Are you sick? I can help."

Arian straightened her right leg out and inhaled with a hiss. She pulled her skirt up and revealed a wooden stump in place of a foot.

Sorsha's eyes widened. "What happened?"

Arian leaned forwards and untied the woollen wrapping that secured the stump to her leg. "Frostbite, a year ago. They cut the foot off and burnt the flesh, but it still hurts." She pulled the wood and a cushion of crumpled beige linen away. The foot had been cut at the ankle, and although the flesh had healed, it was red.

"Let me see what I can do," Sorsha said as she sat by Arian's leg.

Arian nodded, and Sorsha placed her hand onto the flesh. As the heat ran from her heart, she wondered what would happen. *Does it work on old wounds?* She removed her hand and examined Arian's leg. The flesh was no longer red, it had become scar white. Sorsha pressed into the skin near the bone and studied Arian's face. "Does it hurt?"

Arian shook her head.

"Interesting. I wondered if I could grow you a new foot, but I suppose it doesn't work like that, does it? It just heals the injury. But hopefully, this makes it easier for you, anyway. Why didn't you ask for my help before?"

"I didn't want to in front of Serenn," Arian said as she fitted the cushion and wooden stump back onto her leg.

"Why not?"

Arian fumbled with the woollen wrappings and did not look up.

"Are you afraid of her?"

Arian glanced at Sorsha without lifting her head, her forehead wrinkling from the effort. "Aren't you?"

"No."

"Really?"

"Why would I be afraid of her?" Sorsha studied Arian's face. Her eyelashes were thick and dark against her pale skin. "How did you get frostbite, anyway?"

Arian sighed. "I was watching the stars for Serenn. Calculating the time until Imbolc. Do you know what that is? It marks the midway point between winter and spring."

"Yes, my mother taught me about the Ancient People's festivals, Imbolc, Beltane, Samhain, and all that." She frowned. "But why didn't you go back inside when you got too cold?"

Arian plucked a twig from the snow and twirled it between her fingers. "I must do what Serenn says."

"To the point where you lose your foot?"

"I'm an orphan. I have nowhere to turn but the tavern or begging. So, yes, I do whatever Serenn wants."

Sorsha swallowed. "I'm so sorry. How did your parents die?"

"They were burnt to death in their house when the Romans attacked. I managed to get out."

"The Romans...they attacked Caercaled?"

"Six summers ago, in the middle of the night. They torched all the houses outside the city walls." She pointed to the farmstead. "All of this was burnt to the ground in the attack. Prince Rhys, Brei and Taran's father, that is, he was killed, as was the great King Uradech."

"But surely you mean a retaliation? The barbarians must have provoked them somehow, the Roman soldiers wouldn't just attack for no reason."

Arian shifted. "Don't call us that. It is the Romans who are the barbarians. They invaded the north hundreds of winters ago, and we've always fought them off, we've always defended our home. But until they leave us be, it's a never-ending cycle of provocation from the Romans and simmering revenge from us."

"I shouldn't have called you that... What happened to Brei and Taran's mother? Was she killed in the attack?"

"She was taken. We assume she is either dead or has been sold into slavery. I hope, for her sake, the former."

"Then why is it Anwen who seems to despise me so much?"

Arian grimaced. "Anwen was also taken with Princess Derelei, their mother, that is, but she escaped. The experience seems to have...left a permanent mark on her mind. I make potions to help her sleep, to ensure she doesn't remember."

"Why didn't their mother, Princess Derelei, escape too?"

Arian shook her head. "I don't know. No one has seen her since."

"No one looked for her? No one tried to rescue her?"

Arian shrugged. "She could be anywhere, Sorsha. You should know better than me that the Romans control vast lands. Where would you start looking?"

"The slave markets would be a start." She paused. "But wait, you escaped a burning house, but your parents died? Weren't you burnt?"

Arian nodded and pulled down the sleeve of her tunic. The skin on her chest and arm was withered and brown.

"I'm so sorry, Arian."

Arian straightened her tunic and pulled her pelt cape tighter around her shoulders. "Don't be. I'm one of the lucky ones."

"What do you mean?"

"Anwen's the only one that the Romans took who came back, but they took so many women, including Princess Derelei. And just look at Anwen. What horrors and abuse must she have gone through because now she is a wreck, a shell of her former self. She wasn't like this before, you know."

Sorsha looked at Arian doubtfully.

"Honestly." Arian smiled. "Anwen is a few years older than me, of course, but I remember her. She was so beautiful and sweet. I used to see her picking wildflowers and walking with Prince Brei, and the way she would smile at him... she had smiles for everyone back then, but for him they were... it's hard to explain, but they made me smile too."

Sorsha sighed. "I wish I could explain to her that she has nothing to fear from me, but Brei has asked that I don't speak to her."

"Don't take it personally. He's protective of her."

Sorsha's mouth twitched. "I get it, he loves her."

Arian glanced over her shoulder towards the farmstead, her voice dropping to a whisper. "He gave up everything to help her get through the trauma of being taken by the Romans. The Eldar Druwydd wanted him to be King of Caledon after King Uradech was killed in the Roman attack. And when the Eldar Druwydd wants something, he usually gets it. But Prince Brei refused to make a claim, and everyone thinks it's because Anwen wouldn't let him."

"Wouldn't let him? The men here do not seem bound by their women."

Arian shook her head. "A lot is said about Prince Brei behind his back. Hardly any of it is good. Many people hate Anwen because she is an upstart peasant, and their relationship had been largely kept under wraps until she managed to escape from the Romans. But when she returned, he bound himself to her immediately and then refused the crown. It was a huge shock. People hate Anwen for taking a king away from them, but others just hate Brei for being weakened by a woman. Personally, I feel sorry for them. He was devastated when she was taken. I remember I had just been apprenticed to Serenn, and I was asked to take him a sleeping draught. It was summer and his fire was out, so his room was dark, and I remember seeing him as a lump on the bed in the gloom, covered in bandages. I heard him crying. Not loudly. It was sort of a soft whimpering, like a lost child that has given up hope of ever being found. I think about that time a lot, and a part of me wishes that someone would feel about me that way, the way Brei loves Anwen." Arian broke the twig in her hands and threw the sticks on the snow.

"Are you allowed to be bound…to a man…like that?"

"No." Arian squinted up at the sky. "I'm not allowed to make promises to anyone but Serenn. But it doesn't matter, no man would tie themselves to a useless cripple, anyway."

"Is being useful the only thing that matters? What about love? Brei loves Anwen despite her…trauma."

"They say Brei is weak, an aberration. For everyone else, women have to be useful to men to earn the promise of their protection, or there's no point."

Sorsha glanced again at the row of roundhouses that made up the farmsteads. "And what about men? Is their purpose tied to their usefulness to women?"

Arian laughed. "Men are useful to women, obviously, but men don't need women to have a place in society. They get that as a birthright. The same is not true for women here."

"But being a Bandruwydd is a position. A position of power?"

Arian shrugged. "Sort of. I think Serenn wants it to be. Really, we are a lesser order of the Druwydds, and we do their bidding. We have particular skills that set us apart, of course, in healing and midwifery.

But the Druwydds are political, they are kingmakers. Bandruwydds do not have that power…unless a new king would give it to us."

"But still, that is a lot more power than a woman otherwise would have? Even a princess seems to have no role other than producing men who can claim the throne. Surely it is competitive to become a Bandruwydd?"

"It is. Normally they are of noble birth, daughters of kings, like Serenn and Eluned."

"Who is Eluned the daughter of?"

"King Uradech, of course. Where else do you think she gets that arrogance from?"

"Is everyone cousins here?" Sorsha laughed. "But I think I understand now why you fear Serenn. Without her you'd be at the mercy of men?"

"And without your powers, so would you."

"Maybe. But only if I chose to live here. I rather like the sound of living alone in the wild. In a wooden hut on a windswept cliff. And I'd have a dog, or a cat, maybe."

Arian laughed. "I don't think so. You'd get bored within minutes."

"How do you know?"

Arian leaned forwards and touched Sorsha's hand with her fingertips. "You have a restless spirit, I can tell. And it's not because you are a Healer."

Sorsha glanced at Arian's ghostly fingers and fought against the urge to pull back. "Tell me, how did an orphan peasant become a Bandruwydd?"

Arian slid her hand away. "Serenn caught me in her chambers making a draught for pain relief, for my burns after the Roman attack, and she apprenticed me instantly. I have a gift, for herbal curatives, potions and poisons, which not even Serenn can rival," she said, her gentle voice hardly rising above a whisper. "I could save or kill someone without them tasting a difference in their wine."

"Could you kill me?"

"If I had help, I think I could. Maybe I'd poison you, while someone else stabbed you in the heart." Arian grinned. "But I wasn't talking about you. You're here to help us."

"Do you know why I'm here?"

"Yes. But it's worth more than my life to tell you. I'm sorry, Sorsha." She shifted and stared beyond Sorsha's shoulder and groaned. "Serenn is coming."

Sorsha turned towards Caercaled and saw Serenn and Eluned emerging from the forest on the fringe of the snowy pasture.

"We have sick to see," Serenn called out. "Urgently!"

Sorsha glanced at Arian, her ethereal face hardened like ice thickening across a pond.

They followed Serenn at an exhausting pace along the river to the city, and Sorsha wondered if Serenn was as callous as Arian implied. She glanced over her shoulder as Arian trailed through the snow, limping behind them. Her stomach tensed, and she slowed her pace, but Arian smiled and waved her on. Winter forest lay to her right, and the wild, curling river on her left soon gave way to the city's stone wall.

Sorsha followed Serenn and Eluned through the Western Gate to the centre circle, where a few stalls were open. A small gathering of customers were purchasing from the weavers and bakers. The smell of fresh bread made her salivate, but they soon turned up a side lane off the centre circle.

Eluned stopped and pointed to an unremarkable roundhouse in the lane. Icicles hung around the eaves like daggers. "Here." Eluned knocked at the wooden door and waited.

It opened, and a harried woman with clumpy red hair appeared. Sorsha could not tell if the woman looked terrified or relieved to see them as she bowed and admitted them inside. The house was windowless and lit only by a fire in the middle of the single room. Thick smoke clung to the roof, and Sorsha ducked to avoid it. There were seven cots of various lengths and widths, and Sorsha counted six young children sprawled around. Lying between two cots was a gigantic pregnant pig, snoring, and a young child lay next to it, stroking its hairy pink skin.

The woman led them to the back of the room, where a man lay, pallid and sweating. His unfocused eyes stared into the smoky gloom, and his mouth jerked as though in a ferocious conversation with himself. Sorsha studied his face, and an uncontrollable pull lured her towards him. It was as though she were tied to a ship's anchor that had just been thrown into the ocean.

Arian and Eluned retrieved sticks from their leather satchels and lit them off the fire. They had been treated with liquid and herbs, causing them to burn slowly and emit a grey fragrant cloud. Kneeling next to the cot, they held the incense sticks close to the man and chanted in low voices. Serenn stood by his head and threw her arms out wide, her face looking up to the roof. She chanted to Nodens, the God of Healing, and Cerunnos, the Horned God, and Lord of Nature. From Nodens she asked for the man to be healed, and from Cerunnos she asked for the stamina of the wolf to course through his veins.

Sorsha, shielded by the commotion, bent down and considered the man. Grey had yet to fleck his dark hair, and his broad, muscled chest rose and fell in jerks. She examined his face and body, searching for signs of a festering wound. But she could find no physical cause for his fever.

The compulsion ensnared her in a transitive state of empathy, and she was certain she could share his feelings. He felt cold, yet he was sweating, his body ached all over and his throat and nose were dry and scraping. She lowered herself closer to him and placed her head against his chest and listened. It wheezed under her ear. She sat up straight and pressed both hands onto his chest. The deep heat surged from her heart, down her arms and into her hands. His breathing became steady, before she moved her hands to his neck, chest, and abdomen. When his eyes refocused and found her face, Serenn pushed Sorsha away and consumed his attention with her chanting.

Sorsha paused by the fire and stared at the man, who was bewildered by the Bandruwydds, smoke screens, and chanting. The compulsive pull subsided, and she returned to dull ambivalence. Sorsha glanced at the pig and the child as she pushed open the wooden door and stepped into the startling brightness of the overcast day.

She waited in the side lane for a few minutes until the Bandruwydds rejoined her. "Are there more like him?"

Serenn shook her head. "You may go."

Sorsha's eyes flicked to Arian, hoping for a smile, but her grey eyes were like a stranger's, and the Bandruwydds departed up the hill for the tower. Ambling behind at a safe distance, Sorsha veered away and resolved to visit the blacksmith, Gwyddion, again. He never seemed to mind that she watched him, sometimes for hours. The process of melting iron ore down, pouring it into a mould, and later hammering it to perfection, was oddly satisfying. She felt that through the magic of metallurgy, he could control his surrounds, to shape the raw untamed world into an image of his own making, in a way that she could not. *I am at the mercy of my fate, unable to control it, or anything else.*

Sorsha sat inside the workshop on a chair in the corner and watched Aaron, Gwyddion's blond and tubby apprentice, raise the wooden handles attached to the forge up and down. Air filled the leather bellows and blew into the fire. Sparks flew in the air, swirling to the ground, but Gwyddion remained steady. Clutching his rough metal tongs, he pulled a flask out of the fire and carried it to a long clay mould that was standing upright in a bucket of sand. The muscles in his arms quivered under his sweat-stained tunic. He poured the red liquid into the mould and straightened with a smile. His teeth dazzled white against the darkness of his soot-baked skin.

"You should have a go," Gwyddion said, as he placed the flask and tongs onto the stone by the forge. "You've seen enough now to be my new apprentice." He winked at Aaron and tucked a lock of black hair behind his ear.

She smiled. "You seem so busy lately, maybe you will need my help."

He pulled a soiled length of linen from his leather apron and wiped his hands. "Funny you should mention it, Prince Taran actually came down here a few days ago, and I've been put on notice that I'm to expand my capacity. A second forge is going to be built."

"What for?"

"What else? War."

"Are you under attack?"

Gwyddion smiled. "No, it is our turn now for vengeance against the Romans."

She gazed into the flames of the forge. "Are you too busy to make me one?"

Gwyddion glanced at Aaron. "A sword?"

Aaron smirked. He could not have been over thirteen, and she scowled at him until his cheeks were tinged with pink. "Yes, a sword. Would you do it?"

Gwyddion studied her for a moment before the edges of the right side of his mouth curled upwards. "As you wish."

SIXTEEN

Winter, 367 C.E., Vortriu

B rei, Taran, and Naoise continued along the ancient road found-
ed by their ancestors. For four days the road led them through
crags and bogs, and around mountains, passing through the
Kingdoms of Ce and of Vortriu, allies from whom the princes needed
no permission to travel. The muddy road was well trodden, especially in
winter when it was too dangerous to travel by sea, and a crisp scent of
damp earth lingered in the air.

When they approached the coastal fort of Caertarwos on the fifth
day, Taran and Naoise seemed to have cracked. Starting as a whisper
and progressively growing louder, they called out the ancestral words of
Caledon.

"The Snake of Caledon never forgets!"

Brei gripped his reigns and focused straight ahead. His head had
been pounding for a few hours already.

Taran glanced at Brei over his shoulder and yelled louder. "The
Snake of Caledon never forgets!"

By the time they sighted the fortifications of Caertarwos, Taran
and Naoise were screaming to each other, on either side of Brei, as he
tried to ignore them. But a smile teased at the corners of his lips.

"What's wrong, Brei-Brei?" Taran said with a childish affectation as
he sidled Ri up as close to Rhuad as he could manage.

"I have a headache."

Taran pouted and turned to Naoise. "Poor Brei-Brei. We should probably stop annoying him, shouldn't we?"

Naoise nodded, his face deadpan. "Should keep our voices down."

Brei braced himself.

In one impossible move, Taran placed his right knee on the saddle and sprang across to Brei, dragging him off Rhuad and onto the ground. Taran, who had somehow landed standing, grinned down at him. Rhuad and Ri trotted off a few paces in front of them while Brei picked himself up and brushed off the mud. Brei waited until Taran was almost doubled over in laughter before he ran at him, tackled him to the ground, and scrambled to pin his arms.

Naoise cackled as he watched them. "You look like my grandpa trying to wrestle his new woman into bed!"

Brei and Taran broke into laughter and released each other. Brei pushed himself up and crumpled Taran's hair. Still wheezing, Taran punched him in the shoulder.

Brei held his side and wondered if he had pulled something in the fall. As he puffed, he looked across to the fortified walls of Caertarwos. A small party of heavily armed riders galloped across the open grassland towards them. Brei glanced at Taran, whose grin had vanished.

As the lead rider slowed to a walk, Brei recognised his red-haired cousin, Talorc, King of Vortriu, glaring down his long straight nose, with no sign of recognition. The riders formed a circle around them. Talorc raised his fist into the air, and his men lowered their spears towards them. "Kill them."

Brei stared at him, too shocked to even unsheathe his sword.

The warriors drew their spears back and lunged forwards to plunge the steel tips into their chests. Brei shut his eyes. The blade pierced his chest and seemed to hover in place. *Have I already passed out?* He opened his eyes and saw the warriors frozen in the stabbing motion, smiling.

Talorc roared with laughter, and the warriors removed the spears.

"You look like you've all shit yourselves! Please tell me you actually shat yourself?" Talorc leapt off his horse. He was so tall it seemed there was hardly any distance to make. "Heard you children, screaming like cats at each other." Talorc beamed. "So I thought I'd send out a welcome party."

Taran embraced him. "Talorc!"

"It's been too long!" Talorc motioned to Brei. "Brei, come here!" He opened his arms wide and enveloped Brei in a crushing hug.

"It's good to see you, cousin," Brei wheezed.

Talorc released him but kept his hands on Brei's shoulders and stared into his face. "You are well, Brei?"

"As well as ever."

"Good man!" Talorc slapped him on the back and turned to Taran and Naoise. "Didn't I just kick you out, Neesh?"

Naoise grinned. "I thought you might miss me?"

Talorc raised a red eyebrow. "I think I'll have Branwen examine your head, boy. Come into the city, let us feast! Tonight, we drink to my cousins and to our mothers!"

Caertarwos was a promontory fort that clung, wild and windswept, to the cliffs of the sea. They entered the walled city through a corridor of stone. Carved into the walls were pictures of bulls, from where Caertarwos, "Fortress of the bulls", got its name.

They spent the night in the wooden hall with Talorc and his younger brother, Drest, drinking mead flavoured with heather. Talorc leaned across the long wooden table towards Taran, who sat opposite him. "You spoke with the Damnnones?"

Taran nodded. "And King Nechtan at Caermhèad. We saw Cantigerna, she'd probably have asked us to send you her regards, but we tried not to talk about you."

Talorc jerked forwards, and Taran recoiled, then smiled.

"Did you speak to King Alwyn?"

Brei shook his head. "No, we didn't go to Altclud. We only spoke to the warriors at Gowan."

Talorc gulped more ale and belched. "Apparently old Alwyn is near death. His son, Coel, is positioning himself to take the throne."

Naoise frowned. "How can he take the throne, he's not a Prince of the Blood?"

Talorc pulled a face. "Don't be thick, Neesh, they do it differently there."

"How do you know all this?" Brei asked.

"I have spies everywhere. I know everything."

Taran snorted. "And yet you don't know the plots that grow beneath your nose." He winked at Naoise.

Naoise's cheeks flushed, and he mouthed "fuck you."

Taran leant back and laughed.

Brei sipped more ale and tried to keep the confusion from his face.

"And you think we should raid down south, is that what you're getting at?" Talorc asked.

Brei nodded. "Attack them while they are weak. Then, because we can enter through the Great Wall, we can take our horses."

"For more plunder. Yes, yes, it is appealing." Talorc drained his silver goblet of mead and signalled to a servant hovering by the edge of the table that he wanted more. "But why should we limit our ambitions?"

Taran leaned forwards. "What do you have in mind?"

Talorc paused as the servant poured fresh mead. Another servant hurried forwards with a glowing poker and dipped it into the cup. It sizzled and spluttered for a few seconds before the servant removed the poker and, bowing, hobbled away.

"Well, you will remember my queen, Princess Maeve, of Attacot?" They nodded.

"Our children, of course, belong to Attacot, but I visit sometimes, and I have become quite friendly with her father, King Derine. It seems to me that they would be keen to join us." Talorc picked up his goblet and drank.

"Why stop there?" Naoise asked.

Brei turned, surprised to see Naoise contributing something other than banter.

Talorc smirked. "Do you have anything else in mind?"

"My father is a Prince of Ulster, I could visit him and see if his brother, the king, would be interested."

"The eldest sons inherit in Ulster, don't they? Who is in line for the throne?" Talorc asked.

"My cousin, Prince Fergus. He's an arsehole."

Talorc smirked. "I've heard. I had thought of them, but they seem more interested in warring with Attacot and Cait and taking the lands on the west coast. But perhaps an alliance with Ulster would be beneficial."

Brei exhaled through his nose.

Talorc raised his eyebrows. "This displeases you, Brei?"

"What doesn't?" Taran smirked over the lip of his goblet.

Brei grunted and rolled his eyes.

Sitting next to Talorc, Drest pawed at the king's arm. "I will go with Neesh to Ulster, if you give leave, brother?"

"So that you and Naoise can get up to mischief with no one to watch you?"

"We are men!" Naoise huffed. Taran smirked across the table at Talorc, whose eyes twinkled back over his goblet.

"But" Naoise paused, smiling. "If you are worried, perhaps you would send Princess Eithne to keep us in check."

Brei slapped the back of Naoise's head. Princess Eithne was Talorc and Drest's younger sister. As one of the few direct Princesses of the Blood of Caledon and Vortriu left, she was a prize beyond measure.

Talorc shook his head, but Drest grinned at Naoise.

"Fine, you can go together with an escort of my choosing," Talorc said.

Naoise and Drest cheered and slammed their goblets together, spilling mead across the wooden table.

The moon was full and splashed silvery light across the fortified port as it protruded grey into the ocean. Brei had slipped away, trading drunken banter for fresh air. He ambled along the rocky beach next to the fortress, inhaling the salty breeze. Waves rumbled and hissed as Brei sat, drawing his knees up to his chest. He ran his hands through the cold sand.

"Can I join you?" a voice in the dark asked. Brei turned. Talorc stepped across the sand, swaying with glazed eyes and a drowsy smile.

"Of course."

"It's beautiful, isn't it? The moon on the water like that." Talorc thumped down next to Brei and stretched his legs into the sand. "Sometimes I wonder what would happen if we could all see this, would we ever have cause to fight again?"

Brei wondered how many goblets of ale Talorc had drunk since Brei left the hall.

Talorc sighed and lay back against the sand. "Our ancient mothers and fathers lived peacefully under the moon and stars for so long, and I often think it must be because we have turned away from this sense of awe and gratitude for life itself that we kill each other for land and jewels."

Brei burst out laughing. "So much for wanting a saddle full of Roman heads and a bed full of their women!"

Talorc grinned through half-closed eyes. "Is it too much to want both?"

SEVENTEEN

Winter, 367 C.E., Caledon

Sorsha pushed her palms into her aching eyes. Yet another night had been spent with the Bandruwydds waiting for the clouds to disappear, so they could measure the stars. Serenn had taught Sorsha how to track the passage of time through the stars and the moon phases between the solstices and equinoxes. They counted the nights until Imbolc, the festival that fell between the winter solstice and the spring equinox. It celebrated the arrival of spring and the Goddess Brig. Serenn had explained to Sorsha that Imbolc was a time of hope in the despair of winter. But if the signs were not favourable, it was a time of great depression in the realisation that Brig would not lure the snow away early.

"It is a time to beg Brig to purify the herds during their winter confinement and that she ensure the healthy birth of the lambs on the farmsteads. It is a time to drink milk and ale," Serenn had said. "And the Gods always call for sacrifice."

Druwydds from Rīgonīn were soon to arrive in anticipation of the festival, and people from the small villages and farmsteads around Caledon gradually poured into Caercaled.

"We are going to the river," Serenn said.

Sorsha's eyeballs seemed to drop into her sockets, and she wondered how dark the underneath of her eyes must be. Serenn looked immaculate, no matter how little sleep she had. Her hair was always piled atop her head, held back from her forehead with pins made of bone, and her eyelids forever blackened with charcoal, such that Sorsha got the impression Serenn wished to be both feared and adored.

Sorsha yawned. "Why?"

"Because I require more signs."

Sorsha had spent weeks watching for any animal that might be more active, and she had scoured every tree in the Sacred Forest for buds. "But I've told you all the signs."

Eluned arched an eyebrow. "That the squirrels are active? That is not enough. The snow still stays on the ground, and the oak is yet to bud. Have you seen the boxing hares yet?"

"No."

Sorsha glared at Eluned's back as they walked through the empty, winding lanes. Plumes of smoke rose from the roundhouses as they passed, and a large rooster stood on the thatched roof of Gwyddion's workshop, arching its head to the sky and screeching. They continued walking through the muddy lanes of Caercaled, heading for the empty centre circle.

"The festival will take place here on the night of the next full moon, six waxing moons after tonight," Arian whispered to Sorsha, her head bobbing up and down as she struggled to limp at the same pace.

"How can it hold everyone in Caercaled, let alone the surrounding farmsteads?"

"They flow out into the streets." She smiled. "It's a mess."

Serenn clicked her tongue, turning on them with eyes like slits. "Not a mess for the Bandruwydds."

Arian smirked as they passed through the Western Gate, which was guarded by a small garrison of warriors.

At the riverbank, a white-haired man waited for them, wrapped in furs. His pale blue eyes shone like a rabid wolf, and he motioned for them to follow him. "It's this way." Sorsha stared at Serenn's straight back as they followed him along the river. The old man stopped and pointed to a rocky outcrop five yards into the river. "It's out there."

Serenn squinted at the icy water. "Are you sure?"

"Yes, we hit the rocks two days ago, and I got a good look down there for a moment before we freed the boat. It was lucky we didn't sink!"

Serenn turned to her apprentices. "Do you have the rope?"

Arian nodded, the hint of colour disappearing from her pale cheeks.

The old man gaped. "You're not going in there, are you? It's terribly cold, you'll die soon as you get back to the shore."

Serenn smiled. "The Goddess of the River will protect us."

He dropped his head. "Of course. Praise the Gods."

Arian had removed her furs and stood in a black woollen tunic on the bank. Sorsha's gaze flicked to the stump strapped to the end of her leg as Eluned tied a rope around Arian's thin waist. They waited on the riverbank while Arian limped one hundred yards upriver. Pausing for a moment at the river's edge, she limped as fast as she could and dived into the raging water. The river hurled her downstream, towards them, and into the path of the rocks. Fighting against the powerful current, Arian swam out to the middle of the river, and within a few seconds she smashed into the outcrop. Water tore against her back as she clung onto the rocks.

"It's on the left side, closest to the southern bank!" the old man yelled.

Arian leaned under the water. "It's stuck!" She gasped.

Serenn closed her eyes and chanted prayers to the Gods, and Eluned joined in. "*Dour, dobur-ban-doiuis, arbeissi!*" ("Water, dark water Goddess, have mercy!")

Arian kept trying to pull something up off the rock, but it seemed the prayers to the dark water Goddess were not working.

"Shall I fetch her a stick or something?" Sorsha asked, as she scanned the forested bank.

"I've got it!" Arian screamed, holding a black rock high above her head.

"Pull her in," Serenn yelled.

Eluned and the old man heaved the rope. Water sprayed onto the riverbank as the rope twirled and slacked with each heave. As they pulled, the water gushed over Arian and pushed her under the current. Sorsha snatched up the rope behind Eluned and pulled until her hands burned. When she finally hit the bank, Serenn wrenched Sorsha off the rope and pushed her towards Arian. Sorsha fell to her knees in the icy water and dragged Arian onto dry ground, hoping it was not too late. Arian clutched the black rock with blueish-grey hands, her body convulsing. With one arm cradling Arian upright, Sorsha pressed with her free hand into Arian's chest until she ceased trembling.

"Is it better?" Sorsha whispered, her eyes darting back and forth across Arian's pale face, searching for a sign she was not about to die.

A shaking arm extended upwards, and Arian handed Serenn the rock. "I'm okay."

Eluned tossed a fur cape around Arian's shoulders and walked back to Serenn's side to gaze at the rock.

"What is it?" Sorsha asked as she pulled the fur cape snug around Arian's shoulders and held her.

"We shall see," Serenn whispered, pulling a dagger from her waist. The oval-shaped rock was the size of Serenn's hand, and she prised it open with the knife and looked inside. She turned it around to show Arian and Sorsha. Nestled on a grey bed of mushy slime lay a shining white pearl.

"We will have an early spring," Serenn beamed. "The Gods have blessed us with a gift, as a sign of the harvests to come."

"So, there will be a sacrifice at Imbolc?" Sorsha asked.

Serenn rubbed the pearl between her thumb and index finger. "Oh yes." Her voice lowered. "We must praise Brig for delivering us from this winter."

Eluned and Serenn hurried back towards Caercaled, leaving without a backwards glance for Arian. Sorsha helped Arian to stand. "Why did Serenn make you do that? Surely Eluned could have?"

Arian shook her head. "Eluned is the daughter of the great King Uradech. Serenn would not risk her life. They are kin."

"But she doesn't mind risking yours."

Arian smiled, her ghostly beauty shining despite the drenched mop of blonde hair plastered to her cheeks. "Let's head back, I'm exhausted."

Tall pines by the river's edge creaked in the rising wind as Arian hobbled on her sodden stump. Sorsha reached out for her hand as she slipped for the second time.

"It's okay." Arian limped up the icy bank and onto the firmer path that snaked around the river to the Western Gate.

"How do you put up with all this?" Sorsha asked as they trudged in the compacted snow along the path. "I'd be so bitter if I were you, but you just smile and say everything is fine."

Arian laughed. "But everything is fine. I'm lucky to have my life, and so lucky to have my apprenticeship. What is there to be bitter about?"

"It's some kind of dark magic to only see the good in life, Arian."

"Why don't you feel lucky? You have an unending number of lives ahead of you, think what you could achieve with all the knowledge you will accumulate throughout time?"

The path forked sharply west to their left and lazily east to their right. They took the path to the east without pausing, the land rising with gentle ease towards the Hill of Caledon.

"But my mother forced me to accept this Gift. It doesn't feel lucky when it is forced."

Arian stopped limping and stared at Sorsha. "I mean this with affection, Sorsha, but do you realise how whiny you sound? I was forced to feel lucky to be alive because I watched the flesh from my parents' bodies melt in the flames. Very few people are privileged enough to lead lives without sacrifice, to live a life without being forced to do something they would rather not."

"I..." Sorsha looked down, her eyes following paw prints in the snow that followed a pair of large boots.

"And if you're so angry about being forced to accept the Gift, why do you want to go back to your mother?"

"Because… It's complicated."

Arian reached out and held Sorsha's hand. "You're angry that you were torn from your old life, and you miss home? I get it. It's confusing because, despite everything, you love your mother and you know it would have been awful for her having you assassinated. But deep down I think you realise that the same compulsion that drives you to heal people can also drive a Healer to do anything the Gods want. It's the Gods you should be angry at, Sorsha, not your mother."

A tear crept from Sorsha's eye. "This place is horrible, it's so different from home. So cold. So harsh. I just want to find a way to make it work, to appease the Gods but live in the south, in Britannia."

Arian withdrew her hand and walked away. The crunching of her footsteps seemed so loud, and Sorsha's stomach sank as she watched the small lump of furs limp along the snowy path.

"Arian, I'm sorry!" Sorsha called, running to catch up.

"You don't need to apologise, Sorsha," Arian said without stopping. "I'm sure there will come a day when I'll see the good fortune in this too."

EIGHTEEN

Winter, 367 C.E., Vortriu

Brei waited in the stables with Rhuad, as Taran and Naoise prepared their horses for departure. He wanted to return to Anwen and the twins, but he had seen blue skies for the first time in many moons, and a guilty part of him would have preferred to stay longer.

"Prince Taran?"

Brei twisted towards the door. Dressed in a long, white, flowing tunic, the Eldar Druwydd stood in the stable entrance. Ever since he had refused to claim the throne of Caledon, Brei had the impression the Eldar Druwydd disliked him.

Taran bowed. "How may I help you?"

"Serenn, of the Bandruwydd order in Caercaled, has asked a favour of you."

Brei frowned and wondered why Serenn had not asked Taran herself before they left Caercaled.

"What does she want?"

"She needs a new Torc. There is one that is ready, but it is in Rīgonīn. Are you able to detour on your way home to transport it for her?"

Brei frowned. *Who is the Torc for?*

"Are you not coming down for Imbolc?" Taran asked.

The Eldar Druwydd smiled, his cheeks cracking. "I will spend

Imbolc in Rīgonīn. Some of the Druwydds will attend, but they left for Caercaled days before you arrived. It is a wonder you did not pass them, they stayed with King Alpin at Banntuce."

"We did not visit King Alpin. But of course, it would be an honour. May we escort you back to Rīgonīn? Are you travelling today?"

"Yes, that would be appreciated. I have planned it in the hope that you would say yes."

They set out for Rīgonīn, three warriors leading a pilgrimage of five Druwydds. It was a long day's ride from Caertarwos, and the journey took them south, away from the coast towards the mountains. During their breaks from the saddle, Taran and the Eldar Druwydd sat huddled together, talking in low voices. *What's he up to?* Brei knew his brother was not any more devoted to the Gods than he was.

Rīgonīn was a sacred, royal village, where religious and royal jewellery was made. It sat between the Kingdoms of Ce and Vortriu and was controlled by the Druwydds. The great fortress of Rīgbre, the "Hill of Kings", which flirted with ruin but had never been abandoned, guarded over the valley from the north of where Rīgonīn lay.

They approached the wooden palisade that encircled the tiny village of Rīgonīn after night had fallen. The wind picked up and the torches bolted to the palisade flickered as they approached. Brei, Taran, and Naoise stopped to allow the Druwydds to catch up before entering the sacred village.

A Druwydd, hooded and carrying a torch, pushed open a door from within the palisade and walked out to meet them. He gazed up at the warriors, still mounted, and lifting his torch high above his head, let the light fall on the faces of the Eldar Druwydd and his companions. The Druwydd bowed. "Princes, my lord Eldar Druwydd." He turned, and Brei followed the white robes inside the palisade towards the village.

They crossed an embankment and ditch that encircled a paltry collection of rectangular wooden buildings, long houses, and workshops. As they reached the inner circle, the light from the burning torch hovered across an enormous standing stone that guarded the way. Etched on the standing stone was the image of a large man, carrying an axe over his shoulder. His teeth were all fangs, and his nose protruded like a dagger. Brei shuddered, recognising the Axe of Sacrifice.

The Druwydd led them from the entry stone across into the village, where another standing stone met their arrival. Carved into the rock was the Kaelpie of Vortriu, a sea monster resembling a horse-seal. Above it was the Salmon of Ce.

They pulled their horses close to one of the longhouses and dismounted. Light from within shone through the wooden beams. Brei stretched and handed his reins to a young Druwydd in training. His bones ached, and he longed for a hot meal away from the wind. He cracked his neck and watched Taran assist the Eldar Druwydd to dismount. Brei's stomach tensed. Even after the boy had led Rhuad away, Brei remained in the howling wind and watched as Taran walked arm-in-arm with the Eldar Druwydd into the longhouse.

"Brei?" Naoise called from the doorway.

Brei followed Naoise into a lavish hall with a roaring fireplace in the middle. Along each side of the fire were long tables with low benches. Rīgonīn was a neutral sacred site and often played host to war treaties between the northern kingdoms.

Naoise waved Brei over to sit with younger Druwydds in training. Brei sat next to Naoise but watched Taran and the Eldar Druwydd in furtive conversation throughout the meal. He chewed on a leg of lamb, gnawing and sucking until there was nothing but smooth white bone.

"Brei?"

"What?" Brei said without looking at Naoise. Taran sniggered with the Druwydds across the table.

"Are you okay?"

Brei dropped the bone on his plate and turned to Naoise. "What do you think they have been talking about all day?"

"Taran and the Eldar Druwydd?"

"Yes."

"You haven't heard them?"

"Obviously not, Neesh."

Naoise lowered his voice. "It's the strangest thing if I heard right, but they've been talking mostly about Sorsha."

"Sorsha?"

"As far as I can gather, the Torc is for her."

"But she's not of noble blood from any bloodline I know of, is she?"

Naoise shrugged. "To be honest, I'm not that interested, so maybe ask Taran."

Brei grunted and turned back to look at Taran. He had gone. Brei scanned the long table, but Taran was nowhere to be seen. He reached for his goblet of wine and, as he clasped his hands around the metal, he felt arms from behind. Brei's goblet tumbled over as the arms gripped him around his neck. Wine spread across the table and dripped between the wooden slats onto his deerskin pants. The Eldar Druwydd smiled across the table, blurry, as if from a dream. The grip around Brei's neck was not tight. He turned his head and recognised the thick blond hair tied back into a bun.

"Taran?"

Taran released Brei, and sat on the bench next to him, facing away from the Druwydds. He looked tired but more peaceful and happier than he had for days.

"What's going on?" Brei asked.

Taran slapped Brei on the back. "The Gods are with us, brother."

"What do you mean?"

Wood creaked and Brei turned to see the Eldar Druwydd rise. The hall fell silent as the old man raised his left hand in the air. "It is the sixth night of the waxing moon, and there is mistletoe to harvest. We must make our offering to the Gods." He paused and pointed at a blond, pink-cheeked, young man. "Broichan, son of the old King Drest of Vortriu, has the honour of harvest tonight. My Princes of the Blood, you are welcome to join the Druwydds and observe the ritual."

"I want to watch." Taran smiled, the light from the fire lighting up his blue eyes. "Naoise? Brei?"

Naoise finished his ale in one gulp and leaned close to Brei and Taran. "I'm in. I've heard it's horrendous." He grinned and wiped the ale foam from his mouth.

Brei nodded and rose from the wooden bench. Only Princes of the Blood and kings were permitted to view the mistletoe-harvesting ritual. Even Bandruwydds could not watch. Brei had seen a mistletoe gathering once before, as a young child many winters ago. All he remembered about the ritual was an eery sense of unease. A feeling he had long since associated with Rīgonīn itself.

From the hall's entrance, the Eldar Druwydd smiled at the princes. Double wooden doors thrust open, and the white-robed Druwydds walked in single file into the night. Some were old men, like the Eldar Druwydd, with long, greying or white beards. Others were young boys in training, while some were in their prime, like Brei, Taran, and Naoise.

They followed the procession of Druwydds carrying flaming torches out of the village and towards the nearby woods. Brei recalled the Eldar Druwydd's words, "the sixth night of a waxing winter moon". He glanced at the sky. Clouds shrouded the moon, and Brei wondered how the Druwydds knew the moon was in the correct position for the ritual. *They could tell us anything, and we would all just smile and nod.*

As they entered the wood, the Druwydds chanted in deep, melodious voices. Brei's mouth twitched as he remembered an Imbolc festival from childhood. Taran had joked that the prerequisite for joining the Druwyddic orders was the possession of balls the size of a ram's.

They proceeded through the wood in single file to a grove of ancient oak trees, where nine Druwydds stood on a thin covering of fresh snow at the base of the largest oak tree, holding flaming torches and wearing robes of thin white linen that flapped and pulled against their knees in the howling wind. Brei swallowed as a young apprentice carried an axe with an overlong wooden handle to the Eldar Druwydd. *The Axe of*

Sacrifice. Brei glanced at Taran and Naoise, and the light from the torches flickered across Naoise's face. His eyes were wide, and he stood close to Taran.

Heavy hooves trampled through the wood behind them. Naoise jumped and reached for his sword, but Taran grabbed Naoise's wrist as they turned towards the noise. From the black forest, two grey-haired and bearded Druwydds each led a white bull into the grove. The princes stepped aside to let them pass. One bull snorted as they led it to the Eldar Druwydd. Taran draped his arm around Naoise's trembling shoulders. *I forget how young Neesh really is.*

The Druwydds steadied the bulls by their halters as they waited at the base of the oak tree. Holding the long Axe of Sacrifice, the Eldar Druwydd chanted. Broichan, fresh-faced and eager-eyed, leapt up and grasped the lowest branch of the ancient oak with both hands. He swung both legs up onto the branch and climbed to the highest branches. Guttural chanting filled the grove as Broichan ascended. The light of the torches was unable to pierce through the gloom at the top of the tree, and Brei wondered how Broichan would find the bright green balls of mistletoe. One flaming torch had dwindled so low against the ravages of the wind that it extinguished with a pop.

From the canopy of the oak tree, Broichan yelled "I've found it!"

The Eldar Druwydd nodded to three Druwydds who, handing their torches to the remaining six, stepped forwards. They unfurled a length of white linen and held it aloft at the base of the tree. The Eldar Druwydd raised the Axe of Sacrifice into the air and, with a whoosh, Broichan jumped from the tree. As the axe came down and sliced through the neck of the closest white bull, the boy thumped into the linen.

The bull brayed and sank to its knees. Brei clenched his jaw as blood spilt across the bull's white throat. The second bull grunted, wide-eyed, and struggled against its halter. Chanting continued as the Eldar Druwydd released the axe once more and sliced the throat of the remaining bull. It wailed and charged forwards a few steps before it tripped and crashed to the ground.

Dishevelled but unharmed, Broichan handed the Eldar Druwydd a sticky, bright green ball of intertwined plant sprouts with tiny white baubles. Closing his eyes, the Eldar Druwydd held the mistletoe ball high above his head, and the chanting stopped.

The second bull groaned and dropped limp onto its side. Its breathing laboured, rasping, and haggard, until its stomach heaved no more. Three Druwydds dragged the bull by the legs. Blood streaked across the snow in its wake, and they lay the bull next to its brother. Chanting once more, the Druwydds placed the white linen onto the blood pooling from the bulls' necks. White swiftly turned crimson until all threads were soaked and the bulls lay dead amongst the gnarled roots of the ancient oak tree.

NINETEEN

*G*ravel pressed into Sorsha's heels as she hunched beneath the low stone roof of a passageway, making her way towards a light flickering in a chamber. As she bent to pick up the crackling torch lying on the ground, the flame extinguished. Everything was black, and she could hear footsteps coming up the passageway towards her, growing louder and faster. Cold sweat dripped from her armpits and rolled down her arms. The footsteps entered the chamber, and an icy breath rasped against Sorsha's face.

Sorsha choked and opened her eyes. The hearth glowed in her room, splashing orange light around the walls. *It's just the nightmare again.* She tried to control her breathing, but she could still hear the footsteps, echoing in the stairwell, growing louder. Soon the steps were on the landing. The wooden floorboards creaked outside her door. *I wish I had a sword.* She pushed herself up off the bed. A soft knock, only just louder than the snapping fire, as though unsure it wanted admittance.

"Hello?" Sorsha called, retreating into the shadows that would emerge behind the door once opened.

The door to her room groaned open, and the orange glow of the fire fell across broad shoulders and blond hair.

"Taran?"

Unsheathing his sword, Taran turned towards her voice. "Sorsha?"

134

She moved into the light. "I wasn't sure who it was."

He pushed his sword back into the leather scabbard. "Did I wake you?"

"No, I'd just… So you're back from Caertarwos, then?"

He nodded.

"Did it go well?"

"Yes. We had to spend a night with the Druwydds at Rīgonīn, which delayed our return. Was everything okay while we were away?"

Sorsha pressed her lips together and nodded. The light of the fire shimmered across the hilt of Taran's sword, drawing her gaze to the leather scabbard. It was tooled with a spiralled knot design and capped at the end with a curved bronze chape with two glittering snakeheads on either side. "Would you teach me?" she asked.

"Teach you what?"

"To fight with a sword."

"Now?"

"No, but tomorrow maybe?"

"Fine." He shrugged. "Naoise's gone out to the tavern and I could do with a peaceful sleep for once. But I just wanted to check in now because I am on patrol early tomorrow and I'm not sure when I would have seen you." Taran yawned. "Goodnight, Sorsha."

Wind whistled through the thatched roof covering Serenn's chamber at the top of the tower. The dried herbs hanging from the rafters rustled. Flames under the decorated cauldron flickered, and grey steam tumbled up the chimney set into the wall. Eluned dozed in a chair by the hearth, her auburn head rolling and jerking. Seldom had Sorsha seen Eluned undertake anything close to the work justifying an apprenticeship. Instead she seemed consumed by the pursuit of relaxation in Serenn's absence, and dog-like sycophancy in her presence.

Twirling carved streamers danced and curved into knots across the lid of a small wooden box. Sorsha eased off the lid. It had perfect join-ery, and she plucked up a shrivelled leaf from inside the box. The green was fading, but she recognised the slender foliage that came to a point. "This is Nerion?"

Arian placed the pestle she was using to grind herbs in a stone mortar on the bench and turned to inspect the leaf in Sorsha's hand. "The merchants call it Nerion, yes. We call it Ankudol."

Death leaf. "What do you use it for?"

"Serenn uses it to communicate with the Gods."

Sorsha pressed the leaf back into the box. "We had a Nerion bush back home. It had the most beautiful pink flowers. What are you making?"

"A restorative to mix in with wine."

Sorsha watched Arian press the pestle into the leaves. The sound of stone crunching against stone echoed around the breezy chamber.

"So, are you leaving us?" Arian whispered.

Sorsha kept her eyes on the pulverised leaves. "I've not got permission from Taran, so no."

"Have you asked him?"

"No, I've barely spoken to him, and I wouldn't know what to–"

"Sorsha?"

Both Arian and Sorsha jumped and twisted towards the doorway. Elfinn, the king's son, stood in the stone archway, puppy-eyed and smiling. "Sorry to disturb. May I speak with you, Sorsha?"

She wiped her hands on her tunic. "Yes."

Eluned rose from the chair by the fire and grabbed Sorsha's hand. "Serenn needs your help here," she hissed.

"I will come back to help after," Sorsha said. She searched Arian's face for a clue as to Eluned's erratic behaviour, but her pale cheeks were flushed, and the crushed leaves seemed to occupy her gaze.

Sorsha brushed Eluned's hand away and walked across the cham-ber to join Elfinn in the flickering glow of the landing. "What is it?"

Elfinn had brown hair, like his father, and the same sad, wide eyes. "My father said you helped him last time?"

Sorsha nodded and followed him to the gloomy staircase and down to the king's room. Inside, the king's floor was lavishly decorated. Tapestries of curling knots and beasts in greens, reds, and blues hung from the stone walls, and the fire in the hearth burned as large as the one in the hall below. King Gartnait knelt by the fire, grey hair plastered to his bone-white forehead, and his cheeks pinched red with fever.

"King Gartnait, is it your stomach?" Sorsha asked as she knelt in front of him.

He groaned.

She slid her hands into the gap between his stomach and his knees. "May I, my lord?"

He screamed as she pressed her hand against his tensed stomach. Heat tingled from her heart, down her arms and into her palms. Gartnait's muscles relaxed underneath her hands, and he sat up, gasping. She frowned. The urgency to heal him had not yet left her. She pressed her palms into his forehead, his chest, over his lungs and his heart. Finally, his breathing returned to normal, and she looked up at Elfinn and smiled. Elfinn bent down and helped his father over to the enormous bed, resplendent with too many pillows for one man to use.

"Thank you," Elfinn said, returning to Sorsha by the fire.

"I don't understand how he can be unwell so soon?"

"He's not been well all winter," Elfinn said, his hazel-green eyes flicking to his father lying in his bed of feather pillows. "Without you, he would have died by now."

"Without the Gods. It is their work, not mine."

Fabric rustled as Elfinn stepped closer and he clasped her hands. "Do you know why you have come to us? Is it for my father? To save him?"

"I don't know why, Elfinn, I'm sorry. I wish I knew."

Elfinn nodded and released her hands. "Either way, I am grateful you're here."

"Thank you, Elfinn," she said and left the chamber. After closing the door, Sorsha paused on the landing, resting her hand against the cool stone. *Why is he so sick again? Does my power only work temporarily?*

Footsteps shuffled from the darkness of the staircase. Sorsha jumped and stared into the shadows, hoping it was not Anwen. Despite sleeping below her floor, Sorsha had avoided Anwen throughout the winter.

"What were you doing?" Taran whispered, stepping into the light of the flaming torch bolted onto the landing wall.

"The king was ill… I was visiting him."

Taran's chin rose as he looked over her head towards the closed door of the king's chamber. "I was looking for you. You said you wanted me to teach you to use a sword?" He motioned with his hand towards the lower stairs. She hesitated and scanned his stern face. *Perhaps he's guessed I'm a Healer.*

The light from the torch sparkled in his eyes, and he smiled. Sorsha dropped her gaze and walked down the staircase, with Taran following behind, until they stepped into the veiled light of the morning sun that filtered through the clouds.

"Hello, Beli," Sorsha said to the black mastiff. The dog sat up in the recessed alcove at the entrance of the tower and wagged his tail.

"Let's go to the stables," Taran said. She followed him down the slope, and he turned to her as he pushed opened the stable door. "The snow is too thick in the forest, and I assume you don't want a crowd?"

"Won't it bother the horses?"

"If it does, then they'll need to get used to it. Warhorses hear a lot worse in battle." He unsheathed his sword and motioned for her to stand next to him in the main aisle of the straw-covered stables. "Hold it," he said, handing Sorsha his sword.

The top of the hilt split into two pieces and curved upwards on either side. The effect was replicated in reverse at the base of the hilt before the polished iron blade.

"Hold the blade out with just one hand and keep it there."

It was not heavy, less than a bucket of water. But within a minute, the muscles in her arm and shoulder tensed, until her arm shook. Taran smiled and told her to lower her arm. "Now the other side, you need to get used to the weight before I can teach you to wield it."

Taran watched her again until her arm shook and asked her to lower it.

"Shall we go again?" she asked and held out the sword once more.

Taran raised his eyebrows. "You're strong for a woman."

"But women are not trained, are they? Just boys?"

Taran nodded. "I've been training since the time I had seen three winters."

"How old were you when you fought your first battle?"

"Ah…" He glanced at the straw strewn over the stable's floor. "It's been maybe five or six summers since the Romans attacked so I must have seen fourteen or fifteen seasons."

"I'm sorry to remind you of it."

His eyes darted to her face. "You didn't remind me of it. It's always in my mind."

She twirled the sword in her hand, and Taran folded his arms across his chest as he watched her. "What now?" she asked.

Taran picked up a stick that was leaning against the wooden pen. "Are you left-handed?"

Sorsha nodded.

"Push your left hand up to the guard… the metal bit that juts out before the blade. And put your right hand on the very end of the hilt. Yes, like that."

Taran mimicked the position on the stick he held.

He positioned his body side-on to her, and he stepped his left leg out and bent it as he swung the stick from his right shoulder. "The power all comes from your legs. Always swing from the opposite shoulder to where your leg is pointing, and your toes should point at your target."

Sorsha twisted her hips, stood side on, stepped out on her right leg and swung the sword from her left shoulder.

Taran nodded. "Pretty good, actually. Try that a few times, swinging from each side."

By the time Sorsha's stomach growled for lunch, she felt she understood the basics of stance. "Can I try hitting your stick?"

"We're not really there yet, but sure, one hit and then lunch. I'm starving."

Sorsha positioned herself into the attacking stance. Taran mirrored her and, stepping forwards, swung his stick. Sorsha swung the sword from behind her left ear and jumped forwards onto her right foot, slicing Taran's stick in two.

Taran dropped the broken pieces on the ground and grinned. "Lunch."

Sorsha handed Taran his sword, and he pushed it into his leather scabbard.

"You'll be too sore to do this tomorrow. Your arms and shoulders will ache when you wake up."

"But if I am not, will you teach me more tomorrow?"

"Sure, but I promise you'll be terrible sore tomorrow."

As she followed him back to the tower, she rubbed her hands over her wrists, arms, and shoulders, feeling heat flow from her heart and into her muscles.

After her rounds with the Bandruwydds, where she had healed the broken arm of the baker's daughter, Sorsha searched the tower for Taran. She found him walking to the stables. "Are you going for a ride?"

"Yes," he grunted, without looking at her.

"Can I join you?"

He glanced at her over his shoulder. "If you want."

They descended through the Sacred Forest and spiralled down the tiered city until they cantered out through the Western Gate. Sorsha rode on Ri, while Taran had borrowed Dylan's fiery chestnut horse, Laxsaro, "Flames". The wind roared in her ears and her black braid streamed behind her. She wanted to spread her arms and fly. Ri seemed to sense her elation and sprang into a gallop.

Sorsha sped past Taran, and she soon forgot him. The icy lake shimmered as tiny rays of low-lying winter sun peaked through the clouds, revealing distant, snow-covered mountains. Ri slowed as they approached the lake's edge, and Laxsaro's hooves crunched through the snow behind her.

"I've never seen anything so beautiful," Sorsha whispered and turned to smile at Taran.

He leaned forwards in the saddle and followed her gaze. "They don't have mountains where you're from?"

"Not like this. We have grassy hills and forests, but nothing like this. I miss home so much, but when the mist clears from the lake…it sort of takes my breath away. I could look at this all day."

"It will be summer eventually, and the clouds will haunt us less. Then you'll see the mountains almost every day."

She dropped her gaze to the brown leather saddle and fumbled with the reins.

"But that's not what you want?" His voice was gentle, but his eyes narrowed.

"No… I want to find my mother."

Taran shifted in the saddle. "And where is your mother?"

"In the Kingdom of Gwoddodin, at a village close to the Great Wall," Sorsha said, reciting a line she often practised in her mind as she fell asleep.

"And you want me to take you there?"

"You don't have to, but if I had a horse, could you tell me the way?"

He shook his head. "You know I will have to go with you. If you can wait until after Imbolc, for the thaw, then we can go. It will be too treacherous to travel until then."

"How long will that be?"

Taran turned Laxsaro's head and clicked. "Perhaps a moon… Yes, at least a moon."

"How long does it take to get to the Great Wall?" Sorsha squeezed Ri's sides with her ankles and steered the reins to follow.

"Not long, a day or so if the wind is right." Laxsaro quickened his pace into a canter.

"The wind?"

Taran glanced back at her. "We'll travel by boat."

TWENTY

Winter, 367 C.E., Caledon

The frosted needles of a fir tree grazed Brei's cheek as he stalked through the forest to the north of Caercaled. At his side, Dylan panted clouds of mist into the dawn air. Clutching a bow and arrow, they walked under the dense forest, keeping the sound of the river close on their left side. Brei noticed a line of tracks in the icy ground and stopped. *Wolves.* He pushed his grey hood off his face and scanned the forest for movement. A twig snapped behind him and he spun around, raising his nocked arrow.

"Sorry, Brei!" Dylan squealed, dropping the stick he had broken in two. "It's just so boring."

Brei lowered the arrow and rolled his eyes. "You're as bad as your brother. And I thought you wanted to beat him?"

"I do!" Dylan's cheeks reddened. "Naoise has been such an arsehole to me lately."

"Shh!" Brei grabbed Dylan's shoulder. "If you want to win, you need to shut up."

They continued in silence, until they came to the clearing Brei had been looking for. "Sit down," he said, pointing to a pine fallen in a storm long ago. He crouched behind the weathered log and peered into the clearing. Mist hovered above the river and drifted up the riverbank, sloping into the clearing. They could see up into the forest for a few yards before the grey trees disappeared into the fog.

"What do we do now?" Dylan whispered, brushing his tumbling black hair off his sweaty brow.

Brei settled into a cross-legged position and leant his bow on the log in front of him. "We wait."

Clouds of red peeled across the sky and soon vanished into the pale light of morning.

"Brei?"

"Mmm?"

"How come you took Neesh to Caertarwos but not me?"

Brei kept his eyes on the clearing. "I didn't take Naoise. He just came. You know how he is."

"Do you think the kings will agree to Taran's plan?"

Brei tore his eyes away from the clearing. "Taran's plan?"

"Yeah, you know, to raid below the Great Wall."

Brei brushed the white swan feathers of his arrow back and forth. "I don't know."

"Do you think I'd be able to fight if they say yes? I keep dreaming about it, what it will be like. I'm so excited. What's it like, Brei?"

Brei turned back to the clearing and watched a squirrel leap between the branches of two oak trees and disappear into a hollow. "What's what like?"

"You know…killing."

Brei glanced at Dylan. He knew Dylan was the age Taran had been when the Romans had attacked Caercaled, and yet it seemed impossible. Taran had already been a warrior, training every day in combat and sitting at the hearth of the king's floor each night listening to Gartnait and King Uradech discussing politics and trade.

"I don't know, lad. You sort of…you become all eyes and arms." Brei turned back to the clearing. "It's why you need to be blooded. I can't explain what it feels like."

"Well, what does it feel like to stab someone?"

"Like butchering a kill."

"I haven't—"

"Shh!"

A shadow moved through the mist along the edge of the clearing, heading for the river.

"Nock your arrow slowly," Brei whispered, without taking his eyes from the shadow.

The pale glow of morning fell across the velvet point of an antler. As the stag moved further into the light, Brei counted six points on each side. The red stag arched its muscled neck and sniffed the air before it dipped its head down to the river.

"Now," Brei whispered.

The bowstring creaked as Dylan stood up from behind the log. Dylan let loose the arrow, and it spun over the stag's back. "Fuck!" he hissed as the stag leapt into the air and fled across the clearing.

Brei swung around and pulled back on his bowstring and released his arrow just in front of the stag's path. The deer ran into the line Brei had imagined it would take and the arrow buried into its neck. Groaning, the stag thudded into the ground head-first. Ravens cawed and took to the air.

"Brei!" Dylan screamed as he jumped over the log and ran for the carcass. "Brei! That was amazing!"

Brei stepped over the log and followed Dylan, who grasped the antlers and beamed up at him. "I can't believe you did that. Cernunnos has blessed you."

Brei crouched by the stag's head, and the deer drew a haggard breath. He pulled his antler handle dagger from his waist and handed it to Dylan. "Put it out of its misery."

Dylan's eyes widened. "How?"

"Its heart is just under its front leg."

Dylan looked at the stag but did not move.

"You don't have to," Brei murmured.

Shaking, Dylan handed back the dagger. Brei plunged it up under the stag's front leg, and it coughed, drawing its last breath with its tongue hanging out. The colour in Dylan's plump cheeks vanished, and he looked up at Brei with a sheen across his eyes.

Brei put his hand on Dylan's shoulder and smiled. "Go get the horses, lad. And then we can be home in time for lunch."

As he watched Dylan sprint into the forest, Brei ran his hand through the stag's red coat, and imagined a new pair of pants Anwen might make for him. While he waited for Dylan to return, he rolled the stag onto its back. He cut from the pelvic bone to breastbone and removed the entrails, being careful not to damage the hide. On each leg he sliced open the skin from hoof to knee and twisted and hacked off the leg. He bundled the legs together, ready to tie onto one of the horses. Finally, he rolled the carcass over and splayed the abdominal cavity open to drain the blood.

Dylan soon led Rhuad and Laxsaro into the clearing as Brei wiped his bloodied dagger through a handful of icy leaves. Dylan glanced at the entrails, swimming in a pool of red.

"Thought I'd spare you that part," Brei smiled. "But next hunt you must at least watch. When I was your age, I could field-dress a deer with my eyes closed."

Dylan nodded, his cheeks blanching once more. "But you had your father and King Uradech to teach you... My father lives in Ulster, and King Gartnait has no interest in me."

Brei considered the boy and grunted. "This is going to be a big job," Brei gestured to the carcass. "I've tried my best to lighten it up, but he's a big boy. Remember to bend with your knees and don't twist and lift, or you'll hurt yourself."

Heaving and lifting, Brei and Dylan managed to get the carcass strapped onto Rhuad. The stag's antlered head fell limp against Rhuad's stomach, and lines of blood streamed down his back. Brei tied the bundle of legs to Laxsaro's saddle, and they led their horses from the clearing.

"Do you think Taran will be jealous you won?" Dylan asked as they headed south along the forested river towards the Northern Gate.

Brei shrugged. "I don't think Taran bothers much with jealousy. If there's something he wants, he devotes himself to achieving it. Jealousy is for men who can't commit to what they want."

"Are you never jealous of Taran?"

Brei glanced up at the bony fingers of oak branches beneath the pale sky. "If I am, it's my own fault."

As they approached the garrison at the Northern Gate, the warriors on guard cheered.

"Brei's got a six-pointer!" Owain yelled, slapping Brei on the back.

Brei smiled. "He's a big buck, isn't he?"

Cináed joined them and lifted the hind leg of the stag. "Champion's portion, Brei!"

Brei's cheeks burned, and he glanced back at Dylan. The boy was silent, and he stood away from the men, stroking Laxsaro. "We've got to get this up for butchering before it spoils," Brei said. He clicked to Rhuad and led him through the Northern Gate, suffering further slaps on the back until they were clear of the garrison. Dylan trailed behind as they took the steep winding path to the tower.

"I wish I'd shot the stag," Dylan said, barely audible over the sound of the horses' hooves clopping on the rocky path.

Brei looked at him. "Plenty more hunts to beat Neesh at, lad."

"I'd never forget the look on Naoise's face if I ever got the champion's portion at the feast… It was such a good shot, Brei."

Brei nodded and turned back to face the road as it wound up the Hill of Caledon. They led their horses to the stables. Just as servants were helping them to pull the stag off Rhuad's back, Naoise and Taran returned with a young, three-pointed buck slung over the back of Naoise's horse.

"Is that *the* six-pointer?" Naoise yelled.

Taran lifted the small buck off his horse and draped it over his broad shoulders. "Nice work, Brei!" Taran grinned, reaching both arms back and supporting the deer's head and hind legs with his hands.

Brei cleared his throat and slapped Dylan on the back. "No, Dylan shot it."

Naoise raised his eyebrows. "Really?"

Brei looked down at Dylan and smiled at the boy.

"I won!" Dylan said, smiling from ear to ear.

The stag roasted over an enormous fire in the great hall of the tower. Night had fallen, and the hunters gathered to celebrate the hero of the kill and to feast. A servant girl sliced off a venison leg, wrapped the bone in a length of cloth, and handed it to King Gartnait. He smiled as he carried the massive piece to the table. "The champion's portion!" Naoise, Taran, Brei, and Elfinn cheered as Gartnait placed the leg in front of Dylan.

Naoise and Dylan's sister, Aífe, leant across the table and said "Well done, Dyl!" Aífe had fiery red hair that fell about her heart-shaped face in ringlets. Brei sat opposite her, with Anwen and his daughters. Owain, Cináed, and Gruffydd, senior warriors with distant noble blood joined them in celebrating Dylan's triumph. Taran sat between Naoise and Elfinn, who were already well into their cups.

The servants placed glossy red plates before them, piled high with venison. Wine and mead flowed in all their goblets. As they ate and drank, Owain, Gruffydd, and Cináed made Dylan recount the kill once more. Dylan told the story with vigour, as though he and Brei had switched places, and his hunting prowess grew more impressive with each rendition.

"I still can't believe you missed the shot, Brei. I've never seen you miss a target before," Taran yelled across the table.

Brei shrugged and winked as he caught Dylan's eye. Naoise shov-elled a handful of meat into his mouth with his hands and stood up. "Dyl! Dyl, I am proud of you. Come, let me congratulate you."

Dylan jumped off the bench and strode around the table to embrace his brother. With their black-haired heads pressed together, it was impossible not to see the influence of their father, the youngest son of the King of Ulster. Naoise pushed Dylan back and stared at him. Holding the boy by both shoulders, he belched into his face. Dylan squirmed and tried to get away, but Naoise held him still for the duration of what Brei thought might have been the longest belch he had ever heard. The hall erupted into laughter, and tears streamed down Taran's cheeks. Even Gartnait laughed, in a way Brei had not seen him do since the last summer before he fell ill. Dylan traipsed, red-cheeked, past Brei and seemed to head for the door.

"Just ignore him, Dylan," Brei said, reaching out for Dylan's hand. The boy snatched his arm away and marched outside as Naoise and Taran howled. Beli jumped onto him, and Dylan dropped onto his knees and patted the dog. Brei turned back as Aífe and Elfinn collapsed on the table, laughing.

Ceridwen tugged at Brei's sleeve. "Can I play with Beli too, Papa?" With her blonde hair and blue eyes, she looked just like his mother, Derelei. Brei bent and kissed his daughter on the forehead. "Don't go further than the entrance." Ceridwen smiled and skipped out into the moonlight. She stopped in front of Dylan. Brei watched her speaking. He could not hear what she said, but eventually Dylan smiled. She sat next to Dylan, and Beli rolled onto his back, and together they scratched his belly and laughed.

Brei turned back to the feast. Naoise and Taran were now rolling up their sleeves, and Naoise slammed his elbow onto the table and waited for Taran to grasp his hand. Taran finished rolling up his tunic over his swollen bicep, and he flexed as he reached out for Naoise's hand.

Owain whispered to Cináed and passed something small. Elfinn glanced at his father before he also pressed something into Cináed's hand.

Gartnait was deep in conversation with Aífe and Gruffydd and seemed not to notice until his nephews started the arm wrestle.

"Come on, Taran!" Owain and Elfinn yelled, and Aífe ran over to watch.

Gartnait spun around as Taran slammed Naoise's arm into the table. "Boys! You are not betting in my hall, are you?"

"No, Father. We'd never." Elfinn stepped forwards and smiled at the king, while holding his hand out behind his back and accepting something from Cináed.

Brei rolled his eyes and turned back to the entrance to look for Ceridwen. Hooded in black cloaks, Serenn and her apprentices stood in the moonlight. Sorsha knelt next to Beli and patted his ears as she spoke to Dylan and Ceridwen. As if sensing his eyes, Sorsha glanced at Brei and rose. Her eyes flicked past his head and penetrated the room. Brei glanced behind him and saw Taran staring at her. When Brei turned back, the black cloaks of the Bandruwydds shimmered under the moonlight as they walked towards the ramparts and descended into the Sacred Forest.

Anwen stood up and called Ceridwen to her. Clutching Nia and Ceridwen's hands, she led them from the hall and up the staircase. Brei sighed and wondered if he should finish his goblet before joining her.

As he made up his mind to follow Anwen, he glanced again at Taran. He was staring at the table and seemed not to notice Naoise elbowing him for attention as he arm-wrestled Cináed. Brei slid along the bench until he was opposite Taran. "Everything okay?"

Taran opened his mouth, but Naoise bumped him and grunted, heaving against Cináed.

Brei slid further along the table, and Taran followed.

"She wants to leave," Taran murmured.

"Sorsha?"

Taran nodded. "I've spoken to the merchants anchored in Caerd-wabonna, and there's a boat that will take us to Caeredyn."

Brei raised his eyebrows. "Caeredyn?"

"Yes, but I'll take her overland through Gwoddodin to her village. She says it's near the Great Wall."

Brei leaned forwards. "Gwoddodin are close allies with the Romans."

"If you're going to suggest she's a spy, I'll–"

"No, of course not." Brei frowned. "Just be careful. Are you taking her back for good?"

Taran did not raise his head. "Maybe. Yes."

"She doesn't belong here, Taran."

Taran jerked his head up. "Serenn wants Sorsha returned to Caledon."

"Why?"

"You only care because Anwen is still cut up about her." He sighed and ran his hand through his hair. "I'm sorry that she is, Brei. Honestly, I am. What the Romans did to her… But it has nothing to do with Sorsha, and you know it. And the thing is, I want Sorsha to stay here too."

Brei frowned. "I didn't realise you liked her. I thought you were going to find a princess somewhere, to father future kings with?"

"I don't. And I am. I just…" He drummed his knuckles on the table. "Serenn wants her here, so I want that too." Taran stood and walked from the hall.

TWENTY-ONE

Winter, 367 C.E., Caledon

orsha tiptoed, hunched over, through a narrow stone passageway. At the end of the passage, she reached a chamber, and on each of its three walls were cavities with cleaned, exposed bones and skulls laid out on stone basins. There was no sound but that of a wooden torch lying on the ground. With her finger, she traced one of the circular carvings on the wall. A cold drought blew down the passageway, and the torch popped and extinguished, plunging the chamber into darkness. Footsteps echoed along the passage and then entered the chamber and stopped.

"Do you know what happens to kings who fail their people?" a woman's voice asked from the shadows.

Sorsha's skin prickled as more frigid air circulated through the chamber. "They are killed three times," she heard herself answer, but her voice sounded muffled, as though she were watching a memory.

"And then what happens?" the voice whispered in a shrill pitch.

"They are preserved in a bog, unable to pass into Tirscath. They are shamed for all eternity."

As Sorsha spoke, the footsteps scraped in the dirt towards her.

"And what will happen if you fail?"

The voice was in front of her, and stale breath wafted against her face. Sorsha tried to move her legs, but they were numb. Icy fingers closed around her neck, and thumbs pushed into her throat. Sorsha tried to scream, but *against the force of the thumbs, she only coughed. There was a loud crack, and the torch reignited, lighting up the face of her assailant. Jet black hair framed a pale face, and large eyes the colour of emeralds glared at her. Sorsha opened her eyes into the darkness and screamed, and this time it echoed around her.*

"Sorsha?"

Hands groped at her, catching her wrists, and she screamed once more. *Am I destined to join the pile of bones in the chamber?*

"Sorsha, it's me, Taran. Stop screaming or you'll wake the entire floor." He pulled her into his chest, crumpling her arms against herself.

"Taran?" She trembled, unable to stop herself from shaking. Tears clung to her cheeks.

Taran pushed her upright and studied her. "What happened?" Long blond hair cascaded over his muscled arms, and at his chin his hair kinked as though it had been tied back for too long.

"She was killing me." Sorsha rasped in between shallow breaths.

"Who?"

"The woman. She had black hair and eyes like my mother's."

He wiped her cheeks with his thumb and smoothed the hair back from her sweaty face.

"It felt so real," she continued, as the assassin's face lingered in her mind.

Taran remained silent and motioned for her to lie on the pillow.

"I didn't want to die," she said as she lay back and turned her face towards the fire. "But I was being punished for failing to do something... I'm not sure what." She turned to look up at him. "I know it doesn't make any sense, but...it means something, and I wish I could ask my mother."

"Not Serenn?"

"Maybe," she said, gazing into the flames again.

Sleep had almost reclaimed her when Taran cleared his throat. "I meant to tell you, a trading ship landed in Caerdwabonna a few days ago. When I am on patrol I will ask when they intend to depart and whether they can carry us to Gwoddodin."

Her throat contracted as though the hands still clasped around it, and she coughed.

"Are you cold?" He pulled a fur from her bedding over her legs and feet.

She shook her head. "What time is it?"

"Early. You should sleep some more."

"Is it Imbolc tonight?"

"Yes."

Sorsha pushed herself up. "Then I should get up. Serenn mentioned she needed me for something. Will you be patrolling the borders tonight?"

"No, I did last night. Tonight I get to enjoy the festival." He smiled, his white teeth flashing in the fire's glow.

She rolled her eyes. "Fun."

"It is fun. Will you come?"

"Like I said, Serenn needs me."

"Right… I'll leave you to it then."

As he closed the door to her room, she yawned and stared at the roof. A lone moth fluttered its wings and flew across the room before it circled back to its spot on the warm stone above the fire. There was a pull that kept her in the north. Whenever she saw a limping villager or a child with a scrape on its knee, she ached with a desire to ease their distress. But she knew that was something she could not help but feel. The Gift forced her to care and bolted her to Caledon like a torch against the wall, destined to flicker against its will until it withered, spent of body, its spirit fading to smoke.

The moth was joined by another, and Sorsha watched as they clung together above the flames. She had been single-minded in her ambition to leave Caledon, to be rid of the barbarians living between cold, damp walls and yet, as her plan crystallised before her, she thought of Arian. *Arian is not a barbarian.* Sorsha glanced at the foot of her bed, where moments ago Taran had sat. *And neither is he.*

Sorsha pressed her feet into the rough grain of the wooden floor, deciding that she would ask Serenn about her nightmare. She crept up the gloomy staircase and into the narrow, airy space of Serenn's floor.

The only light came from the fire under the shadows of the cauldron. Serenn sat on the chair by the fire and Eluned stood stirring the cauldron. Rows of dried herbs, dead animals, and a bright green ball with white flowers hung from the rafters of the roof. *Mistletoe.* Arian worked at a grey wooden bench, chopping dried leaves and sprinkling them into a stone bowl.

Serenn motioned to the empty chair by the hearth. The fire danced across her face, illuminating it and then throwing it into shadows. In the moments when her face was engulfed in shadow, only the whites of her eyes shone out from within the thick veil of black charcoal that covered Serenn's eyelids.

"You're up early. Do you want to know what I have planned for you for Imbolc?" Serenn asked, her voice croaking, and Sorsha wondered how long she had been sitting in the smokey room.

"No."

Serenn frowned.

"I mean, yes." Sorsha yawned. "But I also wanted to ask you about a dream I had."

"A dream?" Serenn leaned back and crossed her hands over her well-fed belly.

Sorsha relayed the nightmare. "It felt so real. As if her fingers really were against my throat."

"The woman said you had failed, did she say at what?"

"No."

"And the woman, do you think you know who she is?"

"No. But her eyes were like my mother's."

Serenn tilted her head to one side. "What colour eyes do *you* have?"

"Me? Ah, grey. Blue-grey, I think. I have not seen my reflection since I…"

Serenn nodded towards Arian. Her delicate hand hovered over wooden bowls of varying size, a grinding stone, and metal objects that

Sorsha could not quite make out, until she grasped the stem of a metal paddle. Limping across to the hearth, she handed it to Serenn. The side facing Sorsha was adorned with a swirling circular pattern.

Serenn leant forwards and passed the paddle to Sorsha. "Try not to be…alarmed."

Sorsha grasped the metal handle and turned the decorative side over. The green-eyed woman from her dream stared back from the polished silver. Sorsha sucked the air in through her teeth with a hiss and looked away. Arian removed the mirror from Sorsha's hand.

The whites of Serenn's eyes were startling against the black of her lids. "Did you see?"

"I saw."

Serenn leant back into her chair. "I can't help you with this, but there are others who can."

Stone crushed against stone, and Sorsha turned to see Arian back behind the wooden bench, grinding with a mortar and pestle. She poured water from a silver jug and mixed it with her fingers.

Sorsha turned back to Serenn. "Do you mean my mother? Taran said he will take me to her."

"Perhaps. But there are others. Other Healers that have been sent to the Ancient People of the north. But we can discuss this another time. Today we give thanks to Brig."

Eluned ladled the liquid she had been stirring in the cauldron into four goblets. She handed one first to Serenn, then two others to Sorsha and Arian. As Sorsha sipped the concoction of wine and herbs, Arian came to her with the bowl. Taking Sorsha's arm she painted it dark blue with her soft fingers.

When both arms were painted, Serenn rose from her chair. "Take your dress off." A sleepy cloud rolled across Sorsha's mind, and she obliged.

Arian continued painting until her entire body, except for a band on her right arm, was smeared in dark blue. Sorsha sipped the scalding wine as Eluned un-braided her hair and brushed it out. Serenn then stood in front of Sorsha and, chanting praise to the Goddess Brig, painted long swirling strokes on Sorsha's forehead, down her nose and right cheek. She moved to Arian, on whose face she drew lines that ran from her forehead, down her eyes, and onto her cheeks, and Eluned soon received the same pattern.

By the time Sorsha had drained her cup, her fingers tingled, and she swayed as she bent to place the goblet on the ground. Eluned caught Sorsha's arm and raised her, taking the goblet from her and refilling it.

Serenn smiled. "Good. Now sit."

Sorsha lowered herself back into the chair by the hearth. Her breathing was so slow she wondered if time was still working.

"I will introduce the Druwydds to you tonight." Serenn's voice rasped.

Sorsha nodded and wondered if she could crawl down the stairs back to her room to sleep.

"Drink."

Sorsha's eyes refocused at the sound of Serenn's command, and she sipped the fragrant, boiling liquid. It scorched her throat, but her tongue was already numb.

"But I don't want there to be any question as to where she belongs," Serenn was saying to Eluned. "Vortriu already have two, they do not need another!" Her charcoaled eyes rolled towards Sorsha. "Finish your drink."

Sorsha gulped.

Arian took the goblet from Sorsha and held onto her hand. Sorsha tried to smile, but her muscles felt numb and Arian's ethereal face moved in and out of focus. Through the haze, she had a vague awareness of Eluned hovering by her right arm, and that Serenn was whispering to her. Something scratched Sorsha's arm, all the way around her bicep. It tickled. She closed her eyes and her mind wandered happily through the vineyards and golden fields of barley on her parents' estate.

Arian shook Sorsha with gentle hands and poured water down her throat. Her tongue and mouth tasted peculiar, as though she had been eating sand from the river. The side of her face that had been closest to the fire was hot, and her head ached. She placed her hand against her temple until her eyes refocused, and she noticed an itchy pain in her right arm. She lifted her bicep. There was a thick band of black ink etched into her skin, and inside the band were two ovals on either side of a curved square. On the ovals were the flames of Belenus, the God of Light, and through the square that connected them was a bent arrow.

Sorsha's cheeks flushed. "What the fuck, Serenn?"

Serenn lowered her goblet to rest it on the arm of her chair. "Don't heal it. I needed you to be branded, and it was less stressful for all of us this way."

Sorsha scowled. "Less stressful for you."

"It's done now." Serenn shrugged.

Sorsha studied the tattoo. "So it is true, what the Romans say. This is why they call you the Picti."

Serenn frowned. "Picti?"

"It means 'Painted People' in their tongue, and it refers to all the people above the Ruined Wall."

"But there are many kingdoms above the Ruined Wall!" Eluned said. "And we are all very different. I'd hate to be confused with the Attacot or the Damnnones. They are not like us at all."

Sorsha shrugged. "They know you have differences, but to them you are all equally barbarians. So, what do you want me to do tonight?"

"A minor role, for the Druwydds."

"You want me to heal someone?"

"I want you to heal the innocent man."

"The innocent man? Will I know who that is?"

"No, but the Gods will."

"Fine." Sorsha yawned.

"Excellent. Now to finish dressing you." Serenn clapped her hands. "Stand up."

Sorsha rolled her eyes and stood. Adorning Arian and Eluned's usual black robes were large gold belts and a skirt of beads of jet and gold, and around their necks, a golden Torc was wrapped. Arian dressed Sorsha in matching robes and a similar skirt of gold and jet beads. Her robes were sleeveless and ended at her shoulders, ensuring her new tattoo was visible. Eluned hovered behind her and fitted a golden Torc around her neck. The metal was cold against her flushed skin.

Serenn stood in front of her and straightened the Torc so it rested against her clavicles. "I had Prince Taran bring this for you from Rīgonīn."

Eluned pushed a Torc bracelet onto Sorsha's arm. It wrapped around her left bicep and shimmered in the firelight. Serenn draped a circle chain of silver around her hair and hung from it the large pearl they had caught in the river so that it sat in the centre of her forehead.

On top of Serenn's head, Arian secured a leather cap, on which Eluned and Arian lowered a deer skull with massive antlers. They tied it under her chin, and Arian fanned out Serenn's dark blue braids to hide the rope that secured the headdress.

"Will you have more to drink?" Serenn nodded to Arian to pour her another cup of the intoxicating liquid.

Sorsha hesitated, but she accepted the goblet with a sigh. She sat by the fire with Arian and Eluned, and they drank in silence. By the time they had finished their second goblet, the sound of drumming soared into the chamber from the centre circle. As the drumming quickened to a violent pace, a melancholy horn blew, filling Sorsha with dread. But Serenn did not make any effort to move. For a long time, they waited, drinking four cups before Serenn roused them.

Sorsha followed the Bandruwydds from their chamber to descend into the spiralling gloom of the staircase. The sound of drums and cheers roared in her ears. Carvings of salmon, wolves, and bulls leapt out at Sorsha from the walls. As they passed the landing on each floor, shadows from Serenn's headress took on a life of their own, mutating and pulsing in opposite directions to their owner's movements.

When they emerged from the tower, night had fallen, and the stars shone around the shimmering full moon. A path had been lit through the Sacred Forest by warriors holding torches. Most of them were unfamiliar to Sorsha, and blue swirls covered their faces and golden Torcs adorned their necks. The king and Elfinn waited for Serenn to join them before they made their way to the festivities. The men wore only pants, even the king, and their chests were tattooed with a crescent atop a broken arrow. Encircling their biceps was the tattooed Snake of Caledon, and sitting below were massive bronze armbands. Other men dressed in long, flowing, white robes also waited for them. *Druwydds.*

At the edge of the Sacred Forest, Sorsha gazed down into the city, where a giant fire had been lit in the centre circle. Around it, dancing and cheering, were hundreds, perhaps thousands of people. The drums echoed, and the horn blew again, long and dismal.

Flickering torches continued to line their path along the main lane, where villagers had gathered to watch the procession. They had almost reached the centre circle when Sorsha noticed Deryn and Brin, standing as torchbearers. As the procession entered the circle, the crowd had parted to form a clear path to the massive bonfire in the middle. The beat of the drums grew faster. When they were close enough to feel the heat of the fire, she saw Brei. Shadows danced across his chiselled, angular face. His arms were painted, but his muscled chest was bare. Carved into it was a crescent with curled swirls inside it, and over the top of the crescent was a broken arrow bent in a "V" shape. Around his bicep was a black ink band and inside, an enormous snake curled across a bent arrow. Below the serpent he wore a bronze armband. His brown, wavy hair came to his collar bone atop which his golden Torc glistened. She held his gaze as she passed him, close enough to touch.

The faces of the gathered crowd seemed to swirl, and the paint on their faces pulsated. Taran stood by the fire, and the sparking orange flames appeared to leap behind him and lash at his face. His blond hair was still loose and sprawled down his back. Across his broad chest and muscled arms, he had the same tattoos as Brei. She looked down as she passed him.

The king, wearing a silver crown, climbed with Elfinn to a wooden throne on a raised platform to the left side of the fire. The Druwydds chanted as they entered the circle, making guttural, elongated sounds. It was difficult to focus on the crowd through the fog in her mind, but she could sense the anticipation. Sorsha followed Serenn to the fire and stood by her side.

Warriors dragged three bound and unpainted men into the circle as Serenn and the other Bandruwydds sang in a haunting wail. They sang about the winter, about the urgency for spring, and the end of the suffering. The men were brought before Sorsha and Serenn, and the Druwydds encircled them, their flowing white robes blocking the crowd. Two of the men stared at the ground. Their greying tunics were grubby and their skin blotched with dirt. The man in the middle gazed up at her, his wide eyes awash with tears. An insatiable urgency rose inside Sorsha to help him.

Raising a decorated dagger in the air, Serenn chanted to the Gods. Sorsha closed her eyes, and the roar of the crowd disappeared. When she opened her eyes, all she could see was the dagger. It glinted in the flames, held aloft in Serenn's claw-like hands. Serenn bent down and placed one hand on the head of the first bound man, and with the other she sliced along his throat with the shimmering dagger. The wound was deep red, but the blood seemed to hesitate, as if unwilling to abandon the protective embrace of the flesh. Serenn slashed at the throats of the other two men. Blood tumbled from the open wounds, spilling down all three necks. The man in the middle continued to stare at Sorsha while he choked, blood dribbling from the corners of his mouth.

The Druwydds formed a close circle around them, preventing the crowd from observing. Sorsha knelt as the drums roared. The blood pooled on the ground and crept towards her knees. Serenn nodded to Sorsha. "Individuals perish, but the Ancient People survive."

The drums stopped, and all Sorsha could hear was the low chanting of the Druwydds. Sorsha shuffled closer, her knees wet with blood, as she studied the men. Their gurgling breath caught in their throats as they were supported in a kneeling position by the Druwydds. She knew she could not save all of them. *This is the test.* Tingles rippled through her hands, itching to be put to work. *Individuals perish, but the Ancient People survive.*

Giving in to the pull, she placed the palms of her hands on the throat of the man in the middle. She swayed as heat formed in her chest and surged along her arms. The man spluttered, and his chest heaved as she withdrew her hands.

The heads of the other men hung limp over their necks and Sorsha watched as their sluggish bodies fell forwards. She was barely aware of the surrounding huddle when Arian carried a white cloth over to the surviving man and wiped the blood from his throat. A deep, white scar remained. The Druwydds stopped chanting and gathered next to the king, leaving Eluned and Arian to drag the bodies to the fire. Warriors soon assisted, seeming to notice how ineffective Arian was with her limp, and the bodies were thrown onto the pyre. The fire hissed as it accepted the offering. A warrior led the saved man away, the scar along his throat the only evidence that he had been so close to death.

Sorsha remained kneeling in the pool of blood. A strange smell, like roasting pig, wafted over her. She glanced over her shoulder at the corpses. The flames engulfed the bodies, throwing the scent of pork into the air.

Serenn raised her arms and cried. "There will soon be an end to winter!" The crowd cheered, and the drums resumed a rapid beat that drew people forwards to dance.

Sorsha stared at the ground, watching dancers reflected in the pooling red. The dancing bodies appeared monstrous, and the acrid pork stench of the corpses filled her lungs. A wave of nausea passed from her stomach into her chest as the dancers threw their torsos back and forth, jumping, swirling, and screeching.

"Are you okay?" Someone had their hands on her shoulders. She blinked. *Gwyddion.*

"Can you help me stand? I feel sick."

Gwyddion bent down and placed a hand on her elbow and lifted. Lines of blue and white marking his face blurred together and spun. She stumbled, fell to her knees, and vomited into the fire. Her vision cleared and seemed to zoom forwards into the flames, magnifying the corpses as tongues of fire licked their faces. The skin had charred, but the bodies remained intact. Incessant drumming and screeching swirled around her as she heaved once more. A strange sensation tickled her right hand, and she looked up to see it was resting in the fire. It was numb. The flames lashed her, the skin was melting, but she heaved again without removing her hand.

Sorsha felt herself being lifted out of the fire, as Serenn's painted face floated in and out of focus.

"Sorsha!" Serenn's voice seemed to start soft and grow loud.

But Sorsha was not interested in trying to stay awake, and she closed her eyes. A caustic aroma burnt her nostrils, and her eyes snapped open as Serenn pressed a soft cloth hard against her face. Sorsha pushed the cloth away and pressed her left hand into her face. The familiar sensation of heat flowed from her heart to her hand, and her head cleared.

"Put me down."

Gwyddion did not move.

"It's okay. I'm fine."

Through the dancing crowd, she saw Taran pushing past people towards her.

"I am serious, put me down, Gwyddion."

She looked down at her hand. The paint had melted off, and the skin was red and mottled white. Gwyddion lowered her to the ground, and Serenn took her by the wrist and examined her hand.

As Taran approached them, she pulled away from Serenn's grasp and put her hand behind her, placing the palm of her other hand over it.

Taran pushed in front of Gwyddion to speak to her. "Are you okay?"

"Yes, I'm fine. I was just a little sick." She smiled. "Serenn was over-generous with her wine."

Gwyddion stepped forwards, his shoulder grazing Taran's. "But your hand?"

Sorsha held it up. "My hand is fine, Gwyddion. I think you've also had too much wine!"

Gwyddion frowned. "But the fire–"

"What about it? Honestly, no one can handle their drink around here." She laughed. "Now, if you'll all excuse me, I'm going back to the tower." She spun around and pushed through a group of half-naked teenage dancers covered in swirling dark blue paint.

"Sorsha!"

She turned around.

"Here," Gwyddion said, holding out a plain leather scabbard hanging off a leather belt. "Your sword is ready."

Flames glinted in the hilt of a sword sticking out from a long scabbard. Her hands trembled as she held the beautifully worked metal.

"Here, let me." He held out the leather belt and passed it around her waist. The hairs on the back of her neck prickled. She pushed Gwyddion away and finished tying the belt herself. Once tied, Sorsha pulled the sword from the leather scabbard. It had been hammered and polished to perfection.

"It's so beautiful. I feel like I should pay you more than I did." She glanced through the crowd of dancers and saw Taran and Serenn still by the fire, watching her and Gwyddion.

"Of course you cannot pay me more." He smiled as a strange intensity grew behind his black eyes.

A fresh wave of nausea rose into the pit of her stomach. "I really am not feeling well, if you'll excuse me." She stepped backwards and melted into the Imbolc dancers.

TWENTY-TWO

Brei and Gruffydd patrolled along the river, a half-hour ride from Caercaled. Usually, Brei was accompanied on patrol by Taran, but he was not expecting him back with Sorsha for many days.

"When will you ride to Caertarwos?" Gruffydd asked, the grey flecks in his brown hair glinting in the sun.

"When Taran gets back."

"Any idea where he went?"

Brei shrugged. "Somewhere in Gwoddodin."

"Why?"

"To reunite Sorsha with her family, I think."

"I still can't work it out, how her story is supposed to work. The Romans attacked her in Gwoddodin, but she ended up in Caledon? More than that…there's something about her that makes me uncom-fortable. I could have sworn at Imbolc that I saw the fire reflect yellow in her eyes, like it does in a dog or wolf." Gruffydd shivered. "To be fair, I was drunk, but she gives me the creeps. And what were the Druwydds doing with her?"

"I don't think anyone saw, did they? It looked like she chose the sacrifices. Which makes sense, I guess. Did you notice the tattoo on her arm? They've branded her a Bandruwydd. And Taran said he was returning her to Caledon because Serenn wants her here."

"Seems reckless to take her into Gwoddodin when he vouched that she was not a spy. But then, Taran has always been a little reckless."

"Mm. And yet when the time comes, the warriors will choose him as king."

Gruffydd sighed. "We all make our choices, Brei. You didn't have to bind yourself to Anwen."

Brei clenched his jaw and scanned the river path again, but there were no signs of activity. "How are preparations coming along?"

"Gwyddion has the second forge set up, and the Eldar Druwydd sent us one of his Druwydds from Rīgonīn to assist the new apprentices with making swords, spears, and shields."

Brei nodded. "Good, Gwyddion knows what he is doing."

"And what about you? What is the plan once you are in Caertarwos?"

Brei adjusted his seat in the saddle. "The kings of the Northern Alliance will hear Talorc's plan, well, our plan, but it must come from Talorc, of course."

"No doubt Taran will interrupt with some dramatic speech."

Brei glanced at him from the corner of his eye. "He is one for speeches." He looked at the river. The water was so clear, flushed with the snowmelt. "The journey will be slow, King Gartnait is coming with us."

"Gartnait looks so frail these days."

"He seemed to have recovered, but this morning I heard his moaning again. He visits Serenn daily and then walks back to his chambers in a sour mood."

"What do you think that's about?"

Brei shrugged. "Serenn doesn't have the cure for everything within her herb stores. He's also demanded that a wagon be brought for a skin tent, and provisions for a week."

Gruffydd snorted. "King Uradech never needed a tent. He'd camp under the stars, like the rest of us."

"Exactly what I thought. But Naoise said that Talorc also now travels with a tent and a cot with blankets and pillows."

Gruffydd shook his head. "Absolutely soft."

They ambled along the glistening river while the warm sun shone on their backs. In Brei's mind, he imagined wielding his sword in the heat of an attack on unsuspecting Roman soldiers. He could almost feel the jarring of pressing metal into human flesh. He did not know what had happened to his mother, but he knew viscerally what had happened to Anwen. It was enough to make a less steady man fly into a bloodthirsty rage. *It is almost too much to have to wait to see the fields of dead Romans groping around in the mud, crying out in agony.*

As the afternoon sun began its lazy descent, a rider appeared around the river bend, a grey blur in the distance. As the rider drew closer, Brei realised it was Taran. When Taran saw them, he spurred his horse into a gallop.

"Sorsha is not with him?" Gruffydd enquired.

"So, it seems."

Brei frowned as Taran disappeared around a bend in the river. The afternoon wind picked up, and they continued their patrol along the river until the sun set. As they rode along the bank towards Caercaled, the sky grew a deep purple. By the time they were back in the city, the sky was an inky black punctuated by the white lights of the Gods. Brei entered his chamber, where the fire was crackling. The twins and Anwen smiled up at him. He reached down to touch Anwen's cheek before taking his boots and leg wrappings off. It was almost too hot for indoor fires, even within the coolness of the stone walls.

"Any news?" Anwen asked, as she passed him some bread and a leg of hare.

"No, nothing. Have you seen Taran?"

Anwen shook her head. "I thought you said he would be gone for some time?"

Brei grunted through his full mouth.

"I hope he doesn't come back too soon. With that woman gone, I've been able to sleep for the first time in a moon without clutching a dagger," Anwen said, and began to rub her index finger and thumb back and forth.

Before Brei could respond, Nia crept to him and tapped on his shoulder. He put his arm around her and waited for her to speak. She put her mouth against his ear and whispered, "I saw Taran, Papa, riding a strange horse. I tried to say hello, but I don't think he saw me."

Brei kissed her and turned back to Anwen. "What did you and the girls do today?"

"We walked to the farmstead to visit Mother. She will need help with shearing the sheep soon."

Brei turned to the hearth and stared into the flames. *Why would Taran leave Sorsha?*

"Brei?"

"Sorry, yes, I agree."

Anwen smiled. "Good, I'll tell her you will do it soon then."

"Do what?"

"Shear her sheep."

Brei sighed. "Tell her I'll send down Dylan or Naoise to help."

Anwen pursed her lips. "Don't bother with Naoise. He is so unreliable these days. He's almost always in Caertarwos."

Brei raised his eyebrows. "Is he? Why?"

"To spend time with his cousins," Anwen said and smiled.

Brei turned to the fire again. *What if something happened to Taran on the journey? Perhaps Sorsha has died?* Brei wondered if it was bad to hope.

The following night Brei and Taran rode out from the stables on patrol together. Under the ancient trees of the Sacred Forest they rode in silence, and left the city through the Western Gate. On the fringe of the forest near the farmstead they stopped their horses. Brei breathed in the scent of damp, rotting leaves after the snowmelt.

"You all right, brother?" Brei asked. Taran did not respond. "Did something happen?"

"Why do you care?"

"Because you vouched for someone accused of spying for the enemy. Taran, it was a condition of her staying here that you would watch her, and yet…here you are alone."

"You're infuriating, you know that, don't you?"

"If that's what you think, but still, I'd like to know where she is."

Taran bowed his head, his hands fiddling with the leather reins. "We got to the mouth of the River Forth, to the harbour city there, Caeredyn, and now she's…" He paused and cleared his throat. "And now she's gone. She wanted to go the rest of the way on her own, and I searched Caeredyn. Went as far into Gwoddodin as I dared, but I couldn't find her. And so, yes, here I am…alone."

Gwyddion hammered the blade that would be Taran's new sword. In the back of the forge, a Druwydd instructed an apprentice as they huddled near the furnace, demonstrating the use of the bellows. The sharp clang of metal on metal rang around the wooden workshop.

Taran put his foot up onto the blacksmith's chair and leaned forwards. "This should have been done yesterday. How long until this fucking sword is ready?"

Brei shook his head, but Taran glared at Gwyddion.

Gwyddion stopped striking the blade and looked at Taran. "Where is Sorsha?"

Taran removed his foot from the bench and drew himself up to his full height. "That's none of your business."

Neither the Druwydd nor his apprentice seemed to be doing any work anymore.

Gwyddion rested the hammer on the anvil. "When she asked me to make her sword, I thought it was strange, but I knew you were bound in obligation to her and that you'd be responsible for her crimes. But now I've heard you lost her in Gwoddodin. And it got me thinking. Would you make a deal with the Romans in exchange for the throne? To be a bought-and-paid-for king, like those jokes in Gwoddodin?"

Taran lunged before Brei could prevent him and grabbed Gwyddion by the throat, picking up the sword simultaneously. He pressed the sword into Gwyddion's abdomen. "How dare you speak to me like that! Don't make the mistake of thinking you are irreplaceable, blacksmith."

Brei glanced at the Druwydd by the furnace, and he stepped closer. "Taran."

Taran turned his head and seemed to consider the Druwydd. He looked back at Gwyddion and squeezed his throat. "Finish the fucking sword today." He released the smith, threw the sword on the ground, and spat. "Bring it to me tomorrow." He turned around and brushed past Brei as he left the workshop.

Brei picked up the sword and placed it on the anvil. "Will it be done tonight? I'll come back and get it, save you having to deal with him again."

Gwyddion wiped the soot off his forehead with his wrist. "The whole thing with her is strange, and it's making him strange."

"Taran would die before he betrayed Caledon. Will you have it ready?"

"Just needs polishing now. Aaron will do it, won't you?" He looked at his apprentice. "I'm going to be at Elwyn's getting sloshed enough to forget I don't want to knock your lord brother's head off."

Brei stepped towards Gwyddion and put his hand on the hilt of his sword. "Finish the sword now, Gwyddion. Finish it now, while I watch."

A week later, Brei passed through the stone passageway carved with bulls and dismounted outside the gates to the fortress at Caertarwos. Taran closed his eyes, wincing as he dismounted. "I thought we would never get here. My arse has never been this sore."

Brei nodded. What usually took five days had taken seven. King Gartnait had forced them to rest every hour. His pallid skin was perpetually sweaty, and he frequently relieved himself, though it did not appear he was drinking any more ale than the others. Brei noticed he would often mutter nonsensical sentences to himself on the theme of, "she came to us, she belongs to us, she belongs to me."

"The vultures will start circling when they see this," Taran muttered as they watched Naoise and Dylan help the king down from his horse.

Brei swept a rock away with his boot. "You better make your case here then, if you can."

Taran's finger paused as he pulled Ri's reigns over his head. "Would you support me, Brei? This time?"

Taran's blue eyes widened, and in Brei's mind he saw him again as a boy of only fourteen. Blood still stained his blond hair as he stared through the crowd of warriors gathered under the Great Oak. Brei swallowed as he remembered how he had said nothing. How Taran had begged him with his eyes, and Brei had abandoned him with his silence.

"I should have supported you." Brei cleared his throat. "Why didn't you tell everyone what I did?"

Taran grabbed Brei's shoulder. "Because you're all I have left."

Brei looked over Taran's shoulder as the clopping of horses' hooves ushered more men into the windswept fortress. The kings of the north had arrived.

TWENTY-THREE

Spring, 367 C.E., the Saxon shore

Clouds shimmered against blue, moving fast for the first time in days. The boat had drifted, listless, along the Britannic coastline, spending days bobbing on the calm sea, before the wind burst into the red sails, and they sprinted along the smooth white cliffs. Sorsha rested her head on the side of the boat, watching fluffy rabbits, horses, and bears float overhead. Occasionally a seagull circled and shrieked, dragging her back from her daydreams.

In her hands she twirled a U-shaped brooch with a long flat bar. A snake slithering around the "U". "The Snake of Caledon," Taran had murmured as he clasped it to a forest green cape he had gifted to her as they left Caercaled. "The colour of your eyes."

A salty sea breeze blew her hair across her sun-drenched face. She closed her eyes, and she was there again.

The merchant ship had taken Sorsha and Taran from Caerdwabonna to Caeredyn, the harbour city swirling in the mists of the Kingdom of Gwoddodin, the kingdom her father had told her tales of. Taran had found them an inn in the harbour market for the night. He smiled as he told her of his plans for their journey by horse to find her parents' village near the Great Wall. "We can practise more with your new sword," he said.

The tightness in her chest became unbearable. The longer he spoke of the adventure they would have, the more she wondered if she would be sick. Two days before they had been due to depart Caercaled, she had spoken to Captain Antonius, a merchant and Roman citizen who spoke Latin, and she had bartered a Torc bracelet for the captain's role in helping her escape.

"Caercaled will be so different when we get back," Taran said as they shared a meal at the inn. "The Shining Lake will be full of life, otters and birds of prey, squirrels everywhere, and the trees and grass. Everything will be green. And I can take you up to the mountains, the real ones, in northern Caledon. You'll love those." His eyes were animated, like a child showing his parents an ants' nest. Sorsha smiled, not trusting the lump in her throat to let her speak. "I think I'll get some more ale from the innkeeper. Do you want any?" Taran asked.

She stood with an abrupt jerk. "Let me. I need the amenities anyway." Her heart thundered, and for a panicked moment, she was terrified he would hear it. She crossed the room on shaking legs and, as she closed the door, the coppery light of the fire danced across his face as he smiled back at her.

Her mind raced as she walked past roundhouses under cover of darkness. She refused to look behind her, and she broke into a run when she saw the merchants, who had made ready for her as promised.

Suddenly, the air chilled, and invisible hands seemed to clasp around her neck. She choked and fell to the ground as the green-eyed woman from her nightmares flashed in her mind. Shards of rock pressed into Sorsha's palms as she tried to stand. Scrambling against the invisible hold, she ran to the harbour, and Antonius held his hand out as she sprinted across the wooden jetty. Once in the boat, she pressed her back against the mast, digging her nails into her palms. Water splashed, and the chains rattled against the side of the boat as the crew wrenched the anchor up. A gust of wind filled the red sails with a stretching thud. Blood pulsed violently in her neck and she wondered how long until they curved out of the bay into the open water. "Even if he is watching," she whispered to herself, "even if he hates me for this, one day his soul will disappear from the Earth and I will have no reason to feel guilty." She closed her eyes and, in the darkness, the woman with frozen hands waited for her.

A seagull screeched and Sorsha opened her eyes to the bright white clouds, chasing each other across the sapphire sky. Sometimes she wondered whether he had looked for her. Whether he was still looking. *He didn't deserve it.* Her eyes tingled and a tear escaped down her cheek. *He vouched for me, saved me, and showed me nothing but kindness.* Sorsha leant over the edge, overcome with a desire to jump into the deep channel waters. She gripped the edge of the boat as hard as she could, her nails crushing into the wood. Through the pain, Arian's grey eyes and silvery hair appeared in her mind. "This journey you feel you must take… I wish it led here, instead of away." Arian's last whispers echoed in her mind. Shaking, Sorsha placed her hands into her lap, and she looked down at her fingernails, bloodied and broken. *I deserve this.*

Sorsha gazed at the land that passed, at what Captain Antonius called the "Saxon shore". High on the smooth white cliffs were a series of enormous fortresses built by the Romano-British to defend the island against the threat of Saxon pirates who terrorised merchants and soldiers alike. The cliffs rolled into green hills that sloped to meet the sea, and occasionally the shimmering grey ocean would push into the land through a wide natural harbour where it met the brackish water of a river.

The merchant crew did not speak to Sorsha. She seemed almost invisible, though she knew they would hold her to the gold she owed them. *It is a terrible thing to give up a sacred Torc. But like everything else I have done, it was a necessary sacrifice that had to be made.* Sorsha spent the chilly nights on the ship half-awake, twirling her new sword in her hand, trying to fight off the sleep that brought passageways and gloomy chambers whenever she closed her eyes.

As they sailed up the Thames to Londinium, her body was stiff, and her skin burnt from days in the sun. The land was swampy, and she wondered, as she gazed at the outline of buildings and a bridge, at how a city could exist in such terrain. They docked at a wooden pier just within the defensive wall on the city's eastern side. An enormous stone building was wedged in the corner by the river, between a wall running north to south and another that ran east to west along the shoreline. To the west, a long bridge spanned from one side of the river to the other. People and horses and carts crossed the bridge in both directions.

She remained on board as the crew disembarked onto the wooden quay. Silt covered the wood, which in parts was rotting, and a pungent scent of fish, mud, and smoke filled the air. Horses and carts rolled over the dirty road set above the riverbank, and traders were unloading boats docked along the quay. Sorsha had never been to Londinium and her heart leapt at the possibilities that lay in a city so large. But by nightfall, Captain Antonius assisted Sorsha onto a merchant cart, and she had no time to explore the city. The cart trundled out of the city gates and along the paved roads leading through smaller towns and villages for a week until, on a sweltering afternoon, the merchant cart finally arrived in Corinium Dobunnorum.

The fields leading to the walled city swayed green in the gentle breeze, and the rhythm of cartwheels on the road was soon joined by the bustling sounds of prosperity. Corinium Dobunnorum was a large city lying at the crossroads of the paved roads heading from Londinium to the west and from Aquae Sulis in the south to the northern city of Lindum Colonia. The city was surrounded by thick stone walls that could be seen for more than a mile. On the northeast side wound the River Corrin, across which stretched a large stone bridge that led to a formidable, double-turret, arched gate tower.

Sweat dampened the underarms of her thick woollen tunic and the soles of her leather boots, but she kept on her forest-green cape to conceal the sword that hung at her waist. The rectangular terracotta tiled roofs and whitewashed walls glistened in the sun, and the white stone pillars of the buildings and marble statues seemed to sing to her. When the cart reached the main road, Sorsha jumped off and ambled along the straight cobblestone street that ran the city's length and which she knew would take her to the gate tower on the other side.

Corinium was laid out in straight lines at right angles to each other, with two main streets crossing in the middle. Each block was filled with organised commerce, and Sorsha's chest swelled with a nostalgic pride as she passed stone carvers, schools of art for mosaics, glassmakers, and goldsmiths. In the shopfront of a draper, she stopped to admire a wall fresco, painted in vibrant hues of greens, reds, and golds, depicting women in voluminous tunics and flowing pallas. Sorsha continued on, passing the high walls and columns of the great forum and basilica, until she reached the walls and exited the gate tower on the other side of the city.

Leaving the road that led out of the city, Sorsha cut across a dirt track towards green hills, following until she saw fields of barley bordering a vineyard her father had planted. They stretched in rows before a manor house perched on a gentle hill. Sorsha smiled as the green leaves came into view. The white stone pillars of the entrance sparkled, and her heart was lifted by the sight of familiar slaves working as she passed. A young girl squatted at the base of a vine and looked at her warily. Sorsha's stomach tensed as she remembered no one would recognise her. *I wonder if I look like a barbarian.*

"Is the mistress of the house in?" Sorsha called to the girl.

The slave bowed her head. "No, she's not in. She's gone to the markets at the forum."

"Thank you." Sorsha turned and headed back along the dirt track, retracing her steps through the fields towards the city walls. *I hope she will still be there.* Her heart raced. *What if she is still angry at me?*

Sorsha hurried under the stone gate tower and onto the cobbled main street, dodging horses and groups of people talking fast but walking slow until she reached the basilica's high, white walls. Intricately carved marble pillars adorned the building, and statues inlaid the walls. She recognised her father's favourite column, dedicated to the God Jupiter. Bacchus, the God of Wine, perched atop with two bunches of grapes set either side of his curly hair. She climbed the steps and crossed the marble foyer. An overweight, bald man in a red toga brushed past her, and she followed him outside to the forum.

The market stalls were organised in an open-air courtyard, surrounded by the long rectangular buildings of official city business to make a square. Pushing through the crowd, she searched the faces of the throngs of slaves in drab tunics, and citizens draped in togas and colourful pallas, for her mother. A blonde woman wrapped in a marigold palla chatted to a man selling loaves of bread. *Is that her?* Sorsha pushed past a tall slave with olive skin. *No, it's not her.* Her stomach dropped, and she held her breath until her heart slowed and she could continue along the long line of stalls. The smell of cinnamon from a spice merchant transported her momentarily to Serenn's gloomy chamber. *There.* Her mother was a few stalls further, admiring reams of dyed cloth.

Sorsha approached the stall and stood next to her mother. She tried to catch her eye, but her mother was examining a silk. A pale green palla covered most of her hair, but her mother looked the same as Sorsha remembered. Blonde hair flecked with white, full glossy cheeks, and eyes the colour of emeralds.

"Hello," Sorsha whispered. Her mother looked up and smiled. Within an instant it vanished into a frown.

"Mother. It's Lucia," Sorsha whispered.

"Is it?" She smiled and embraced her. Sorsha closed her eyes and breathed in her mother's woody scent of frankincense oil.

"Lucia, darling," her mother whispered in her ear, "I have worried so much whether you'd survived. I found your body so close to the edge of the stone circle I wondered if it had actually worked." She held Sorsha away and stared into her eyes. "I know you didn't want to leave, but look at you, you look just like the Gallar in Tirscath."

Sorsha's eyes filled with tears, and she leant forwards to kiss her mother on the cheek. "Can we talk?"

Her mother nodded and led her to a quiet edge of the market. "Is something wrong? Where were you sent?" Her mother switched from Latin to the Ancient Tongue.

"North." Sorsha swallowed. "So far north, to Caledon, far above the Great Wall."

"I expected further north actually, to the Kingdom of Vortriu, or to Ulster. That is where my other firstborn daughters have been sent."

"You knew I'd be sent to live with barbarians?"

"Barbarians? Do they think they are barbarians?"

Sorsha pressed her lips together for a moment before answering. "No. But they live so differently to here."

"And different means barbaric, does it?"

Sorsha bit into the side of her cheek, thinking of Arian. "No, it doesn't. I'm sorry, I shouldn't have said that. But it doesn't matter anyway. I'm back now."

Her mother grabbed her hand. "Lucia, you're not being serious, are you?"

"Please…please don't say I have to go back."

"Don't tell me you came here for yourself, without a purpose from the Gods? Is there no one who suffers? Have you been told they do not need help?"

"I have been healing the sick and injured in Caercaled."

Her mother rubbed her hands over her face. "Lucia, you would be dead if not for the Gift. You have no home other than the one the Gallar chooses for you. You exist for the Gods and for them alone, do you understand? We are not people in the way they are." She motioned towards the people in the market, flittering between stalls, chatting and smiling. "We are here to protect and to heal. Throughout all the lives you will inevitably lead, you will find that you are controlled by the Gods. I'm surprised you managed to get so far south alone, you must…" She paused and studied Sorsha's face. "You must be having such terrible dreams."

"I am… The most awful nightmares. What do they mean?"

"It is a warning. A warning of what will come to pass should you stray from the path that has been set for you. You will die. The Gods will make you take the life they have gifted you."

"So, we can never live for our own pleasures? We are just tools?"

"It may help you to think that way, yes. I know it takes great strength to say goodbye to the ones you love, believe me. But focus on your work. It will be less painful if you do. Think not of the individuals but of the Ancient People, and I think you will not hurt anymore."

Tears crept over the edges of Sorsha's eyes. "I can't go back."

"Lucia, please" her mother's voice sounded steady, but the redness of her eyes betrayed her. "I am just as bound to the will of the Gods as you are. I know you didn't want this, but I had to force you to accept the Gift. You don't know yet, but you will, what it is to have the fate of thousands played out through you. We are Healers. We are the children of the Gallar of Tirscath. We are here to ensure the survival of the Ancient People. Individuals may perish, but the Ancient People survive."

Sorsha felt her nose running. "I don't care. I don't care about them. You don't know what I went through to get back to you. You can't send me back, I won't do it."

Her mother slapped her across the cheek. Sorsha blinked rapidly, her ears ringing.

"I will not allow you to bring me into this. I don't want to be punished for your weakness of character. How do you think I know about the dreams? I've had them before." Her mother grimaced. "Oh yes, Lucia, I know exactly what haunts you. But I grew up. I rose to the challenge of what has been assigned to me, and I got on with it. You exist so that our people may survive. Stop thinking you are special and that you deserve free will, because you don't. You deserve nothing but death, and every day the Gods allow you to live is a gift. You will never stop being at the mercy of the Gods and the plans they have for the Ancient People."

Sorsha dropped her gaze to the cobbled pavement. *I'd rather die than live at the mercy of others.* Her stomach churned, and the darkness of the chamber swallowed her mind. She choked as the icy fingers closed around her neck. Her mother held her shoulder and helped her to steady herself as she gasped for air.

"Why did you want to leave, anyway?" her mother asked, her voice gentle. "Have they mistreated you? I would have thought you would hold a position amongst the nobles, which is how it was for me before the Romans."

"No, they don't mistreat me. I am, as you say, treated like the Band-ruwydds."

"Then what?"

"I missed…" Sorsha lifted her chin up, "home. I missed the baths and my silk sheets."

Her mother smiled. "Lucia."

"I…" Her throat ached, and her voice cracked as she spoke. "I missed you. And I felt like I squandered our last years together, and I wanted you to know how sorry I am for what I put you through…for refusing the Gift."

Her mother kissed her forehead. "You were my quietest firstborn, Lucia, always off riding alone or lurking in dark corners at parties, refusing to speak to the other children. But you were also my fiercest, most headstrong. Of all my firstborns, of you, I was most proud. You are going to achieve great things for the Gods, I've always known it. And just look how tall and strong they've built you. You remind me of a Healer I once knew who fought with Queen Boudicca against the Romans."

"Who? Was it one of your firstborns?"

"Her name was Morrigan. No, she wasn't mine. She was much older even than me." She paused as a man with a wheelbarrow filled with spices trundled past their secluded spot. "Lucia, be strong." She dropped her voice to a whisper. "It is what it is, and you must accept it. Immortality is a long business. You cannot have regrets, you cannot carry grief because you will endure alone and carry those aches for eternity. Believe me when I say that time never feels so slow as when you lose someone you love, when you turn regrets over and over in your mind for hundreds of years." Her mother squeezed Sorsha's shoulder and smiled. "Now I must go, Lucia. Be strong, and even if you cannot be happy, you have a purpose, and that will sustain you, trust me." She placed her hand on Sorsha's cheek and held it there for a moment and stared into her eyes before she dropped her gaze and turned away.

"Wait!"

Her mother stopped and turned slowly.

"Did you ever..." Sorsha paused, wondering how to phrase it. "Did you ever go looking for your mother? Did you ever have questions?" Sorsha stared at her mother's face. *I want to memorise it forever.*

"Yes. I came looking for my mother."

Sorsha's stomach tightened. "What did she say?"

"Nothing. She was dead by the time I found her."

"You mean, she had gone to the stones? The Gods sent her away?"

"No... No, the woman in the chamber silenced her screams forever." Her mother turned and melted into the crowded market.

Sorsha stood in the forum, in the city she had grown up in, and watched her mother walk away, knowing she would never see her again. People obscured Sorsha's view, but then her mother would pop up again, an insignificant speck in the crowd. Sorsha waited, her breath catching in her throat, until she could not see her mother at all.

TWENTY-FOUR

Spring, 367 C.E., Vortriu

Waves thundered against the cliffs below the fortress of Caertarwos. The rocky peninsular was made an island by two circular walls of stone, one enclosing land that sat higher than the other. Princes and Princesses of the Blood lived inside the roundhouses of the higher rampart. The largest of these was the hall of the Kings of Vortriu. Inside, the hall seemed to constrict as the men assembled. The Kings and Princes of the Blood met, as was customary when there were matters of importance that may affect future rulers. Kings sat on wooden benches on either side of a long table while their brothers and nephews stood behind them and observed.

King Talorc brushed a stray lock of fiery hair behind his ear and stood. "Thank you for coming, cousins, we have matters of great importance to discuss. I wish to thank my uncle, King Gartnait of Caledon, for sending his nephews Taran and Brei to bring this plan to me. The plan I wish to discuss with you today."

Brei glanced from Gartnait, thin and sweaty, up to Taran, who stood behind him. Taran's golden Torc rested on his collarbone above his uncovered, tattooed chest. Brei picked at the sleeves of his linen shirt, regretting every thread. He glanced at the snake tattoo on Taran's arm. *The Snake of Caledon*. He studied the tattoos of the other men in the hall. Across their chests all wore the crescent and broken arrow that signified they were warriors. But their armbands were different depending on which kingdom they were from. Naoise and Dylan also had the Snake of Caledon tattooed around their biceps. Talorc and Drest had the Kaelpie of Vortriu. King Alpin had the Salmon of Ce, while King Cailtram of Cait had a bear.

Talorc cleared his throat and continued. "You may have heard the rumours that the position of the southern oppressors beyond the wall has weakened. Their eyes have turned back to Rome. Now is the time to strike. Now is the time for revenge for our people, past and present."

A wave of murmuring rippled around the room.

"How do you know their grip on the south has weakened? How will we get through the Great Wall?" Cailtram, King of Cait, asked. Just older than Talorc, he was tall, strawberry blond, and hungry-eyed.

Talorc smiled. "My cousins Taran and Brei have spoken to the warriors of Damnnonia in the south who have said that—"

"Let them speak for themselves then," yelled Alpin, King of Ce. He was younger than Gartnait, but had the markings across his forehead of his lost youth.

Taran cleared his throat. "Talorc is right, Brei and I led a scouting party to the south, and while in the Kingdom of Damnnonia they told us the Roman's grip on Britannia had significantly weakened. The men at the Great Wall are being bribed, and they are letting in raiding parties of the Damnnones." He paused and glared around the room. "Maybe those of you up north in Cait have not felt for a long time the long arm of the Roman army, but the Caledones remember, we lost our uncle King Uradech and our mother, Princess of the Blood of Vortriu and Caledon, only six summers ago."

Talorc looked across the table at Taran. "His vengeance can be ours, cousins, and the glory can be enjoyed by all the Northern Alliance."

King Alpin leaned back. "This sounds more like a blood feud for Caledon. Why should Ce join?"

Taran shook his head. "The Romans have been wolves at our door for hundreds of winters, and though they are now weakened, do not be so naïve as to think they will not return. Now is our chance, not only for revenge but to plunder and cripple them so they will never return. Our united efforts will be the beginning of universal liberty for the north and for our distant cousins in the south. Don't think you are safe, Alpin of Ce, though you hide in the safety of the mountain fortress of Banntuce. Don't forget that your lands are surrounded by sea. But even the sea is not a refuge when the Roman fleet lingers. Therefore war, which is always honourable to those who are brave, is surely now the best opportunity, even to those who are ravaged by cowardice?"

Taran paused and glared at Alpin and Cailtram. "And what of our ancestors? What of all our fathers, grandfathers, and their fathers, who died at the hands of the Roman savages? Did they not put their hopes in us? We are the future they fought for. We must claim the freedom they should have lived in. You think you have nothing to fear, Alpin, and Cailtram, but you have been defended to this day by your remoteness. The mountains, the moors, and the jagged cliffs. All these have kept you safe. But we men of the north are at the edge of the world. There is no kingdom beyond us. There is nothing but waves and rocks. And then there are the Romans, whose arrogance and brutality we cannot escape by submission. For we are all debased by slavery, and they will make slaves of us all. The Romans, these plunderers of the world, after exhausting their lands by their own destructions, their avarice compels them to seek more. Don't think they won't regroup. And when they find themselves wanting, they will come for us, as they have before. They will ravage and slaughter in the name of 'empire', and when they have made a wasteland of our homeland, they will call it peace." Taran drew a breath and stared around the silent hall. "Do you want their peace, brothers? Or do you want the freedom our ancestors died to give us the chance for? Revenge or Tirscath!"

"Revenge or Tirscath!" Talorc roared.

Alpin and Cailtram stood. "Revenge or Tirscath!"

The Princes of the Blood joined, and the hall echoed with the war cries of their ancestors.

"What are the Druwydds saying of the scheme? Have you had them consult the Gods?" King Cailtram asked as the cheers died down.

Talorc motioned to his brother, Drest, who sprinted from the hall. The room broke out into a rabble of conversations as they waited for Drest to return with the Eldar Druwydd.

"You got to make your claim, after all," Brei whispered to Taran.

Taran turned to him, his face relaxed. "Every day, I make my claim."

Drest returned, followed by the Eldar Druwydd, his white robes flowing behind him. Talorc smiled at the white-haired man. "Thank you for coming. We seek your counsel upon communion with the Gods about our plan to seek vengeance and glory in the south."

The Eldar Druwydd nodded, his wrinkled face passive. "Tell me your plan, and I will consult the Gods."

Talorc cleared his throat. "We are yet to agree on the details, but we plan to bribe the soldiers to allow us to pass through the Great Wall into the south, for vengeance."

"I will require a new moon in which to consider it."

Talorc's eyes widened. "That will be two weeks from now!"

The Eldar Druwydd bowed low. "I will communicate the wishes of the Gods to you the morning after the new moon." He straightened and glided out of the room.

Talorc stared after him, a frown cutting into his smooth brow. "Enough talk! Let's enjoy some wine, the only good thing those Roman bastards have given us!"

Brei watched the kings and princes mill about, talking. Servants entered the hall carrying silver pitchers and trays laden with chicken, apples, turnips, kale, bread, and cheese, along with wooden barrels of wine and goblets. Brei sat down at the end of the table, and Taran, Naoise, and Dylan joined him. A full pig was brought into the room and placed into the middle of the table.

"Good, I'm starving," Naoise said, signalling to one of the serving boys to bring them meat. Dylan reached across his brother to grab a loaf of bread. Jostling boys soon surrounded the carcass, trying to get in to carve pieces of flesh for a king or a prince. Their boy, with a blond mop of hair, hurried over to their end of the table and heaped carved pork onto a glossy red dish in front of them.

"And wine too, son," Brei said, patting the boy on his back. He scrambled away as they helped themselves with their hands to pork and bread, and he soon returned with a jug, almost as large as him, and sat it onto the table for them. Naoise picked up the jug and poured wine into silver goblets embossed with vines and sprawling leaves.

From the middle of the crowded table, Talorc rose and raised his hands. When the hall fell silent, he lifted his goblet high in the air. "Here's to two weeks of good food and wine!"

Brei joined the others in cheering before turning to Taran. "I should send a rider to Caercaled to tell them of the delay."

Taran nodded, his mouth full.

"Are you staying, Brei?" Naoise asked.

"I think we must, seeing as it is our proposal."

"I'm certainly not leaving," Taran said. "This is where all the action is."

Naoise laughed. "Well, I wasn't asking you! You have nothing to go back home for, unlike Brei."

"Anwen has her mother, and Gruffydd is maintaining the garrison in our absence," Brei said and sipped his wine.

"I hope they get up a celebration tonight, with dancing," Naoise said as he glanced around the room. "It's a stag fest in here."

Taran swirled his wine in his cup, watching the contents closely. He glanced up at Naoise and smiled. "It's simpler that way, though, isn't it?"

Naoise smirked. "Simpler, maybe. But I wouldn't mind a dance with Eithne."

Taran raised his goblet to Naoise. "Her being my first cousin aside, that would be a pleasant prospect."

"Cheers to no rule against second cousins," Naoise said, and grinned as he clinked Taran's goblet.

TWENTY-FIVE

Spring, 367 C.E., Britannia

Sorsha lingered in the forum market long after her mother left, frozen in a shaded corner, drawing the scowls of nearby vendors as though she might be a thief. She meandered through the stalls and stepped across the marble foyer and out into the hectic cobbled street. It was not until an unapologetic slave thrust into her shoulder that she decided to visit the temple of Banduiu-Cwrrabon, "Goddess of the River Edge".

Turning down a narrow street heading northeast after the forum, she followed the cobblestones until she came to a tall, circular building. In the vast sea of rectangles that formed Corinium, it was a rare sight. The temple was of Roman construction, but it was dedicated to the Ancient Goddess who had watched over the River Cwrr since the dawn of time.

Inside, the temple was a single, cavernous room made of plain stone. There was a peace in the stark grey tones that could not be produced by sparkling marble. A stone altar stood in the middle of the austere temple, lit by a small arched opening in the wall. Carved roughly into the base of the altar was a relief of three seated women. The middle woman held a child, while the other two held bundles of offerings. On the other side of the altar was a carving depicting the Roman God Mercury, standing next to the Ancient Goddess Cwrr with a cauldron filled with water from the river. The temple was empty, and the air hung with the musk of disuse. Sorsha crept to the altar and fell to her knees in front of the three carved women, who represented the three sides of the Goddess Cwrr.

"Tell me what to do," Sorsha whispered to the stern faces of the Goddess. *How many of my mother's people, the Dobunni, have worshipped the Goddess Cwrr? How many Healers have been in this temple?* Sorsha pressed a shaking hand against the stone Goddess. "Individuals perish, but the Ancient People survive."

The setting sun encircled the arch window with red, as though it were alight. Darkness fell and, through the arch, stars pricked tiny holes in the carpet of dark sky. Sorsha lay awake throughout the night, watching as the stars faded, inky black wavering on grey. When fingers of golden dawn crept into the temple, she decided to go to Aquae Sulis. *I want to bathe in the hot springs and visit the shrine to Sulis.*

Wrapping the green cape Taran gave her around her shoulders, she stepped out onto the cobblestones and walked to the edge of town, to the paved road called Fossa. The road was unnaturally straight and connected Aquae Sulis to Corinium Dobunnorum. She followed the road south, taking her past a great stone arena, which had once housed gladiators but now held dog fights, until she reached Aquae Sulis by the afternoon.

From the road, Aquae Sulis, the "Springs of the Goddess Sulis", looked like any other town in Britannia. A thick stone wall and ditch encircled the settlement, and a single gate tower on the northern side permitted traffic in and out. Inside the walls was a sacred refuge, a sanctuary for temples to the Gods, both of the Romans and the Ancient People.

Sorsha walked under the gate arch and along a straight main street, trailing behind a group of female pilgrims dressed in beige raw-spun tunics until she spotted the high, barrel-shaped roofs of the hot spring baths. As Sorsha stood on the threshold to the temple sanctuary, she paused to admire a monumental archway inlaid with a stone relief of two delicate nymphs beside a spring flowing from a rock. Steam billowed from the shadows of the archway that led to the spring of the Ancient Goddess Sulis. Sorsha watched the pilgrims disappear into the steam and wondered if Sulis would be disappointed that she had strayed from the path the Gods had chosen for her.

Sulphuric vapours filled her lungs as she entered the women's bathhouse, where Corinthian pillars surrounded a large square pool of cloudy water. Four women reclined in the pool, chatting amongst themselves. Sorsha removed her belt and laid her sword by the edge of the pool. As she did so, she noticed their voices died down and the women seemed to watch her.

She nodded at them, pulled off her tunic and cape, laying them on the stone floor next to her sword, and stepped into the warm water. Her skin tingled as she submerged. *I haven't had a bath for months.* She waded to the corner opposite the group of women and laid her head back against the stone. The high, vaulted ceiling was so beautiful that it almost hurt her to see it again. She closed her eyes and inhaled the pungent fumes drifting off the water.

"May we join you?" The group of women had waded over to Sorsha's corner of the pool. "We were wondering where you came from?" asked the closest woman. She had the kind of bronze skin and dark eyes that made Sorsha wonder if she was from Rome itself.

"Corinium Dobunnorum."

A mousy-haired woman with blue eyes glanced at the other woman. "Really? How curious that you carry a sword, then. We assumed you must be from the north, near the Emperor Hadrian's Wall, perhaps."

"I have come from there, yes, but I was born in Corinium Dobunnorum."

The bronzed woman smiled, and the rouge on her lips cracked. "Yes, we thought that must be it, how thrilling!" She bit her lip and glanced at her companions before turning back to Sorsha. "Now tell us, have you seen one of the painted men, the barbarians? Are they truly as fearful as they say?"

Her tone was not at all fearful, and Sorsha was left with the impression that the woman hoped that Sorsha had indeed met one. Sorsha shrugged. "Yes… I've spent some time beyond the Great Wall." She remembered her mother's words. "But they're not barbaric…just different."

The women exchanged a mixture of glances, Sorsha thought, perhaps excitement, and feigned horror. The mousy-haired woman leaned forwards and whispered. "Is it true that they mark themselves with paint…permanently, like slaves?" The women seemed elated, and they giggled.

Sorsha sunk deeper into the water, ensuring her tattooed arm was submerged. "Yes, they do. But it's not like slaves. The symbols are for honour."

"What do the symbols mean?" the tanned woman asked.

"There's a symbol that looks like a broken arrow on a shield. All the warriors have it. I think it means victory. But there are others, such as a snake curled around an arrow, which is a territorial marking."

The women's eyes widened, and they made collective "ooh" sounds.

"I've heard they are like the Gauls and are absolutely dripping in gold and silver," the youngest in the group said.

"Well, the nobles are. I think a lot of the farmers and workers also like to wear brooches and bracelets, but they are not allowed to wear the Torcs."

"What is a Torc?" the dark-eyed woman asked, and Sorsha noticed her staring through the water at her arm. *Why didn't I cover up my tattoo?*

"It's a crescent-shaped necklace made from twisted ropes of gold. It sits around your neck like this," she motioned to her clavicles. "Two golden orbs sit at either end."

"You know such an awful lot about them," the tanned woman said.

"Yes, I was lost up there and…a family looked after me. But I am back now."

"What's that on your arm?" the mousy-haired woman asked.

Sorsha glanced down. "It's… That is to say, they painted one on me." She lifted her bicep out of the water.

They gasped and ran their fingers over the design. "It's beautiful!" the dark-haired woman said.

The mousy-haired woman's finger traced the circles. "Beautiful but so barbaric!"

Sorsha also studied the tattoo. *It is beautiful.*

"Was it terrible?"

Sorsha looked up. "Was what terrible?"

The dark-haired woman was inches from her. "Being lost up there, having to rely on those barbarians."

"It was terrible, yes, but not because of the people…not all of them anyway. Some of them were very nice. It was terrible because I was so far away from my home, from my mother. But I think I would feel that no matter where I was, even if it was in the heart of civilised Rome. It would feel terrible to be away from my family in a strange land."

The dark-haired woman nodded. "I think I know what you mean. Britannia is not my home, either. In fact, it feels quite barbaric to me, so foreign!"

"Does it not go away, though?" Sorsha asked. "That feeling like a part of you is where you grew up, and you're not really whole anymore?"

The dark-haired woman smiled. "Yes, there will always be a part of you where you grew up, where your family are, but I think I have found that you have so many parts, there is so much of you that to lose a small part is not so bad."

"But you are not going back there, are you?" the youngest woman asked Sorsha.

She hesitated before answering. "No." She slipped further into the water until it reached her chin. Invisible hands slithered up her chest and grasped around her neck until she coughed.

"I'm Cecily, by the way," the dark-haired woman said, sliding down next to her. "Where are you staying while you are here?"

Sorsha gazed up at the vaulted ceiling and rubbed her throat. "I haven't decided yet, actually."

"Then it's settled. You must stay with us. We have plenty of room in our little dwelling here." Cecily winked at her friends. "My husband is the Provost of the Storehouses of London, in the service of the illustrious Count of the Sacred Bounties. We know the count personally."

A dolphin and two seahorses swam together in a sea of tessellating stone tiles. Sorsha admired the mosaic that clung to the wall above the elaborate dinning table, piled high with delicate treats.

"Tell him, Lucia, how you got there. Oh, it is the most thrilling tale, Marc," Cecily said to her husband across the table. Marcus, a grey-haired man with red cheeks, was perhaps twice the age of his glamourous wife. Their "little dwelling" was a whitewashed manor house on the main street. It was vast and made for entertaining lavish summer parties.

Sorsha inhaled, before recounting the lie she had told Cecily in the baths. "My father was a merchant, and I went with him on a trading voyage. But there was a storm, and the ship was wrecked. Everyone drowned, but I managed to come ashore. If the Caledones hadn't—"

"The who?" Marcus interrupted.

"The Caledones, the people from the Kingdom of Caledon. They are one of the kingdoms above the Great Wall."

"You mean the Picti?"

Sorsha swallowed. "Yes. If the Painted People had not found me, I would not have survived."

A serving girl offered her more wine, grapes, cheese, and olives. The meal seemed exotic, and Sorsha had to remind herself that it was nothing out of the ordinary here.

"They cared for her, darling. Can you imagine that?"

Marcus nodded. "The civilised savage. It is true then, what Tacitus wrote about the barbarians?"

"What do you mean, darling?" Cecily purred.

"Tacitus, sweet one, the stories about the barbarians by Tacitus."

"I'm afraid I don't think I've read Tacitus."

"I'm afraid you neither think nor read, darling," Marcus said as he kissed her jewelled hand.

"My father used to read Tacitus's stories to me," Sorsha said as Cecily poked her tongue out at her husband.

"Will you tell me the story then, Lucia?"

"It's the story of General Agricola, and his battles around the empire. But I think you mean the part where he was fighting in the northern wilds of Britannia?" Sorsha glanced at Marcus, and he nodded with a smile. He picked up a silver goblet and held it aloft for the serving girl to refill. Sorsha noticed the girl's red hair and pale skin. *I wonder where she is from?*

"Go on, dear," Cecily said, patting Sorsha's arm.

"Ah, Agricola, yes. Agricola had control of Britannia, and he led an exploration to discover the north. He was so clever... It took him several years, but slowly he pushed up into the north, building forts all the way along and garrisoning them in case of attack. He was almost unopposed until there was a great battle in the mountains. At the battle, the barbarians' leader, Calgacus, said 'If we don't fight the Romans, we will be enslaved because the Romans are everywhere, and everywhere they go they massacre the people and ruin nations. And yet they call the result a success.' Calgacus was much more eloquent than I, of course, or Tacitus rather. He is portrayed as rather civilised for a savage, and Tacitus clearly respected him and wrote that he was brave and exotic, with his fearsome warriors with chariots. Of course, the story goes that Agricola massacred them and sent them running for the hills. If it wasn't for the general being called back by the emperor, Rome would have turned the entire island into Britannia. That and, I suppose, the discovery that the climate was so terrible no one would want to live there anyway." Sorsha paused and sipped wine from her goblet.

Cecily snorted. "Well, I don't understand. How does unjustly criticising Rome make someone civilised? He just sounds like a savage. Now tell me, is it true that they are cannibals?"

Sorsha thought about the sacrifice at Imbolc and the smell of human flesh burning on the fire. "Not that I ever saw."

Cecily's nostrils flared. "You know, I have never understood why the barbarians, not just the ones on this island, but the Alamatti too, why they insist on fighting against us, fighting against civilisation. Their lives would be happier with Roman order."

"Well, I think that was what Tacitus was trying to point out, my dear, through the words of Calgacus, that perhaps the imposition of foreign rule, no matter how civilised it looks to us, perhaps to those who are being colonised, it is akin to slavery." Marcus sipped his wine and studied Sorsha. "Did you think the Painted People were happy, Lucia?"

Sorsha frowned. "I think so, yes. At the most basic level they were no different to us, and their domestic lives are much like ours. They have cities and houses made of stone, but the buildings are round and they do not shine white in the sun. They are religious, like the people here were before the Romans came. When it comes to it, they are the same people. I could speak their language because my mother taught me the Ancient Tongue. The people there were not without their troubles, in the same way that people in Aquae Sulis are not without their complaints."

Cecily leant forwards. "The people are happy in Aquae Sulis."

Sorsha smiled and bowed her head towards Marcus. "I think people can have troubles and complaints and still be 'happy'. The curse stones thrown in the water to the Goddess Sulis Minerva are a testament to the troubles and complaints of the people of Aquae Sulis, and yet I would agree with you that people here, on the whole, are happy. You will also agree, I am sure, that crop yields continue to decline, that the plague affects you here too. The Painted People have their own troubles and complaints, and yet I would also say they are happy."

"Perhaps you are familiar with Cicero, Lucia? He thought happiness comes from moral goodness. Do you think the barbarians can be happy in the same way we can be?" Marcus asked and then deposited a plump grape into his mouth.

"My father had a copy, but it's been a long time since I read it. If I remember it correctly, Cicero thought that happiness is based on the goodness or morality of an individual, is that not so? Happiness does not belong to any race. Even the citizens of Rome were good and bad. So if Romans can be bad people and therefore not happy, then I would think the test is down to the individual rather than the race. And so you must forgive me, but I do not know you, and so I do not know if you are moral yourself. Therefore, I cannot say if you are any happier than anyone from within the Painted People."

Marcus laughed. "Well, perhaps we need not examine it further. I take the point, though, that we cannot paint all barbarians with the same brush. But they certainly do not seem to be capable of the same happiness that I could be capable of when I have reason and law and live in an aesthetic city."

"But they do have reason and law." Sorsha leant forwards. "Yes, it is different from ours, but they still have it. And their city was…harsh and unrefined. But it was within nature. They incorporated the trees into their city in a way no one would have the patience for here. I hated it at first, the lack of grand public buildings and art. But it wasn't that they didn't have those things. They did. Their art is carved into their skin, and their grand public buildings were not basilicas and forums but standing stone circles within the woods. Just because it is different does not mean it doesn't exist. Perhaps we are afraid of the Painted People because they are different and we do not understand them. It is not because they are fearsome or immoral or unhappy. It is because we allow our fear of difference and the unknown to blind us from recognising that, when it comes down to it, we are all the same.

We live, we love, we feel sad, and we die. And so do they."

Cecily drummed her manicured nails on the table. "But if what you say is true, if they are not so different from us, that does not fit with what I've always been taught. They are barbarians who need civilising. Enemies who must be kept at bay."

"It is convenient, though, isn't it?" Sorsha said. *Why am I defending them?* She pressed her nails into her palms. "If we call them barbarians, then they are unquestionably not like us. And so when we invade their lands, there is no awkwardness. We invade their lands, and when the barbarians fight back, they are called the enemy. I am not experienced in politics or warfare, but it seems to me that we first create a barbarian, an enemy, and then we take away their lands."

TWENTY-SIX

Spring, 367 C.E., Vortriu

"If we get an agreement, will you lead the men from Caercaled?" Talorc asked Taran, handing him another goblet of wine.

"That will be our uncle's job," Brei said.

Talorc glanced around the hall at the few stragglers remaining and dropped his voice to a whisper. "He looks almost too weak to carry on."

"He got better, but lately he got sick again," Dylan said.

"Gartnait needs a Healer," Talorc said, taking a swig from his goblet. "We have two here in Caertarwos. Maybe I'll send one back with you."

"A Healer?" Dylan said. "Like the Gallar? Are they real? I've never seen one."

"Haven't you?" Talorc grinned. His brother, Drest, rolled his eyes as Talorc pulled a dagger from his belt. Dylan inhaled as Talorc drew the blade down his arm from wrist to elbow. Brei stared as the blood pooled and dribbled onto the red hairs on his arm. From the corner of his eye he saw Taran and Naoise looking concerned. It was as if none of them had ever seen blood before.

"Get Branwen," Talorc said to a serving boy. "They just arrived, out of nowhere. The first one, Morrigan, was sent to us from the Druwydds at Rīgonīn, and a few months ago Branwen arrived. Warriors found her lying in a stone circle a short ride from here to the east. With no clothes. And they both have green eyes like you've never seen."

Brei looked at Taran, but he seemed to avoid Brei's eyes. The servant returned, followed by a young woman with light brown hair that fell long and wavy about her shoulders. She wore a black tunic with flowing sleeves that rustled against her skirt. She walked to Talorc and stood behind him, her eyes lingering on his wound.

"Branwen, meet my cousins, Taran, Brei, Naoise, and Dylan."

She looked at them with her head angled down. Her eyes were the same startling green as Sorsha's. Taran lowered his goblet to the table with a thud.

Branwen leant forwards and put one arm around Talorc's shoulder. She positioned her other hand onto his wound. She looked up again, and Brei felt like he had plunged into a dark tunnel, and at the end, in the dark, she was waiting for him, her eyes glimmering green in the gloom. Branwen removed her hand from the wound and stepped behind Talorc again.

Brei could see that all the colour had drained from Taran's face. Talorc smiled and wiped the blood off his arm in one deft motion to reveal a thin, healed scar.

No one said anything. Even Naoise was still.

"Thank you, Branwen," Talorc said, taking her hand and kissing it. Her eyes were cold, but she smiled.

"I was thinking of sending Morrigan to Caercaled. How do you think she would like that?" Talorc asked, without releasing her hand.

Branwen's smile disappeared. Unblinking, she bent forwards, so her face was in line with Talorc's, and she whispered, "Only the Gods may command us." She straightened and pulled her hand from his grasp, then retreated from the hall.

Talorc laughed and shook his head. "They would as soon as kill you as heal you. But great in a tight spot, they can't help but heal us. The Eldar Druwydd says they are descendants of the Gallar from Tirscath."

Naoise shook himself as though covered in cobwebs. "She reminds me of Sorsha. Is she a Healer, Taran?"

Taran cleared his throat. "Sorsha is no one's concern but mine."

"But in the stories of the Gallar they are sent to all people, all the Ancient People," Dylan said.

Taran made a fist on the table, his knuckles turning white. "She is not your concern."

Talorc chuckled. "You got yourself a Healer? Clever lad! You'll be invincible!"

"They're only bound in obligation," Naoise smirked. "If you were truly clever, you'd have yourself bound in protection."

Brei remembered how eager Taran had been to rescue her at Sorsha's trial. *Had he known what she was? When the Bandruwydds pulled down her tunic to inspect something on her chest, what did they see?*

The following day the welcoming festivities began. Talorc had been eager to get to business and had delayed the usual welcoming celebration until the next morning. The day began bright, but a sea wind soon blew clouds over the sun.

The grassland at the centre of the lower rampart was transformed with wooden tables, so that the villagers and farmers could join the celebrations too. Inside the upper rampart, the long table inside the hall was laden with meats and bread and wine. An enormous bonfire had been prepared on the land near where the workers and farmers had gathered and where they would later dance. At midday, the drummers and horn blowers arrived and set up around the fire.

Brei sat in the hall with Taran, sipping wine. The sound of drums, periodic horns, and cheering echoed into the dark, smokey hall. Naoise had left them as soon as he could, to follow Talorc and Drest's sister, Eithne, who was helping them to open the dancing.

"Do you feel like dancing?" Brei asked Taran.

"Do you?"

"Almost never, but I'll watch if you want to dance with the Princess of Cait, she would be quite a prize."

"Indeed, but I care more about getting Caledon than I do for getting a throne for my sons."

Brei smiled. "At least you're honest in your self-interest."

"Naoise doesn't care about his children. He just knows that the closest he'll get to being king is being bound to Eithne and fathering one," Taran said and gulped the rest of the wine from his goblet.

"I think we should get out of this room, at least. Maybe we could just watch?"

"It is said that the Romans kill their kings when the ambition of the younger men boils over. There was a son who killed his father and he became their king," Taran continued, with no sign he had heard Brei.

Brei grimaced. *He must be drunk.* "Let's get some fresh air."

"Do you think the Gods will favour us? I am eager to get down there, to break some Roman skulls."

"Who knows? But as eager as I am for an answer from the Druwydds, I don't think we'll march out any time soon. Summer is the wrong time for an attack. It leaves our families and farms too exposed. We need the insurance of winter before we can strike. You know this," Brei said.

Taran didn't reply, instead barking at a servant to bring wine. The boy poured wine into Taran's cup and reached for Brei's goblet, but Brei raised his hand. "No, I'm fine." The boy nodded and skulked back to his corner.

"You know, I've been thinking about last night," Brei whispered. "Is Sorsha really a Healer?"

Taran scraped his chair back and stood up. "You know, I think I will dance with the Princess of Cait, after all."

As Taran walked out of the hall, he snatched the jug of wine from the serving boy's hand and disappeared. Brei leaned back and continued to sip his wine until, by nightfall, he felt drunk enough to venture outside.

The sun had only just set when fresh sea air misted against Brei's face. Across the horizon the clouds were lit up blood-red, and the flames from the bonfire were so large that they almost surpassed the hall's height. As Brei listened to the intense rhythmic drumming, he saw the dancers bending and contorting their bodies to the music.

Brei scanned the scene for familiar faces. *Naoise is making a fool of himself dancing with Eithne, who, to be fair, is behaving just as foolishly, running her hands over his bare chest like that.*

Talorc was deep in conversation with King Alpin, King Cailtram, and King Gartnait. He was sharing a very animated story and, after a minute, they erupted into a chorus of loud laughter. Brei looked around and saw Taran sitting on the fortified wall by the sea. He was accompanied by Drest and a jug of wine. Brei wandered towards them.

"Nice of you to surface, Brei," Taran yelled.

"We've just been taking bets on which farmer's daughter had detained you this time," Drest smirked as he passed him the jug of wine.

Brei rolled his eyes and accepted the jug from him. He brought the jug up to his mouth and tipped it up. "It's fucking empty!"

Taran and Drest heaved in silent laughter. "Oh, be a lamb and fetch us another, won't you, Brei-Brei?" Taran said.

Brei lunged for him, and Taran sprung from his spot on the wall. Brei caught him by the waist and tackled him to the ground, laughing.

TWENTY-SEVEN

Spring, 367 C.E., Britannia

Sorsha spent the night sleeping on a feather mattress under cool silk sheets. But all the softness and luxury in the world could not shield her from the dark passageways and green eyes that haunted her. When she was not sweating through her nightmares, she lay awake, looking at the whitewashed roof. *How long can this slow, sleepless torture endure?*

When she awoke the next morning, she was greeted by the handmaiden with bright red hair. The maid wore a metal collar around her neck, the mark of a slave. *I wonder if she came from Caledon.*

"Hello," Sorsha whispered in the Ancient Tongue.

The girl almost dropped the brush that she was handing to Sorsha. "Hello," she whispered.

"Where do you come from?" Sorsha asked.

"Caermhead, Kingdom of the Maetae. Where do you come from? Your accent is so strange." She blushed.

"Yes, it is," Sorsha smiled. "I am from here, from Corinium Dobunnorum, but I have lived in Caercaled, in the Kingdom of Caledon." She lifted the sleeve of her tunic and showed the girl her tattoo. The girl opened her mouth and crept closer to inspect it. Her finger hovered, tracing the design in the air without touching her. "You are a Bandruwydd?"

"Sort of."

She gazed into Sorsha's eyes. "Your eyes are so green. My grandma used to tell me stories about the Gallar, with eyes like yours."

"Have you ever seen a Healer before?"

"No, but my grandma said she had. But it was such a long time ago. My grandmother saw her when she was a child and then one day the Healer was found dead in the circle of stone."

Should I tell her? What's the harm? "I am a Healer."

The girl's hand slid as she untied Sorsha's braid. "Really?"

"Yes. Are you happy here? Are you treated well?" she asked the girl as she brushed out Sorsha's long black hair. The girl stopped what she was doing, and Sorsha turned to look at her. "It's okay, I won't say anything."

The girl stared at her feet and then back up again. "They don't beat me or anything, so I am lucky because not every slave can say that. But no, I don't think I, or anyone taken from their families, could be happy. How could we ever?"

Sorsha remembered the slaves who had served her growing up. "Were you taken six years ago? Six summers?"

"Yes, I think that's right."

"With others?"

"Yes, there were many women, taken to a city far from here, where we were sold. I was in a lot with some other girls. The provost bid for us to serve his wife...for the most part." She blushed again.

Sorsha took the girl's hand in hers. "I'm sorry this happened to you. What is your name?"

"Nyfain."

"Nyfain... That's a lovely name."

"What is yours?"

"Sorsha."

Nyfain frowned. "Where is that name from?"

"Ulster, I think. It was the only name I'd heard that wasn't Roman, and I panicked when I had to choose a name."

"You got to choose your name?"

"When I first became a Healer, I was sort of reborn but as an adult. And when I met the Caledones, I had to think of a name."

"And 'Sorsha' was the best name?"

Sorsha smiled. "They already suspected me of being a Roman spy, so the name didn't help things, no."

"In my kingdom, princes from Ulster often marry Princesses of the Blood, so maybe it's not such a strange name," Nyfain said as she pulled Sorsha's hair tight into a fresh braid. "Will you go back?"

Sorsha shrugged. "I don't know."

"I'd love to see the north again, even if my family are all gone."

Sorsha watched Nyfain as she packed away the brush and walked out of the room. *I wonder how much a slave costs.*

Corinthian pillars rose from the marble floor, high up to the vaulted roof of the steaming baths below. Sorsha and Cecily were assisted back into their tunics and wrapped in flowing pallas by Nyfain and Cecily's slave, Fortunata. Sorsha's baths had become so frequent that a sulphuric tang clung to her skin. Displaying her wealth through her slaves, Cecily allowed Nyfain and Fortunata to wear voluminous tunics in pale shades of blue and yellow, and gold armbands. Nyfain's fiery red hair was curled and piled high on her head, in the style of her mistress.

Spring was withering into a scorching summer with so little rain that there was already apprehension, even in the sacred city of Aquae Sulis, that there would be a bad harvest. Throughout the weeks she had spent in Cecily and Marcus's luxurious apartments, Sorsha had thought more about Nyfain and the other slaves taken from the north. She wondered at how blindly and easily she had accepted it, just because society told her they were different. *I wonder whether Taran's mother survived. He thought she had been taken to be a slave. I wonder if Cecily would know how I could find out.*

Sorsha followed Cecily along a stone corridor surrounding the bath complex and out onto the narrow path leading to the nymphs' grand archway. Through the archway, they entered a courtyard within which there stood a tall, white, rectangular building with decorated pillars supporting a vaulted, triangular roof. Sorsha and Cecily climbed the marble steps and joined Marcus in prayer at the temple to Sulis Minerva.

Inside the temple was a great stone altar, with reliefs of the Gods carved into it. Earthy frankincense and fruity myrrh filled the air, covering the sulphuric scent of the baths. On the wall high above the altar was a geometric border surrounding a large male head with wavy hair, like serpents. It was the Gorgon that the Goddess Minerva wore on her armour. In front of the altar was a towering bronze statue of the Goddess Sulis, a woman with almond eyes and a thick crown of curly hair.

Sorsha bent to her knees before the altar while Marcus and Cecily roamed the cavernous temple in silence. *Sulis Minerva, forgive me. Help me. Ask the Gallar that I be given a new mission.* Tears squeezed past her closed eyes and rolled down her cheeks. *Don't make me go back.* She pleaded with the bronze face of the Goddess as she had done countless times in her former life. *Help me, Sulis.* The Goddess' vacant eyes stared back at her, and Sorsha swallowed down the crushing disappointment of yet another unsuccessful morning spent praying to a Goddess who was not sympathetic to her plight.

Sorsha got to her feet and rejoined Marcus and Cecily, who waited by the decorated entrance pillars. As they walked out of the magnificent temple and into the whitewashed courtyard that backed onto the bathing complex, Sorsha turned to Cecily. "Would it be possible to find a slave if I knew her name and where she was taken from?"

Cecily raised her preened eyebrows and turned to her husband, who mirrored her surprise.

"There was a woman taken from the family who helped me. I don't know if she is dead but if she is alive, then she would be a slave, and I would like to buy her and take her home. As a thank you, you see, for her family saving me?" Sorsha felt her cheeks flush.

Cecily nodded, but she did not smile. "That would be very difficult to work out, but the slave market is in Londinium, so you would have to go there and check the records."

Marcus smiled. "Such a noble idea, Lucia, and yet, sadly, I fear it will be wasted on those not civilised enough to appreciate altruism."

"Even so, I would like to try. Would she have been taken to the Great Wall or to Londinium?"

"Oh, Londinium, for sure, if they wanted a good price," Marcus replied, as though they were talking grain.

"Do you know someone there?"

"Flavius, he runs the slave market. He will have all the records. He speaks a fair bit of barbarian too by now, of course. And you do too, don't you, dear?"

"Yes, many of us can still speak the Ancient Tongue."

Cecily laughed. "I don't know why they waste their time teaching their children a dead language."

"I suppose nothing is truly dead until there is no one left to remember it," Marcus said, smiling at Sorsha.

"But let us talk of fun things," Cecily grinned. "There are to be gladiators at the amphitheatre in Corinium Dobunnorum five days from now. Real gladiators, not just the usual bull-baiting. I even heard there might be a bear. Shall we go, Lucia? Marc must attend on official duties, so we can sit in the stands, away from the commoners. How would you like that?"

"I never really went to the arena. I saw bull-baiting once, but I didn't see the fun in it."

Cecily clutched her hand. "When its real men, it's so much more thrilling than animals. Trust me. You'll love it! And we have such lovely apartments in Corinium Dobunnorum, near the governor's residence. We know the Governor of Britannia Prima personally."

TWENTY-EIGHT

Spring, 367 C.E., Vortriu

The new moon plunged Caertarwos into darkness as a procession of chanting Druwydds cloaked in white glided into the city through the stone passage carved with bulls. A crisp, salty breeze blew up the cliffs and the Druwydds' torches shuddered, splashing orange light across their billowing robes and bare feet. Brei, Taran, Dylan, and Naoise stood on the wall of the upper rampart and watched the Druwydds meander between the roundhouses of the lower rampart. Eithne climbed up onto the wall next to Naoise and was joined by her brother, Drest.

"Where are they going?" Naoise whispered to Eithne.

"To the temple of the Goddesses. But only the Bandruwydds will enter. There is a staircase that dips down under that hill, and below is a stone chamber with a pool of fresh water. It is a beautiful room, painted with scenes of the Goddesses. Few have seen it. Only the Bandruwydds, Healers, and Princesses of the Blood may enter."

"Not even Queens?" Taran asked.

"Only women of the royal bloodline may enter," she smiled at Naoise. "Though I suppose if a Princess of the Blood married her cousin who was a King, then she may enter as Queen."

"What do they do in there?" Brei asked.

"I'm not sure exactly, but I think they use the water to consult with the Goddesses. I went down there one time, and one of the Healers, Morrigan, was staring into the pool, talking, but she was alone."

Brei shivered. The Druwydds' chanting grew louder, humming behind the hill until black-clad Bandruwydds emerged from the subterranean chamber. The procession moved further away towards the cliffs until only pricks of light from their torches hovered in the distance. Eventually, the rolling hiss and thud of waves hitting the rocks drowned out the chanting.

Taran jumped off the rampart and sat on the ground, leaning his back against the stonework.

"Go get us some ale, Dylan," Naoise said, pushing his brother off the wall.

Brei slid to the cold ground next to Taran. *It's going to be a long night.*

Someone was shaking him.

"Soldiers are attacking."

Brei opened his eyes. His father, Rhys, stood over him as he lay in his bed in Caercaled.

Brei yawned. "What's wrong?"

Rhys strode to the other side of the room where Taran lay in his cot bed, a mop of short blond hair covering his sleeping eyes. Rhys leant over the boy and shook his shoulders. "Taran, get up, son. Roman soldiers are attacking Caercaled."

Brei sat upright. His vision blurred from the sudden movement. "Where have they attacked?"

Taran opened his eyes and squinted up at their father.

"The farmsteads are on fire, and they've slaughtered the garrison at the Western Gate," Rhys replied.

Brei leapt out of the bed and grabbed his pants, which were hanging over a chair. "Are there survivors from the farmsteads?"

"I don't know, Brei. Gruffydd just rode up to the tower to sound the alarm. Taran, get dressed now. We need to defend the city."

Brei could hear screaming from the rooms below. In the stairwell his uncle, King Uradech, was speaking with someone. "Stay here with Derelei. Don't leave the tower. You'll be safe here."

Brei jammed his feet into his boots and grabbed his sword and shield from under his bed. His fingers trembled as he secured the leather scabbard belt around his waist.

King Uradech walked into the room with his brother Gartnait, and Gartnait's son, Elfinn.

"Are you taking the boys with you?" Uradech asked.

Rhys nodded. "We need everyone if we are to save the city."

Uradech grasped Rhys on the shoulder. "Good man. We'll try to push the Romans out of the city, but Gruffydd says they're fanning out and burning houses. This is going to be difficult."

"Who will remain here to guard the women and children?"

Uradech shook his head. "I can spare no one. Derelei is armed, of course, but that's the best we can do. Naoise and Dylan are too young and will remain with the women, but I have left them with daggers." Uradech turned to Taran with a strained smile. "Ready, lad?"

Taran nodded. He had barely seen fourteen winters, and yet his face was set with the confidence of a man who had seen thirty. They left the tower and stepped into the moonlight. In the warm summer air Gruffydd and the king's guard waited for them with torches. King Uradech took a torch from the hands of a warrior and held it above his head.

"Defend our homes, brothers, or we will meet again in Tirscath!" Uradech yelled, and he ran towards the outer ramparts and into the Sacred Forest.

The nauseating scream of women in pain echoed in the dark. Brei's mind lurched to Anwen, and his mouth turned dry. They followed King Uradech through the trees and into the city, where flames glowed against the dark horizon. At least a hundred Roman soldiers were fighting Caledon warriors in the centre circle. The market stalls were ablaze, as were all the roundhouses near the Western Gate.

"Head to the centre circle!" Uradech yelled as they sprinted towards the flames. Crowds of screaming women and children clogged the lanes as they descended through the city.

"Shelter in the tower!" Uradech yelled to villagers scrambling up the hill away from the soldiers. A woman fell in their path, and Brei skirted around her. He looked over his shoulder as he kept running and saw Taran had stopped to help her stand. Brei clenched his jaw and kept pushing through the fleeing villagers.

The heat from the fires increased as he drew closer, and the scraping of metal echoed over the screams. Warriors, men he saw every day, were slashing at the Roman soldiers. Metal covered the soldiers' chests and heads, and they carried large round shields. King Uradech charged through the crush of men and cracked his sword into the helmet of a Roman. The soldier fell, and Uradech stabbed into his neck. The warriors roared and pushed forwards against the soldiers.

Brei stayed close to his father and Taran as they moved forwards to engage. The space was so crowded it was difficult for the warriors to swing their swords. Covered in armour, the Romans pierced through the warriors' uncovered chests with ease. A Roman blade plunged through the stomach of a warrior in front of Brei, and out through the warrior's spine. The warrior fell to his knees, screaming as blood streamed down his back.

The soldier glared at Brei, his eyes glinting in the fires' light. Brei raised his sword, as best he could in the crush, and swung at the Roman. The soldier stepped back and knocked Brei's sword away with his shield. As Brei tried to swing again, the soldier lunged at his abdomen. From the corner of Brei's eye, he saw someone jump towards the soldier and stab him in the exposed part of his neck with a dagger. The soldier collapsed as Taran looked up at Brei. Taran grasped Brei by the shoulder. "Courage, Brei," he yelled and ran through the gap in the Roman line, swinging at a soldier with a strength unnatural for a boy of his size.

Brei ran after Taran in the mêlée and faced a tall Roman. The Roman *raised his sword and lunged for Brei's head. Brei swerved to the right and plunged his sword into the gusset gap underneath the soldier's armpit. The Roman fell to his knees as Brei pulled his bloodied sword from the soldier's side and stabbed it through the man's throat. Blood sprayed from the Roman's mouth, his eyes locked on Brei's. But Brei had no time to enjoy his victory as another soldier was upon him. Brei pulled the sword from the dead man's neck and lunged at his next opponent, ducking as a spear was hurled at his head.*

In a blur of bodies and metal, the warriors pushed through and overwhelmed the soldiers, encircling them until the Romans surrendered.

With shaking fingers, Brei returned his sword to his leather scabbard. We have won. *His mind turned to Anwen's face.* They don't need me. The battle is over. *He ducked out of the circle and sprinted along the deserted lane to the Western Gate. He ran along the river towards the flames that had engulfed all the buildings of the farmstead. Horses screamed in the stables as the fire claimed the building, but he pressed on, racing to the last roundhouse before the forest.* Please don't be dead.

A body lay before the door of the burning house. Brei stooped over it and recognised Anwen's father. He was covered in blood, and his intestines swam on his stomach in a pool of glistening red.

"Where is Anwen? And Morfydd? Are they inside?"

The man coughed, and blood dribbled from the edges of his mouth and down his chin. "They took Anwen. I tried to stop them, but they took her."

"Where? Where did they take her?" Brei yelled, his voice breaking.

Anwen's father raised a wavering finger towards the forest. "They are long gone now." His breathing laboured, and Brei held his hand as he died.

Brei jerked awake at the sound of chanting, opening his eyes to a procession of feet passing along the upper rampart wall at Caertarwos. The pink light of dawn shimmered on the faces of Taran, Dylan, and Naoise. Brei dragged his hands over his face, wiping off a cold sweat. He stood up and watched the Druwydds and Bandruwydds return through the carved bull stone passage, their robes sodden to their knees. Across the lower rampart, where the hill rose and dipped, two women surveyed the procession. One he recognised as Branwen, her auburn-haired companion was, he suspected, the other Healer, Morrigan. Brei glanced at Taran, who watched the Healers, a slight crease in his forehead as the women disappeared down the invisible steps under the hill.

As the last of the procession entered the upper rampart to meet with Talorc, Brei yawned and lifted his arms above his head to stretch.

Talorc beamed. "The Gods have spoken, and the same need for vengeance for the crimes of these barbarians against our fathers, mothers, and those who have gone before us, drives them as it drives us. We will have our southern invasion!"

Taran jumped onto the wall of the rampart and yelled "Revenge or Tirscath!" The gathered kings and princes cheered. The Eldar Druwydd whispered to Talorc, but Talorc waved his hand at the Druwydd and walked away. Seeming to have aged a hundred years in one night, the Eldar Druwydd hobbled away, assisted by two apprentices.

Talorc bounced around, shaking the hands of the kings and princes, grinning. "Wine!" he yelled, which was greeted by more cheers.

Brei groaned, staring up at the pale pink sky. "I think I will go for a swim."

"I'll join you," Taran murmured, jumping off the wall.

"Are you coming, Neesh?" Brei asked, but Naoise was staring across the upper rampart to the King's Hall. Brei and Taran turned to look and saw Eithne had joined her brothers, Talorc and Drest. Taran grinned and ruffled Naoise's thick black hair. Naoise turned and tried to punch him, but Taran stepped out of the way, dancing around him, and slapped him on the back of the head before running towards the small hill above the mysterious chamber.

Brei smirked and jogged after Taran. His stomach tightened as he saw Taran's body disappear behind the hill. First his knees, then up to his waist, until only his head bobbed above the grass, before it too disappeared. Brei reached the knoll and looked at the stone staircase as it sloped down under the hill. At the base was a square doorway made of stone. Inside, the chamber was black, and Taran stood at the last step on the balls of his feet, seemingly frozen. Murmuring rose from the chamber, and it was as if Taran was talking to the darkness. After a few minutes, he turned and climbed back up the stairs, not meeting Brei's eye until he reached the top.

"Well?" Brei asked.

"Well what?" Taran said without stopping, and he continued over the lower rampart.

"Why did you go down there, and who were you talking to?" Brei asked, struggling to keep up as he followed to the beach on the other side of the headland.

Taran did not answer, but as their boots sunk into the sand, he stopped. "I had a question."

"Did you get an answer?"

"Yes," he grunted, pulling off his boots. He strode across the sand and dived into water that was so flat in the dawn stillness that it appeared Taran had dived into a pink mirror reflecting the sky.

TWENTY-NINE

Summer, 367 C.E., Britannia

"Kill it! Kill it!"

A frenzied roar rose from the crowd, drowning out the snarling dogs. Sorsha closed her eyes as an animal howled, low and thick with misery. Her stomach churned. *Put it out of its suffering. Please.* The animal gasped and let out a strangled groan.

Sorsha opened her eyes as the crowd erupted. On the dirt floor of a large stone amphitheatre, just outside the walls of Corinium Dobunnorum, the brown bear sprawled, motionless, in a pool of its own blood. The bear had been tied to a pole, while five mastiffs attacked it. Moisture gathered across her eyes, and she blinked rapidly, willing the tears to disperse.

"I told you to put money on the dogs, Lucia!" Cecily saidd as she brandished a slip of red fabric in the air to gain the attention of the bookie. The folds of her red palla covered her dark brown hair, which was puffed high atop her head, and around her arms, golden bracelets glittered in the sun.

Sorsha surveyed the crowd. Thousands had gathered for the fights and were clearly excited by the bloodshed. Some seemed annoyed and must have bet on the bear. But others, like Cecily, had drunken smiles and waved slips of crimson fabric above their heads. Sorsha swallowed. *This is just foreplay.*

A slave dressed in a shabby tunic approached Cecily and, in exchange for her piece of red fabric, pressed ten gold denarii into her hand before he moved on to the people sitting behind them. "I bet you've missed this?" Cecily purred as she slipped the gold into a red silk purse.

"I've only been once before." Sorsha's skin prickled as a chain gang of five men were hauled across the arena floor. They were pale, and some had hair of fire.

"You'll enjoy this," Cecily whispered.

The crowd hushed as the Governor of Britannia Prima strode into the arena, resplendent in a white toga that draped over thick purple bands running either side of the shoulders of his tunic. "Citizens! Behold! From the depths of the coldest corners of the north! I give you the Picti!"

Slaves removed the chains from the warriors, and the crowd gasped.

"How will the barbarians of the north match up against the gladiators of Carthage?" the governor roared.

The crowd screamed and stamped their feet. Sorsha craned her neck to see ten armed men enter the arena, wearing protective armour and carrying shields. She looked back at the northern men, who were shirtless and without a weapon. *Surely, they will at least give them a sword?*

The sound of a gong reverberated around the arena just as Marcus jogged up a wooden staircase and into the box Sorsha and Cecily were sitting in. He smiled at them as he took his seat, handing Cecily a cup of wine.

Sorsha studied the gladiators, the sun shimmering off their dark olive skin. *How is it possible that Rome conquered Carthage when their warriors look so formidable?*

Seemingly well practised at herding, the gladiators separated two men from the group. One gladiator lunged at a red-haired man, splitting open the man's stomach. Sorsha sucked the air in through her teeth. For a frozen moment, the crowd hushed. The silence was broken by the splat of guts slopping to the ground. The crowd screamed again and drummed their feet like thunder.

"How is this entertainment when they are not even given a chance?" Sorsha hissed.

"Why do you care, Lucia? They are animals."

"Kill! Kill! Kill!" the crowd chanted.

Sorsha watched the man's face writhe in agony as the gladiator lifted him up by his hair. *I'm going to be sick.* A second gladiator swung his sword and beheaded the northern man. The crowd leapt into the air and roared as the victorious gladiator paraded the head around the arena, waving up at his screaming fans.

Sorsha gazed up at the grinning red faces in the crowd. "Cecily, I need to go for a walk."

"Are you not well, my dear? The sun is hot today. I'll take you back to the apartment."

Sorsha shook her head. "No, thank you, I'll be all right. I know my way around Corinium, and I don't want to ruin your day." She forced a smile and accepted a kiss on the cheek from Cecily's rouged lips.

By late afternoon, groups of exhausted, drunk, and sunburnt patrons returned through the tower gate and poured into Corinium Dobunnorum. Sorsha walked against the tide of the crowd and headed back towards the stadium. Inside the tiered stone amphitheatre, slaves bustled through with brooms, and two heaved a bag of sawdust across the stadium floor, scattering it over pools of blood. She walked through a wooden gate and crossed the dirt floor into the centre of the stadium, imagining what it would feel like to have a crowd of people screaming at her while she fought for her life.

"Can I help you, lady?"

Sorsha turned around at the sound of a lightly accented, soft voice.

A young man with olive skin waited with his arms behind his back. His nose was sharp and his black eyes reminded her of a hawk.

"I just wanted to see what it was like. It seems terrifying."

He nodded. "It is."

"You are a gladiator?"

He shook his head and drew his right arm from behind his back. In place of a tanned limb was a mangled stump ending above where the elbow should have been.

"They let you live?"

He licked his brown lips. "I try to be indispensable."

"How?"

"I train the gladiators."

Sorsha smiled. "Impressive. Where are you from?"

"Carthage. But I haven't been there for a long time. Not since I was ten."

"You became a slave when you were ten?"

His gaze dropped to the sawdust on the ground. "No, lady, I was born a slave. But I was sold to my current master when I was ten. Where are you from, if you don't mind me asking, lady?"

"I'm from Corinium Dobunnorum, but I spent the winter in the north with the Painted People."

He raised his dark, preened eyebrows. "That almost seems un-believable, but things are making sense now."

Sorsha tilted her head. "What things?"

"The fact you are down here when everyone else is drunk and gone home. The fact you are trying to imagine what it would be like to be a gladiator. And I saw you leave early. You looked like you might throw up."

"You saw me?"

"It is impertinent, I know." He dropped his eyes to the ground and a faint crimson flushed his olive cheeks. "Forgive me."

She studied his face. *If not for his tattered robes, he could be anyone.* She smiled. "Could you do me a favour?"

"If it is within my power, lady, but note that not much is."

"Are there any Painted People alive? I'd like to speak to them if I can."

"Two men survived, but one may be dead by now. I can take you to their cages, but I don't know if you should see them. It is not for ladies such as yourself."

"They are kept in cages?"

He nodded.

"What is your name?"

"They call me Hannibal. But they call all Carthaginian gladiators Hannibal."

"What was the name your mother gave you?"

"Mago."

Sorsha smiled. "Well, my name is Sorsha. Please take me to see him, Mago."

Mago bowed and led her across the arena floor and through a wooden gate to a line of iron cages fixed atop unhooked carts. He pointed to the closest cage, where five men leaned against the bars. Three were olive-skinned and bore the same sharp noses and almond eyes as Mago.

"Are these your countrymen?" Sorsha asked.

"From Carthage or the surrounding African province, yes."

One man was dressing the shoulder of another with a linen bandage. They glared at her from behind the iron bars.

She stepped towards the cage. "Who are the other men?"

Two men with lighter skin leant against the bars with their backs to her. Their wrists were bound and hung through the bars behind them.

"My master says they are from the Alamanni. They do not speak Latin. They arrived here only a few weeks ago. We keep them bound because they are dangerous."

Sorsha approached the back wheel of the cart.

"Stay back, lady Sorsha, I do not want them to harm you."

The Alamanni men did not turn as she placed her right hand around a bar and gazed up into the cage. The Carthaginians watched her but did not move forwards.

"Hello," she whispered in Latin to the Carthaginian, whose shoulder was bandaged. "Is your arm badly hurt?"

His black eyes searched hers, and he shook his head. "A scratch."

She glanced to her right, where the Alamanni men sat inches from her. The closest man was now staring down at her. His strong features and blue eyes reminded her of the men of Caledon. She reached across to where his bound hands poked through the bars and she placed her hand into his. He winced when she touched him, but then she felt his hand close around hers. *I wish I could help you. I wish I could spare you the horrific death that awaits you.*

"Lady Sorsha, you wanted to see the Painted Man?" Mago whispered behind her. "I think he will die soon, and my master will be back any minute."

As she released the Alamanni's hand, he closed his eyes and turned away.

Sorsha followed Mago along the cages of men to the sixth cart, where two of the occupants had the palest skin of them all. Their red hair shone in the fading evening light. One man lay on his back, his hands covering his stomach, and another man sat cross-legged by his head, holding his hand. Blood dripped down the sides of the cart and onto the dirt-encrusted wheels.

Sorsha strode to the cage and reached through the bars. "Push him towards me," she said in the Ancient Tongue. "I can help him if you bring him closer."

The dying man turned his head and gazed at her. "Who are you?"

"I am…" She paused. The tide of empathy rose inside her, and she pressed up against the bars. "I am a Healer, from Caledon. Let me help you."

She stretched her fingers out towards him, willing herself to reach, but he turned his head away and stared at the wooden roof of his cage. "I don't want to be healed," he croaked.

"Why not? You are moments from death."

The corners of his mouth twitched. "I know. And it will be such a relief."

Sorsha glanced at the man who sat by the dying man's head. "I don't understand."

The man placed his hand on his companion's shoulder. "If you heal him, what will you be saving him for? Are you planning on freeing us?"

Sorsha lowered her eyes to the blood running along a spoke of the wheel.

"I thought not," said the man. "So you would save him now, only to go back out there tomorrow. To fear for his life in front of thousands of drunken faces laughing at him. To watch his countrymen have their limbs torn off by bears or other slaves. And lie in the indignity of a cage with the smell of his waste in his nostrils." He pointed to a wooden bucket in the corner of the cage.

She clasped the warm bars with both hands as tears fell from her cheeks. "When were you taken?"

"It has been so long I don't even remember. Many moons and winters have passed."

"Were you taken from Caercaled?"

The man nodded. "They captured mostly women, but we were only boys when we were taken. They've only just started using us for the fights now that we are big enough."

"Was Princess Derelei taken with you?"

"She was for a time. But when they loaded us onto boats, she was not on ours. And she was not at the markets in the big city, either."

"Lady, my master is coming," Mago hissed.

Sorsha glanced behind her and saw an obese, red-cheeked man ambling towards them.

Sorsha wiped her cheek. "How can he not care that he kills defenceless men for sport?"

"My master is not his enemy." Mago frowned. "None of these men are. They may wield the sword that killed him, but they are not his enemy. Neither is my master. It is the crowds who seek the blood. They are his enemy."

Sorsha stumbled along the stone passageway, towards the flickering light in the square chamber. A lit torch lay on the ground and the wood crackled, but a gust of wind blew it out, plunging the chamber into darkness. She straightened and backed herself against the stone wall, listening to the footsteps getting closer. Someone was running up the passageway towards her. Sweat pooled on her forehead and along the top of her lip.

"No! Stop it!" she screamed as emerald eyes closed in on her.

Sorsha sat up, panting, and opened her eyes. Staring around the room, she took in the grey outlines of Cecily and Marcus' splendid bedroom furniture. She rolled over and closed her eyes, determined to sleep. Once more, icy fingers slid up her chest and closed around her neck. Groaning, she pushed the palms of her hands into her eyes, but the icy fingers tightened their grip. She shuffled to the window and peered out into the dark. The cool air washed over her sweaty face and body.

I have to go back.

Sorsha yawned. The skin under her eyes was heavy and swollen.

"Are you tired?" Nyfain asked.

"Yes." She had stayed awake to watch the sunrise, afraid to close her eyes again. But Sorsha had made arrangements to leave for Londinium that morning, instead of returning with Cecily and Marcus to Aquae Sulis.

"Thank you for all your help, Nyfain."

The girl bit her lip.

"You'll be okay, won't you?" Sorsha whispered in the Ancient Tongue.

Nyfain looked at the ground.

"Would you come with me?" Sorsha whispered.

Nyfain's head snapped up, and her eyes swam with hunger. "Where?"

"Londinium, first."

"Will you go back to the north?"

"Maybe. I think I have to."

Nyfain knelt down and took Sorsha's hand. "We don't belong here, Sorsha."

Sorsha pulled her hand back. "I'll speak to Cecily and see if I can… er…"

"Buy me?"

Sorsha's cheeks flushed. "Yes." She closed her eyes and turned away from Nyfain. "I'll see what I can do." She left the room without looking at Nyfain again and walked into the reception parlour, where a green and gold mosaic of a hare was inlaid on the floor. Sorsha skirted around it, not wanting to walk across the hare's face.

"Lucia!" Cecily called to her from the dining room. "Lucia, it is so sad that you want to leave us today! Why can't you stay?"

Marcus shook his head. "Leave her be, Cecily. She is not your daughter."

Cecily pouted but smiled as Sorsha joined them at the table.

Sorsha reached for a bunch of grapes from the opulent fruit platter in the centre of the table. "You have both been so generous to have me for so long. I do not know how I will ever repay you."

Cecily waved her hand. "Think nothing of it. In fact, I have a gift for you." She pointed to a silk purse placed above Sorsha's plate.

Sorsha glanced at Marcus, and he smiled. "Open it."

She pulled open the strings. It was full of gold denarii, perhaps one hundred. Sorsha put the purse down. "This is too much, please."

"Think nothing of it. It has been so illuminating to have you here," Marcus said, reaching out and tapping her hand. "Is there anything else we can do for you for your journey? We have prepared a week's worth of food, although it should only take you three or four days by horse."

Will it seem ungrateful if I also ask for Nyfain? She shook her head and reached for a cup of water. But her stomach tensed as she sipped. *Is awkwardness really a reason to subject someone to a lifetime of servitude?* Sorsha cleared her throat. "Actually..."

Marcus and Cecily looked up from their breakfasts of fruit, honey, and fresh bread.

"I was wondering about the handmaiden who has been serving me, Nyfain. I've grown quite fond of her. Instead of this generous gift, could I, perhaps, have her instead?"

Marcus raised his eyebrows at his wife, and Sorsha knew she had stepped too far.

"But, of course, you must have the slave," Cecily said, beaming. "And you must keep the gift. Have both."

Marcus smiled and returned to his honeyed bread.

Sorsha swallowed. *Nyfain is nothing more than a horse to them.*

THIRTY

Departing at dawn, Naoise and Drest sailed for Ulster from the harbour at Caertarwos. Meanwhile, Brei and Taran travelled to the southern kingdoms. Both parties had been entrusted by King Talorc to draw more allies to their cause, but Brei wondered how much Naoise and Drest could achieve beyond gambling and sinking tankards of ale. Much to his disgust, Dylan had been left to escort King Gartnait to Caercaled.

Their journey led them through Ce, and King Alpin had invited Brei and Taran to stay at his fortress on Banntuce, "Mountain of the People of Ce". The land rose as they rode south-east with the Ce contingent, climbing away from the coast's rugged beauty. Outstretched before them was a patchwork of moorland and forest, and the rough road was indistinguishable from the muddy bogs that lingered even as the spring sun warmed the land.

By late afternoon, they approached the mountain range. Whilst not as high as those in the west, the mountains were steeply peaked and, on one peak, the distinctive ramparts of a ringed citadel enclosed a circular stone tower. Like many of the north's fortresses, it was well located, with a view far across the moorland, reaching to the lands of Vortriu and the ocean. When they arrived, Brei looked out to the west, where small peaks jutted up in the distance, and he knew that one would be

Rīgbre, and below it the Druwyddic centre of Rīgonīn. He thought of the Torc they had been asked to escort back to Caercaled, and he wondered where Sorsha was now. Brei glanced at Taran, who had followed his gaze.

They walked through the stone ramparts and into the inner sanctum, where armed warriors stood guard. Next to the tower, the Kings of Ce had built a hall, which had a thatched roof, raised high in a pitched triangle, and Brei felt it was much airier and pleasant than in the dark stone hall at Caercaled. Large deer antler and bull horns were mounted on the hall beams, and two long tables were placed in the middle.

"Papa!"

A boy who had seen perhaps twelve summers ran towards King Alpin, a grin on his face.

"I don't think you have met my son, this is Cal. Son, these are Princes of the Blood of Caledon and Vortriu, Prince Brei and Prince Taran."

Brei looked at Alpin's son. Cal was a handsome boy, with the same tanned complexion and brown hair as his mother, who came from Gaul.

"The meal is almost ready, Father, would you like some mead?"

"I think a cold mouthful of water first. Brei, Taran, would you like to see our mountain well?"

Taran was gazing across the hall at a group of ladies with the same tanned skin as Cal, and Brei thought he recognised Alpin's lady, Balinee, and his sister, Luan. "No, I think I will introduce myself to the ladies," Taran said and drifted across the hall.

Alpin watched him go. "He won't have any luck there. Luan is already promised to Prince Drest of Vortriu."

"When will the binding ceremony take place?" Brei asked.

Alpin gestured for Brei to follow him out of the hall. "Beltane is the season for it. It is an excellent match. The Kingdoms of Ce and Vortriu are neighbours, and now they will be allied with blood."

They walked across the inner fortress. The mountain air was cooling as the sun began its descent. Alpin led them to a semi-circle wall of stone, only a yard wide, surrounding a spiralling staircase that sloped into the shadow. Brei followed Alpin down the steps into humid darkness.

"My boy is not too much older than your girls, I think?" Alpin said.

Brei grunted. *No doubt he will seek a match for Cal with Nia or Ceridwen.*

They descended until water covered the stairs, and they stopped. A wooden bucket floated across the grey water, attached to the side of the stone wall with rope.

"Is it true that Taran has his own personal Healer?" Alpin whispered in the echoing well.

"How did you know?"

"Naoise told anyone who would listen. So, it is true?"

Brei pressed his hand against the cold, damp stone. "I don't know."

"I've heard Taran has the Eldar Druwydd in the palm of his hands."

Brei's chest tightened. "Taran's business is his own."

"Indeed," Alpin said as he pulled up the wooden bucket of water and brought it to his lips. "Ah!" He swallowed and handed the bucket to Brei.

When they had drunk and washed their faces of the grime from travel, they walked back up the spiral staircase.

"What do you hope to achieve from all this, Brei?"

"All of what?

"The campaign beyond the Great Wall?"

Brei paused on the final step. "Revenge."

Alpin smiled. "Naturally. But for you personally, is that all you want?"

"I want what Caledon wants."

"Is it the same for your brother?"

Brei sighed. "I know what you're getting at, but I don't see why it is your concern. If you must know, I have no quarrel with Taran and I won't be drawn into any schemes. If you want to align Ce with Caledon through my daughter and your son, I will not oppose that, but if you're trying to find any rifts between my brother and I, you will be disappointed."

Alpin laughed. "No offence meant, my friend, but I am gladdened by your consent. I will bring Cal to Caercaled to meet your daughters at the summer meeting for this conspiracy of yours."

Brei shielded his eyes with his hand as the early summer sun pierced through the canopy of the Sacred Forest.

"It's Beltane tonight," Anwen said. "Will you come to the farmstead early to see Mother? She complains that you never visit her."

"She's not high on my list of priorities, Anwen. I've got to ensure everything is ready for when the kings arrive in Caercaled, and I have to make sure that quarrelsome blacksmith, Gwyddion, is producing enough swords and spearheads each day. It's summer now and we are running out of moons until our attack. I still have to train boys and farmers how to use those swords, if they are to join the warriors in battle. And then there's the harvest. You know the warriors are all expected to help on the farmsteads, so I'll be going to Gruffydd's lands soon. If I have any free time, Anwen, I will spend it with you and the girls, not Morfydd."

"I'm sorry, Brei, I didn't mean to upset you. I know how hard you are working."

Golden strobes of light floated across Anwen's freckled face as the oak tree they stood under swayed in the gentle summer breeze. Her copper hair hung loose about her shoulders and a strand blew across her face. Brei brushed it away and sighed. "I'm tired."

"You're hardly sleeping, maybe you should have a rest. We could bathe in the Shining Lakes?"

Brei shook his head. "It's not the work. It's what King Alpin said to me at Banntuce."

"That you should think about your future?"

He nodded. "I'll not deny that I think about what will happen when Gartnait dies. I think about the king's death more than one should be allowed to. But I keep coming back to what Gruffydd said to me. That I made my decision already."

"But so many moons have passed since then. So many nights and winters. You can make a new decision if you want to, my love."

Brei gazed up at the green leaves of the oak tree and inhaled the sweet summer scent of warm air. He squeezed Anwen's hand. "What Gruffydd said is just an expression of what the rest of the warriors think of me. That I am the man who could have been king but chose not to be. That I chose not to because…"

"Because you wanted to bind yourself to a peasant farmer's daughter?"

"There's never been any point denying it, darling. You know I love you, but what I did…is not easily forgotten. And then what about Taran? Ever since that night, he has worked tirelessly to position himself with the warriors, with the Druwydds and Bandruwydds, to take the crown when it is next available. He is loved."

"That doesn't mean you have to support him, though. If you don't want to. Do you want to be king, and, if you do, why do you want it? Taran has always given me this… I'm not sure how to explain it… but a sense of darkness, of desperation in how much he wants to succeed."

"I know. He tries to hide it, but I see it too. But he's only like that because of me."

"Because you didn't support his claim?" Anwen frowned. "Why would you when he beat you almost to death in trying to ensure he was the only possible claimant?"

"It is because of that, yes, but there are things you don't know… That's not why he beat me. I have told no one what happened the night of the attack, except for Taran. There's a part of me that knows I owe him. And then there's a part of me that questions if he is the best one to lead us. I wonder if he only wants the crown for his own ambition, or if he would be like me and be a father to Caledon. But then, surpassing all of that is you, Ceridwen, and Nia, and I remember how selfish I am. Because I would betray my kinsmen in a heartbeat if any of you were at risk."

Anwen embraced him, her face pressing into the linen tunic that covered his chest. "I don't believe you would betray your kinsmen, Brei. You are not capable of that. I know you would find a way to protect us all." She raised her blue eyes to his. "I believe in you."

Brei tightened his arms around her small body. *I don't deserve her. If she knew what I did to Taran, she would despise me. I would be a terrible king.* He sighed and kissed the top of her head. *Then why do you still dream of the Eldar Druwydd raising the crown onto your head?*

A horn wailed from the tower above them. Brei turned and scanned the forest. They were still alone, but voices drifted towards them. Chanting.

"The Druwydds are going down for Beltane," Anwen whispered.

"The procession will take hours. They don't light the fires until sunset. Maybe we could sneak off to the lakes?"

"Brei, that's not like you." Anwen grinned.

Brei kissed her. "Let's go."

Two giant bonfires blazed on either side of the stables at the farmstead. The Eldar Druwydd had led a procession of white-robed Druwydds and black-cloaked Bandruwydds from the tower through Caercaled, and along the bank of the River Tae to the cleared pastures adjoining the farmstead.

The Eldar Druwydd stood at the stable, wearing a leather cap over which the skull and antlers of a stag were affixed. Serenn stood next to him, glaring out at the farmers and villagers from Caercaled who had gathered for Beltane. Her usual charcoaled eyes had been enlarged with white paint circles, while the rest of her face was painted dark blue with woad. She also wore her deer antler headdress, and blue braids fanned across the black robes covering her bony shoulders. Brei did not enjoy Serenn's company at the best of times, but he found her presence unbearable when she was decorated for a festival.

King Gartnait and the Princes of the Blood, Brei, Taran, Naoise, and Dylan, stood between the two fires, facing the stables. A hush, feverish with anticipation, fell across the farmstead. Both sides of the lane that divided the farmstead's roundhouses were lined with people craning their necks to get a better view. The Eldar Druwydd chanted a rumbling incantation to Belenus, the God of Light, calling upon him to protect the cattle and sheep as they prepared to release them from their winter captivity for summer grazing.

Brei glanced at Taran. In the glow of the flames, the tattoo of victory, the crescent overlaid with a broken arrow, glistened across his broad chest. In contrast, King Gartnait's collarbones jutted out of his tunic, as though he were already a corpse waiting for its skeleton to be de-fleshed by ravens.

The Eldar Druwydd lifted his arms to the sky and Brei's eyes followed to the cloudless indigo blanket pierced with shimmering stars and a waning moon. The drums started, slow at first but then with a menacing, increasing beat. Taran and Naoise brushed his arms on either side as they walked forwards to the stables. Brei walked in line with them, with King Gartnait and Dylan on the outer edges. They reached the double wooden doors and waited for the Eldar Druwydd.

Inside the stables, cattle and sheep brayed and stamped. The Eldar Druwydd removed a dried sprig of mistletoe that had been lain across the doorknobs. As one, the Princes of the Blood and the king opened the stable doors. The doors were thrust wide, and Brei leapt out of the way as a black bull charged through. Behind the bull, farmers drove out the rest of the herd of cattle and sheep with horns and clapping.

The Druwydds and princes watched from the sidelines as the terrified animals were driven between the two fires. Horns blew into the night, and the Druwydds' chanting echoed around the farmstead. But the hooves of hundreds of animals stampeding thundered on the soft ground, louder even than the drums that now beat at a ferocious pace.

When the animals were through the fires, they galloped along the lane crowded with people on either side until they escaped into the freedom of the pastures. Revelling in their newfound liberty, the cows called to each other, and their low cries rang across the hills throughout the night.

When the last sheep had been enticed out, the drums stopped and the Eldar Druwydd stepped between the fires and raised his hands to the sky. "Belenus has blessed us and will protect our herds for the summer grazing! Light your hearths from the Beltane fires, have no other light but Belenus tonight!"

A wooden flute whistled, and the drums returned to a lively beat as villagers approached with bundles of broom and lit them. Blazing torches bobbed in a glowing line from the farmstead, along the River Tae to Caercaled, and all the way to the tower, until Caercaled sparkled with fires blessed by Belenus, the God of Light.

THIRTY-ONE

Summer, 367 C.E., Britannia

The paved road from Corinium Dobunnorum led Sorsha and Nyfain east through forest, over bridges, through villages and between hills. At times it was busy with travellers and often plagued by carts flicking dust and rocks into their faces. At the crossroads town of Verulamium, they stayed overnight in an inn and washed off the dirt before continuing their journey south. After a week-long trek, the stone wall surrounding Londinium rose before them, shimmering on the horizon in the afternoon sun.

They had taken it in turns to ride the horse, to spare their feet eight hours a day of walking on hard paved roads. As they approached the city gate, Sorsha led the horse while Nyfain sat astride. A sea of stone tombs and monuments lay just outside the walls. Roman soldiers stood outside the gate and on the ramparts, but Sorsha and Nyfain passed through the cool shadows of the stone gate unopposed. On the city side of the gate, Sorsha stopped the horse next to a foot soldier. "Excuse me, we are looking for the slavers' market. Which road do I take?"

He approached her horse and stroked its neck, smiling at her with dark eyes, and brown hair poking out under his gold-gilted helmet. "Follow this road east. Once you hit the city walls again, follow the wall to the south around the big fort and head to the river, and there are the slavers and cattle pens."

"Thank you," she said and clicked to the horse to walk on.

The road they followed through the city was straight and wide and lined on either side with buildings stretching to the east for what felt like a mile. Public buildings were in various stages of repair or ruin, and the forum had long since burnt down. Londinium bristled like a geriatric lion, once adored but now reduced to mere existence.

The slave market was indistinct from the cattle auctions, with its auctioneer platform and holding pens. As they approached, a chain of men was led off the platform, a rope tied to each of their necks. Leaving Nyfain with the horse, Sorsha walked across the dirt yard to the plump and sweaty auctioneer and his tall assistant who were talking to the customer who had purchased the lot. Sorsha glanced at the chained men with their dark hair, tanned skin, and mournful eyes. *They are broken.* One man struggled more than the others to walk upright, and he had a bandage around his torso, soaked in blood. The compulsive wave to heal swept over her, and she stepped closer.

"Stay back. These slaves are fresh and dangerous," the man who had purchased them yelled.

"But this man is dying."

The purchaser marched over and inspected the man and then rounded on the auctioneer, his face red. "You've tried to mislead me! This one only has a day to live!"

The auctioneer scurried across the yard, his pudgy belly jiggling as he ran. "I swear the blood was not coming through like this before. You know I value you as my greatest customer and I would never sell you damaged goods knowingly."

"Take it out of the lot. This one is worthless, maybe practice for the gladiators, but even then he can barely stand. A pig would put up a better fight." He chuckled as he kicked the man, who stumbled and fell, causing the rope to drag the other men down with him.

Sorsha ran and caught him. "I will help you," she whispered to him in the Ancient Tongue, though she did not know if he could understand.

The auctioneer snapped his fingers to his pale assistant. "Cut this one loose and kill him. He's not worth the grain to feed even for a night."

"I will take him!"

The original purchaser, the auctioneer, and his assistant all turned to Sorsha.

"I need a farmhand, and I will try to nurse him back to health." She looked over to Nyfain, who nodded.

The assistant cut the dying man loose, and Nyfain came over and helped him to stand up. While the purchaser and auctioneer haggled over a new price, Sorsha and Nyfain huddled with the slave. His face was drained, and the skin pulled tight against his sharp nose.

"Do you understand me?" Sorsha asked in the Ancient Tongue.

"Do you understand me?" Nyfain whispered in her different dialect.

Something flashed in his vacant eyes, and he nodded. Sorsha slid her hand under the sodden bandage and pressed into the wound. Heat pulsed from her heart and flowed down her veins into her palms. His breathing returned to normal within moments, and his dark eyes refocused.

"Listen to me," Sorsha pressed her lips to his ear. "You must pretend you are still injured, or they will take you back."

He nodded and doubled over, groaning.

"Take him to lie over there," she said to Nyfain in Latin. Sorsha walked across the yard to the auctioneer, her blood-soaked hands trembling.

"Thank you for spotting that dead weight, I am much obliged," the original purchaser said to her, pressing a silver coin into her hand.

She shivered as the remaining men were led away from the market, an uncomfortable urge rising inside her to free them all.

The auctioneer wiped sweat from his bald head. "And what are you still doing here?"

"My sincere apologies for the inconvenience caused, but better you were able to sort out a new deal here than have lost a valuable customer forever."

He glared. "What do you want?"

"I would like your help to find a slave that might have come through here, six years ago, from the Painted People. I come on the recommendation of the Provost of the Storehouses of London. Are you Flavius?"

"Marcus sent you? Hmm. Yes, I am Flavius, but that will be difficult."

"I will pay you for your trouble."

"Yes, handsomely. But it will take a few days. Do you know the slave's name? Description? Tattoos?"

"Yes, Derelei is her name. Female, blonde, tall. I'm not sure if she has any tattoos, she might have an armband with the Snake of Caledon…that is, a snake curled across a broken arrow."

Flavius stepped over to a small writing desk beside the platform the slaves had stood on and scratched on vellum with a quill and ink. "Your name?" he drawled without looking up at her.

"Lucia of Corinium Dobunnorum."

"Hmm. And why do you want to find this slave?"

"She is the mother of my handmaiden," Sorsha gestured to Nyfain. "I wish for them to take care of my household."

He frowned, and his eyes travelled from her face to the sword that hung at her waist.

She reached into the coin pouch on her belt. "Here, ten denarii should more than cover your time in searching the records."

He reached out to take the coins, but she snatched her hand back. "Paid upon delivery of the information I seek."

"Of course." He licked his lips. "And if I do not find her?"

"I'll still pay you. Most slaves come in first through this market, do they not?"

Flavius nodded.

"So, if she was not taken here, then either she is dead, or she was taken directly to a fort at the wall?"

"Most likely. Now, if that is all you want, I have other business to attend to. Come back in three days."

Sorsha walked back to Nyfain. The slave put his arms over Nyfain and Sorsha, and they heaved him back to their horse and helped him to mount. *It's almost harder to pretend that he is injured than it would have been to get a real injured man on a horse.*

Once he was mounted, Sorsha led the horse west along the wall. The buildings nearest to the river seemed to be large manors, with gardens, white walls, and sloping roofs covered in red tiles. They soon reached a gate that opened onto the bridge spanning the river. She remembered when she had seen it from the river on her first visit to Londinium and how it had seemed like the world was full of possibilities. A cart laden with sacks of grain trundled from the bridge, through the gate, and along a road that led north back into the city. Sorsha pulled at the bridle and they followed the cobbled road to the north, where the density of people and buildings increased. Women wore long tunics to their ankles with bright-coloured pallas wrapped around their shoulders and tucked under their arms. A few men wore togas over their tunics that came to the knee, but most disregarded such formality. They bustled along the street that narrowed to squeezed wooden buildings with a mixture of shop frontages on the ground floor and squalid-looking houses on top.

Fresh baked bread wafted down the street as people purchased goods from the alcoves at the buildings' base. At the end of the street, a high, vaulted, triangular roof towered above the other buildings. It was the remains of the old forum and basilica. Next to the baker was a triple-storied tavern, and they rented a sparse grey room in the upper storey. On a wooden floor was a cot barely big enough for Sorsha and Nyfain to have shared. Sorsha led the man to the cot, and he sat down.

"Ask the innkeeper for some water, bread, and cheese," she said to Nyfain. "And a cloth!" she yelled as Nyfain disappeared out the door.

Sorsha bent down in front of the man and removed the bloodied bandage.

He fingered the scar that now lay where his mortal wound had been an hour before. "Thank you… How…?" was all she managed to understand. He spoke a similar language to the Ancient Tongue, but it had diverged enough that it was barely comprehensible.

"I am a Healer… Gallar. I heal from the Gods," she said, trying to speak as simply as possible, while she scanned his body for any other signs of injury. The rope had burnt his neck, and his feet were bloody from marching barefoot.

By the time Nyfain returned, Sorsha had tended to the rest of his wounds. As Nyfain bent down to wash him with a bowl and a cloth, he wrenched the water bowl from her and gulped. Nyfain returned with more water, and when he was clean, they sat on the floor together and ate.

"Where do you come from?" Nyfain asked when he finished eating and had lain back on the cot bed against the wall.

"Overwater… Gaul."

"From Gaul? But Gaul has been part of the empire for hundreds of years." She paused and switched to Latin. "You speak Latin?"

"Yes, I speak Latin, but I don't like to. My village refused to pay taxes to the Romans. The Saxons raid our villages, but the Romans don't protect us anymore. Yet they still demand taxes."

"What happened to your village?" Nyfain asked in the Ancient Tongue.

He shrugged. "All burnt…gone."

"What is your name?" Nyfain asked.

"Dioras."

"I am Nyfain."

He smiled and repeated, "Nee–fan."

Nyfain looked at the ground.

He watched her, a smile still playing on his lips, and then turned to Sorsha. "Name?"

"I am Sorsha."

"Saw—sha."

His eyes followed Nyfain, who had risen to tidy away their meal.

"You don't need to do that." Sorsha stood and took the water bowl from her hand. "Sit, and rest."

Nyfain looked troubled.

"Please, I don't want you to serve me. You are free." She looked at Dioras. "You are both free, and you may leave whenever you want."

Neither said anything.

"Of course, you may stay with me. But you are free, and I am not your master."

"I have nowhere else to go," Nyfain said. "I will stay."

"Dioras, I can help you get back to your family?"

He shook his head. "My village burn... I stay."

They spent the next three days exploring Londinium. It was difficult to understand Dioras in the Ancient Tongue, but he seemed happy to listen to Sorsha and Nyfain, who made an effort to converse with him. Dioras was old enough to have been a father but had not been bound when he was captured, a fact that Nyfain had been most delicate about extracting. Dioras, though mostly silent, smiled and shone from his eyes, seemingly pleased by all he encountered, and Sorsha shuddered at the horrors that had led him to such a disposition.

On the third day they paid their bill with the tavern and returned to the slavers' market. Flavius seemed astounded to find Dioras alive. Flavius informed them he had searched their records for the last seven years and could not find a Derelei that matched the description. "Likely as not she is dead," he continued. "But if you are desperate to find her, the forts along the wall are crawling with slaves for the soldiers, and they need not come through the Londinium markets. The soldiers just take them straight there."

"What will we do now?" Nyfain asked after Sorsha had paid Flavius.

"We head north. To the Great Wall."

THIRTY-TWO

Summer, 367 C.E., Caledon

B rei, Taran, and Dylan stood on the hill at the ruins of Caerdwabonna and scanned the River Tae. With them was a guard of
warriors they had taken from Caercaled that morning. An os-
prey circled overhead and dived into the water, returning to a pine tree
on the bank with a fish thrashing in its beak. Brei gripped the reins in
his hand, and the leather tightened and creaked under his grasp.

"There," Taran murmured.

In the distance, coming in from the ocean, three ships paddled
against the river current. The boats drew closer. Fifteen to a side of men
rowed the boats in sync. Men sitting at the aft of the boats yelled out
"Pull!" to the rowers, and the oars creaked against the rusted metal
handles as they plunged into the river and hauled the boat forwards.
"Pull!"

Taran clicked to Ri, and they cantered down the grassy slope
towards the sandy riverbank. As the first boat came closer, Brei recognised his cousins Talorc and Eithne. Next to them, standing on a
platform, were three men with tied-back hair and cropped beards. In
the second boat was King Alpin of Ce and his son, Cal, surrounded by
an entourage of Ce warriors. Naoise and Drest were in the third boat
with King Cailtram of Cait and a black-haired man who Brei could
only assume was Prince Fergus of Ulster.

They waited on the bank until the ships approached, heaving against the current. When the first ship swung into the landing bay, the warriors rushed into the river to drag the boat in.

"Cousins!" King Talorc called out as they pulled the ship across the sand.

Naoise leapt from his boat before it had been pulled ashore, and he waded to Talorc's boat and reached up for Eithne. She smiled, her golden hair flowing over her shoulder as she took Naoise's hand. He picked her up and carried her across the shallow water and up high onto the riverbank where the ground was firm.

"Naoise! I hope you will show the same courtesy to your king!" Talorc yelled.

Brei laughed and turned for Naoise's reaction, but Naoise was otherwise engaged with Eithne's mouth. Talorc jumped over the boat's edge into the river and waded across to the shore, followed by the three strange men. Brei had assumed the three men were standing on a platform on the boat, but he realised as they stopped before him that they were a foot taller than Talorc.

"Cousins, this is Prince Ælfric, son of the King of Saxons."

Brei grasped the prince's hand and smiled. "We are sorry King Garnait is not here to greet you himself."

"And these are his cousins." Talorc pointed to the tallest of the Saxons. "This is Wulfraed." The man nodded. "And this is Edmund. Only he speaks the Ancient Tongue." Talorc introduced Brei and Taran to the men, and Edmund spoke to Prince Ælfric in a strange language that sounded as though it had been conceived in the depths of war.

Prince Ælfric smiled. His teeth were milky against his swarthy skin, and while his overlong hair was tied back from his face, stray strands of black fell over his forehead. "Prince Brei, Taran," he said in a deep, thickly accented voice.

Taran's jaw tensed momentarily before he smiled and offered his hand. "Prince Ælfric."

Prince Ælfric murmured something to Edmund, who translated, "Prince Taran, your cousin Talorc has told me much of you."

Taran nodded, and a strained silence fell between them. The two remaining boats were hauled into the bay, and they were soon spared when Drest, King Alpin of Ce, and King Cailtram of Cait and their men joined them.

"Who are they?" Cailtram asked, nodding towards Prince Ælfric and his cousins. King Cailtram was in his prime, and his strawberry-blond hair hung at the nape of his tunic, resting above a silver penan-nular brooch with two bear heads carved into the ends.

"Saxons," Brei replied.

King Cailtram seemed surprised. "Were you expecting them?"

"Talorc has cast his net wide."

"Did you succeed with convincing King Nechtan and King Alwyn?" Cailtram asked.

"King Coel now," Taran said. "King Alwyn was taken by the plague, but his son was successful in his claim to the throne."

"And did you speak with Coel? What are his views? The Damn-nones would be a crucial ally, being so close to the Great Wall."

"They will, indeed," Taran nodded. "But Coel wouldn't let us into Altclud because of the plague. But he agreed to attend this meeting. He is our first cousin on our father's side, you may recall, and I am sure he will be keen to hear what we have to say."

"Is he young?"

Brei shrugged. "He has seen as many winters as I."

"Good," Cailtram said. "We don't want to deal with a boy king."

"Don't worry," Taran said. "The Eldar Druwydd would not have suffered a boy king."

"When will the southern kings arrive?" King Alpin asked.

"King Nechtan arrived from Caermhead not long before you did. King Coel and King Derine of Attacot have been in Caercaled a few days."

King Alpin lowered his voice. "The Attacot are a strange race.

I wonder how Talorc stands it, spending so much time with King Derine."

"I expect Talorc doesn't mind it when his children, with Queen Maeve, will inherit the throne," Cailtram replied.

The sound of men splashing into the water, calling to one another to coordinate the unloading of cargo, stifled the conversation and soon almost one hundred men, kings, princes, and their warriors stood on the riverbank.

Brei cleared his throat. "Shall we go up to the tower?" he yelled, but no one seemed to hear.

"Cousins! Friends! Your attention, please!" Taran's voice, booming across the crowd, grated against Brei's ears.

The men turned to Taran in unison.

"We have a few hours' ride from here to Caercaled. Horses are waiting for you and your men can follow on foot. Your ships will be guarded. We have watchtowers all along the river." Taran gestured to the hills. "If we make a good pace, we'll be there in time for the feast." He patted Talorc on the back and led his horse between the men. Brei did not move. He watched Taran's broad back disappear through the crowd of warriors, his mind flipping from respect to jealousy with every step Taran took.

"What's in it for us?" Prince Fergus of Ulster asked. "And don't tell me it's plunder and women. Ulster wants land." He pointed to King Derine. "Your land."

King Derine stood up. "Piss off back to Ulster, you're not getting any more Attacot territory. Talorc should be the one to gift land, it is not my venture."

Brei leant against the wall in the tower's hall in Caercaled. The kings and princes assembled around the long wooden table, but there was not space for all. The rest of the men stood behind, drinking ale, and some men spilled outside. Brei closed his eyes. After two days of feasting, his head ached, and his Torc dug into the back of his neck. He rubbed it as he studied Prince Fergus, who was older than Talorc, old enough to be king.

"We shouldn't be fighting amongst ourselves," Taran said. "The Romans are an enemy to all. We should seize the opportunity."

"Sit down, boy, I've had enough of the Snake of Caledon trying to charm us," Fergus spat. "Talorc, let's be real. You need ships, the Saxons' pirate fleet is not enough. You need Ulster, and Ulster wants land. I want Attacot land or I will return to my father and we will raise our goblets to you from across the sea while you fail in Britannia."

Talorc ran his hand over his face. "Vortriu and Caledon can pay you in silver now."

Brei frowned and glanced at Taran whispering to King Gartnait, who sat next to him.

Fergus shook his head and leaned his elbows on the table. "Land."

"Ah, Caledon will..." Gartnait stammered and coughed. His son, Elfinn, stepped towards him and blocked Brei's view.

Taran finished Gartnait's sentence for him. "Caledon and Vortriu will offer silver to Attacot, in compensation for losing land to Ulster."

"Talorc, this would be your son's land," King Derine said.

King Derine was as old as Gartnait, but he reminded Brei of the great King Uradech.

"So be it," Talorc nodded.

King Derine shook his head. "Fine, take it, Ulster scum."

Prince Fergus grinned and gulped ale from a silver goblet.

Talorc sighed, the darkness under his eyes betraying his exhaustion. "Then we are agreed?"

Kings Cailtram of Cait, Alpin of Ce, Coel of Damnnonia, Gartnait of Caledon, and Nechtan of the Maetae all nodded. The Saxon Prince Ælfric and Prince Fergus of Ulster bent their heads slightly.

The Eldar Druwydd waited at the entrance to the hall, but his appearance at the meeting seemed to have gone unnoticed. Brei raised his hand to catch Talorc's eye, and he nodded towards the old man robed in white.

Talorc spread his arms wide. "And now we work out the specifics!" he yelled and beckoned the Eldar Druwydd forwards.

"Ale, first!" King Cailtram yelled.

Talorc grinned. "Yes, ale!"

Brei accepted a wooden tankard from a serving girl. As he took it, she bowed and avoided his eyes. He looked over at Taran, who clutched his usual silver goblet. Brei clenched his jaw as Taran turned and caught Brei's eye, and he swung his long legs over the low bench and pushed through the crush of men towards Brei.

"All right, Brei?"

"That was a bit tense," Brei whispered as Taran stood next to him, his muscled shoulder warm against Brei's.

"No one has the motivation that we do. Except maybe King Nechtan. The Maetae were hit as hard as we were by the Romans."

"Everyone else does it for greed?"

"Take or be taken from."

Brei lifted his wooden tankard to his lips and gulped. He wiped the foam from his mouth with the back of his hand. "Prince Fergus was too harsh with you."

"I don't care what Fergus thinks of me. Do you think I do?"

Brei glanced at Talorc and the Eldar Druwydd conferring with three other Druwydds in white robes. "I just remembered what you said when we were in Caertarwos that every day you are making a claim and I didn't want you to be disheartened."

"Why do you care? Would you rather it was you who speaks?"

"No." He sighed and looked at the grey stone floor. "And yes. Sometimes I do. Sometimes I wish I was like you."

"You can always jump in first, Brei. It is your right too."

Brei looked into his brother's blue eyes. *He is always going to be that boy I betrayed. The boy who protected me.* "I know you want it more than me you have more heart. Merit and right have little to do with it. In the end it is heart that is the difference between winning and losing."

"What are you saying?"

"I'm saying that when Gartnait dies, I will support your claim." His stomach sank as he said the words. The room seemed to spin, and the voices faded. His body thrust forwards into Taran's embrace, but he felt nothing.

"I hope you won't be disappointed in me," Taran whispered. But Brei could not hear him over the pounding pulse in his ears.

"We are agreed on the details, then?" The Eldar Druwydd sighed after over three hours of logistical discussions that drew progressively shorter and more slurred responses from the kings as the ale continued to flow.

The Eldar Druwydd ran his hand through his long white hair. "One more time. King Coel will subjugate Gwoddodin. Gwoddodin is loyal to Rome, and if bribes do not satisfy them, King Coel and the Damnnone warriors will prevent them from attacking us as we travel through the south to the Great Wall. King Coel will also bribe the Roman soldiers on the minor towers on the Great Wall. We will wait by the wall next to the towers that have been bribed until they signal that it is time for the attack. Then they will drop torches along the wall for us to follow to where the big forts are, and they will let a small group of men through the wall. That small party will run ahead to the fort each kingdom is targeting and will sneak in and set fire to as many buildings as they can to create a distraction. King Derine will lead the Attacot to attack one fort, while King Nechtan and each of the northern kings will attack the remaining forts simultaneously. There are sixteen major forts, but our spies tell us that only six are garrisoned with enough soldiers to get in our way, so we will attack those." The Eldar Druwydd turned to the Saxons. "And Prince Ælfric will lead an attack by ship along the eastern coastline."

Ælfric drained his silver goblet of wine, watching the Eldar Druwydd in silence over the rim.

"And" the Eldar Druwydd bowed low to Prince Fergus, "the magnanimous Prince Fergus will lead the Ulster ships down the west."

Brei smirked as he caught Taran's eye.

Talorc pushed himself up from the table. "But that is just the initial attack. After that, our path will take us through the middle of Britannia. We will burn and plunder everything in our path." Talorc smiled. "And in the spring, Prince Ælfric and Prince Fergus will continue down the coastline, attacking the coastal fortresses and towns."

Talorc raised his silver goblet into the air. "The Gods have blessed us with a good harvest. We must keep the forges burning from now until long after Samhain. We need swords, spears, and arrow tips. There is work for all our peoples. Vengeance will be ours. We begin our attack on the winter solstice. Revenge or Tirscath!"

THIRTY-THREE

Sorsha, Dioras, and Nyfain travelled at night, sparing the one horse they had between them the exhausting summer heat. During the day, they found cool, leafy hollows and rivers to sleep by. The villages and towns they passed on the road were littered with buildings in desperate need of repair, and many buildings were abandoned. Villagers often warned them of marauding bands of robbers and murderers, and so with the denarii Sorsha had received from Cecily, she purchased a second-hand iron blade for Dioras and a dagger for Nyfain.

To ward off boredom, as they waited for the cool blanket of night to travel under, they would play at target-throwing with Nyfain's dagger. One scorching afternoon, after waking from a heavy sleep, Sorsha walked to a bubbling stream flowing near the shaded spot she had been sleeping in and bathed her aching feet. She stretched out her arms and let the mottled light play on her skin as it filtered through the green leaves above.

Laughter rang from the trees as Dioras teased Nyfain. "So close! But not close enough."

Sorsha turned to see Dioras give Nyfain a playful push towards the tree they were using as target practice. Nyfain retrieved the dagger from the ground, fallen just short of the old oak's trunk, and handed it back to Dioras. He grinned, "Watch me closely this time."

Standing side-on to the tree, he bent his front leg, drew his arm back, and released. The dagger landed with a thump in the "X" they had carved into the tree.

Nyfain shook her head, smiling as Dioras skipped to the tree to wrench out the dagger. "Here, I'll show. It's your arm. Need you to follow," he said, handing the dagger to Nyfain. As he positioned her, his hands barely seemed to touch her body.

Sorsha looked back at the river. It smelt fresh, and the sound of the water gurgling over pebbles and rocks was lulling her back to sleep. She leant on the ground, sinking into the soft silt as it took her weight, and dangled her feet in the cool water.

"Did you see that, Sorsha?"

Sorsha turned towards Nyfain. She had landed the dagger at the tip of the "X". Sorsha smiled and closed her eyes again. Birds twittered in the trees above her, and she drifted to the vineyards on her parents' estate. In her mind she chased her brothers along the rows of grapes, the sun catching the backs of their heels as they ran.

"Sorsha!"

She had just closed her eyes when Nyfain and Dioras started calling her again. Frowning, Sorsha struggled back into consciousness.

"Sorsha!" Nyfain yelled.

Sorsha's eyes snapped open.

A grizzled-looking man stood over her with a lopsided grin. "Hello."

Sorsha sat up, taking in his tattered tunic and military-issue metal vest. He reeked of ale and stale urine. She looked up the bank to the trees, where two men held Dioras and a third restrained Nyfain. The hilt of Sorsha's sword hilt dug into her side. *Has he seen it?* "What can we do for you?" she asked, not moving from her seated position on the bank of the stream.

"So much, lovely, so much," the man leered. He turned to his companions. "Won't these two do so much for us, lads?"

As he laughed over his shoulder, she shifted her weight and leant back over the scabbard and entwined it under her leg.

He turned back to her and crouched down. "Now, what is a pretty girl like you doing out here?"

"Let my friends go, and I'll tell you," she said.

He stood up straight, laughing with a harsh crackle. "Should we let them go, lads?" He turned again to his companions.

She crossed her left hand over her waist and clasped the hilt of the sword while the other men laughed. They seemed young, almost boys.

"No, no, there's not enough of you to go round for what we have in mind, lovely. And anyway, this Gaulish bull here will fetch a pretty coin at the slavers' market."

"Fine," she said, raising her chin, "but let her go, at least. I can guarantee I'll be enough."

He smirked. "And why do you think that?"

Sorsha motioned with her finger for him to come closer. He crouched down, and she rose onto her knees, smiling. "Do you know what I'd do first?" she whispered.

He licked his lips. "Tell me."

"Well…" She grabbed his hair and, at the same time, pulled her sword out from its scabbard and jammed the blade against his neck. The man just spluttered, shocked at how quickly he'd lost control of the situation. Sorsha jumped up, yelling "let them go" to his companions.

"Go on then, do him! Less of us to share you with," said the blond man holding Nyfain, while one of the men holding Dioras pulled out a dagger and wedged it against his throat. Blood dribbled from the cut and down his neck.

Sorsha's heart raced. *Don't panic.* She let her hostage go and kicked him to the ground, then ran towards Dioras and Nyfain.

The second man holding Dioras stepped forwards and thrust out his sword to meet her. When she was upon him, she ducked beneath his arching blade and slashed at his legs. He groaned and fell forwards. She looked up at Dioras, but his wide eyes darted behind her and he shook his head. Before she could turn, a blade crushed against her throat. She looked up and saw the first ruffian glaring down at her, blood streaming down the side of his neck. *Fuck.*

"You filthy bitch," the man snarled in her ear with rotten breath.

The other man was struggling to stand. She squeezed her sword. The blade against her neck was cold, and from the corner of her eye she saw Nyfain. Tears streamed down her face. A wave of nausea rippled through Sorsha's stomach and she looked up at the sky. *May the Gods give me strength.* She wrenched her body forwards, and the blade pushed into her neck, gouging through the skin and veins. The ruffian sliced the blade across her throat as she swung her sword wildly behind her and made contact. With a thud, he dropped his sword and fell on the ground groaning.

Sorsha crawled away and tried to stand upright. She convulsed, and blood sprayed from her mouth. As she held her hand to her searing throat, she stared at Nyfain and Dioras, still held captive. Steaming blood spilt down Sorsha's neck and Dioras's eyes told her how grotesque she must look. Heat flowed from Sorsha's heart, down her arm and into her hand, but she could not finish the healing as the first ruffian lunged for her again. She adjusted her grip on the hilt and leapt towards him, slashing the blade across his neck. Her arm jarred as the sword wedged into his spine. *It's stuck.* She lifted her boot onto his chest and wrenched the sword out of his neck.

The man collapsed, and she turned to the other man just as he sprinted towards her. *Shit.* At the last moment she dropped once more and slashed at his already bloodied legs. He stumbled, and she jerked her sword up into his abdomen. Screaming, he fell to the ground, clutching his stomach. Blood gushed through his dirty linen shirt and oozed through his fingers.

Sorsha panted as she glared at the two remaining men holding Nyfain and Dioras. An intense rage pulsed through her. The same compulsive intensity as when she healed people, but now it was the inverse. It was an insatiable desire to kill.

The man holding his blade against Dioras's neck shuddered. "Stay back, stay back, witch, or I will end him!"

Without taking her eyes from the bandit, Sorsha walked to within a foot of Dioras. The ruffian's lips trembled as she leaned forwards and whispered. "You touch him, you hurt a single hair, and I will pull the guts from your body. Slowly, ever so slowly. I'll string out your intestines until I can find my way back through the forest with them."

His eyes widened, and she struck his face with the hilt of her sword. Screaming, he released Dioras and dropped his blade. Dioras scrambled to pick up the fallen dagger as the bandit slipped while trying to flee. He grabbed a fistful of the man's hair, yanked his head back and sliced his throat.

Sorsha, smiling, stepped towards the final man, who was holding Nyfain. "Now I'm wondering why you're still here."

He screwed up his face and spat at Sorsha.

"Drop your head," she said to Nyfain in the Ancient Tongue. Nyfain obeyed as Sorsha swung her sword up from the left to plunge it into his neck. He released Nyfain and slid to the ground, the sword wedged into his flesh. Sorsha pulled the sword out of his neck and swung again, but it became stuck in his neck once more as he fell forwards onto his knees.

"You're not strong enough." Dioras unsheathed his sword. Drawing the blade to his ear, Dioras swung his sword across the bandit's neck. The head leapt off its neck and fell with a thud onto the ground. Sorsha looked at the straw hair, flecked with blood.

"Those villagers weren't joking," Dioras said as he held Nyfain.

Sorsha wiped the spit off her face and clutched her neck to finish the healing. The rage dissipated like a fog withering under the sun. As her breathing returned to normal, a tremor spread across her hands and fingers. Dead eyes across the clearing stared up at her. Waves of nausea crashed through her stomach, and she collapsed on the ground and pressed her head against her knees.

"Are you okay?" Dioras asked.

"I barely remember what I did. I just wanted to save you both." She looked up at Dioras and Nyfain. "Everything sort of blurred... I didn't mean to..."

"They would have used us and killed us, Sorsha," Nyfain said, her voice choking. "They were bad men, and they deserved what they got."

Sorsha nodded, but her hands still shook. She curled them into fists and dug her nails into her palms until they bled.

The sun was now setting and the purple sky swam with orange. "We should go," Dioras said. "Take everything we can from them and let's get out of here before there's any more trouble."

Nyfain found a pouch with a hoard of silver denarii in a saddlebag while Sorsha strapped a shiny dagger to her boot. As they set out onto the road on the ruffians' horses, under the milky light of the moon, the milestone to the Great Wall was marked "XLI".

"We'll reach the wall by morning if we hurry." Dioras clicked to his new horse and pushed into a gallop.

THIRTY-FOUR

Summer, 367 C.E., Caledon

Talorc raised a silver goblet in the air. "When the snow starts falling, we go through the wall!"

"Revenge or Tirscath!" Taran yelled.

The hall echoed with cries of "Revenge or Tirscath!"

"And" Talorc raised his hands. "And! I have more news."

The kings and princes fell silent, many utilising the pause to fill their mouths with ale.

"I am pleased to announce that my sister, Eithne, and my much begrudged but still loved cousin Naoise are to be bound!"

Naoise, who had been dwarfed by Ælfric and his Saxon cousins Wulfraed and Edmund, popped his head out from behind them and leant forwards across the table to grasp Talorc's hand.

"I will return Eithne to Caercaled along with my army when we march, and they will be bound here in Caercaled before we depart for the wall. Eithne says she wants to delay it for as long as possible. No doubt she is hoping Naoise will perish in battle, and she'll only have to put up with him for one night." Talorc winked as the hall filled with laughter. Then he raised his goblet once more. "To my Neesh and Eithne."

"To Naoise and Eithne!" the princes and kings cheered.

Whistling reverberated around the hall and Brei wondered if he could slip away to Anwen and the twins, who had remained on the third floor, along with Aífe. Brei surveyed the stone hall to see if anyone was looking, but no one seemed to notice as he nudged his way behind King Cailtram and escaped up the dark, spiralling staircase. The noise from the hall below was still deafening, but his shoulders relaxed as he pushed open the wooden door to his floor. Anwen and Aífe were sitting by the fire talking to the twins, and it sounded as though Anwen was telling them a story about faeries. He smiled and sat on the ground by Anwen's feet.

"How's it all going?" Aífe asked as she brushed a stray red curl from her porcelain face. "They sound either really pleased or furious."

"We have an agreement."

"Will Prince Ælfric be in peril?"

"And why are you worried about him, particularly?"

"No reason." Aífe smiled and looked into the flames. "He is awfully good-looking, though, isn't he?"

Brei grimaced and cracked his neck to either side.

"Is your neck sore?" Anwen asked softly.

"Killing me. I will be so glad when this is all over."

Anwen pulled him closer to her, and he shifted so that she could massage his shoulders.

"But then you'll be risking your life. You can't be glad for that?" Aífe said.

"But I can. Standing around, being still, that is the killer."

"Will Dylan go raiding with you, Papa?" Ceridwen asked, her blue eyes wide.

"Yes, Dylan is old enough to go to war, so he will join us."

Nia gazed up at Brei. "Will he die?"

"Maybe. I might die too." He pulled at one of Nia's auburn braids.

"I don't want you to die, Papa," Nia whispered, and she crawled to sit in his lap.

"I don't want to, either, but sometimes we have to take risks for the things we want. I want revenge against the Romans."

Ceridwen tilted her head to one side. "But not all Romans are bad, are they, Papa?"

"Yes, they are," Anwen snapped.

Nia looked up at Anwen from Brei's lap. "But, Mama, how do you know? Have you met every Roman?"

Anwen bit her lip and looked away.

"Brei! There you are. Need to speak to you." Talorc stood in the doorway. Standing next to him was Taran, and his face was set as if stone.

Brei brought Anwen's hand to his mouth and kissed it. "I'll be back soon," he whispered.

He stood up and walked into the passageway to join Talorc and Taran. King Gartnait and the Saxons, Princes Ælfric, Edmund, and Wulfraed, waited for them on the landing.

Brei closed the door to his floor. "What is it?"

"Prince Ælfric has made a proposal to Aífe," Taran said.

Brei frowned. "Should we get Naoise?"

"Both Naoise and Eithne have gone missing." Talorc grimaced.

Edmund whispered into Ælfric's ear, and a wry smile played on the prince's lips.

"Taran, Brei, what do you think?" Gartnait asked.

Taran answered first. "Is it even something you would consider, Uncle?" He turned to Ælfric. "Would you take her to Saxony?"

Edmund translated, and Ælfric raised his chin and considered Taran before he murmured something back to Edmund. "Of course Prince Ælfric will take her to Saxony," Edmund replied.

"Out of the question," Taran said. "A Princess of the Blood must always remain in her kingdom." Taran looked at Talorc. "You cannot possibly be entertaining this, cousin?"

Talorc shrugged. "It's an alliance that I am drawn to, I will admit. And we need Saxon ships, just like we need Ulster's."

Taran glared at Ælfric. "As if you need the alliance to raid the Roman coasts."

Prince Ælfric ran his hand over his cropped black beard as Edmund translated for him. He smirked as he responded, and Edmund translated. "We don't, but perhaps Prince Ælfric needs an excuse not to raid your cities."

"Haven't you seen how many kings have gathered here?" Taran laughed.

Ælfric smiled as Edmund translated for him. "Yes, Prince Ælfric has seen how divided you are."

"And you would like to continue that divide, wouldn't you?" Brei said. "Rob us of the chance to shore up another alliance?"

Edmund and Wulfraed conferred with Prince Ælfric. "Aífe said yes to Prince Ælfric. That is all that matters."

Taran lowered his voice to a whisper. "Aífe is vain and would say yes to any man of consequence, no matter how little that consequence is."

"I think…I think Caledon say no, Talorc," Gartnait wheezed, and he turned his head away as he coughed.

Talorc shook his head. "I should never have let Eithne carry on with Naoise." He slapped Ælfric on the back. "Not to worry, my Queen Maeve is pregnant again. If it's a girl, you can have her, for yourself or your sons. That will give you an alliance with Vortriu, Caledon, and Attacot."

Brei's lip curled, and he looked at Taran, who was watching Ælfric and his cousins descend with Talorc into the shadows of the staircase.

"Nothing is as distasteful as a man who breathes only for his own ambition," Gartnait whispered.

"Yes, ambition will be the death of you." Taran smiled and put his hand on Gartnait's shoulder. "Are you well, Uncle?"

"Truth be told, my lad, I've not felt well for some time, and now that she's gone…" Gartnait looked at the stone floor. "I might retire early. Yes, I'll go to bed. Can you tell Elfinn? Otherwise, he'll worry."

"'She'? Who did he mean?" Brei whispered as they watched Gartnait hobble down the stairs.

Taran had a strange expression on his face that Brei did not recognise. He looked tired, as though the last three days had drained all the energy from him, and what was left was a half-man, robbed of his best years.

"Taran?"

"It doesn't matter," Taran murmured and put his hand on Brei's shoulder. "I'm going to speak with King Coel. See if we can't get an alliance out of Aífe, after all."

Brei watched Taran walk down the stairs. The torchlight threw shadows across his eyes as he glanced back at Brei and grinned, his face once more transformed.

THIRTY-FIVE

Summer, 367 C.E., Britannia

The dawn was red beneath grey clouds as Sorsha, Nyfain, and Dioras crossed a stone bridge over a wide river and passed through the fortified wall surrounding the civilian town of Coria. It lay at the junction of the road leading north through the Great Wall and the road that ran east–west between the forts along the wall. The small town was part fort and part commercial settlement. The main lane was lined with red-roofed warehouses filled with military supplies. On the western side of town were two large, elevated granaries and, on the northern end, aqueducts flowed to a large public fountain.

They led their horses through the town, searching in stables and inside the granaries, but a slave matching the description of Derelei could not be found. In an expansive square courtyard next to the public fountain, Sorsha eyed two Roman soldiers and approached them.

"Hello, can you assist me?" Sorsha said.

One soldier glanced at her sword before responding with a grunt.

"I'm looking for a slave. She's tall, blonde, middle-aged and goes by the name of Derelei. Have you seen her? She would have come from the north about six years ago."

The soldier seemed puzzled by the question. "Why on earth do you think I'd know where she is?"

"Oh." Sorsha stepped backwards.

"But I can ask the commanding officer's wife, she keeps several handmaidens here."

Sorsha smiled. "Thank you."

He disappeared into the building and returned with a young woman, draped in red silk and fine white linen.

"You are looking for a slave?"

"Yes."

The woman pursed her lips. "What does she look like?"

The woman appeared disinterested as she listened to the description of Derelei, and Sorsha wondered if she even knew what her own handmaiden looked like.

"No, I don't think any of my slaves match that description, but you could check with the Tribunus up at Vercovicium. Or in the town Vindolanda. I'd try there as well."

"Is it nearby?"

"An hour's ride west to Vindolanda. And Vercovicium is a big fort at the wall itself, not far north from Vindolanda."

Sorsha thanked her and rejoined Nyfain and Dioras. It was raining as they rode west from Coria to Vindolanda. They spent the remainder of a miserable morning searching through the town in intermittent deluges. By midday, Sorsha sensed Nyfain and Dioras had had enough, and she left them to seek shelter in a wood outside Vindolanda.

Sorsha continued north to Vercovicium. The rain pelted her face, and she could not see more than a yard ahead. Hills rose as if from nowhere, green shadows beneath the swirling grey clouds. Pulling back on the reins, she stopped the horse, shielded her eyes, and gazed towards the hills. Lightning cracked across the sky, illuminating a stone wall that clung to the ridge like a spine. In the middle of the wall was a fortified settlement, and Sorsha cantered towards it, before dismounting to lead her horse up the hill to the huge wooden gates.

"I am here to see the Tribunus," she said, smiling at the Roman soldiers on guard. Wrapped in sodden red cloaks, they waved her in, and she walked to the pillared house of the Tribunus in the centre of the fort, leaving her horse at the stables. There was no one around, no soldier guarding the entrance. On the steps that led to an ornate door, she hesitated. *What is the penalty for trespass?* She climbed the steps and waited in the entrance hall. Footsteps echoed behind her, and she turned to see a tall woman in a tattered tunic with her blonde head bowed.

"Derelei?" Sorsha whispered.

The woman stopped and looked at her. Around her neck was a thick metal collar.

"Derelei, is that you? I come from Brei and Taran," she whispered in the Ancient Tongue.

The woman appeared to tremble. Her eyes were bright blue. *Like Taran's.* Hanging from the metal collar was a bronze tag the size of a man's fist. Inscribed on it, Sorsha read:

I have run away.
Hold me.
Return me to my master
Lucius Antonius
for a gold coin.

"Is your name Derelei?" Sorsha whispered again.

"Yes," she croaked. "Who are you?"

"I am Sorsha. I have come to take you home, Princess."

"How?"

"I will have to buy you."

"But...I don't understand."

Sorsha stepped closer and gently touched Derelei's shoulder. "It's going to be okay. I'll explain everything later. But can you find your mistress and ask if I may speak with her? Don't say who I am."

Derelei nodded, but her brow was furrowed. She hurried across the entrance hall and disappeared into a corridor.

Sorsha gazed around the whitewashed hall, noticing a turquoise and gold fresco of deer nibbling grapes above two beautiful birds. *I wonder if this is the last Roman painting I will ever see?*

Footsteps echoed along the corridor, and a woman appeared with black hair streaked with white. "Hello, you wish to speak with me?" Her Roman accent was thick.

"Yes. I wish to make a commercial proposition to you. May I?"

The woman nodded.

"I wish to buy your slave here." Sorsha gestured to Derelei, who lurked in the corridor at the entrance to the hall.

The woman laughed. "Oh, she is not for sale. And anyway, she is so old."

Sorsha jingled her silk purse of denarii. "I will pay in silver."

"Why would you pay such a price for a worthless slave?"

"She is the mother of my handmaiden, Nyfain, a loyal and trusted servant, and I wish for them to work in my household together, as a reward for loyal service." Sorsha slipped open the purse and held out a coin. The woman grasped for it, but Sorsha kept it out of her reach. "You may have all the denarii in this purse for the slave. Do we have a bargain?"

"Yes." The woman stepped forwards and tried to snatch the purse from Sorsha's hands. "Take her."

"Unlock her collar first, and you can have the silver."

The woman pulled a key from her pocket and exchanged it for the purse. Sorsha stepped behind Derelei, inserted the key into the keyhole at the back of the collar and turned it. The lock clicked and unclasped. The collar fell off, revealing Derelei's red and scabbed neck.

Sorsha guided Derelei down the steps to the horse in the stables. Derelei trembled, barely able to put one foot in front of the other.

"Put your foot in the stirrup," Sorsha murmured.

With vacant eyes, Derelei starred at Sorsha and did not move.

Sorsha reached for Derelei's hand and squeezed it. "You're okay. I promise. I'm going to look after you and take you home, okay?"

Derelei was so frail it was easy to lift her up into the saddle.

Sorsha led the horse down the muddy hill to where the land flattened. The rain was lighter and, as she grasped the pommel of the saddle to mount, she glanced at Derelei. The woman's shoulders were shuddering violently.

"Derelei?"

She crumpled forwards and wailed as she heaved over the side of the horse and vomited.

Sorsha walked in front of the horse and examined Derelei. Tears shone on her cheeks.

"Is it real?" Derelei gasped.

Sorsha nodded as she gently wiped Derelei's mouth and forehead with her hands.

"I dreamt every day that someone would come for me," Derelei whispered. "But the days became years, and I stopped dreaming. Each day dragged, and I wished for death. I even tried to hasten it, but every time they caught me." Her hands trembled against the horse's neck. "I gave up so long ago of ever being free. So, this can't be real. Is it that I am dead? Is this Tirscath?"

Sorsha clasped Derelei's trembling hand in hers. "It is real. You are free and alive in the land of the living. And I am going to take you back to Caercaled, to your sons Brei and Taran."

Derelei looked around at the fields of grass and forest. "I…" Derelei paused and shook her head. "I haven't spoken the Ancient Tongue for so long, for six years." She pressed her fingers into her cheek. "It's almost as though the muscles in my mouth have forgotten how to form the words."

"Derelei, Princess, I need to get you away from here. Please sit up, and I'll take you to meet my companions. They were also slaves, but they are free now." Sorsha squeezed Derelei's hands. "I can't promise that you will ever feel how you did before they took you. I'm not going to tell you that, because it's not true. But what I can promise is that you will feel so much better than you did yesterday. And you never have to go back."

THIRTY-SIX

Autumn, 367 C.E., Caledon

B eli began barking outside the tower as Brei and Taran sat in the hall, sharpening their blades. They both snapped their heads up, hearing the urgency of the dog's whining, and they strode outside into the bright afternoon light. Brei's knees went weak when he saw her. *Mother*.

The sun shone on her golden hair as Derelei smiled at her sons, tears streaming from her wrinkled eyes. Taran lifted her down from the horse. His shoulders shook as he held Derelei in his arms and glanced at Brei over his shoulder. His face was wet. "Brei, come here," Taran said with a shaky voice.

Brei stepped towards Taran and his mother. She smiled through glistening tears. His eyes prickled, and he felt the first tear slide hot down his cheek. "Mother," he croaked. Taran pulled him into their embrace, and Derelei kissed his cheek. They pressed their heads together, their shoulders heaving as they cried.

Over Derelei's shoulder, Brei glimpsed Sorsha sitting astride a powerful stallion as black as her hair, which hung in a long braid over her shoulder. With her was a girl with long copper hair and a man with skin like bronze.

Footsteps echoed in the stairwell, and Brei stepped out of the embrace to see Anwen, her mouth open. Sorsha clicked to her horse and trotted towards the stables. Her horse had an unusually high step when it trotted, and Brei wondered absently where she had acquired such a beast.

Derelei straightened and wiped her cheeks with the sleeve of her blue tunic. "It's Anwen, isn't it?" She glanced at Brei as she stepped towards Anwen.

Anwen nodded, her cheeks reddening.

Brei looked from Anwen to his mother. *I never imagined I'd have to explain this to her.* He cleared his throat. "Come in and have dinner. And, ah, meet your grandchildren."

Derelei smiled, and his shoulders relaxed. "This is Nyfain and Dioras, my travelling companions," she said, gesturing towards the pair. "Did Sorsha leave?"

"She shouldn't have come back," Anwen hissed.

Derelei looked Anwen up and down. Brei thought he could see an argument going on inside her head. Disgust that her son had tied himself to a peasant, and sadness for what had befallen both women at the hands of the Romans.

"Anwen, why don't you go back in and ask the servants to prepare a feast?" Brei whispered, gently squeezing her hand. "Tell King Gartnait that Derelei is back."

"How are you even here?" Brei asked when Anwen had gone inside.

"I don't know. It all seems impossible. And Caledon has changed so much since I left, hasn't it?" She looked at him directly in the eye "Peasants marry princes now."

"Let's not quarrel, Mother. It is what it is, and we have more important things to discuss."

Derelei glanced behind her and waved to Dioras and Nyfain to follow her into the hall. They walked into the hall as servants brought wine, ale, and food. Anwen, Naoise, Dylan, and Aife joined them.

"What happened? How did the Romans get you that night?" Taran asked as he helped himself to a leg of venison.

"We were all asleep when the horn of Caledon blew. Gruffydd... Is he still alive?"

"Yes."

"Good," Derelei smiled. "Gruffydd had been on guard with the garrison at the Western Gate when he saw fires at the farmstead. Roman soldiers had slaughtered most of the garrison at the gate." She paused to swallow a piece of cheese. "Everyone in the tower was in a panic. King Uradech and Gartnait and his boy... Where are Gartnait and Elfinn, by the way?"

"King Gartnait is not well, Mother. Elfinn is at his side," Brei said.

"*King* Gartnait? I see. Well, as I said, you and Taran and your father...you all left in such a panic. Uradech had told me to watch the women and children. And I meant to. But I was worried about my boys, I was so worried about you. So, I slipped out."

Derelei reached across the table and patted Aífe's hand. "I'm sorry for leaving you. After I left the tower, I went to the Sacred Forest to watch the battle. The city was on fire. For a while, it looked as though the warriors of Caledon had succeeded. But then a second wave of soldiers attacked and overwhelmed them. I moved closer to see what was happening. Women and children, screaming in terror, ran past me towards the tower. The roundhouses were on fire, and I could hear pigs squealing inside as they burnt. I saw Taran and Rhys cornered and fighting off a group of soldiers. As I edged closer, I saw Uradech on the ground. His eyes were open, and I remember wondering if he could see me. But he never blinked. He never moved." She paused and slid her goblet across the table, back and forth as though deliberating in her mind what she would say next. "And then something hard hit my head. I'm not sure what, perhaps the hilt of a sword or a fist. But when I woke up, I was in a boat heading down the river towards the ocean. I was tied by my neck to other women from Caledon and the Maetae." She rubbed the scar that curved around her neck. "And I've had rope or metal around my neck since that day, until Sorsha rescued me. It feels strange without it now. To imagine my life before I wore it."

"How did you get back home?" Taran asked.

"Perhaps we should start with you, Nyfain?" Derelei said. "She rescued you first."

Nyfain was about to speak when Gartnait strode into the hall with Elfinn. The king was walking straighter than Brei had seen him in months.

"Sorry I'm late, I wanted to speak with Sorsha." He smiled at Elfinn and accepted a goblet of wine from the serving girl, Eiry. "Derelei, you have no idea how many nights you have filled my dreams. I am so glad you are back, sister." Gartnait waved his hand as he sat down. "Please, continue your story."

"Ah… well…" Nyfain began. Her voice was soft and melodic, like a trickle of water rushing over pebbles. "Sorsha was staying with the provost's wife, and I was helping her to dress for the morning. She started speaking to me, in a tongue I was not expecting to hear from her." Nyfain continued to tell the story of Sorsha leading them to a great city and searching for Derelei at the slave market.

When she finished, Dioras began to tell his story, with an accented, stilted voice. "I knew I would soon die. That is when I noticed Sorsha and Nyfain watching me. They cut me loose, and Sorsha spoke to me. She wanted to know if I could understand her, and when I nodded, she…she put her hand on my wound and–"

"Dioras!" Nyfain hissed.

Brei tilted his head.

"Go on," Derelei said, her eyes glinting.

Nyfain shook her head. "I don't think Sorsha would like us talking about her like this."

"No, she wouldn't," Taran said. "What happened after?"

"After we rescued Dioras, we rode north for the wall. It took us such a long time, we were rather delayed at one point." Nyfain paused and glanced at Dioras.

"Delayed by what?" King Gartnait asked, leaning forwards on the table.

"Bandits," Dioras said. "But we fought them off."

"The bandits?" Dylan asked. "But how many men were there?"

Dioras glanced at Nyfain before answering. "Four. They had daggers on our throats. It was something I'll never forget, seeing how Sorsha fought–"

"Anyway," Nyfain interrupted, "when the men were dead, we took their coins and horses, and…when we finally got to the wall–"

"Stop, stop, stop!" Naoise waved his hands. "Are you saying that Sorsha…that she killed four men?"

"I knew it," Anwen shuddered. "I knew we were right to fear her."

Brei tried to catch Anwen's eye, but she was staring into her lap.

"Then what happened?" Dylan asked, his eyes ablaze.

"When we were close to the Great Wall, we searched through the towns and forts until we found Derelei," Nyfain said.

"Sorsha took me away from the house of the Tribunus," Derelei continued. "And then we rode along the river to the coast, and Sorsha sold our horses to pay for passage on a merchant ship to Caertarwos. I visited Talorc alone, and he gave us horses to travel home with. I remember when he was only Naoise's age, it's strange to think of him as a king now."

Brei could see see that Anwen's face was red, and she was scraping her index finger up and down her thumb. He stood up. "I think our guests are tired, Eiry. Have you made up a house for Nyfain and Dioras?"

The serving girl nodded. "Yes, Prince Bridei."

Dioras and Nyfain rose, glancing at Derelei before they followed the servant out of the hall. Taran watched them leave, then stood up abruptly and disappeared from the hall, stomping up the stairwell.

"I want to speak with you outside," Derelei said to Brei.

"Let me put Anwen and the twins to bed, and I will meet you in the Sacred Forest under the Great Oak."

The sun was setting by the time Brei met Derelei.

"Now tell me why Gartnait is king, and you are not? My brother is a good man, but he is not a king."

"I never made a claim for it."

Derelei's face remained expressionless.

"Don't look at me like that. I've had enough time to live with it. I don't need you to re-open the wound."

"If I had been here to speak for you, you would be king."

"Yes, probably." Brei shrugged. "But it's Taran who wants it. I think he dreams about it every night. It's him you should speak for now." He looked up through the broad leaves of the oak as the red-gold glow dwindled into twilight. "Did they…mistreat you?" Brei's voice shook as he asked the question he was not entirely sure he wanted the answer to. "They took Anwen and…did unspeakable evil to her."

Derelei looked away, through the forest. "Sorsha told me what happened to Anwen. I can't speak of it, Brei… You already know."

"I will avenge you for the six years they stole from you. For every second of pain they caused."

She reached for Brei's hand and squeezed it. "I know, Brei. I know you will. But if I had my way, I'd have you stay here with me and make up for the years I lost with you. I fear the Romans will take more than years from me. They have already taken my brother and your father."

When Brei returned to the tower, Serenn had just delivered Anwen's nightly sleeping potion. Anwen sipped her potion with one hand and grated the back of her thumb with her index finger on the other hand. Brei sat on the bed and slipped his arm around her waist. "Anwen, nothing can hurt you. I am here, and you are well protected by everyone in the tower and the garrison at the city gates."

"Who will protect me from her?" Anwen's voice quivered. "And who are these people she has brought back with her? Who is that warrior? How could you allow him to remain in the upper rampart?"

He kissed her delicate hand. "Darling, you heard the story. He was a slave. Why would he be aligned with the Romans? And why would Sorsha risk her life to rescue my mother if she was our enemy?"

Anwen turned to him, the goblet shaking in her hand. "Sorsha is a monster, Brei. I know she is. She'll lure us into a false sense of security only to slit Nia and Ceridwen's throats in their sleep."

THIRTY-SEVEN

Autumn, 367 C.E., Caledon

Sorsha rode to the stables and dismounted. The horse nuzzled her, and she pressed her face into his black shoulder and breathed in the bouquet of grass and dirt. *I wish I didn't have to come back here.* She slid her hand down the horse's neck to the saddle and undid the strap with trembling fingers. She hung the saddle on the railing of the horse pen and rested her hands against the cracked brown leather. Tears slid down her cheeks. Her shoulders shuddered, and she slipped to the ground. Icy fingers pushed up into her throat and squeezed.

Retching on all fours, Sorsha gasped for breath. "Why can't you leave me alone? I came back!"

The stable door creaked open, and she looked up. Elfinn ran across the stables and crouched on the straw beside her. "Are you ill, Sorsha?"

Sorsha doubled over and leant her face on her arms. "Yes."

Elfinn's hand was warm on her back. "I...I know this isn't an ideal time, but my father is dying."

Sorsha bit her arm and screamed into it. Elfinn pulled his hand away.

"I'm sorry. I'm just tired." She stood up.

"Can you heal yourself?" Elfinn whispered as they walked from the stables.

"It's not that kind of sickness."

Outside the tower, King Gartnait was sat on the ground, his back against the stone wall. His grey skin stretched into a smile when he saw her.

"My lord." Sorsha crouched before him.

Clammy hands clasped around hers. "I was so forlorn when you left. I became so ill again, and there was nothing Serenn could do for me. None of her potions worked."

"Where is the illness?"

"My stomach." He coughed. "And I have a fever."

Sorsha slipped her hands out of his. "May I?"

He nodded and closed his eyes.

She placed her hands on his stomach. The king smelt of mustiness, of someone who rarely ventured outdoors. Her hands moved across his narrow chest and continued up to his neck and his head. "Will you turn around, my lord?"

The king shifted onto his knees and she pressed her hands into the back of his head and down his knobbled spine.

"Do you feel better?"

Gartnait turned around, smiling. "Yes, thank you, thank you!" He grasped her hands again and brought them up to his greying lips, kissing them with his eyes shut.

Elfinn assisted his father to stand. "I am so glad you have returned. Will you join us in the hall for a feast?"

"It's not my place," she murmured. Elfinn nodded and she watched them walk inside the tower to the hall. Sorsha looked for a short while at the trees in the Sacred Forest gently swaying, and then she crept around the tower, dragging her hands along the jagged edges of the stone. Beli ran to her when she reached the entrance. She crouched down and allowed the black mastiff to lick her face.

"Don't give me away," she whispered as she slipped inside to the stairwell. Her boots echoed on the steps, and she paused, unlaced, and removed her boots. Then she crept up the cold, spiralling stone staircase to the fourth floor. When she reached Serenn's chamber, it was damp and dark, save for the fire cowering under a gigantic cauldron.

Serenn's charcoaled eyes cracked as she smiled. "You came back to me."

Sorsha slid into the chair by the fire opposite Serenn and watched Eluned braiding her dark blue hair. Each braid was as thick as a thumb, and at the end of each braid Eluned affixed an amber bead. Wood clunked against the floor as Arian emerged from the shadows and limped across the room. Her ethereal face was even paler than Sorsha remembered and seemed to blur into the golden white of her hair. Arian held out a goblet of wine and smiled down at Sorsha. "I missed you," she mouthed.

Sorsha took the cup and, for a moment, her fingers lingered on Arian's icy hands. "Are you sick?" Sorsha whispered.

Arian's eyes flicked to Serenn, who was chiding Eluned for pulling her hair too tight. "I can't sleep," Arian whispered and limped away.

"Where did you go?" Serenn asked.

Sorsha watched as Arian limped to the workbench along the furthest wall from the fire. With a mortar and pestle, she began crushing herbs.

Sorsha turned to Serenn. "I found Derelei."

Serenn's eyes widened. "You brought her back?"

"I made my journey worthwhile."

"You didn't find your own mother, then?"

Sorsha slumped further into the chair and closed her eyes. "I found her."

"I see. So, you understand things now?"

"Mmm."

"Good, because we have a plague."

"Right. And the king was sick again."

"Was?" Serenn frowned.

"Don't worry, I healed him. Just in time, too." Sorsha yawned. "I wonder why he keeps getting ill."

"Maybe it's something he is eating?" Eluned smirked.

Serenn reached up and slapped Eluned. "Don't make jokes at the king's expense." Serenn sniffed and smoothed the folds of her black robes. "It could be anything, Sorsha."

Stone grated against stone, and Sorsha peered across the gloomy room at Arian as she ground her herbs. Her eyes were wide, and she glared at Serenn and then up at the rafters. Sorsha followed her gaze to a bundle of Nerion hanging upside down from a string. She stood up and walked to Arian. "Who are those herbs for?"

Arian held the bowl up.

Sorsha frowned as she recognised valerian roots and mistletoe. "A sleeping draught?"

"For Anwen. We give it to her every night, remember?" Arian's screaming eyes seemed at war with the calmness of her voice.

"Have your wine, Sorsha," Serenn said with a husky rasp.

Sorsha's eyes lingered on Arian's pale face, and she wondered, as she returned to the chair by the hearth, if the poor girl had finally cracked under Serenn's harsh treatment. As she drank the bitter wine, voices seeped up the stairwell from the hall. Every nerve in Sorsha's body tensed. She knew Arian wanted to speak to her, but she itched to leave the claustrophobic stone room that reminded her of the closing walls of her nightmares. "I can't be inside right now," Sorsha said, standing. "I'll see you in the morning, and we can visit the sick."

Serenn nodded, her charcoaled eyes intense over the lip of her goblet.

Sorsha hesitated as she reached the landing and checked to ensure she was alone in the shadows of the stairwell. Still barefoot, she glided down the cold stairs and slipped outside. Beli licked her face as she pulled her boots on, and then she ran to the stables. Hurriedly she placed a soft woven halter on the black horse and led it out of the

Western Gate and into the glowing forest. The setting sun burned behind the hill to the west, covering everything in a hazy veneer of red gold.

Everywhere the forest teemed with life that she had never seen there before. Fuzzy red squirrels chased each other through the trees, and birds fluttered by overhead. Grass, twigs, and wildflowers covered the forest floor, and the shadows of trees and shrubs danced in the breeze as the sun dipped below the horizon. She breathed in deeply, inhaling the sweet early autumn air carrying the scent of leaves, soil, and grass. The roar of the river and the twilight birdsong filled the air as her arms tingled in the breeze.

Sorsha stopped their meandering walk when the moon splashed silver across her face. She turned to her horse. Derelei had given him to her in Caertarwos, a gift from King Talorc to thank Sorsha for saving his aunt. The horse's face was chiselled and his ears short. At seventeen hands high, he was tall and muscled, like a draught horse. But he was nimble despite his size, and his neck was long and arched beneath a black, silky mane.

Sorsha kissed his nose. "What should I call you, sweet prince?"

The moonlight glistened on his jet-black coat.

"You shine so brilliantly in the sun and the moon. I will call you Nema, 'Shine'."

She hugged Nema's head as she watched the moon rise through the trees, listening to the soft hooting of an owl waking up for the night.

"Hello."

Sorsha turned, and Taran was standing behind her. She had not heard a single twig snap. "Hello," she said, stroking Nema's neck to hide the tremor in her hands.

Taran stepped closer and placed his hand on Nema's withers. "He is beautiful."

"He was a gift from King Talorc. His name is Nema."

His eyes were gentle as he moved his hand along Nema's flanks.

"You came back." Taran moved closer, sliding his hand slowly across Nema's shoulder until his fingertips brushed hers.

Sorsha moved her hand away, her heart beating faster. "I didn't come back for you."

He dropped his hand to his side. "I know you didn't, Sorsha." He swallowed. "Or, at least, not in the way you are thinking. But you did come back for me. Even if you don't know it yet."

She frowned.

"You found my mother," he whispered. "Why didn't you tell me that was your plan? I could have helped you." He smiled. "Or at least I would have known you were okay."

"I didn't intend to find Derelei. And I don't understand, why did no one try to find her before?"

"We all assumed she was dead. And we can't exactly just walk down to the Great Wall and start asking around, can we?"

"Right. Well, I wasn't sure if you would let me go if you knew."

"You're right, I don't think I would. Or I would have wanted to go with you, to protect you. Although, it sounds like you don't need any protecting, do you?"

"I'm supposed to help you. You're not supposed to help me," she murmured.

Taran held her gaze for a moment, his eyes glinting in the moonlight. "I just wanted to say hello. But now I must get back to my patrol, Owain is waiting for me."

"How did you find me?"

"I tracked you from the stables." Taran smiled and bowed his head. "Good night, Sorsha."

Into the darkness he walked away, and she watched him, knowing she could see him for longer than he would realise. She pressed her face into Nema's neck and closed her eyes.

Sorsha waited until the moon was low on the horizon before she led Nema back to Caercaled. *Everyone should be asleep by now.* She tiptoed up the staircase to the second floor and into her old room. She crawled into the cot and under the soft sheet and kicked the furs off. Her eyes closed and, for the first time in many moons, she did not dream.

Her muscles tensed. The air in the room shifted, as though someone was moving near her. She opened her eyes and saw the blurred outline of Anwen hovering above her. "What are you doing?"

Anwen raised her arm and plunged a dagger into Sorsha's chest.

Pain seared through her, and her breath caught in her throat. Sorsha looked into Anwen's eyes as Anwen's hand lingered on the dagger. Tears trickled down Anwen's cheeks. "Anwen, it's okay, I'm not going to hurt you," Sorsha wheezed.

Anwen leapt off the bed and sprinted out of the room, her footsteps echoing up the stairs to the third floor.

Sorsha exhaled and looked at the hilt of the dagger wedged into her chest. Made of bone, with the Snake of Caledon carved into it. Warm blood pooled across her chest and dripped into her armpits and, as she breathed, the wound pulsed. *Why is the pain so much stronger than other times I have been hurt?* Her senses were heightened, and she felt all the exquisite pain of the flesh that was open, the coolness of the blade. Even the crackle of the fire seemed louder, and she could hear her blood circulating with a whooshing sound, like waves.

THIRTY-EIGHT

Autumn, 367 C.E., Caledon

"I killed her."

The sound of Anwen's heavy breathing woke Brei and, in the darkness, he could hear her sobbing. *She must have had a nightmare.* He reached for her. "Anwen, darling, what's happened?"

She snapped around, her wide eyes glinting in the low light of the fire. "I killed her," she whispered.

Brei shuffled to the edge of the bed and pulled her into his arms. "It's just a dream, darling. You haven't killed anyone." Her skin was icy, as though she had been outside.

She pushed him away. "No, I really killed her, Brei. I couldn't help it... It's all I could think about. Taran spoke to me after dinner, and he said something, I forget exactly, but something about how she wasn't one of us, and I felt like I had no choice. Otherwise, she would have killed us, Brei."

Brei yawned. "Who did you kill?"

She looked down at the floor, as if she could see to the rooms below, and whispered. "Her."

"Sorsha?"

Anwen bit her lip, and the skin on his arms prickled. "Stay here and I'll go check, but I am sure you just had a dream. Climb back into bed, darling, I'll be back up in a minute."

Brei crept down the stairs to the second floor and paused on the landing. *It's just a dream.* He opened the door to Sorsha's room and found her sat by the fire, resting her head on the back of the chair, staring into the flames. Brei sighed. *She's alive.* Flames glistened in a puddle beneath her chair, catching his eye. Following the trail of red up the leg of the chair to her sodden tunic, his gaze finally rested on a bone handle protruding from Sorsha's chest. *That's my dagger.* The floor creaked beneath him, and her eyes flicked to his face.

"Have you come to finish me off?" she said, her eyes flashing yellow in the fire.

Brei stepped backwards, his chest frozen, and he wondered if he was still breathing. "Did Anwen really do this?" he croaked.

"She missed."

"Why are you not...fixing it? *Can* you fix it?" he whispered, stepping into the room and hovering next to the empty chair. Beads of sweat slid down the sides of his head through his hair.

She looked into the fire. "Yes, I can fix it."

He studied her face. *She looks so calm.* "Why don't you, then? Isn't it hurting you?" He fought to keep his voice from shaking.

"Yes, it hurts...but it's distracting," she said, without turning away from the fire.

"Distracting from what?"

She looked up at him, and her eyes were green again. "From everything." Her voice choked, and a thick tear slid down her cheek.

He bent onto his knees next to her so that his face was level with hers. "It's okay," he whispered and placed a hand on hers.

She recoiled, and the muscles in her jaw tensed. "But I'm not okay. And I'm never going to be okay." She was breathing fast, and the dagger rose and fell with her chest.

"You can heal the wound. You'll be okay."

Sorsha shook her head and smiled. "I'm not worried about this. I'll heal it in a moment."

Brei's muscles relaxed. "What you are worried about, then?"

"I'm never going to see my mother again." She pressed her lips together. "I am all alone, and that's the way it has to be. I am a blade. Nothing more."

"Is your mother dead?"

She shook her head. "Only dead to me. And there is nothing I can do to go back. The Gods won't let me leave here. Instead, I have an eternity of servitude. Alone."

"Maybe you should fixate less on the past and instead think about the future. Because you can't change the past. I always tell Anwen that."

Sorsha laughed. "Does it work for her? If it was that easy, don't you think I would have done it?" She leant her head into the back of the chair. "What future do I even have? There is no future for me, there is no 'me' anymore. I'm not even sure I am a human. I'm a mere shadow of a human, who belongs in Tirscath. A slave of the Gods, a tool. I am here for everyone else's benefit but my own. There is no joy, no hope. There is only an eternity of loneliness while I serve my purpose…and eventually watch everyone around me die. Winter after winter after winter, I alone will remain. You are all ghosts to me." She closed her puffy eyes, but the tears continued to slide down her cheeks.

"I don't understand what you are saying… Do you mean you are immortal?"

"Not exactly."

"What do you mean, then?"

"It's complicated. All I know is that I died before. And if I die again in the right way, I live another life. But that life will always be one of servitude."

"You are forced to help people?"

"Yes, but the force…it's like a compulsion. When someone is hurt, it's as if there is nothing else in the world that I can do other than help them. I have no control."

The blood was drying tight against her skin. Brei watched it turning brown and cracking. The gnarled rise of a scar on her chest poked out above the collar of her tunic. "Is that scar from when you died?"

She nodded. "I was shot in the heart with an arrow. Just before you found me."

Had Taran seen the scar before the trial? The fire caught in her eyes, turning them luminous yellow again. He shuddered and sat in the chair opposite her. "I don't understand why you can't enjoy life, even if you're forced to heal people."

She slumped lower in the chair. "Do you remember how painful it was when your mother and Anwen were taken? Or when you lost your father and uncle?"

"Yes."

"Well, imagine if you lost everyone you loved, Anwen, the twins, Taran, they all died. And there was no comfort for you, no release from the mourning because you would go on forever. You would feel that pain, the pain of their absence, for hundreds and hundreds of winters."

"I don't know what to say, Sorsha." Brei gazed into the fire. "But I feel like that pain would be better than being alone forever."

She shook her head. "Loneliness is just another kind of pain, Brei. A dull pain. For me, it's not worse. I'll never see my family again. That is a raw pain, sharp, that lingers just below the surface of my skin. I'd rather be alone than to mourn for all eternity. And I think, deep down, you know that is worse."

Brei tried to push away thoughts of Anwen dying. They sat in silence, staring into the flames. *Have I neglected Anwen so much that she would do this? I saw her sipping her sleeping potion. She shouldn't have been able to wake up.* Brei cleared his throat. "Are you going to tell Taran about Anwen?"

"I'm not a monster, Brei. I understand the fears that plague her in the long hours of the night. The doubts that are ever-present in her mind. When the irrational terror sets in her heart, she has no more control than I do."

Brei clenched his jaw. *Sorsha is a monster, though, just not the bad kind.*

"Is Anwen the reason you never made a claim to the throne? Or did you just never want to be king?"

"I wanted to be king. From as far back as I can remember, before Taran was born, probably. But Anwen was so broken. I had to make a choice."

"Do you regret that choice?"

"Sometimes. Sometimes I tell myself and others that I do. I don't know why, though. Because from the moment I met her it set the wheels in motion for all the other choices I made in life. I loved her for so long that it became who I was. And when the time came, I could not have made a different choice to the one I made."

"But what about now? What if King Gartnait died?"

Brei ran his hand across the stubble of his jaw. "Now I could do it, yes. Especially because Mother is back. But now it is different."

"Why?"

"Taran is…" He swallowed. "It means more to him now than it does to me. Anwen and the twins changed me. I'm not willing to sacrifice all for the pursuit of my own interests. I would rather follow Taran than challenge him, because challenging him would require my complete commitment, and I don't want to take that part of me away from my family."

The fire crackled and whirred as they fell into silence again. *I need to check Anwen is okay.* Brei yawned and stretched his arms above his head. "Would it be okay if I, ah…had my dagger back now?"

Sorsha closed her eyes and ran her hand through her hair, as though she had a headache. "I suppose so." She pulled the dagger out with one forceful upwards motion. Fresh blood oozed down her chest, re-wetting the dried blood. She looked at the wound for a few moments before she placed her palm over it. Her hand hovered there for a minute, and she closed her eyes. Then she wiped the dagger with her tunic, smearing red across the beige linen.

"Here you go." She smiled as he reached for the dagger. "Anwen will be okay, Brei. I will stay away from the tower. I'll stay as far away from Caercaled as I can. You might never see me again."

Brei glanced back as he left and saw Sorsha on her knees, soaking up the blood from the floor with the skirt of her tunic.

THIRTY-NINE

The infant paused its incessant wailing to cough. Hoarse and rasping. Sorsha pressed the back of her hand against the baby's forehead. "The coughing fever," she whispered to Serenn as the baby screwed up its red face and continued to wail. "This will be quick."

Serenn walked across the grubby roundhouse to the firepit in the middle of the room. "We shall call on the Gods Nodens, Cernunnos, and Brig to save your child."

The young mother nodded, her bottom lip trembling. Her red hair was tied in a bun at her neck, a dirty apron was wrapped around her rough spun woollen dress, and her hands were covered in the flour she had been grinding when the Bandruwydd arrived. She was bound in protection and provision to a simple man, a hunter repurposed as a warrior for the forthcoming campaign. Soon he would leave for the south, and there would be no one to protect or provide for them.

Eluned passed a smoking stick to Serenn, releasing an earthy herbal fragrance into the stale air.

"Nodens, God of Healing, save this child and protect him through the long nights of winter," Serenn said, raising her arms to the roof. Sorsha waited until she was certain that Serenn and Eluned's chanting had consumed the mother's attention before she placed her hands on his chest and forehead. Within moments of the child's healing, Eluned swooped down and wrenched him from Sorsha's arms. Serenn and Eluned chanted over the baby and blew smoke from the cured sticks into his face. He coughed, small and sweet.

"The Gods have expelled the sickness from his body!" Serenn said.

The boy's mother rushed to Eluned. "Thank you, thank you so much!" she sobbed as Eluned passed the child into his mother's arms.

Sorsha was already forgotten, if she had been noticed at all, and she left the roundhouse and waited outside. Although she knew this was her last patient for the day, she lingered in the muddy lane for Serenn. Sorsha intended to interrogate Serenn, as she had done every day since she returned from the south. The door to the roundhouse creaked open and Serenn and Eluned stepped out into the mud.

"I have nothing to say to you, Sorsha. Just like I didn't yesterday. And just like I will have nothing to say tomorrow," Serenn said as she brushed past Sorsha.

"Where is Arian?" Sorsha yelled to Serenn and Eluned's backs.

A man leading a pig between the row of roundhouses jumped, his eyes wide. "Come along, pig," he murmured and pulled at the rope around the pig's neck.

Eluned swung around, her mouth contorted. "For the hundredth time, she is busy!"

Sorsha glared at Serenn and Eluned's black cloaks fanning behind them as they scuttled around the last roundhouse on the row and disappeared. Since Sorsha's return, the forests surrounding Caercaled had transformed from green to violent red and orange. Every day Sorsha met with Serenn and Eluned in the city to heal the sick, but even as the leaves crumpled to the ground and the first snowflakes fell, Arian was nowhere to be seen. Sorsha yearned to seek her out, but after Anwen's attack she had kept her promise to Brei and not ventured near the tower again. In a way, she was grateful for the excuse to avoid its confined, damp walls, which reminded her of her nightmares. But she feared for Arian's safety, and Sorsha wished bitterly she had spoken to her properly the day she returned, to find out what Arian had been trying to tell her.

Mud squelched beneath her boots as Sorsha stomped along a path leading between a row of roundhouses. Villagers jumped out of her way. They feared her. "The strange Bandruwydd from the south," she had once heard a villager whisper, "she's a spy." Since her return, her senses had ignited. Whispers in houses were as loud as drums beating for a festival. An ant crawling across dead leaves in the dark was as clear to her as a bird flying across the sky on a sunny day.

The row of roundhouses ended, and she passed below the naked branches of oak and yew until she reached the city wall. The Northern Gate was garrisoned with warriors she knew, despite the lack of conversation they had with her. Owain and Gruffydd were senior warriors, calm watchers of events. Cináed was a troublemaker, good-natured but with a taste for riling men up into scrapes he could bet on. Brin and Deryn were young and were happiest when they could stand on the sidelines to holler and jeer. Sometimes Princes Naoise and Dylan would join them, for entertainment more than assistance. Fifty or more men were stationed at each gate, all with their unique perspectives on life and yet all with the same reserved aversion for Sorsha. As she approached the gate, the men fell silent, as they always did, and stood back to let her pass. When she had first returned to Caercaled and the sweet smell of late summer still lingered in the air, she had experimented with hellos or smiles. But the men met her with stony faces. Now, as winter approached, she avoided their eyes altogether.

An oak-lined path ran from the Northern Gate to the River Tae, and eerie branches stretched across the path, as if yearning for a skeletal embrace. As the days grew colder, the wind blew mist off the river, cloaking the forest in a veil of wispy white. Sorsha continued along the trail and past the holly bushes growing rampant beneath the oaks, threatening to overgrow the path. Red berries shone within the spikey green leaves, and Sorsha watched as a brown thrush flew into a bush and disappeared to its nest. The path forked, and she followed a thinner trail through the misty trees until she reached a clearing.

King Gartnait had been so pleased to have Sorsha back that he made generous gifts to her companions Nyfain and Dioras, including a small roundhouse that had become vacant after the last occupant perished from the coughing fever. As their body was burnt in a pyre outside the house, Dioras, Sorsha, and Nyfain moved in.

Paltry rays of sun streaked through the fog onto the slanting thatched roof of the roundhouse. Nyfain was hanging linen garments on a rope affixed to the roof and stretching to the trunk of a nearby tree. She turned and waved as Sorsha walked across the clearing. Dioras sat on a stump, striking a rock along the length of his new sword. He looked up and smiled.

Through the first moon of autumn, Sorsha had stayed with them, but as the nights grew longer, Sorsha would linger in the forest alone with her horse, Nema, until well after sunset, unable to tear herself away from the serenity of isolation. While she did her rounds with Serenn in Caercaled, Nema returned to the stable Dioras had built next to the roundhouse. Now, Nema's black head popped out over the half-door, and he whinnied to welcome Sorsha's return.

"I missed you when you came home this morning," Dioras said, with a coy smile.

Sorsha kissed Nema and glanced at Dioras over her shoulder. "You were out cold. Were you drinking with the Caledon warriors again?"

"Yes."

"Any news?" Nyfain called over.

"Just the same," Dioras said. "They are leaving for the Great Wall as soon as the solstice approaches. Their excitement, I will admit, is endearing, and I've been wondering if…"

"You want to go with them?" Sorsha turned to him.

"I do. Is that so bad?"

"Why would it be bad?"

Dioras shrugged. "You don't seem that keen on the warriors or on killing Romans."

"I have nothing against the warriors. But I know when I'm not welcome."

"They all think I'm brave for living with you," Dioras said. "They think you're an evil spirit let loose from Tirscath."

Sorsha smirked. "An improvement on the whole spy thing, I suppose."

"I still don't know how you get away with healing people and everyone thinking its Serenn," Nyfain said to Sorsha. She then turned to Dioras. "I think you should go. I'm sure it would be exhilarating to kill some Romans soldiers. I know I would go if I could."

Dioras and Nyfain smiled at each other, and Sorsha turned back to Nema.

"Sorsha, I should have mentioned this earlier," Dioras said. "I was talking to Taran and Naoise last night."

Sorsha grunted and kept patting Nema's shining black coat.

"Taran said he feels badly for not seeing you for so long. He said he'd come visit us today."

Sorsha spun around. "Why?"

Dioras cleared his throat and pointed across the clearing. "Like I said, I should have mentioned it earlier. He's here now, so you can ask him yourself."

Taran waved and jogged across the clearing as Sorsha shook her head at Dioras.

"Taran!" Dioras jumped up to shake his hand.

"Nyfain." Taran bowed his head as he shook Dioras' hand.

"Thank you for visiting us, Prince Taran. It is an honour," Nyfain smiled.

Sorsha turned around and continued to pat Nema.

"Have you been well? I trust the roundhouse is suitable?"

"Yes, it was ever so generous of the king to arrange it for us," Nyfain replied, her voice higher than usual.

"You'll both let me know if there's anything I can do for you?"

"Of course, thank you," Dioras said with a breathless enthusiasm that made Sorsha's fingers curl.

"Well, if you'll excuse me for a moment, I have to speak to Sorsha."

Twigs and leaves creaked as Taran walked towards her. Keeping her back to him, she kissed Nema.

"Hello, Sorsha." Taran leant next to her against the half-door of the stable and smiled.

"What do you want, Taran?"

"Nice to see you, too."

"Forgive me. But as you've not spoken to me since I got back, I assume you're here because you want something."

"I didn't think you…" He frowned and stepped towards her. "I'm sorry, I thought–"

"It's fine." Sorsha smiled. "It's just been hard coming back here, and I didn't quite realise until just now that I actually wanted…"

Taran's eyes glistened. "What did you want?"

"No one has visited me. Not a single person since I've come back." Tears threatened her eyes, and she tried to frown them away. "Serenn and Eluned make me help them in the city, and I live here with Dioras and Nyfain, but no one has come to see me. Not your mother. Not Arian. Or Brei."

"Why would Prince Bridei visit you?"

Sorsha blinked. "Of course he wouldn't." She shook her head. "It's very kind of you to take the time out of your day to come here. Is there something I can help you with?"

Taran drummed his fingers on the top of the stable half-door as he considered her. "I just wanted to say goodbye. The day after Naoise and Eithne's ceremony, we depart for the Great Wall."

"Goodbye, then," Sorsha said, and turned back to Nema.

Taran stepped closer, and his fur cape rustled against her forest-green cloak. "I know what you are."

"'What'?" Sorsha bit her lip as a tear slipped down her cheek. "Not 'who'?"

Taran reached out and touched her elbow. "Who. I'm sorry."

Sorsha pulled her arm away. "How long have you known? You knew at my trial, didn't you?"

Taran ran a hand through his long blond hair. "I knew you were valuable. Serenn and King Gartnait wouldn't have been willing to bind someone as important as Naoise to you if there wasn't something in it for them."

Sorsha raised her eyebrows. "So that's why you did it?"

His blue eyes flicked to the ground and back to her face. "Are you angry?"

"No." She sighed. "Actually, in a way, I'm relieved." She smiled. "No offence."

He laughed. "Some offence taken."

"But I'm also confused. Why did you bind yourself to me, and then when I came back, you had nothing to do with me… Are you still angry at me for leaving you in Caeredyn?"

"I was angry. Furious, actually." Taran's eyes narrowed. "But not with you. Why did you really go to the south? It wasn't just about your mother, was it?"

Sorsha raised her chin. "To escape."

"Right." Taran squinted up at the sun fighting through the mist. "Why did you come back?"

"I didn't come back because I wanted to."

Taran's face was calm. "The Eldar Druwydd said you would come back to me. He had predicted you would come to Caledon in the first place. There is a prophecy."

"Come back to you?" Sorsha frowned. "What is the prophecy?"

"You must go to Rīgonīn to hear it, Sorsha. Promise me you will go?"

"I'll think about it."

Taran reached for her hand and squeezed it. "Promise me. There are others, Sorsha. Other Healers. In Caertarwos. They told me they are waiting for you to find them. There is a staircase under a hill that leads to a chamber. They will find you there. Promise me you will go?"

Sorsha's stomach tightened, and she looked up into his blue eyes, shining like turquoise.

Taran cleared his throat. "Serenn told me about what happened with Anwen. If I had known, I wouldn't have…" He swallowed. "I'm sorry."

"It's not your fault. It's not her fault, either. Poor Anwen, is she all right?"

"You forgive her? You're not angry?"

"Of course I forgive her. I understand why she did it. She's troubled, and I feel nothing but sorrow for her."

Taran dropped her hand and grimaced.

"What's wrong? What's happened?" Sorsha asked.

"Nothing. Nothing, it's just that you're so…" He laced his hands behind his head and turned to face the clearing.

Sorsha reached out for him, her hovering fingers inches from his back.

He turned around and frowned at her outstretched hand. "How would you remember me if I died on this campaign?"

Sorsha dropped her arm to her side. "I don't know, I barely know you. But you've always been kind to me. And I thought we were friends before I…before I left you in Caeredyn. I'm sorry, Taran, you have no idea how horrible I felt about betraying you after all you had done for me."

Taran studied her with an intense gaze, his eyes darting across her face as though he was searching for something. "We are friends, Sorsha," he sighed. "I was never angry with you. But I wish I'd not stayed away now." He shook his head. "Serenn told me to, but I wish I hadn't."

"Why did Serenn tell you to stay away?"

"Serenn doesn't matter." Taran stepped closer and grasped her hand once more. "Sorsha," he squeezed. "If something happens to me, think of me like you think of Anwen." Bending his head, Taran kissed her cheek. "Goodbye, Sorsha." He turned and walked across the clearing, a dark shadow enveloped by mist.

FORTY

Autumn, 367 C.E., Caledon

A wet snowflake landed on Brei's eyelash. He swept it away as he gazed across the Shining Lake, watching the snow tumble in the wind and melt on the water.

Between the lake and the ridge of snow-dusted hills, King Talorc led a small party of riders. A horn blew, announcing the king and his warriors, a line of cavalry, followed by marching spearmen. Brei raised his hand and Talorc greeted him in kind, spurring his horse on.

"How was your journey?"

Talorc pulled up next to him and reached out his arm to grasp him. "It's getting much too late in the year for ladies to be travelling, so it's a good thing Eithne is staying here."

"It's a shame that they are to be bound on the eve before we depart. Surely we could give them one day?"

Talorc shook his head. "The muster has to begin tomorrow if we are to make it to the Great Wall to join the other kingdoms on the solstice. The Eldar Druwydd has warned me I may have left it too late already." Talorc looked back at Eithne as she approached and then back to Brei. "Still, I wouldn't put it past Naoise to have secured his succession before he leaves."

"The Goddess Brig be with him," Brei snorted. "Talorc, you should

292

know that Gartnait is not well, not well at all, and he'll be unable to make the ceremony."

Talorc scratched his red beard. "This is a tragedy, of course. But with tragedy comes opportunity."

Brei grunted. "For Taran, perhaps."

Eithne and her brother, Drest, rode up to them. She smiled, radiant and golden as he last remembered her.

"I will accompany you to the tower, where rooms have been made for you on the king's floor. The ceremony will start in the afternoon," Brei said.

"I hope the weather holds out," Eithne said and smiled. "Talorc has been absolutely beastly in chiding me for waiting so late in the year for it."

Talorc leant forwards and gave her a little shove. "You should have listened to me, then, if you didn't want to be teased, darling Eithne."

Eithne rolled her eyes and urged her horse into a canter.

Bouquets of dried purple heather had been draped over the branches of a tall ash tree in the Sacred Forest. The fiery leaves clung stubbornly despite the lateness of the season.

Naoise was bare-chested, his Torc glinting in the pale light, and Eithne stood at his side in a pale blue tunic, threaded with silver. She seemed to float, and, in that moment, she was the most beautiful creature Brei had seen. He pressed his hand into Anwen's and squeezed.

Serenn presided, wearing her deer skull and antlered headdress, as she called upon the Goddess Brig to bless Naoise and Eithne with fertility. On Belenus, she called for guidance to light their way when the world grows dark. From Taranis, she asked for strength, and from Cernunnos, Lord of Nature, she asked that he remind the couple of their duty. Around Eithne and Naoise's wrists, she bound them together with a rope made of gold, twisting like a Torc. "I bind you before the Gods in protection and provision," Serenn said and dropped their hands.

Eluned and Arian stood a few paces away from Serenn. Dressed in black, their faces were painted with swirls of dark blue. Brei's stomach tensed as he felt Sorsha's absence more than he wanted to admit. He had not seen her since the night she had been stabbed, and yet it seemed she was always in his mind, her tears filling his dreams. Brei stood back, his arm around Anwen, and forced a smile as Naoise and Eithne passed them to return to the tower. When he turned back to the tree, Taran strode towards him, and they embraced.

"Talorc just told me that the Eldar Druwydd is concerned about the plan," Taran whispered.

"Why?"

"Apparently he's overheard Talorc bragging about the plunder they're going to take."

Brei glanced at Talorc. "So he was serious when he said the Gods would only allow revenge?"

"Talorc is worried."

"This is a problem."

Taran nudged Brei with his shoulder. "We can talk about it later. Shall we go back in?"

Brei nodded his head towards Anwen.

Taran glanced at her. "Fair enough," he said and spun around. "Talorc!" he called and pushed through the crowd towards the king.

Brei re-joined Anwen. Her face was strained, and he took her hand. "Is everything okay?"

"Is she going to come back when you leave?"

"Who?"

Anwen bit her lip. "Sorsha."

"No," he sighed. "Darling, let's go inside and join the feast."

Anwen nodded, and they walked up the hill through the Sacred Forest to feast in the hall. The long table heaved under the weight of meat and wine. Drummers, a flautist, and a horn blower played a melody that echoed around the hall. In the city, a bonfire had been raised in Naoise and Eithne's honour and mead supplied to the people. Fear and excitement gripped Caercaled as drummers and dancers congregated around the fire to celebrate the union of Caledon and Vortriu and the impending attack on the south.

Brei sat with Anwen, the twins, Dylan, and the Bandruwydds. Opposite, Taran sat in the middle of the table with King Talorc, Naoise and Eithne, Aífe, Elfinn, and Derelei.

"Where is this Healer, then?" Talorc asked Taran, and the voices in the hall seemed to speak quieter.

Taran leaned his head towards Talorc and whispered. His eyes flicked to Brei's and then back to Talorc. "Sorsha's not coming with me. She's going to Caertarwos."

"Why is Sorsha going to Caertarwos?" Dylan asked. "Are you going too, Anwen? And what about Aífe and Derelei?"

Aífe craned her neck forwards. "What about me?"

"Are you going to Caertarwos with Sorsha?" Dylan asked her.

"Brei," Taran lifted his chin. "Smack Dylan over the head for me."

Dylan ducked under the table before Brei had even moved.

Brei smirked. "Nia, Ceridwen, kick Dylan for Uncle Taran."

Ceridwen grinned, and she kicked under the table. Dylan squealed and reached up and tickled her under the arms. Brei smiled as Ceridwen giggled.

"Brei, tell Dylan to stop," Anwen said.

He pressed his lips against her ear. "Just let things play out as they will." Brei turned back to Taran and smirked.

Taran raised his goblet to him and grinned. "He's better than Naoise, though."

Naoise slammed his goblet of ale on the table. "No one is better than me!"

Talorc rolled his eyes. "Everyone here is better than you, Neesh."

"Take that..." Naoise belched, "back."

Talorc laughed. "If you are able to walk out of this hall, I will take it back."

Naoise drained his goblet in one gulp. "Challenge accepted." He withdrew his dagger and severed the golden tie that still bound him to Eithne. She glared at him as he untangled his legs from under the table, swung them over the bench and stood up.

Derelei shook her head as she patted Eithne's arm, the muscles in her cheeks fighting a smile.

Naoise swayed and put his hand against the wall. Aífe swivelled around and said in a drawn-out voice, "left foot, right foot."

Talorc leant back and pulled Naoise's leather pants down so that his snowy cheeks poked out. Naoise frowned and gazed around the hall. "Bit draughty in this hall, Elfinn." He grinned and raised his index finger in the air. "You should, you should," he released a wet belch, "you should really tell King Gartnait to fix that." He started to walk without hitching his pants up and, as he approached Aífe, she slid her foot forwards, and he plunged to the floor. Talorc and Taran roared with laughter.

"He… is," Aífe gasped between heaves of silent laughter, "out… cold."

Eithne sipped her wine without turning her head to look.

"Hey, Eithne," Taran yelled.

Eithne clenched her jaw and looked the other way.

Talorc nudged her. "Hey, Eithne."

"Eithne." Taran threw a gnawed bone at her. "Did you see Naoise?"

Taran and Talorc heaved with their heads together.

Brei was laughing when he turned to see Anwen's stony face. He grinned and kissed the top of her head.

As night fell, Brei walked into the Sacred Forest alone, to the treeline, where the forest gave way to the city below. He watched the red light and shadows from the bonfire dancing across the faces of the buildings.

The pace of the drumming was fast, and people were cavorting around the fire, laughing and singing.

"What are you thinking about?"

Brei turned. Derelei stood close behind him, smiling. "Nothing," he said.

She stepped closer and took his hand. "Tell me."

"It was just something Talorc said when we were in Caertarwos... about war."

"What did he say?"

"That if people could see the same beauty that he could, would there still be wars? There was a time when we all lived peacefully. I was just thinking about them down there, and then us, up here. We go on about foreign enemies, but even within our own community, we have wars, we have differences."

"And you think of this on the eve of battle because you have regrets?"

"No, I want revenge. I want to do this." He paused and wondered if he should tell her. "But the Druwydds have put a condition on the venture. No looting. And I'm worried."

"Worried because you all intend to plunder and ravage?"

"Well, obviously. And I've been thinking about why the Gods would be against it. We're all trying to get more than the next person, aren't we? We were once content and peaceful and now... So few are supported by so many, and yet we are still not satisfied."

Derelei shrugged. "This is the world we have, and if you don't take it, someone else will."

Brei turned back to watch the people dancing and singing around the bonfire.

"Speaking of taking. Gartnait is gravely unwell."

Brei nodded. "I know. He has been sick since last winter. And then miraculously gets better. I guess Sorsha must have helped him. But he's been declining for weeks now."

"Why hasn't Sorsha helped him again? Where is she? I've not seen her since we returned."

"She won't come near the tower because of Anwen, and Gartnait can't walk anymore."

"Did you ask Sorsha to stay away?"

"Something like that."

"Well, Gartnait will be dead within days if she doesn't help him."

Brei sighed. "We're all going to die, Mother. Maybe it's just Gartnait's time."

Brei's head pounded. "Anwen." He let out a strangled hiss. "Water!"

The cot bed creaked as Anwen got up, and she soon pressed a cool goblet into his hand.

Brei groaned as he sat up. He gulped the water and cracked one eye open. "Is it morning?"

"Yes, warriors are already mustering inside the upper ramparts."

Brei slid back down onto the pillows and groaned. "Why did we drink so much?"

Anwen smiled. "Why indeed?" She opened the door to their chamber. "The twins want to say goodbye, Brei."

He ran his hands over his face. "Give me a minute."

Across the floor, the door swung open as though it had been kicked. "Brei!" Taran yelled from the stairwell. Already wrapped in his wolf's pelt cape, he carried his H-shaped shield and his sword hung at his waist.

Brei shook his head. "Of course you're not hungover! You're unbelievable."

Taran chuckled. "Get up and see Naoise. He can't stop throwing up." Taran skipped off down the stairs, shouting, "Neesh! Get up!"

Brei took the retching sounds from below as Naoise's answer. He swung his feet off the bed and steadied himself.

Anwen helped him to dress into his thick winter skins. She fastened his wolf's pelt cape with a penannular brooch bearing the Snake of Caledon. "It's too much to say goodbye, Brei." Her bottom lip quivered. "I know you're doing this for me, but I want you back. I want you to come home."

He held her against his chest and kissed her head. "I will."

When Brei had said goodbye to Nia and Ceridwen, he joined Taran, Naoise, Dylan, Talorc, and Drest at the stables. Naoise's face was pale, and he leaned against the stable wall and convulsed as they laughed at him. Naoise stood up and wiped his mouth. "I will strangle you all in your sleep if you say one more thing."

"Naoise!" Taran yelled in Naoise's ear. "Neeeeeee shaaaaaaa!"

"Fuck off!" Naoise yelled as Taran danced away. "I swear to all the Gods, Taran. One day I am going to kill you!"

Talorc ran up behind Naoise and tackled him to the ground, pushing his head into the snow. Naoise heaved himself onto his knees and vomited. Taran, Talorc, and Brei were doubled over, tears streaming from their eyes as Derelei walked towards them, smiling. "Leave the poor boy alone."

Naoise groaned and rolled onto his back. "Derelei, make them go away. I need help. I am literally dying. I may already be dead. We don't know."

Derelei shook her head and reached her hands out to Brei. He embraced her. "My boy, my eldest boy and darling. Please be safe. I don't want to lose you again." She glanced at Taran as he feigned an attack on Talorc. "Don't let Taran get to you. You were born to be a king. You are so strong when you believe in yourself. I believe in you. Promise me you will be strong."

Brei's eyes prickled. "Mother," he croaked, "I'm sorry about Anwen. I know you forbade me from binding myself to her, and the minute I thought you were dead, I betrayed you."

Derelei shook her head against his. "Hush, Brei, my darling, say no more of it. I will not have our final moments be like this. I forgive you. When I was a slave, I learnt what really matters in life, and who you love will never be a problem for me." Derelei looked at him, her blue eyes shining with tears. "I'm so proud of who you are, Brei. When others see weakness because of your choices, I see strength. You are so strong, let yourself use that strength for Caledon, I know you could be a great king."

"What about Taran?" He glanced over at his brother. Taran pushed Naoise away and fended off an attack from Talorc. They wrestled in the snow until Taran ended the game by putting the king in a headlock.

"Taran has much growing up to do before he will be ready."

"You don't give him enough credit, Mother. He is a strong leader and he will be my king."

"You have a soft spot for him, of course, but don't let that blind you. I've heard what happened between you two."

He bit his lip. "Mother, listen to me, I have to tell you this before I leave."

"What is it?"

"Taran didn't try to kill me."

"Oh darling, don't be so naïve."

"Mother, please just let me finish. The night Caercaled was attacked…I choked. It's one thing to train with your friends, but it's another to face someone whose very survival depends on ending your life. I was terrified in the face of the enemy, and when a Roman soldier came bearing down on me, I could barely lift my sword. But Taran stepped in and killed him. He saved me. And…" Brei glanced at the snow that surrounded their feet. "And when I thought the battle was over, I snuck away." He nodded his head. "I snuck away to the farmsteads that were burning, where Anwen was, and searched for her. Her father lay dying and told me they had taken her, and so I searched all night for the soldiers, but I couldn't find them. And when I came back at dawn, I saw that a massacre had taken place. I admitted to Taran what I had done, and he belted me for it. As he was right to do, Mother. I deserved to be executed for it. And instead of telling everyone about it, he protected me."

Derelei's eyes widened, and she shook her head. "This cannot be true, Brei."

He squeezed her hands. "Believe me, Mother, Taran saved me twice that day. And when he made a claim for the throne of Caledon, I could have spoken up, could have endorsed him. I had already decided not to stand for the crown. Do you know what held me back from endorsing Taran? Jealousy. Because when it comes down to it, I am a small man. You think I made this big sacrifice? You think Anwen asked me not to make a claim? Well, she didn't. You and Father denied me permission to bind myself to her, so I was going to run away with her. It was always her. I sacrificed nothing. Caledon is Taran's. He is pure and strong, and I believe in him, and so should you."

"Brei, hurry up and kiss your mummy goodbye. The men are leaving!" Naoise mimed kisses in the air and grinned.

Brei rolled his eyes and kissed Derelei's cheek. "I'm sorry, Mother."

She opened her mouth as if to speak, but Brei turned and strode through the snow to Rhuad, his heart pounding.

When they had mounted their horses, Talorc led them forwards. Derelei, Aífe, Eithne, Anwen, and the twins waved to them as they passed the tower. Even Serenn and Eluned had made the long descent down the stairs to say goodbye and, like black ravens, they watched the men depart for war.

His stomach tensed, and the leather reins creaked under his grasp. As the warriors passed through the gap in the wall, Brei could see the greys, browns, and whites of warhorses waiting in the Sacred Forest for King Talorc to lead them to the Great Wall. Brei could hear the snapping leather of a bridle, the metallic crunching of a bit against teeth. A thousand warriors waited in the forest.

"Warriors of Caledon and Vortriu!" Talorc yelled. "The solstice is upon us! For glory! Revenge or Tirscath!"

The warriors beat the hilts of their swords against their shields. "Glory! Revenge or Tirscath!"

Talorc marched down the hill, riding three abreast with Brei and

Taran to either side. The warriors parted as they rode through, and they beat their shields as they passed. Brei twisted in the saddle to look behind him. Warriors were mounting their horses and falling into line, and behind them men on foot carrying round-butted spears followed. Forest gave way to city, and the people cheered when the warriors appeared, lining the main lane all the way to the Western Gate. Women, children, and old men waved to them and clapped.

The warriors wound their way down to the centre circle where the bonfire from the night before still burned. Drummers played a steady marching beat that Brei felt in his heart. Taran wore a bull's horn around his neck and blew into it. A long, low note against the beating of the drums. The hairs on Brei's arms prickled.

"Revenge or Tirscath!" Talorc cried.

"Revenge or Tirscath!" Brei roared with the warriors, and he beat his sword against his shield. The crowd cheered louder, and Rhuad tossed his head. Brei leaned forwards and stroked his neck as he smiled at an old man on the road.

"Kill one for me, lad!" the old man yelled.

They passed through the Western Gate and farewelled the depleted garrison that would remain to protect Caercaled. Brei glanced behind him again when they passed the farmstead. The line of warriors stretched around the bend in the river and out of view. He turned and smiled at Taran, who was staring into the distance, his features tensed. Following Taran's gaze, Brei saw Sorsha on the edge of the forest with Nyfain. Snowflakes whirled around Sorsha's head. As they drew in line with her, a gust of frigid air blew a strand of black hair, and it danced across her forehead. Horses' hooves clipped on the ground as the warriors continued, and they passed her without acknowledgement. The snow fell thicker, and Brei looked back, but Sorsha had disappeared into the swirling white.

FORTY-ONE

S moke plumes billowed over the city walls as Sorsha lingered outside the Western Gate. The wailing of female voices cut through
the icy breeze. Sorsha approached Brin, a warrior who had
remained at the garrison. "What are they celebrating?"

He wore a thick cape of animal pelts, and his hood was lowered
over his head. "It's not a celebration, lady. The king is dead. Can't you
hear the women keening?"

Sorsha froze. "How did he die?"

The man frowned. "It seemed sudden to me, lady, but I heard Owain
and Gruffydd say that he had been sick since the leaves started falling."

Why didn't Serenn send for me? She nodded to Brin and passed
through the gate into the city. The lane that ran from the gate to the
centre circle was lined with grieving people. A massive pyre had been
built in the centre and black smoke puffed from soaring flames. Sorsha
pushed through the crowd of mourners, edging her way towards the
front. The fire was scorching against the frosty breeze. A body reclined
on a bed of wood, nestled within the angry flames. Elderly women
from the city sat around the base of the fire, keening with intense melancholy.

Sorsha scanned the gathering of people until she saw Serenn standing to the left of the pyre with Eluned and Arian. *She's alive.* Her heart

raced as she pushed through the crowd towards Arian. Heat from the flames bristled against her cheeks, and she stopped. Anwen stood behind the Bandruwydds with Derelei, Eithne, and Aife. Sorsha hesitated. Arian caught Sorsha's eye, and her stony face rippled with anguish. Sorsha motioned with her hand, and Arian limped through the crowd of mourners to meet her.

"Arian," Sorsha whispered, her throat tightening, "what happened to you? I haven't seen you for so long, I thought..."

"I'm fine, Sorsha."

"But did she hurt you?"

Tears shone in Arian's eyes. "It will heal."

Sorsha reached forwards and squeezed Arian's delicate hand. "Let me help."

Arian pulled her icy hand away. "Not here." She glanced over her shoulder at Serenn and Eluned comforting the Princesses of the Blood.

"Did you know King Gartnait was sick again?"

"Oh Sorsha, I'm so sorry." Arian's brow contorted. "I tried to tell you about the king. But Serenn saw me and she's kept me away from you ever since."

"Why didn't she want me to help him?"

"I want to tell you. But she'll kill me. You need to speak to Serenn and ask her yourself."

Sorsha looked over Arian's head at Serenn in her black robes. "When?"

"The Bandruwydds are taking the ashes to the cairn on the night of the full moon."

"I have to wait three more days to speak to her? Why can't she speak to me now?"

Arian shook her head. "That's what she said. She sent me over to tell you to meet her at the standing stone circle on the night of the full moon. Now I have to go, I'm sorry. Serenn is going to be furious I've spoken to you for this long, and she'll..."

"She'll what?"

"Goodbye, Sorsha." Arian turned and limped back through the mourners to re-join the Bandruwydds.

The keening wail rose above the voices of the mourners, and a log snapped and exploded in the fire. Sorsha retreated from the city and returned to the roundhouse. *Serenn knew Gartnait was ill again. She must have.*

The silvery light of the full moon pierced through an opening in the clouds and sparkled against snowflakes whirling in the wind. Sorsha waited inside the standing stone circle, pacing around the snow-carpeted perimeter.

A branch cracked and flickering torchlight penetrated through the trees. The black-robed Bandruwydds emerged from the dark forest. Arian held the flaming torch above her head, and Eluned carried a clay pot decorated with the Snake of Caledon. *Gartnait's ashes.* Serenn glanced at the sky as a cloud crossed over the moon and plunged her face into shadow. Sorsha still saw Serenn vividly, and the whites of her eyes shimmered from within the hollows of her charcoaled lids.

"Lead the way, Serenn," Sorsha murmured.

They walked around the standing stone circle and then processioned in a straight north-easterly line up the hill until the forest gave way to grassland on the other side. Sorsha followed. Eventually they came to three tall stones, and the Bandruwydds touched them as they passed, chanting to the Gods of the mountains. Sorsha knew that it was possible to see the great mountain ranges from the stones during the daylight hours. When they reached the furthest stone in the line, they turned left and trudged to the north. After a mile, they came to a frozen stream and walked across, one at a time, before entering a forest. They walked on, through black conifers and naked white oaks, until they approached a clearing. Within the clearing was a tall mound covered in snow. At the base, Sorsha could make out a stone archway.

Arian dipped her head under the arch and disappeared inside. The light from the torch flickered within the mound as Serenn and Eluned followed.

Sorsha swallowed. *It's like my nightmares.* She stepped towards the cairn. *But there is no passageway. It's not the same.* Ducking under the archway, she stepped inside the cairn and could hear chanting. The corbelled stone roof was inches from her head. There were two stone walls on either side of a middle path, creating four distinct areas within the chamber and, inside each, a stone basin had been carved into the ground. Skulls and bones rested on the basins inside the first two quadrants on opposite sides of the path.

She continued along the path between the walls and passed into the third and fourth quarters of the chamber. Serenn held the clay pot of ashes above her head and called to the Mother Goddess. She lowered the pot to the stone basin and stood up as Eluned and Arian stopped chanting. Silence descended over the cairn, broken only by the crackle of Arian's torch.

"Did you know the king was sick again?" Sorsha asked.

Serenn stiffened. The fire caught in the breeze that blew into the chamber, and shadows leapt across Serenn's faintly lined face. "Yes, I knew."

"Why didn't you call for me? I could have saved him again."

The corners of Serenn's mouth cracked into a smile. "Individuals perish, but the Ancient People survive."

"You killed him, didn't you?" Sorsha glanced at Arian, who was holding the torch above her head, tears trickling down her pale cheeks. Sorsha stepped towards Serenn. "You were poisoning him this entire time, weren't you?"

"He thought the potions were helping him," Serenn said and smirked.

"But why didn't Elfinn try to find me?"

Serenn shrugged. "I told him you had gone away again... But

enough of that. What's done is done. Taran wants you to go see the Eldar Druwydd."

"Why do you care what Taran wants?"

"We want the same thing. We are united in purpose."

"No." Sorsha shook her head. "That's impossible. Taran would never do that."

"Oh, Sorsha." Serenn smiled. "Taran has felt slighted since he was fourteen, when he was overlooked for the throne of Caledon. He was tinder waiting for a stray spark. All the Eldar Druwydd had to do was whisper in Taran's ear, and the fire burned on the fuel of his own ambition."

Sorsha's heart pounded. "I don't believe you. It was all you."

"Taran was just as complicit in the poisoning as I was. We worked together. His hardest task was keeping you away from Gartnait. You kept healing him, and your powers lingered in his veins for weeks."

"Taran kept me away? How?"

"Why do you think he was so happy to take you to the south?"

Sorsha's eyes prickled. "But I ran away from him."

"Yes...that was unexpected, and he was furious with me for that. But the Eldar Druwydd and the Healers in Caertarwos assured him you would return. And you did, didn't you? You couldn't help yourself. You even went a step further and delivered him his mother, the final key to securing what he wants most."

"But..." Sorsha's voice shook and a hot tear slid from her eye.

"But then you came back too early, didn't you? Your power was just starting to wear off from Gartnait. He was almost dead when the kings met here to agree on the invasion. And then you returned and immediately healed him. So, we had to keep you out of the tower then."

"How did you do that? I stayed away because of Anwen." Sorsha glanced at Arian, whose face was contorted with tears. "No!" Sorsha screamed.

Serenn laughed huskily. "Who knows better the fragile state of Anwen's mind than me, the one who prepares her nightly sleeping potions? I gave her a potion but left out the sleep-inducing valerian roots and mistletoe. All Taran had to do was hint you were not like us, that you were a monster who had returned to take her back to the Roman soldiers. She would have been in such a frenzy. I don't think she knew what she was doing." Serenn smirked. "And again, you were a good little lamb, weren't you? You stayed away. I have heard that Healers prefer to sleep under the trees anyway, so I convinced Taran it would not harm you."

Tears clung to Sorsha's cheeks. "I don't want to hear any more of this. You and the Eldar Druwydd are vile. Manipulating us like puppets. Taran would never have done this if you hadn't exploited him. Neither of you will reach Tirscath!"

Serenn laughed again. "Taran's ambition is the work of the Gods. He has as much free will as you do. If the Gods did not want this, they wouldn't have sent us such an obliging little wolf pup, would they?"

The blood in Sorsha's veins pulsed hot, and her cheeks flushed. She glared at Serenn and turned to leave.

"Go to Caertarwos to see the other Healers, Sorsha. They will take you to the Eldar Druwydd," Serenn croaked. "But I don't know why I'm saying this you won't be able to help yourself, will you? Even now I bet there is a compulsion rising inside you, luring you to the north."

Sorsha spun around and raced at Serenn, grasping her by the neck. The amber beads affixed to Serenn's blue braids clicked together. Sorsha squeezed her fingers into Serenn's throat. "The minute you fall out of favour with the Gods, I will be here. I will be here waiting, and I will take the life from your eyes."

Serenn shoved Sorsha away. "You'll pay for this. I know how to give a Healer the permanent death. Not just for you. For your little Maetae girl as well, what's her name?"

"Nyfain," Eluned said.

Sorsha stepped backwards, her hands shaking.

"Run," Arian mouthed.

Sorsha stumbled out of the cairn and ran through the forest. She reached the frozen stream and skidded across the ice. Her hands and face landed in the snowy bank on the other side. *I need to reach Nyfain before they do.* She heaved herself up and sprinted down across the thick snow, back towards the standing stone alignment. The stones flashed past her. Cutting through the forest, she jumped over fallen logs and ducked under low branches. The walls of Caercaled glowed in the moonlight. She followed them through the forest north until she reached the roundhouse in the clearing. Throwing herself at the door, Sorsha wrenched it open with such force it tore off its hinges.

"Nyfain!"

The girl stood in the middle of the roundhouse holding a dagger. A strange warmth spread across Sorsha's chest when she saw the dagger. *Good girl.*

"What's happened?" Nyfain asked, wide-eyed.

"Get dressed, forget everything but that dagger and meet me in the stable."

On a beam of the sloping roof, Sorsha extracted her leather scabbard belt and long sword. The metal pin of the belt buckle stuck in the leather hole, and she fumbled with it, her ears ringing until she managed to jam it through. Sorsha walked to the door, dangling on its hinges. "Grab my bow and quiver of arrows. Hurry, Nyfain."

Sorsha ran to the stable, where Nema's black face was poking out. "I need you to ride hard tonight," Sorsha said as she threw a padded saddle blanket onto Nema's back. Nema tossed his head and snorted. "You'll get over it, I promise." She lowered the leather saddle onto his back. Nema exhaled and held his breath as she pulled the girth strap under him. "Don't push your stomach out, Nema!" Sorsha hissed. "We have to go!" Her hands trembled as she fitted the end of the girth strap into the metal belt clasp and waited for his stomach to contract with the next breath in. The wind gusted, blowing hair across her face. She looked up as Nyfain ran to the stable.

"Warriors are coming, Sorsha."

"Fuck. How did Serenn get back so fast?" Sorsha handed Nyfain the reins. "Get on Nema now."

Nyfain wore a thick woollen cape and the quiver of arrows on her back. When Nyfain had mounted, Sorsha led them forwards to the stable door, and she peered around the corner. Four warriors, wrapped in furs with swords drawn, emerged from the trees into the clearing.

Sorsha unsheathed her sword. "I don't want to kill them."

"You just need to wound them enough to get away."

"Right." Sorsha nodded. "I can do that…I think." She reached up for Nyfain's hand and squeezed it. "As soon as there is an opportunity, I want you to gallop to the Shining Lakes. Hide in the wood by the lake's edge. Don't come out until you see me. If I don't return in an hour, ride east to the coast and then follow the road all the way north till you reach Caertarwos. There are Healers there. Tell them what happened."

Nyfain nodded and squeezed back. "Don't worry about me."

Sorsha stepped out into the moonlight and pulled Nema's bridle behind her. "Let us go and I will not harm you," Sorsha called to the warriors. She recognised Owain, Brin, and Deryn but did not know the fourth man.

Owain shook his head. "I have orders from Serenn to arrest you for the murder of King Gartnait. If you put up a fight, I will kill you and the girl."

Sorsha gripped the metal hilt tighter. "Do you really believe that, Owain? I've not seen the king since my return in autumn."

"Serenn says you used black magic to curse him because you are a witch."

Sorsha twirled her sword in her left hand. "Just let us go. I don't want anyone to get hurt."

Brin and Deryn glanced at Owain. His red hair shimmered in the moonlight, but his eyes remained fixed on Sorsha. "Surrender, then."

"Owain, please be reasonable. There's hardly any garrison left to protect Caercaled. Do you really want to risk fighting me?"

"Enough!" Owain spat on the ground and strode towards her. Brin, Deryn, and the other warrior seemed to hesitate and clung to the edges of the clearing.

"Are you ready?" Sorsha asked Nyfain in Latin.

Nyfain nodded.

"You speak the Roman language like a traitor. I remember your trial. They should have executed you. But perhaps I will have the pleasure now."

"Why do you hate me, Owain? I have done nothing but help the people of Caledon."

Owain stopped within two yards of her and braced his sword in front of his face. "Tagging along with the Bandruwydds doesn't count as helping people. And in the absence of a king, Serenn commands me, and I have orders to kill you."

Sorsha gazed at the three warriors hovering by the trees. "Once I've killed Owain, I will spare the three of you if you do not avenge him. He's been warned."

Owain roared as he swung his sword at her. Sorsha danced to the left, and he skidded in the snow, trying to turn.

"Now!" Sorsha yelled in Latin.

Nyfain spurred Nema into a gallop. Owain's eyes widened, and he lunged for the horse. Stepping forwards, Sorsha swung her sword behind her shoulder and slashed into Owain's neck. Snow flung in every direction as Nema galloped through the clearing and disappeared into the forest. Sorsha looked down at Owain. Blood seeped into the snow around Owain's body, as he lay on the ground clutching his neck.

Brin and Deryn stepped forwards.

"Wait!" Sorsha gasped as the empathy pulled her towards Owain. "I will save him if you stay back and let me go."

"Do it," Brin grunted, and they stopped walking.

Owain's hand dropped away, and blood spurted from his neck. Sorsha's chest lurched, and she staggered to her knees. The heat burned through her veins as she pressed her hands into the bloody wound.

Owain gasped, and his eyes rolled around in his head until they focused on her. "You!"

Before he could grab her, she jumped up and stepped out of his reach. "Let me leave," Sorsha croaked. "Please, Owain, just let me go. I won't ever come back to Caledon. I promise."

Owain turned to the other men and nodded. "Go. But if I see you in Caledon, I will kill you. Orders or not."

Sorsha sheathed her sword and ran from the clearing. Through the snowy forest she sprinted, heading east until the trees parted and the Shining Lakes appeared. Sorsha reached the edge of the lake and fell to her knees. She grasped a handful of snow and shovelled it into her mouth. The burning ice melted on her tongue and bathed her parched throat. As Sorsha drank, Nyfain emerged from the wood. Sorsha wiped her mouth, pushed herself up, and walked towards Nyfain's outstretched hand.

"Which way?" Nyfain asked as she pulled Sorsha onto the saddle behind her.

"We head east through the valley of the lakes and then–"

"Sorsha!"

Sorsha turned behind her and squinted at a blur in the distance. At the base of the hill below the cairn, something limped towards them.

"What is it?" Nyfain asked. "I can't see who it is."

"It's Arian! We have to take her with us."

Nyfain turned Nema's head around and spurred him into a gallop towards the hills.

Grasping Nyfain's waist, Sorsha watched as Arian struggled across the snow, dragging her stump through the snow. The stump caught in a drift, and Arian fell headfirst into the snow.

Nyfain grabbed Sorsha's arm. "Sorsha! Over there!" A line of riders in the distance galloped from the city walls.

"Keep going!" Sorsha squeezed Nema's stomach with her boots. *Rhiannon, Goddess of Horses, give Nema the speed of Tirscath.*

Nema's hooves thundered beneath them, furiously kicking up snow.

Arian pushed herself up and staggered towards them, her stump abandoned in the snow. As they reached her, Sorsha leapt from Nema and ran to Arian, hobbling on one leg and clearly in agony. Empathy flooded into Sorsha's chest as Arian fell into her arms.

"Arian, what happened?" Sorsha whispered.

Her face was mottled red and white, and the sleeves of her robes had burnt away. "Serenn took the torch when you left." Arian was trembling. "She held it against my face and…and she said I was going to die like my parents did."

Sorsha pressed her hands against Arian's delicate face. "Shh. It's okay. Serenn is never going to hurt you again." Heat flowed from her heart, and Arian's shoulders relaxed. Sorsha brushed a strand of silvery hair from Arian's forehead. "You're safe now."

The ground shook beneath them as the warriors closed in. More men had joined the pursuit, and now twenty riders bore down on them.

"You two ride to Caertarwos, it will be faster without me." Sorsha scooped Arian into her arms and helped her onto the saddle behind Nyfain.

"No!" Nyfain screamed as an arrow whisked over Sorsha's head.

"Hurry! Don't wait for me!" Sorsha yelled.

"Sorsha, behind you!"

An arrow tore through Sorsha's stomach. She looked down at the arrowhead sticking through her thick woollen tunic. Blood pooled into her hands, and the wound seared and itched around the arrow.

"Sorsha! No!" Arian sobbed.

"Go!" Sorsha slapped Nema's rump. He leapt into a gallop and sprinted east towards the Shining Lakes as another arrow ripped through Sorsha's shoulder. She bit her tongue to distract herself from the pain. The warriors bore down on her and she closed her eyes. *Dark.*

Arrows whirred past, narrowly missing her. The hooves slowed, and the horses, snorting and squealing, pulled up before her. Men jumped to the ground, and their boots crunched in the snow. She opened her eyes. *Light.*

Sorsha rolled on the ground and ducked under the sweaty belly of Owain's horse. The arrows snapped as she rolled, the movement tearing at her wounds. Nausea from the pain blinded her momentarily. Dazed, she pushed up and sprinted towards the hills. Behind her, she heard the warriors swearing as they scrambled to remount. The arrowheads seared in the wounds as her muscles worked, but she pushed herself to run through the snow until she disappeared into the shadowy forest. *Dark.*

FORTY-TWO

Winter, 367 C.E., The Great Wall

A ditch sloped up into a menacing hill crowned with an enormous stone wall. Warriors gathered at the base of the Great Wall that long had haunted their dreams. Thick cloud obscured the moon, but they lit no torches. Rhuad swung his head up and stomped his front hoof. The leather bridle cracked through the silence.

Brei patted his neck. "Shh." He glanced up at a stone tower that rose from the wall. *Nothing.* Brei shivered and pulled his hood down further.

"What's taking so long?" Naoise whispered.

No one answered him.

Brei cracked his neck from side to side. *It's been hours, the sun will rise soon, and we will be done for.*

A shadow passed across the tower. Brei looked up. A Roman soldier carrying a torch leaned out of the window. The soldier waved the torch from left to right and dropped the flame. It landed in the snow but did not extinguish. Along the wall in the distance, Brei saw another torch fall from the wall. He squinted as a third dropped. *King Coel's bribes worked.* Behind the lines of mounted warriors, men on foot pushed to the front with long spears and square shields. Ladders were carried across the ditch and up the hill to the wall. The footmen slowly trudged through the snow to the top of the hill, climbed up the ladders, and disappeared over the wall.

"Let's go," Taran whispered as the last footmen scaled the wall.

The mounted warriors rode along the base of the hill between the mile castles. The fallen torches flickered against the compacted snow, lighting their path. Before they reached the furthest flaming torch, a warrior rode forwards and extinguished it. They waited again in darkness. A mile along the wall, a large fort was lit with torches. Brei gripped the bow, the nerves in his fingers tingling. *This is it.*

A horn blew, low and desolate through the frigid air.

"That's Gruffydd," Taran whispered. "Move out, no noise until you hear my horn. Pass the message along the line and follow."

Brei turned to Dylan and repeated the message.

They walked closer to the fort. Taran pushed up into a trot, and Brei followed. Along the line, hooves crunched through the snow as the rest of the mounted warriors followed towards the formidable wall of stone. They found the fort's double-breasted gate already opened for them.

A horn blew close to Brei. A deep note, like the wail of a cow. He turned and saw Taran with the bull horn to his lips. In the distance, he heard other horns left and right in reply. *Talorc, Alpin, Derine, Cailtram, and Nechtan.* An arrow whirred through the air and narrowly missed Taran's head. Brei reached behind his back and pulled an arrow from his quiver. He nocked the arrow and shot up onto the rampart. The Roman archer groaned and plummeted over the edge of the wall.

"Revenge or Tirscath!" Taran cried.

"Revenge or Tirscath!" echoed along the line. Taran's horse jumped across the snow and galloped up the hill to the gate. Another volley rained down on them as more archers were roused to the attack. Brei continued to release arrows into the ramparts as the warriors charged up the hill and through the gate. He ducked as another arrow buzzed over his head.

Arrows and slingshot stones whooshed down as the horses galloped as fast as they could through the snow. A horse screamed and crashed to the ground as a slingshot stone bore into its shoulder. The warrior leapt from the saddle and continued on foot up the hill. Brei released arrow after arrow into the ramparts as more of his men and horses fell, screaming and groaning in the bloodied snow. Beside him, Naoise and Dylan also fired into the ramparts. One of their arrows struck a Roman, and he fell from the rampart and rolled down the hill towards them.

Brei reached behind his shoulder, but there were no more arrows in his quiver. *Fuck.* He bent against Rhuad's neck and, unsheathing his sword, he pushed the horse into a gallop. "Revenge or Tirscath!" he cried.

The screams reached Brei's ears before he was close enough to see. He galloped through the gate and rode past a Roman soldier lying face up, his dark eyes still open. Inside the fort, rows of rectangular buildings were on fire, their roofs glowing in the smoke.

Warriors were being held back by a large force of over five hundred Romans. The soldiers had formed a wall with their shields, ten soldiers deep and spanning the main road through the fort. Roman archers stood at the back and fired up into the air, slaughtering the warriors that tried to break through the shield wall.

Taran rode at the helm of the line of men and raised his fist into the air. "Pull back to me!"

Brei rode to Taran through a carpet of bodies. "What is it?"

"The footmen haven't been able to break through the other side of the fort. We're outnumbered until they can get in, and we're falling like ashes."

"The archers are the problem."

Taran nodded. "What if you lead a small group to the back to get the footmen in while I keep pressing at the front?"

"I thought they were going to burn the doors down… Do you see how the Romans have trapped themselves? If I can get the footmen in, we can attack from both sides. Meet you in the middle?"

Taran grasped his arm and grinned. "Yes."

Taran separated from him and shouted the plan to the men along the line, while Brei called for Naoise and Dylan and led them back to the gate. "We are going to find the footmen and let them in. The fort looks like it is planned in a square." He scanned the fiery chaos. "We took them by surprise… They wouldn't have planned to hold men back. They've rushed here to the northern side of the fort."

"So, if we sneak around the side, we can get to the southern end and let the footmen in?" Naoise asked.

Brei nodded and glanced at Dylan. The boy's face blanched as he watched warriors being torn down by arrows in the lane. Brei grabbed Dylan's shoulder and smiled. "I know you're going to make me proud, lad."

Tears swam in Dylan's eyes, but he nodded and clenched his hands into fists around the reins.

Brei leaned back in the saddle and turned Rhuad's head around. "Let's go!"

Brei, Naoise, and Dylan galloped along the inside of the wall to the eastern edge of the fort. The smog grew thicker as they rode until it blanketed the path, and they stopped. Flames engulfed the building closest to them, and the walls and roof caved in with a thundering bang. Horses were trapped inside the building, and their screams drowned out the clang of metal and the yelling men. Laxsaro reared beneath Dylan, his eyes wide with terror.

"Grab the reins!" Brei yelled to Naoise, and they pushed their horses towards Laxsaro to prevent him fleeing.

Dylan clutched the pommel of his saddle, his cheeks glistening with tears.

"You're all right, lad," Brei said. "Keep as close to the wall as you can, in single file behind me."

The flames from the burning buildings were hot against his cheeks as he peered through the smog. His eyes burnt, and he choked on the acrid smoke, but they did not come across any Roman soldiers as they

ollowed the outer wall to the southern end of the fort. Naoise jumped
up, stood on the saddle, and looked over the wall.

"Can you see them?" Brei asked as he held Naoise's horse still.

"Yeah, they're pushing each other over the wall a bit further down."
He lifted onto his tiptoes and craned his neck. "But soldiers are slaugh-
ering them as they come over. Shit."

"How many?"

"Thirty? Fifty?"

Brei ran his hand through his sweaty hair. "Fuck."

Naoise crouched and sat back in the saddle. "I'm willing to give it a
crack. Revenge or Tirscath, right?"

"If we can distract them for a bit while more men jump over, we can
finish them off." Brei nodded. "Dylan, jump over the wall and tell the
footmen to give it all they've got to launch themselves over the wall."

"But you and Neesh can't fight them on your own." Dylan blanched
again.

Naoise grabbed a fistful of his brother's hair. "Get the fuck over
there now."

"Okay, okay!" Dylan squealed.

They watched as the boy stood on the saddle and jumped over the
wall.

"Are you ready, Neesh?" Brei asked.

"Let's do this, Brei-Brei."

They rode along the southern edge of the fort at a walk. The noise
of battle grew louder. The thunder of metal scraping on metal, and men
wailing as their insides were pierced and emptied of blood. Wood
exploded in flames and horses screamed.

A mass of Roman soldiers, wearing golden helmets and chain
armour tunics, thrust spears up the walls as warriors clambered over.

Brei pulled his sword from his scabbard. "Aim for their necks and
legs," Brei yelled and squeezed his boots into Rhuad's stomach, urging
him up into a gallop. Naoise held his sword over his head and screamed,
"Revenge or Tirscath!"

The soldiers stumbled and turned to face them as Brei charged forwards and slashed down at the neck of the closest soldier. Blood sprayed up onto Brei's leg as the soldier fell. Naoise swung manically, left and right, pushing his horse into the Roman spears and knocking them over.

Along the top of the wall, warrior after warrior heaved himself up and dropped into the battle. The air was hot and thick with smoke and the smell of blood. A soldier launched a spear in the air, and Brei ducked to avoid it. He glanced over his shoulder and saw a warrior on the wall tumble forwards, the spear pierced through his stomach. Brei roared and spurred Rhuad towards the soldier and wrenched his sword through the Roman's neck. The soldier spluttered, blood spewing from his mouth as Brei kicked him in the chest to dislodge his sword.

Soon the ground was littered with Roman bodies and blood. The faces of the dead squelched into the bloodied mud beneath the warriors' boots as they streamed into the fort.

To the north Brei could see rows of Roman archers standing two hundred yards in front of them between burning buildings, firing on Taran and his men.

"Kill the archers!" Brei screamed. "Embrace Tirscath and slaughter them all!"

Brei spurred Rhuad on but kept him in line with the sprinting men. He raised his sword into the air above his head and screamed until his lungs felt like they would burst. The archers turned and fired on the mass of screaming warriors, but many fell before they had time to identify their assailant. Rhuad hurtled into an archer, knocking him to the ground, and Brei brought his sword down on the head of another soldier beneath him. The blow hit the helmet and knocked the soldier to his knees. Brei pushed Rhuad forwards as soldiers within the compacted shield wall struggled to turn. He slashed at another Roman, and a jet of red blood oozed from his neck. Brei grinned into the faces of men fighting for their lives. He gazed behind him through the myriad of warriors, the flames glistening in their sweaty faces. Naoise hacked at a

Roman's neck with a square cut axe until the head fell to the ground.

The footmen swarmed into the battle, covering the Romans like locusts. Metal clashed against metal, and men groaned as they fell in a blur of anarchy. Brei's shoulders soon ached as he slashed his way to the middle. The warriors crushing in on the Roman soldiers from the other side were close enough for Brei to recognise their faces. *Where is Taran?* Brei pushed Rhuad forwards and thrust his sword deep into the neck of a soldier who stood weeping with his arms raised. Brei glanced around as other Roman soldiers dropped their swords and shields.

"No prisoners," Brei yelled. "Kill them all!"

The warriors surged past him and slaughtered the unarmed soldiers until they were reunited with the other half of the Caledon warriors at the end. Brei watched a body twitching on the ground below him, blood pouring from a deep gash in the soldier's exposed neck. The man's eyes stared up at him. Brei leaned forwards in the saddle and rested his arms on Rhuad's neck while he watched the Roman die.

"Brei!"

Naoise swaggered towards him, blood smeared across his beaming face. He grasped Brei's forearm and embraced him. Brei turned back to the dying soldier, savouring the man's contorted face as he struggled to breathe.

He scanned the crowd for Taran, but the fort was a sea of bodies, bounded by flames. He twisted in his seat to search behind him, his heart quickening as the minutes went by, and his stomach sank.

Then he heard warriors cheering and saw them pointing to the ramparts on the northern side of the fort. Brei looked up. Taran was engaged with a Roman soldier in a sword fight on top of the wall. The soldier lunged forwards with his broad sword, aiming for Taran's stomach. Taran stepped forwards and swung his long sword against the soldier's with a reverberating clang. The warriors below, standing knee-deep among the bloodied bodies, watched Taran. Brei pressed through the men to get a closer view. *That soldier is stronger than Taran.* The sword slid free from Taran's grip with a sickening scrape. Lunging again, the

Roman stabbed his sword into Taran's leather-covered chest. The warriors groaned and jeered.

Brei leant forwards in the saddle, his heart racing.

Taran hunched and stepped backwards. But he picked up his sword where it fell and screamed at the soldier, lurching left to the edge of the wall. The soldier stepped back, and Taran swung his sword into the soldier's neck, slicing from ear to chin. The soldier fell to his knees and grasped at the gushing wound in his neck.

Taran glared at the soldier and kicked the broad sword out of his hand. The warriors cheered. Taran stepped closer and ripped the helmet off the soldier's head. He threw it off the wall, and it crashed with a dull clang to the ground. "Kill, kill, kill!" the warriors screamed.

Taran grinned beneath a film of blood and raised his sword in the air. "I am Taran, Prince of Caledon, and this, brothers," he paused, his chest heaving. "This is just the beginning!"

Taran turned back to the kneeling soldier as the warriors roared his name. Clutching the hilt with both hands, he swung his sword behind his shoulder. Flames flashed in the iron blade as it arched through the air and cut the Roman soldier's head clean from its body. The head spun in the air and thudded against the ground, rolling until it was caked thick with blood and dirt.

AUTHOR'S NOTE

In the author's note to her début historical novel *The Sunne in Splendour*, the late Sharon Kay Penman said that "[w]hile imagination is the heart of any novel, historical fiction needs a strong factual foundation". I am not a historian or archaeologist, but I have written a novel inspired by the work of historians and archaeologists.

A Painted Winter draws on works in the study of Iron Age Scotland, the Picts, the Celts, the Romans, archaeology, mythology, and linguistics. However, this research could only take me so far, as the period suffers from a lack of contemporary historical records. Further, the records that survive are told from the Roman perspective, meaning the Pictish view is not reflected.

"The Pictish Conspiracy" series is inspired by an event recorded by Roman historian Ammianus Marcellinus in the late fourth century of the Common Era (c.e.), which is referred to as the "barbarian conspiracy". I will not relay that account here, as it is full of spoilers for this series. However, it is a fascinating and little-known event in British history.

These events sit on the cusp of the so-called Dark Ages, and many details about the events and people of the time are unclear or unknown. However, as in any age, the people would have spanned the spectrum of humanity, with good people and bad people, sensitive people and brash people, introverts and extroverts and everything in between.

Roman Britain

This book is set in the late fourth century, when Roman power in Britannia was in decline, and this is reflected by the weakening presence at Hadrian's Wall and the abandonment of some buildings in the cities. However, the Roman presence in the British islands dates back to the year 43 C.E., when Emperor Claudius led an army into Britannia with the purpose of conquest and occupation. By 87 C.E. the Romans occupied southern Britannia. From the fortresses the Romans built, cities flourished, such as Londinium (London), *Corinium* Dobunnorum (Cirencester) and Eburucum (York). The Romans' investment in public works still marks England today, with their stone city walls, amphitheatres, and baths.

Between 79 C.E. and 84 C.E. the Roman general Agricola led an invasion into modern-day Scotland. However, the invasion was not a success. Emperor Hadrian realised the north could not be conquered and instead set about defending the Romanised south from the northern 'barbarians' by building a wall. In 122 C.E. the construction of Hadrian's Wall commenced, leading to a mammoth structure across Britain that survives almost entirely nearly two thousand years later.

Emperors Antonius and Septimus Severus ordered invasions beyond the wall in 142 C.E. and 209 C.E. to conquer northern Britannia, but they were also unsuccessful. The Romans managed to hold the south of modern-day Scotland for a time, but they incited the ire of the natives, who defended their territory ferociously and initiated revenge attacks. Therefore, Emperor Antonius commissioned the building of another wall – the Antonine Wall – in 142 C.E. between modern-day Edinburgh and Glasgow. This enabled a short period of Roman occupation in Scotland, but the Antonine Wall was quickly abandoned, and the Romans withdrew to Hadrian's Wall.

For those interested in a more comprehensive analysis of Roman Britain's archaeology and history, there is a wide range of sources. I ecommend Guy de la Bedoyere's *Roman Britain*, Birgitta Hoffmann's *The Roman Invasion of Britain*, and Adrian Goldsworthy's *Hadrian's Wall*.

The Picts

The people of ancient Scotland were, broadly speaking, Celtic and made up of many different Iron Age tribes or kingdoms. These diverse peoples were referred to collectively by the Romans as the Picti, meaning "the Painted People". This name is traditionally thought to refer to the practice of tattooing or painting the body.

Ammianus said that the Picts were made up of two main groups, the Dicalydones and the Verturiones. In earlier records, Roman Cassius Dio referred to the Picts as being made up of the Maitai and the Caledonii. As such, *A Painted Winter* reflects a number of different tribes operating across the area encompassing modern Scotland.

For a general and accessible overview of the Picts, I recommend Tim Clarkson's *The Picts: A History* or Julianna Grigg's *The Picts Re-Imagined*. For a deeper dive, with a specific focus on the north-eastern Picts and up-to-date archaeological insights, I recommend Gordon Noble and Nicholas Evans's *The King in the North* or James Fraser's *From Caledonia to Pictland*.

Language

The Iron Age peoples of Scotland most likely spoke a dialect of Old Welsh. On occasion I use Celtic language, and my interpretations are based on a linguistic estimate of the appropriate proto-Celtic word, based on the commonalities of Celtic languages such as Gaelic, Welsh, and Gaulish. But the specific language that would have been used is, of course, unclear. For example, the word for the underworld that I use in my books is "Tirscath", which incorporates the proto-Celtic estimate of *Tir*, for "land", and *scath*, which can mean "shadow".

In England, modern place names are typically derived from Saxon or French origins, so I use the earlier Latin names for these locations. For example, Bath in Somerset was known as the spring of Sulis, which is translated to "Aquae Sulis" in Latin.

In Scotland, place names are typically now based on Gaelic, and I have therefore adapted names to have stronger links to the Old Welsh language. For example, the Gaelic word *dun*, which means "castle" or "fort" in Gaelic, is replaced with the Old Welsh word *caer*. The Scottish town of Dunkeld, for example, means "fort of the Caledonians" in Gaelic, and I have changed it to Caercaled. "Caledonia" is a Latinised word, and "Caledones" or "Caledon" may be closer to the original.

In Britannia, the people had been colonised for a few hundred years by the Romans and would have spoken Latin. However, there is evidence for the retention of the indigenous Brythonic language in places such as the former Dobunni tribes' lands where Sorsha is from.

The Saxons spoke an old dialect of German and would not have had a good understanding of the Celtic languages. Having said that, the Saxons had contact with the British people, and there is some suggestion that they were already colonising the eastern coastline even before the Romans withdrew from the island. Given the likely contact between the Saxons and the inhabitants of Britain, I have proposed that translators would exist and have used one for Prince Aelfric.

Prince Fergus may have also required a translator. I did not include one as it was already cumbersome enough for Prince Aelfric. Due to geographic and language family proximity, and the royal inter-breeding, the Ulster characters are likely to have understood the Welsh dialect better than the Saxons, and I make a distinction on this basis.

Names

I have largely used linguistically appropriate names for the characters in my book. The majority of Pictish men have names taken from, or derived from, Pictish kingslist. Brei is a shortening of the common Pictish King name of Bridei. Likewise, Cailtram, Nechtan, Gartnait, Uradech, Alpin, Cailtram and Drest are all on the Pictish Kings list. Taran is also listed as a Pictish King, and is derived from the Celtic God Taranis, the God of Thunder. Eithne and Derelei are documented Pictish female names. Naoise is the son of the King of Ulster's younger brother, and his name is therefore based on Irish mythology. For characters who are not 'of the Blood' I have largely used Welsh names, with a few who are intentionally named from Irish mythology rather than Welsh, such as Morrigan and Maeve.

Sorsha is the key outlier. Lucia's birth name is a Latin name, given she was born and raised in Roman-occupied Britannia. However, the name Sorsha has no historical basis whatsoever, reflecting Sorsha's self-perception of being an outsider in all the communities of Britannia.

Women

There is limited evidence about the role of women in Iron Age Scotland. The Pictish symbol stones tend to depict abstract objects and when they clearly depict humans, it is usually men.

However, I have utilised one interesting historical quirk in relation to the Picts, the concept of matrilineal succession. In the Pictish King list, the line of succession does not pass from father to son, but rather seems to pass based on a man's relationship to royal women. Under matrilineal succession, brothers can be kings if their sister and mother are of the royal line, but sons of kings cannot become kings. Whether matrilineal succession occurred is the subject of debate. As Tim Clarkson argues, the Pictish king list indicates that patrilineal did not occur and conforms with what would be expected for a matrilineal society. Clarkson further argues that matrilineal succession remains the simplest interpretation, and I find these arguments persuasive. Personally, I cannot think of a better way in ancient times of ascertaining with 100% accuracy the royal blood of a child than that it is related to its mother.

There is no evidence of anything close to the modern-day concept of marriage. Roman sources describe the Iron Age Scottish people as being polygamous. I am not convinced by this, as it seems more like propaganda to justify treating them as "barbarians". In *A Painted Winter*, the concept of "binding in protection and provision" is the closest thing to a modern-day marriage (and is inspired by the medieval Scottish practice of "handfasting"), but it is entirely fictional. Likewise, the concept of "binding in obligation" is fictional and is a very basic form of contract.

There is some evidence from Roman records and Irish myths of female Celtic priestesses or Druids. I have used this to form my Bandruwydds (*bann* is the Celtic word for "woman", and *Druwydd* is the Old Welsh word for "Druid"). Finally, without giving away spoilers, Sorsha is based on aspects of female representation in the Welsh and Irish myths, as well as the Gaulish Celtic Goddesses.

Sites

As you can see from the list of sites provided at the end of the book, the places visited in *A Painted Winter* are real archaeological sites. I have sought to describe sites in a manner that is faithful to the growing and exciting body of archaeological work in relation to the Picts.

On many occasions I have utilised poetic licence to bring sites to life, such as for Caercaled. There is a tiered fort in Dunkeld as described, and it faces west toward the River Tay. However, it is unclear if there was a tower (broch) on top, but I have placed a large one there based on the Moussa Broch from Shetland. I have also estimated the population size based on the recent excavations on Tap o' Noth in Moray, which suggest a Pictish population of up to 4,000 people living on that hill fort, but there is no evidence that the site in Dunkeld was that large. There is evidence of metalworking on the site, however, so we do know that it was an important place. A much more realistic interpretation of the site has been produced by the Perth & Kinross Heritage Trust's Kings Seat Hillfort archaeology project.

My description of Rīgonīn (Rhynie) is hopefully quite accurate, as there had been some amazing work by the University of Aberdeen's Northern Picts Project on this site, including a 3D model.

Our understanding of the Picts is constantly changing as new sites are excavated. After attending a 2020 lecture by Professor Gordon Noble about the site of Caertarwos (Burghead), it is evident that my description is a tad too advanced for the reality. Initial carbon dating suggested that the site was active in the fourth century and earlier, but more recent work suggests that it was active from the seventh century. However, work on the site continues, and more findings may show that the site was fortified in the fourth century or earlier. Certainly, neighbouring sites like Tap o' Noth and Rhynie were active during the fourth century so I think it is not a stretch to assume that Burghead, on the strategic promontory, would have also been in use.

In Britannia, the sites I have described are real sites based on the archaeological and historical information available. The Corinium Museum in Cirencester has a wealth of information about how Roman Corinium Dobunnorum would have looked and has preserved many mosaics and artefacts from the time. The baths in Aquae Sulis are famously preserved in Bath, but visualising the temple to Sulis Minerva was challenging, and Eleri H. Cousins's *The Sanctuary at Bath in the Roman Empire* was extremely useful. Londinium was in decline at the time of my book, and the forum and basilica had been burnt down in retaliation for the people supporting a rebel emperor. The towns and forts around Hadrian's Wall are fairly well preserved, and I have described them based on my own site visits, as well as the reconstruction images produced by English Heritage in their guidebooks, and Adrian Goldsworthy in his book *Hadrian's Wall*.

Food and clothing

Evidence indicates the Picts had a diet consisting of dairy, pork, and vegetables, such as turnip and kale. For the upper classes, hunting was important, and animals like venison were consumed. Interestingly, for a community who lived with access to the coast and rivers, there is little evidence that the Picts ate fish.

There is evidence of trade with the Romans with finds of red Samian ware pottery, glass, and silver. Pictish jewellery predominantly survives in the form of penannular brooches. The 'Snake of Caledon' brooch combines the Pictish penannular brooch shape and the common Pictish symbol of a snake curved around a Z-shaped arrow.

I have used Torc necklaces for the nobility in *A Painted Winter*. This is based on it being a common Iron Age Celtic artefact and on the descriptions in the poem *Y Gododdin* written in the seventh century, which records the Picts as wearing torcs.

There is limited information about Pictish clothing as organic remains rarely survive in the archaeological record. The Pictish symbol stones record a hooded shawl with tassels (a rare example of which survives as the 'Orkney Hood' on display at the National Museum of Scotland) and typically show women and men wearing tunics. The images seem to show the men wearing tunics that come to the knee (Golspie stone and 'Rhynie man' are good examples). It is unclear if there are pants underneath, but given the brisk nature of the Scottish climate, I have decided that there were. The symbol stones such as Sueno, and Aberlemno show warriors carrying spears (possibly with round utted ends as represented in the Tulloch Stone), bow and arrows, swords, square or distinctive "H" shaped shields, and helmets. Warriors are represented both on foot and on horseback.

The tattoos described in *A Painted Winter* are all found in the symbol stones and metalwork of the Picts. Any time I describe stone carvings, I am describing real Pictish stones. For example, the Rhynie man is described in chapter 18 in Rīgonīn, and the Caertarwos carved bull stones are the stones found in Burghead. I recommend George and Isabel Henderson's *The Art of the Picts* which provides a comprehensive overview of the Pictish Symbol stones and metalwork.

In Britannia, I have generally described the people as wearing togas (men) and colourful pallas (women) wrapped over tunics. I recommend Kelly Olson's two fascinating books *Dress and the Roman Woman* and *Masculinity in dress in Roman Antiquity* for further information on Roman dress. Slavery was unfortunately commonplace across the Roman Empire, and I have tried to give faces and personalities to these often forgotten people. The inscribed slave collar that Derelei wears in chapter 35 is based on real slave collars that were worn at the time.

Religion

In the *Life of Saint Columba* (written by Adomnan in the mid to late 7th century) it was observed that King Bridei of Fortriu was advised by a Druid named Broichan. Based on this observation, and on the other similarities between Iron Age Scottish archaeology and pre-roman England archaeology, I have centred the religion of the Ancient Peoples on the archaeological and historical records of the general Celtic religion.

From the archaeological record, I was inspired by symbols left on stones and items such as cauldrons and bowls that have survived. I have referred to some festivals, including Imbolc and Beltane, and have tried to base my descriptions on the evidence for these festivals found in archaeology and history. For more on religion, I recommend Ronald Hutton's *Pagan Britain* and *The Stations of the Sun*, and Miranda Aldhouse Green's *Caesar's Druids* and *The Celtic Myths*. For an overview of the Celts, I recommend Alice Roberts's *The Celts*, and for a more academic dive into the Celts, I recommend Barry Cunliffe's *The Ancient Celts*. For a specific look at Sulis and the worship of a pagan goddess in the geographic region of the Dobunni tribe, you may be interested in Stephen J. Yeates's *The Tribe of Witches*.

Lightning Source UK Ltd.
Milton Keynes UK
UKHW011406221021
392644UK00004B/85

9 780645 042900